HEART OF THE EMPIRE

HEART OF THE EMPIRE

HANNAH WILLIAMSON

Hannah Williamson

First Printing, 2022

Content Warnings

This book contains a depiction of attempted sexual assault. It is not explicitly graphic, but may be uncomfortable for some readers. For readers who would like to skip that scene, it takes place at the end of Chapter 16, *Zey*, and there are some small, non-graphic references to the scene further in story.

This book portrays scenes of violence.

Contents

Map of Syytala

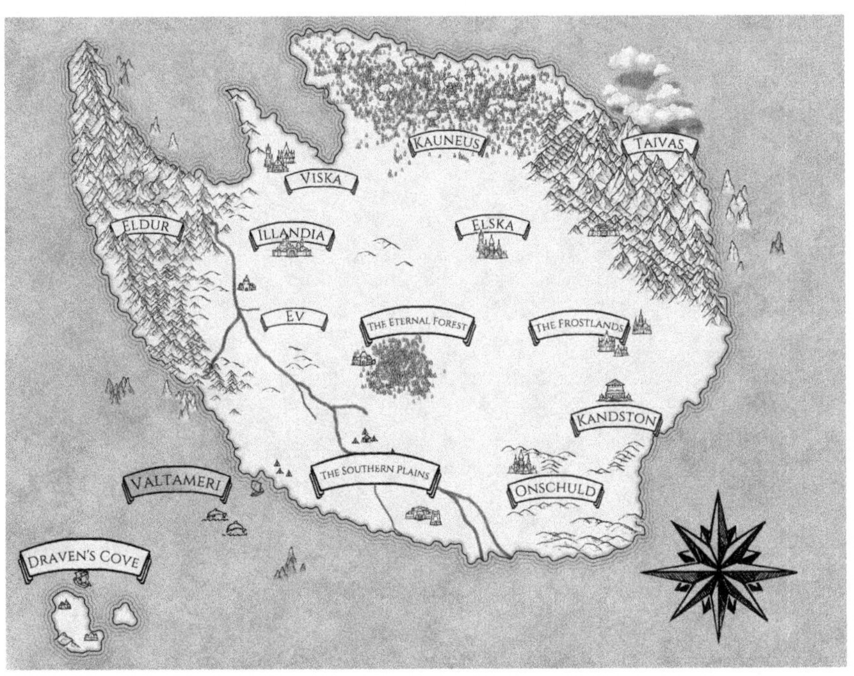

To Mom and Dad
I crafted the book
You crafted the author

Prologue

His words had burned once. The history he wrote with his own hand turned to ash in minutes. The record of lifetimes, gone. But Maddy restarted the work, the burden. Ancient lives such as his witnessed history as it happened. Saw the birth and death of nations and languages. The crowning of kings and queens, emperors and empresses. And war. Warfare and bloodshed filled far too many pages of Maddy's histories.

Yes, his words had burned, but it was his duty to preserve the lives and victories etched in his immortal memory. A little fire wouldn't change that. Besides, he had learned from it. Had started enchanting each and every book with all sorts of protection spells. Perhaps it was a bit much, but Maddy was not one to do things halfway.

He finished scrawling the introduction to his new *Volume II* of *The History of the Empire* and looked up from his work. Eli sat in the chair opposite him, his feet propped on the desk as he read silently. Intelligent as his favorite student was, he couldn't know what was coming. Couldn't understand it in the way Maddy's ancient heart did. The boy was so innocent. Untouched by tragedy. That was all about to change. Any moment, the dam would break. The war would poison him. Maddy watched Eli turn a page. Remembered how it felt to be so content. But those days had long since slipped out of the immortal's reach.

Those were thoughts best left unwatered. Maddy pressed pen to page and continued his work.

As detailed in the previous volume, the Imperial Guardians were chosen - one from each of the twelve kingdoms - to protect and advise the new High

Emperors. I left Volume I off after our training ended, and that is precisely where I begin anew.

The twelve of us were told only that we would be going through some sort of initiation ceremony, and as part of it, we would be given new names. I would no longer be Talis Fabri, but Madara Anluan. The twelve of us were each given the same surname. Brothers and sisters from that moment on. I do not think even The Wizard's Council, with all their schemes and manipulations, understood the power they had handed us. A family. A bond. Crafted not of blood but the sharing of burdens. And of course, magic.

Because they gave us - and the High Emperors - another gift. Immortality.

Maddy paused. He could ramble on and on about the day of The Making. The peculiar, magical high of power surging through his body. The instant connection to his new brothers and sisters. The beauty of the magic itself, dancing through his soul. But this book was meant as a record, not a diary. He pushed the emotional bits aside as best as he could and went on.

The High Emperors were made first. The magic in them is slightly different than that running through my own blood. While both their and our immortality is imperfect - allowing us to die of mortal wounds and nothing else - there are a few key differences. When a High Emperor is killed, he or she is replaced by the person who killed them. This was intended as a protection against future corruption. If an emperor began to serve his or her own desires at the cost of others, they could be removed. This unfortunately leaves good emperors and empresses vulnerable to the dark machinations of those who are already corrupted.

That is why the Twelve Imperial Guardians were made. To shield them from dark powers. To guide them away from selfish choices. But The Wizard's Council was only able to craft the magic through an external power source (see Vol. IV of Spells and Artifacts for details). That power was limited, so they could only give the ability to pass immortality down from one person to another to the High Emperors. When a guardian dies, no one takes their place.

Once more, Maddy hesitated. He had lost his sisters that way. Had lost some of his brothers. Killed by those seeking the High Emperors' power or those who loathed their differences. Heretical extremists and hateful fools often stood in the path of the guardians. But some... some had defeated them. All they did was stand between the High Emperors and death. All they did was stand for their people. All they did was stand. And they were killed for it. Brutal and bloody and-

"You alright, Madd?"

He lifted his eyes to find Eli watching him. When had the boy looked up from his book?

"You looked a little... upset." Eli set his book on the desk, giving Maddy his full attention. Room to speak his heart.

That wasn't going to happen. "I'm fine." He looked back down at the page.

No one takes their place.

If he died in this war, no one would take his place. If any of his brothers died, they were lost. Just lost. Certainly everyone faced the loss of those they loved. Maddy himself had loved and lost again and again. Mortals came and went, taking pieces of his heart with them. But the guardians were constant. Brothers and sisters by his side always.

Until they weren't.

Until knives were driven through faithful hearts. Until wings were clipped. Until hatred won. Until brothers and sisters couldn't stand anymore. Until brothers and sisters dwindled to just brothers.

They had faced war before, but with every guardian lost, it became harder to protect each other. Because that was the secret. They were created to protect the High Emperors, but they would *always* protect each other first.

Maddy dipped his pen in the inkwell. Let it hover over the page. There was so much more to say. Thousands of years of history, even harder to write than the first time. The lives of his dearest reduced to pages and ink. How many chapters before he had the displeasure of recounting Skyli's death? Or Kila, or Satama, or Ráj, or... Dain.

Madara slammed the book shut.

Eli, who had returned to his reading, jumped. "Are you..."

He trailed off as Maddy hopped to his feet and shoved the book back into its proper place. His fingers slid along the spines of his handwritten histories, skipping over empty spaces that once held books now turned to ash. He yanked another off the shelf and placed it on the table. Unfinished, as many of them were. Aware of Eli's eyes trailing him with concern, he quietly flipped through the pages to find where he left off. Hopefully somewhere better than thinking about his dead brothers and sisters. When he found the end, he started reading from the top of the unfinished, final paragraph for context.

Eden Anluan came to fight beside his brother at The Loft. A dangerous choice for a man with no wings.

No. This was not better at all.

Daingeon and Eden led the Taivan army in battle for nine days, Dain from the air, Eden from the relative safety of Taivas' enchanted clouds. In one noticeable incident, Eden was

The sentence ended there. Maddy knew exactly why. He didn't want to write about Dain. Didn't want to think about him. About losing him.

He closed his eyes for a long moment. War everywhere. Through the pages of history. *His* history. His brothers and sisters pressed within, suffering, killing. Bones broken and flesh severed. Finishing blows he couldn't bring himself to face. None worse than Dain. He had been the best of them, and even he had fallen.

Who would he lose this time? Which of his brothers would this war claim? When would it end? When would people realize death was not the answer?

Maddy sat frozen, staring at a page that was no better than the last. Another story he couldn't complete. Not yet. He started to close the book when the door swung open without warning. Both he and Eli turned to see who was there.

"Eden?" His brother's expression was grim. Darker than he'd seen in a long time. Maddy knew the words Eden would speak before he opened his mouth.

"Get ready to leave. We're shipping out."

"Where?" Maddy asked as his heart dropped.

Horror dawned on Eli's face as he realized he was losing Maddy, possibly forever. The war wrapped it's tendrils around the boy at last.

Eden stayed only long enough to give an answer before he left Maddy to prepare.

"Bane."

I

Bane

Screams of the dying echoed through the valley, filling the thick air. Not the ring of steel, the clang of armor, the thud of arrows could drown it out. Blood and bodies decorated the once beautiful valley. Green grass stained red. Flowers trampled underfoot. Clean air turned foul and muddy. And the bodies.

Mounds of them.

The ground gave way beneath Eden's foot with a snap. Steadying himself, he realized it wasn't the ground at all, but the arm of a dead soldier. The sound, bone breaking under his weight. He shifted his grip on Tasa, a sword both old and beautiful, and struck down another soldier in front of him. The broad blade cut clean, spattering blood on Eden's face and in his mouth. Tasting the metallic buzz of blood on his tongue, he spat to the side, moving on before the man's body hit the ground.

Even in the chaos of war, he was striking. Walking tall and determined through the battlefield, built for death and warfare. Unafraid. Cutting down every man in his path. Black hair hung in front of his face. He ran a dirty, calloused hand through it, pushing it away from his icy gray eyes.

Soldiers scurried to escape at the sight of those eyes. Eden, quick and merciless, wouldn't allow it. They fell, bodies like rag dolls. The sword in his hand pulsed, exhilarated by the taste of their blood. The blood of men so easily fooled. Twisted, lost, to politics and lies that Eden didn't like to think about.

One soldier faced him. A strength in his stance Eden had yet to encounter on this battlefield. He was ready. Firm. Strange. Others ran while he stood, but Eden sensed more than that. He came closer, and Eden understood. The curve of the soldier's body, the shape of the armor. It was a woman. A petite little soldier girl.

He closed in. She made her move, lunging forward with a low swipe at his legs, gambling her size meant she was quicker. Eden expected as much, and shifted his sword to block hers. Swearing, she stepped back to recover, hoping he didn't have time to make a move before she could. Eden twisted Tasa around, aiming to cut her exposed side. Fear flashed in her eyes as she reacted, lifting her sword to block him. Eden caught a glimpse of blonde hair peeking from her helmet.

He hesitated.

But not for long. While his hesitation allowed her to block the blow, she wouldn't be so lucky with the next. Using his momentum, he shifted the blade around and under hers, piercing her side. The woman fell like so many others. Insignificant. Another body on the ground. Blonde hair meant nothing, her short stature meant nothing. She was not the person these features represented to him. *She was not her.*

A scream jolted Eden back to reality. He stepped over the woman's body and continued through the bloodshed, cutting rebels down like wheat. Scanning his surroundings, a figure caught his attention through the waves of soldiers and bodies. A wizard on a small hill, standing tall against the onslaught. A blast of magic threw half a dozen soldiers away from the hill, and Eden felt a smile tugging at the corner of his mouth.

The smile vanished before it came. He felt before he saw. A silent scream of danger in his head. There, behind the wizard, a soldier crept up the hill. The wizard's focus was on the rebels in front of him, coming in full force. He didn't see, didn't know.

"Maddy!" Eden screamed, but the sound was lost in the battle.

Springing into motion, Eden's sword cleared a path towards the wizard. "*Hiek*!" he swore in his native tongue, helpless. Too many men, too many bodies between them. He watched as the rebel lifted his weapon - a mace and chain - and swung. Striking the wizard's leg, he tumbled down the hill, out of Eden's sight.

A jolt shot through Eden. Fear, but not his own. Maddy's fear. Accidentally sent to him through their bond. Eden broke through the wall of soldiers and ran to the hill.

He arrived in time to see the rebel looming over Maddy, lifting his weapon to deliver the final blow. "You're dead!" Eden roared as the soldier's arm descended. Swinging his blade hard and reckless, Eden cut the rebel clean through the middle. Not quite fast enough to save the wizard from harm, but enough to redirect the blow. To reduce the impact of the skull-crushing weapon.

Eden shoved the bottom half of the soldier off Maddy, biting his lip to stop himself from swearing when he saw the state of his friend. The left half of the wizard's face was bloody and mangled with large gouges opening the flesh. Evidence of the weapon's menacing spikes. Mercifully, none of them reached his eye, but that didn't stop the blood from spilling into it.

"E-eden," the wizard gagged through the blood filling his mouth.

"Don't speak, save your energy," Eden ordered, lifting the wounded man across his shoulders.

Maddy groaned. Blood from his mouth and head dripped onto Eden's arm.

"I'm not going to be able to fight as well with you on my back," Eden explained, eyes scanning the danger. Enemies on all sides. But the hill provided some cover, obscuring them from allies and rebels alike. Those nearby were either busy facing another opponent, or deterred by the sight of Eden slicing a man in half. They were relatively safe until the rebels grew bold again. Or until they started moving, drawing new eyes their way. "You're going to have to cover us, *halviti*."

"Don't s-swear," the wizard gurgled.

"Don't tell me what to do when I'm saving your ass." Eden took a breath. There. A break in the wall of soldiers. Eden pressed forward. "*Chyddan*, why are you so heavy when you're skinny like a twig?"

As they went, more enemies spotted them. Two of their biggest threats, wounded and encumbered. A group of rebels moved to block their path, taking full advantage of their enemy's impaired state. From his place, lying half-dead on Eden's shoulders, Maddy muttered a spell. Gobs of blood dripped from his mouth and garbled the ancient words, but they worked all the same. A bolt of lightning shot from the sky, blasting away the soldiers and wrecking the hopes of any who thought to try next.

Eden nearly toppled over as he swore, "*Pas*, Madd, warn a guy!"

Maddy let out a pathetic, gurgling attempt at a laugh.

"*Hiekkem velki*," Eden muttered, the Eldurian words natural on his tongue.

"D-don't sw-"

"I know! Don't swear," Eden snapped, moving forward. "Why don't you concentrate on not bleeding or something?"

"I'll try," he wheezed.

"Good," Eden pushed his way through the battle, thankful Maddy's lightning bolt had shattered the rebels' confidence, reinstating a healthy fear that kept them away. They were weakened but not weak. And though annoying, he supposed the wizard was, at the very least, useful. "Look, just don't... don't die, alright?"

Maddy didn't reply.

2

Rolina and the Day

Waves crashed against the fragile boat, knocking it - and the girl within - to one side. Feet flying from beneath her, she fell on her rear. Water splashed in her face as she tried to right herself. With a huff, she started to wipe it from her eyes. Another wave jolted the boat. The force heaved her over, face smacking hard against the wet, wooden floor. She clamored to her knees with a snarl and began tossing water out with her hands. For every scoop she bailed out, twice as much poured in.

"Damn it!" shrieked the girl, blonde hair flying violently in her face. Another wave slammed against the boat, throwing it to the side so suddenly and viciously it tossed the girl out. Reaching for the boat as she flew, her fingers brushed the rim.

Then, water.

Surrounded on all sides, the storm tossed her around until she lost her concept of which way was up and which way was down. She shut her eyes. Perhaps she could feel it somehow, in spite of the storm. Her heart pounded in her chest, amplified by her held breath. If she could right herself, she could swim for air. Maybe even find the boat.

Something unholy grabbed her ankle. Spindly fingers wrapped around her skin.

Her eyes shot open, peering down to identify the creature. A clenched jaw and paralyzing fear were the only reasons she did not scream. She needed all the air she could get. A scream was wasteful. But the thing holding her ankle, dragging her down into the dark, was twisted. Wrong. Its gray body was cracked, dehydrated despite the thousands of miles of water surrounding them. Its eyes yellow like the sun, yet cold as death. Worst of all, its shape. Like it was once human.

The girl tried to kick the thing loose, but the water slowed her foot to a harmless tap. Aware of every second of lost air, she chose a new strategy and bent over to pry its fingers away. Instinct told her to recoil when she touched its saturated, dry skin. But she was more than her instincts. She dug her fingers in, pulling and scratching to break free. Though she tore at its skin - ripping pieces of soggy flesh away to drift in the water - the thing would not budge.

She dared a look beyond the creature, down into the black, hoping for something useful. A rock to smash in the creature's skull. The debris of a shipwreck with a bit of splintered wood to drive into its eye.

Instead, corpses.

Her stomach twisted. All around her at the bottom of the sea, bodies in varying states of decay. Some nothing but corroded bones. Others still flesh, discolored and bloated. A fresh corpse swayed in the water below, the familiar shade of sandy blond hair catching her eye. Shining blue eyes turned hopeless and empty. Recognition seized her. She knew those eyes, that face, no matter how distorted.

She screamed.

The air in her lungs shrieked for renewal, burned, stung, but still, she screamed.

"Rolina!" Firm hands gripped her by the shoulders. She thrashed and fought. The creature had allies, dragging her toward death. But she couldn't see them beyond the ocean and the thing's rotten yellow eyes.

"Rolina!" with a shake, she snapped from the dream. The corpse inches from her face. No, not a corpse. Alive. Full of color and vigor, holding her arms tight. His blue eyes searched her for signs she was still lost inside the dream.

"Iero!" she collapsed into him.

He pulled her against his chest, allowing her to hide her teary face. "It's alright," he ran his hand through her blonde hair. "You're in your room, in your bed, it was a dream."

"In my room... in my bed." She could hear his heartbeat - chose to focus on the tender sound. How alive it was. Her body shook as she clung to him. Her breath sharp and unsteady. But he was there and alive and holding her in safe arms. Minutes passed as her trembling body settled.

"You alright now, Dove?" he asked softly. She nodded into his chest, but made no moves to release him. "Then you should go back to sleep," he eased her away, stroking her arm in a gentle, almost fatherly gesture despite appearing around the same age, "there are a few more hours until morning."

"I don't think I can," she pulled the blankets tight around her body, a shield against the night.

Iero looked at her with tired eyes. The deep sort of tired that clings. A stain that can't be rubbed out. "Try. You don't get enough sleep as it is." None of them did.

Rolina opened her mouth to speak, but found her thoughts interrupted. His clothes. "Why are you fully dressed in the middle of the night?" He even had his boots on.

"I only just got in when I heard you screaming." Scooting off the edge of the bed, he stood and adjusted his leather shirt, dyed gray and crimson in wide, vertical stripes. Three silver clasps secured leather straps that wound to the small of his back. Two daggers lay safe in their sheaths where the straps met, tucked out of sight. Every stitch crafted to meet his rich taste and bad habits.

"Those are your thieving clothes," Rolina noted, reaching up to touch one of the round clasps. A compass rose etched on each one, the eastern point engraved with a criss-cross pattern.

He flashed a devilish smile. "As you can imagine, I'm fairly eager to see my bed." Turning away from her, he added, "You need sleep too."

"Can I go with you?" Rolina did not wait for an answer before throwing the blankets off to follow.

"No, Rolina, you're nineteen. You can handle your own nightmares," he insisted, even as she scurried after him. She was a lady now, and ladies shouldn't be found in the beds of immortal guardians. Even if that immortal guardian had been letting her curl up beside him since she was eight. Even if Iero, with his young, energetic face, was more like a father or an uncle than anything else. "Sleep in your own bed."

She looped her arm through his as they stepped out into the hall. There were a few dim lights left burning in anticipation of the guardians' late night comings and goings. Even before the war demanded every second of their lives, Iero in particular often stayed out deep into the night.

"Not to mention, you give off too much body heat," Iero opened the next door down wide enough for both of them to enter. "It's not natural."

The cold-enchanted room sent a shiver through Rolina as they stepped inside, "I don't give off that much heat, you're just cold-blooded. Like a corpse." A second shudder rippled through her, though it had nothing to do with the cold. The comparison reminded her of the dream. Iero's distorted face, lifeless in the water. She clutched his arm tighter as he shut the door.

"Frostlanders weren't made for heat," he reminded her, tugging his arm away to walk into the adjoining washroom.

Iero's chambers were big. Giant windows with thick curtains that were hardly ever open in recent months. A closet *and* a large wardrobe, as he had more clothes than he could fit in one alone. The wall beside the washroom was decorated with weapons. Mainly daggers and knives, sitting low enough on the wall for him to snatch on his way out the door. Beside them a small, cluttered desk. A painting of Eldur hung above the door, deep reds and browns contrasting the silvery-blue walls. A bookcase on the opposite wall, full of not books, but trophies.

A bracelet snatched off the wrist of an Elskan queen centuries before Rolina was born. Feathers plucked from the wings of Taivans, friend and enemy alike. A silver chalice from a Feinin king's table. A dwarven lock box he had never managed to open. Weapons, so many weapons. The evidence of centuries worth of kleptomania. Treasures and trash alike.

Shivering, Rolina ignored Iero's continuing complaints from the washroom and crawled into bed. Surrounded by white blankets and pillows that mimicked the snows of Iero's homeland, Rolina settled in. His bed was softer than hers, though slightly smaller. Both were large enough for two, but Rolina's bed was crafted to accommodate its previous owner. As a Taivan, they built it wide enough for him to lay with his wings comfortably spread in any direction. When she was little, Rolina would lie in the middle and imagine she could feel the impression of them in the mattress, or that she had wings of her own.

The same way she used to imagine lying in Iero's bed as lying in a fresh layer of snow. Cold, but soft and enveloping. This fantasy crept into her head once more, easing her into relaxation. But she did not close her eyes. If she did, the nightmare might return. The images waiting just out of sight.

Reappearing through the washroom door, Iero wore only a pair of loose trousers. Rolina raised an eyebrow, "Aren't you freezing to death in those?"

"Aren't you sweating to death under those?" he gestured to the mass of blankets overwhelming her. Blankets she knew he only kept for her. "All those layers." Shaking his head in disapproval, he climbed onto the bed beside her. Rolina's eyes followed the enchanted tattoo on his bare shoulder. A compass with the eastern point at the top. The deep blue ink shifted as he moved, always pointing east. Always pointing home. "Get out of my room," he said through a yawn.

"No, thank you," she replied, pulling the blankets close. Iero was a pushover when he was sleepy. And he had a weak spot for her. She grew up under his care, under the care of all six living guardians to some extent or another. They may have been in charge, but she knew how to work each of them.

Lying sprawled on top of the covers, exposed to the chill of the enchanted air, Iero grumbled, "Get out of my bed."

"No," she repeated, scooting closer.

Iero groaned, swiping the air in a half hearted attempt to shoo her, "Go away."

"Go to sleep," she wrapped her arms around his chest, nestling her head against his tattooed shoulder.

"I don't take orders from you," he insisted, already closing his eyes. "It was one thing when you were little, but you're old enough now to..." he yawned again, "to deal with your nightmares alone."

Rolina snuggled up close to him. Content. Safe. She closed her eyes, resting in the knowledge Iero could kill anything her nightmares threw at her. Even yellow-eyed sea monsters. "Goodnight," she said, voice low, peaceful.

"You're like a furnace," he mumbled, half-asleep. Then, after a long pause, he added, "Goodnight."

Day came, throwing light through the window to dance across the bed. Rolina woke, the fears of the previous night washed away by sunlight. The chill of enchanted air like snowflakes on her skin. Safe beneath the snow-white blankets, she imagined herself a frozen princess awakening from a spell. Eyes opening to fall on Iero, foot on his desk, lacing up his boots. Already dressed and preparing for the day. No more than a few hours could have passed between her nightmare and then. How long had the guardian slept? Not enough to smooth out the dark circles under his eyes.

"What were you doing last night?" She half expected him to jump at the sudden sound of her voice in the otherwise silent room. But Iero noticed everything. Had probably heard the change in her breath as she woke, or seen the soft flicker of her eyelashes all the way from across the room.

"Nothing to worry yourself over," he answered, straightening as he finished lacing his boots.

"That's not an answer," she noted, a playful undertone in her voice. As though she was part of the mischief with him.

"I'm aware," he reached for his daggers, strapping them on with practiced fingers.

"Come on, you can tell *me*," she pushed, looking up at him with softness and innocence in her big, green eyes.

Iero didn't even glance at her puppy-eyed face, "That doesn't work on me, Dove." After a pause, he added under his breath, "Anymore."

Rolina made a show of pouting, but the guardian ignored her, pulling on a jacket to obscure his daggers. He went to stand in front of a mirror on the opposite wall and began fiddling with his blond hair. Tossing individual strands this way and that until each one was precisely where he wanted it. Rolina saw no difference. But she was the same. Had learned her own vanity from the man staring at his reflection a few feet away. At least he didn't have to worry about what age would do to him.

I may be a thief and a spy, he told her once, *but if I'm ever caught, I'll be damned if I don't look dashing.*

"The truth of it is, I have my work to do, and you have yours," he lectured, turning his head to see himself from every angle. "Now you're awake, time to get to it." Satisfied, he stepped away from the mirror. Toward the door.

"You can't stay a minute?" she asked, knowing the answer before he opened his mouth to say it. "I never see any of you anymore."

"Never?" he raised an eyebrow playfully, "I seem to recall several hours last night you spent intrusively close to me."

"True," she conceded, but refused to let the issue drop. "There's never any time to *talk* anymore."

The mirth left Iero's voice, replaced by the familiar, deep tired, "Can you blame us? The world is in pieces, Rolina. We're the ones who put it back together." Before she could tell him she wished things were different, that she missed him and the others, he pushed on. "You're nineteen, it's time you stop acting like a girl and start acting like a woman. You have your job, and you can't begrudge us for doing ours."

"I know," she said, her voice quiet. More words would only betray her emotions, would only make him think her more childish than he already did. They all did sometimes, when she displayed too much mortality. When she let her head drift too far into the clouds. Physically, she had passed him up nearly a year ago. He was immortalized at eighteen, his face fresh and young forever. But he was older than dirt and wouldn't let her forget it. Wouldn't let her forget that she would only ever be a child in his eyes.

Her face betrayed her instead. Of course he saw it. The flicker as his words hit. Eleven years of studying her face, he knew when she hurt. "I'm sorry," Iero came to sit on the edge of the bed. "I didn't mean..." but he did. He brushed his thumb down her chin, the only attempt at comfort he could afford. "I would be here. If I could."

Rolina looked at the wall.

"I do have some good news," he said, leaving the words to hang in the air. Bait.

Her gaze returned to the guardian, unable to resist.

"We received an update last night," a spark behind the exhaustion in his eyes, "Madd should arrive home sometime this week."

Rolina forgot her loneliness as the words hit her. Maddy. Home. She had worried and prayed and worried some more since the day he and Eden shipped out. Had felt her heart crack when she heard of his injury. But now her friend, her teacher, was coming home. A wide smile broke across her face, "And Eden? Is he coming too?" She nearly tumbled out of bed with excitement.

"He's still fighting in Bane," Iero answered, a bit of the mirth stolen from the moment.

Then it ended altogether.

"Get up," he ordered, pressing a kiss on her forehead as he stood. "There's work to be done."

Cold air nipped at her skin as she tossed the covers off. Iero offered one last, pitiful smile before he was out the door. The image of Maddy's smiling face fluttered through her head as she followed Iero out into the hall. As he walked away, towards the front exit, she turned and slipped inside her own bedroom.

Alone, she threw her arms out wide and twirled. Her head tilted upward as the nightgown flared around her legs. A laugh escaped from deep in her chest. It was important in times like these to celebrate every victory, if only for a second. Though Maddy was injured, his return was as close to a miracle as Rolina had ever experienced.

The world settled back in her head as she came to a stop. She tugged her nightgown off and marched to her wardrobe. An ornate, decorative thing, and like all the other furniture in the room, older than she was. As Iero said, she had a job to do. Like him, she'd be damned if she didn't look good doing it.

3

Rolina and the Day

Warm spring air touched Rolina's shoulders as she stepped into the gardens. Eyes closed, she took in a deep, calming breath. Savoring the moment. Standing still in The Eternal Forest's perfection. Golden leaves fluttered on trees high above her. The smell of blossoms drifting in the breeze. Magic spilled from every living thing around her. The ground, the earth, sometimes Rolina wondered if even the squirrels were magical. Her eyes opened and she took her first step into soft, lush grass. Her kingdom.

Dewdrops chilled her bare feet as she glided across the gardens. Every spring like the first time she saw it. Blooming and wild and shimmering. Maddy taught her and her brother, Eli, the names of each flower, tree, and plant, but she hadn't listened. When the wizard took them out into the gardens, her young mind couldn't care less about names or species. She took in shapes. Smells. Colors. And then she would look beyond. To the lone figure in the distance. Eden. He always chose the gardens to train. A harsh thing in the midst of perfect beauty.

Inevitably she would slip away from Maddy as he and Eli talked about science and magic and boring plants. Eden was not a person to strike up casual conversations with, nor a person to badger with questions. So Rolina would simply watch. And when she saw enough to understand, she would copy the maneuvers, imagining a sword in her own hand, like his. She pictured monsters and evil men falling before her. Imagined herself a knight, defending innocent villagers from bandits and beasts alike. Eventually Eden broke through her imaginary world and spoke to her. It began with a correction. *Don't plant your feet like that, stay on your toes.* And then he brought her a wooden sword. And then he was training her to fight.

Maddy did not tell her about plants anymore.

Rolina's path kept her in the heart of the forest, away from the military base in all its ugliness. She chose to shut it out during her brief walk. To pretend there was no war or bloodshed hidden just behind the trees. She strode up to the Emperor's Pavilion, an architectural masterpiece, sculpted to capture the natural beauty of the surrounding forest. Support beams shaped like trees and vines. Plants and animals carved into white marble. As she approached, she saw the figures within.

Dimitri sat with one slender leg up on the war table. His face in deep concentration as he studied the maps and documents spread across it. Mercury sat beside him, head resting in one hand as she did the same. Here, the High Emperors were tucked away from public view. Here they could slouch and kick their feet up without fear of how they would be perceived. Even Haven, usually standing alert and on guard a few steps behind Mercury, had caved. The guardian was asleep in a chair, sword sitting across his lap.

Mercury's eyes flicked up as Rolina walked in, "Good morning, Rolina."

"Long night?" she asked, nodding towards Haven. That was usually her chair.

Dimitri didn't bother to look up, brow furrowed as if working out a particularly annoying puzzle, "Just kick him and tell him to move."

Mercury shot her brother a sharp look, "Oh that's a great idea. Abuse the man who just spent all night helping us solve what to do in Onschuld."

A spike of anxiety shot through Rolina as she neared the table. "What's going on in Onschuld?"

Dimitri's eyes finally lifted to hers, "He's fine, Prayer."

Of course Dimitri knew what she was really worried about. The Holy Prince of Onschuld was one of her few close friends. If something happened to Ramarajan, it would break her heart.

Mercury sat up a little straighter and pointed to one of the maps spread on the table, "Kandston has been pushing into Onschuldan territory. However, the Holy Prophet refuses to officially take a stand."

"Meaning he hasn't requested imperial intervention, but hasn't acted against us either," Rolina guessed.

"Would you kick that layabout out of your chair and sit down already?" Dimitri waved a hand at Haven.

Rolina put a soft hand on Haven's shoulder. How was she supposed to wake the gentle soul after such a long night? After all his kindness, all his worry, he needed the rest. "I'll give him a minute."

Mercury continued as if she hadn't been interrupted, "We had to discuss workarounds on how to step in without angering the prophet too much. Otherwise, we could ruin our chance to get him on our side. But we can't leave the Onschuldan border undefended."

Rolina gingerly nudged Haven's legs to one side, placed his sword next to the chair, and squeezed in beside him. He wouldn't mind, he had always been a snuggler. Actually, it was kind of nice. He kept her warm despite the spring breeze fluttering through the open pavilion. "I still don't see why you can't just order them to fight for the empire," she grumbled, though it was a tired argument. "You're the High Emperors, they answer to you."

"Prayer," Dimitri flicked his caramel eyes to her, "Our power is a balance between freedom and command. If we start demanding they fight against the rebellion, they may very well view us as the tyrants Kandston wants us to look like."

"And that could lead them to side with the rebels," Rolina grumbled. She had heard it all before, but the hopeful side of her couldn't help from asking again. From wishing they could end the rebellion in one, brilliant maneuver and bring Eden and the others home. Rolina sighed and slumped further back. Her head landed conveniently on Haven's shoulder.

The guardian let out a little "mmm" sound, but didn't otherwise stir.

"I'm telling you, just yank a strand of that obnoxious red hair and get him out of your chair," Dimitri goaded.

Rolina ignored him, "What did you decide to do?"

The High Emperors shared a look, silently communicating in that way only siblings could.

"What?" Rolina scowled, "Am I not allowed to know?" They did, on occasion, hold something back from her. As close as she was to them, they were still above her. Still dealing with things she didn't - couldn't - understand.

"You're allowed to know," Dimitri said cautiously, then leaned forward. "We sent a letter to Ramar."

Rolina tried to stuff down the jolt of fear that shot through her gut, but it was plain on her face.

"He's *fine*," Mercury promised.

"Certainly," Rolina agreed tersely, "He's fine *now*, but let me guess, that letter is to ask him to act on his own. To protect the border without - no - *against* his father's permission." The Holy Prince could act on his own, yes, but that didn't mean there would be no consequences. His power paled in comparison to his father's. And his father's wrath... well, Rolina supposed she was the only one in the room who knew anything about that.

"Yes," Dimitri confirmed, locking eyes with her. "I understand why it frightens you, but we have to use the allies we have. No matter how young. No matter how beloved."

"Do you really think he can hold the border on his own?" Rolina asked, her voice small enough to keep from breaking.

"Ramarajan and Anish hand-picked his holy guard," Mercury reminded her. "They are some of the best warriors in Onschuld."

Rolina nodded. Ramar often bragged about his strength, but she wasn't sure how much of that was accurate versus a warrior's bravado. Certainly he had always been able to take her down when their arguments devolved into wrestling matches, but he was a whole lot taller than her and she had a bad habit of neglecting her training.

"Besides, do you think Tvor would let his chosen prince die?" Dimitri commented.

He has before, she wanted to say, but kept the comment to herself. The god's protection was not absolute.

Rolina tucked a strand of blonde hair behind her ear and asked, "What do you have for me today?" Better to get to work than keep worrying over someone unreachable.

Dimitri gestured to a stack of papers on the edge of the table. Reports and letters from across the continent and from within The Eternal Forest. As an assistant to The High Emperors, it was her job to sift through them. To decide what to ignore, what to delegate, what to deal with herself, and - most importantly - what to pass on to the emperors. In the last few months her job had become more difficult, and twice as important. Everyone wanted the emperors to hear them. To hear their fear. Rolina sorted their desperation into neat piles and sent them away.

With a sigh, she leaned forward and took the first paper from the stack as Dimitri and Mercury returned to their own work. Her job used to take an hour or two each day. Until the war. Until Kandston's lies poisoned the empire. She read through the paper, a letter from Elska, confirming all seven Elskan princesses would attend the upcoming Tavek celebration. She tossed it to the side. No reply or action necessary beyond a quick note.

As she reached for another paper, she glanced outside. At the trees in the wind. The fresh buds in the garden.

There wasn't time for that.

"I don't understand it." Dimitri spoke to his sister, but Rolina couldn't help but look up. "Redleaf, Bane, Frostlander edgetowns... what does he want there?"

Mercury shook her head, "Your guess is as good as mine," she grumbled.

"How do you mean?" Rolina asked, leaning forward to study the maps herself. Troops from both sides were marked with little figures that looked like they ought to be part of a game. Each one represented a different number of soldiers putting their lives at risk. They reminded her of the carved wooden soldiers she played with as a girl.

"There's only one goal in fighting the Syytan Empire," he said, not in the least bothered by Rolina's intrusion into the conversation.

"To kill us," Mercury agreed.

Rolina sank back into her seat, shrinking away from the awful truth. The warmth of Haven's peacefully napping body welcomed her. She nestled up close to the guardian and hoped no one noticed. She was a lady, not a little girl who needed to be comforted and sheltered from every unpleasantness.

"When we took the empire, nobody knew us. We had to make a name for ourselves first. Prove to the people we would be better than what they had, but Cadogan..." Dimitri's brow furrowed once more.

"He already has support from a number of regions," Mercury finished for her brother. Rolina wondered if they knew how often they finished each other's thoughts. How easily their conversation flowed. "He probably has spies and assassins we haven't flushed out." Mercury stood and leaned over the war table. "We know he's been recruiting under our noses. Only some have publicly aligned with him, but the roots likely go deeper. We have no way of truly knowing the damage. Not yet."

"And if he has as much support as we think-" Dimitri began.

"Why aren't we already dead?"

Rolina gawked at them. "Do you really think he could kill you so easily?" They were the most powerful people in the world, they couldn't be killed on a whim.

"Not easily, no," Mercury said, glancing up at Rolina. "But he did well keeping his plots from us until mere months ago. Why not have us assassinated before we even knew there was a threat?"

"Because he has to do it himself," Rolina reasoned, blind to whatever detail they were seeing. Of course she didn't understand. She was young and mortal and couldn't keep up. An inconvenient child they had to explain every tiny thing to. She sank further back against Haven, but the guardian did not stir.

"To become a High Emperor, you have to kill a High Emperor, yes," Dimitri agreed, "But if he has someone loyal enough, they could kill us, then let him kill them."

Her eyes went wide, "That's horrible."

The siblings shared a look, then Dimitri continued, "He's not acting like someone who needs anymore allies, and that means he either has much more support than the kingdoms are willing to admit, or he thinks he can do this on his own."

"No one can do this on their own." Mercury looked down at the maps, and Rolina wondered if it was an excuse to hide her face. To stop Rolina from seeing the concern there. "Which reminds me, who's his second?"

This, at least, Rolina could comment on. "He's unmarried, no children, no known lovers, no close family," she listed the candidates off one by one. Duke Cadogan was clever and calculated. He would have chosen the person who would rule by his side long before making any public moves. The magic that ran through Dimitri and Mercury's veins would not allow him to kill them both. Cadogan *needed* a partner.

"It has to be someone he respects. Someone he thinks would make a good leader," Mercury agreed, trailing off Rolina's thoughts much like she did with her brother's. A little spark of pride flickered through her. She *was* a part of this strange little family, even if she was an ordinary mortal. "He knows he's going to spend *hundreds* of years with this person, so if he's smart, it's someone he gets along with."

"Learned that one the hard way," Dimitri commented with a crooked smirk.

"Shut your mouth, you love me," Mercury shot back without so much as a blink.

Dimitri continued as if the comment never happened, but the smirk remained, ever-so-slightly at the corner of his mouth, "We don't know who he wants to kill us, or why he hasn't done it already. Or at least *tried* to do it. He's not rallying the people. In fact, he keeps making public appearances and pretty, lie-filled speeches, but his strategies aren't backing him up. He's not helping the ordinary man or striking against imperial strongholds. So what is he doing? Why these places?"

Rolina leaned forward in her seat once more, studying the maps. Hardly any of the marked places were important cities. And they were scattered far and wide instead of concentrated on one kingdom or another. He didn't so much look like he was invading as, "Searching."

The High Emperors turned their eyes on her. "I... I mean, it looks random, so maybe I'm wrong, but he could be looking for something."

Dimitri turned to his sister, "*We* are idiots."

"Speak for yourself. *I* am simply sleep deprived." She turned back to Rolina, "What do you think he's looking for?"

She shrugged, "Power? Something to help him win."

Once again the High Emperors shared an unreadable look. "Sounds like a job for Maddy," Dimitri commented.

Mercury nodded. "Until he's recovered, we'll give the task to less knowledgeable minds." She scratched out a note then snapped to get the attention of a servant waiting just outside the pavilion. "Please deliver this to our intelligence division, dear." Even her orders were sweet as chocolate. The servant hurried away and Mercury turned back to her brother. "If he's looking for something, he'll reveal his interests sooner or later."

Hopefully sooner, Rolina thought, but kept the comment to herself and looked back down at the paper she'd been neglecting. A report from Ev. Rolina stiffened. The rebels had only recently gained a foothold in her home country, but she knew how quickly their infection could spread. She read the report quickly. It mainly focused on cutting off a group of rebels who were on their way as reinforcements to Bane.

Relief flooded through her. Nothing about her hometown, Gaj. Nothing about her parents. Nothing was good. Nothing meant safe. And, it occurred to her, the less rebels there were in Bane, the safer Eden was. The less likely he was to end up like Maddy. Or worse.

She tried to cover up her nerves as she wrote a brief note,

summarizing the report, then tossed it on top of the letter from Elska. She reached for another paper on the stack.

"Prayer."

Rolina looked up, finding Dimitri's eyes locked on her hand. It was shaking.

"What's wrong?"

"Nothing," she promised, "just a little worried about Ev."

Dimitri studied her a moment longer, then went back to his own work, muttering, "Eden will be fine. Nothing touches that man."

"Of course," Rolina said, pretending he was her only concern. Why would the High Emperors care if her parents were safe? They were busy managing a whole continent and crushing a rebellion. What were two farmers to them?

She leaned back and pretended to read the next report. Her mind drifted to her family. To the rebels creeping closer to their home. The tiniest whimper escaped her lips before she could bite it back. At least she was sitting too far away for the emperors to hear such a tiny sound.

"Rolina?" a voice mumbled near her ear.

She turned to find Haven blinking at her groggily.

"You were in my chair."

He raised an eyebrow, "So you sat on me?"

"So I squeezed next to you," she corrected, shrugging.

Haven chuckled, "You're more on top of me than next to me, you know."

She shrugged again, "You were in my chair."

"I told her to kick you," Dimitri commented without looking up from a report he was reading.

Haven squeezed out of the chair and picked up his sword without commenting, "I should be going anyway." He rubbed a sleepy hand across his eyes. "I need to check in at the infirmary."

"Say hello to Eli for me," Rolina said as he strode away.

He gave her a nod as he marched down the stairs.

"What you see in that soft, ginger, meat-head, I'll never know," Dimitri commented.

Mercury crumbled up the document she was looking at and tossed it at him. He didn't so much as flinch as it smacked the side of his head and bounced to the floor. "He's sweet. You could learn a little from him."

"Sweet," Dimitri mumbled under his breath, "Like an idiotic hound."

"Remember, Dimitri," Mercury said sweetly, "hounds bite."

He ignored his sister and tossed the document he was reading back on the table. "The Monathi are gathering the tribes to discuss the war, but it's slow going. Most seem in favor of fighting for us, but others are concerned with leaving the civilians vulnerable. Bolwerk says he's done what he can, and wants to move on." Dimitri looked at Mercury, "Thoughts?"

"Bolwerk knows them best, and we've no time to waste. If he thinks he can't do more there, it's better for him to get on the field," Mercury agreed. "He's one of our strongest."

"And he scares people," Rolina commented.

The emperors' attention turned back to her.

"I just mean, he's intimidating. So it's better to use him as a soldier than a diplomat," Rolina explained, trying to look confident. She didn't want them to think she was talking bad about the Montathi guardian.

"Right," Dimitri nodded, then picked up another paper.

Rolina looked back at the letter in her own hand. About halfway through, she realized she had no idea what it was about. She shut her eyes for a moment, then began again. None of them could afford to waste time like that.

The soldiers on the Kandston front needed more food. Of course they did. Everyone did. A shame to be so close to a land of prosperity, but on the wrong side of the line. How could the leaders of Kandston stand to let people starve simply because they weren't *their* people? How could they do any of it? Lie and twist and work the people up into a rebellion.

She noted the section of the front line where the letter came from. Another for her growing list of people lacking supplies.

And then her eyes drifted again. Out, into the tangled woods beyond the gardens. So many lovely secrets to uncover, so many trees to climb.

So many letters to read.

Rolina turned back to her work.

A breeze fluttered through the pavilion, lightly rustling the papers. It caught her hair, danced around her. She could stand it no longer. "There's something I need to check," she announced, standing suddenly.

Dimitri and Mercury shared a look, one of those secret, silent messages exchanged. As close as Rolina could decipher, it meant something like, *I don't believe her, do you?*

"Go on then, Prayer," Dimitri waved her off.

"Don't dawdle too long," Mercury added.

Permission. Either she had been doing a really good job and earned herself a break, or they needed to talk alone and it was a convenient opportunity. She didn't waste time questioning. Rolina hurried down the steps and tried not to look like she was skipping. Perhaps it was childish. Perhaps she didn't care. Earth and grass and trees, she needed them like breath. Like blood. And when she turned a corner in the garden, tucked out of sight from the pavilion, she ran. Ran before anyone could call her childish. Before anyone could ask why she wasn't working. Before the world could creep back into her head. She ran.

Straight into the woods.

4

Woods

These were her woods. It didn't take half a thought for her bare feet to know where to land. She sprang over a fallen log, uncertain where she was going. She hardly ever knew where she was headed, only that she would never be lost. There was a trick to the place. One learned long ago. When straying from the paths of the forest, there was only one sure way back. She had to follow her feet and not her eyes.

A low rumble caught her attention. Something animal. Something large. One of Kail's creatures no doubt. Over the centuries he had amassed quite a collection. Beasts from across the continent that should never have been in one place. Rolina turned towards the sound to see an inky black panther stalking towards her.

"Chermak," she greeted the beast with a curtsy.

It growled in response.

Behind it came another, this one white, its eyes a shining blue.

"Good morning, Rosalba. I thought it strange to find him alone," Rolina commented, then started towards the animals. "You two are peas in a pod."

Chermak growled at her again.

"None of that," she scolded, reaching a hand out tentatively. Chermak sniffed then pushed his head into her hand. Rolina grinned. "You always act so tough, but you can't resist a good scratch behind the ears, can you?" Rosalba came and rubbed her big, white head against Rolina's back. "You're just a pair of sweeties," she cooed, reaching around to stroke Rosalba's side.

Both cats stiffened, their heads lifting to scan the trees. Rolina followed their gazes as she continued to scratch idly. Two figures walked towards them, far enough away that it took Rolina a moment to recognize the guardians. Iero and Kail.

She grinned and started to lift a hand in greeting. The smile faltered. Kail came out into the woods every day to feed his creatures, but Iero... What was he doing out there?

The pair stopped in their tracks as Kail placed a gentle hand on Iero's cheek.

Rolina raised an eyebrow. Kail had always been a touchy one, but the way Iero froze stood out of place. "Don't tell on me," she whispered to the panthers, then crept closer. She wasn't exactly a master of stealth, but she managed to keep out of sight. The harder part was staying unheard as she slipped behind a nearby tree to listen.

"She's so young," Iero's voice cracked.

She. They weren't talking about her, were they?

"That doesn't make her blameless." The beautiful Fae's voice was sorrowful.

No. She didn't care for that at all. Kail was supposed to be cheerful and strange. Charmed and charming. Not sad. Not worried over his brothers.

"You know she just got married a few months ago."

They weren't talking about her. That was good at least, but then who could they mean?

"Iero you can't think-"

"I'll be making a widower of her husband." His voice was hollow. Desperate.

Rolina dared a look around the edge of the tree. Iero's back faced her, but she saw Kail's thumb trace across his cheek. Tears. Her heart clenched. She shouldn't hear this. Iero was very careful to keep that part of his job away from her. The titles of Thief and Spy he wore with honor but it was this last one that broke him. Shamed him. Assassin.

"I can't do this, Kail." His voice broke again, and Rolina's heart with it.

"You always do this," Kail reminded him, but not unkindly. "You let your head get tangled in visions of widows and orphans and those left behind. It doesn't help, does it?"

"No," Iero said quietly.

"Then stop it."

Iero let out a bitter laugh, "Would that I could."

"You *can* do this. You *will* do this, and you will hate every second," Kail said, then resumed walking towards the panthers. "And then it will be over."

"It's not that simple," Iero continued, trailing after him.

There was only one thing to be done. Get him out of his own head. Certainly, his work would always haunt him, but Rolina wouldn't let it take any more bites of his soul today. She hurried back the way she came, smoothed the wrinkles from her dress, and stepped into view as if she had only just arrived.

"If you don't-"

"Hush." Iero must have seen her.

Rolina pretended to notice them for the first time. She forced her face to light up as she turned to greet Iero and the most handsome man alive. "Kail!" Her eyes swept over him before she could think. She would have been embarrassed if she didn't know how much the guardian adored that sort of attention. Thrived off it. As a convoluted mix of elven, Feinin, human, and at least a dozen other things, Kail's looks had something for everyone. Most people were either attracted to or jealous of him. Oftentimes both.

Of all the guardians, Kail had the least responsibility. And occasionally, he even had a moment to talk. Though she was warned not to linger, she planned to take full advantage of that fact. Kail *loved* listening to her talk. Said she reminded him of some of the Fae he grew up with when he was mortal. "Come to see your animals?" she asked him, noting the bag slung over his shoulder. No doubt filled with the favorite treats of all kinds of beasts.

He turned his tired eyes toward her, fiddling with the necklace he always wore. Three brown feathers on the end of a leather cord, decorated with a few beads. Similar beads on his bracelets tapped lightly against each other with the movement. Though she had encountered nobility and royalty from all twelve kingdoms, she had never seen any bracelets quite like them. But Kail wasn't born royal, and Rolina often wondered if they were traditional among commoners of one of the many races and cultures to which Kail belonged. Mostly because nobility and royalty wouldn't be caught dead wearing anything made of that particular material. Hair. Human or Fae or some other being she didn't know about. Each was uniquely woven with beads or charms. The colors were different as well, each belonging to a different person Kail cared for.

Her eyes drifted to one woven from thick, black hair and decorated with beads of red and silver. Eden's hair. She'd never seen him grow it long enough to make something out of. How many hundreds of years ago was that bracelet made? When did Eden keep his hair long?

Kail glanced over his shoulder as he walked towards the panthers. "Sorry about your nightmare last night."

She followed the look to find Iero walking silently towards them. Still in his own head. Still dreading his task. Rolina pretended not to notice his mood and turned back to Kail. Even if he didn't have as much to do, he was an important member of the imperial court. The pretty, charming one who now had bags under his eyes courtesy of her nightmare. His hearing was even sharper than Iero's thanks to his Fae heritage. "I'm sorry about the screaming." Rolina tucked some hair behind her ear, embarrassed for keeping him awake.

"Screaming?" he raised an eyebrow. Exquisite. Unfairly attractive in his confusion.

"Isn't that what kept you up?" she asked, unfazed. Kail was often dazed in the mornings. A slow waker.

"Screaming... I heard you... in the night," he said slowly, as though trying to remind or convince himself it was real. There really wasn't much going on in that head of his.

His expression was distant as Iero reluctantly came to stand beside him.

"What are you doing out here?" Rolina asked, giving him a chance to speak his mind. To tell her what was wrong and let her help.

Iero shrugged, "Needed to talk to Kail."

It wasn't exactly unusual for Iero to keep things from her, but it was always worth hoping. She would simply have to treat him as if nothing was wrong and hope it was enough of a distraction.

Kail reached into his bag and retrieved chunks of what appeared to be raw meat. Chermak and Rosalba happily devoured the offering. With hands still dripping red from the meat, he pat each of them atop the head. "What about you? Aren't you supposed to be stuffed behind a desk sorting through all that boring stuff?"

Rolina bit her lip.

"Didn't I tell you this morning you needed to get to work?" A sly smile slipped onto Iero's lips. Good. Even the smallest spark of his usual self was enough.

Kail chuckled, waving Iero off, "I'm supposed to be at the palace right now. But I won't tell on you if you don't tell on me."

"Deal."

"I'll tell on you both," Iero teased.

"No you won't," Rolina and Kail said together. They shared a smile as Iero rolled his eyes.

With Tavek coming up, even Kail was busy enough to need opportunities of escape. Guests had been arriving for the past week. Usually that meant Rolina, the guardians, and The High Emperors were all stuck playing the gracious hosts, but with the rebellion growing they hadn't the time. Kail wasn't good at sneaking around like Iero. Or magic like Maddy. Or most things in general. But he was charming. A little charm went a long way in building alliances and strengthening bonds. Rolina would have to do a bit of charming on the night of the celebration, but this year, it was Kail's job until then. She was more than a little thankful for that.

"You should come with me," he said, turning away from the panthers.

"With you?" Rolina's eyes widened and Iero shot Kail a glare she didn't quite understand. The party alone was more than she wanted to deal with. Lately she spent most of her days surrounded by politics and warfare, she didn't need it bleeding into a night that was *usually* about having fun with her closest friends. She hadn't seen Twila in months, nor Ramar since last Tavek. She pouted slightly at the thought. He wouldn't be there this year. His country needed him. Twila probably wouldn't be allowed to attend. Not when her kingdom was publicly aligned with Kandston.

Kail lifted his hand to her chin and ran his thumb across her cheek, "Your face is too pretty to hide behind desks and paperwork."

Rolina snorted.

"Don't be stupid Kail," Iero commented, "*I'm* pretty and I love hiding behind things."

She appreciated the backup. Though in truth Rolina was just as vain and petty as Kail when it came to her looks. Her vanity was as much Kail's fault as Iero. He was always telling her what a cute little thing she was, and teaching her horrid little tricks to use to get her way. A well-placed smile. When to meet someone's eye and when to look away. When to seem shy and coy and when to take control of the room. Like her lessons with Maddy, she had only listened to about half of it, despite her best efforts. "Thank you, Kail, but I'm happy with my job."

"Are you?" he asked, the question so simple and sincere, she wondered for a moment if she was. Of course she was, this was what she was trained for - by the High Emperors themselves. It was just... different lately. Before the war started, it was all about bringing people together. She found herself assisting with things like opening up trade lines between different countries or mediating potentially catastrophic conflicts until they were resolved peacefully. Now it was all starving soldiers and frightened civilians. Keeping people apart with swords and walls.

"I like my job too," Kail continued, unaware he had struck a nerve. He smiled brightly, reminding Rolina of the rumor that Kail was part pixie, and that's why his smile was so cute and light. She asked him once if it was true and he shrugged, saying, *I'm a lot of things, but mostly, I'm me.*

He pressed a kiss atop each panther's head then stood. "Come on, let's go see the nixies. The emperors can't blame you for avoiding work if you're helping me."

Rolina stiffened as Kail gave her arm a gentle tug. "Kail, the nixies always try to eat me."

"That's why I've got to keep them fed," he pat the outside of his bag. "Come on, they won't try anything with me there."

"Kail!"

Both Rolina and Kail jumped at the way Iero snapped. He didn't do that. He was made of mischief not rage. But then, this war had shown Rolina lots of new things she wished it hadn't.

Iero composed himself and slapped on a grin that wasn't quite as playful as before. "Come now, Rolina, you should know better than to let a Fae lead you off into the woods."

"I'm not just any Fae," Kail grumbled, ignoring Iero's outburst, "I'm me."

"And *you* have plenty of trickster blood in you," Iero teased, but it felt flat, forced. He stepped closer to Rolina and slipped a hand to rest on the back of her head. His fingers gently tangled in her blonde hair, ruining all the work she put into styling it just so. "I'm sorry," he said, all too seriously, "I know you need someone right now, but I'm afraid I have to steal even Kail away from you."

"Why can't you talk in front of me?" she asked quietly. She knew the answer. Because it wasn't her place. Because she was just a girl to them. A pretty toy to admire and play with when the mood struck and then be put on the shelf to wait. She hadn't felt so useless before. Not until the war broke out and they all knew their places in it. Not until they went off to be heroes and she was left behind.

"It's not up to me, Dove. Keeping secrets is my job."

"I can keep secrets," she promised, looking into those sad, blue eyes. Every once in a while, she saw his true age behind them. The weight of eternity.

"You don't want these secrets, trust me." He studied her a moment, as if catching a similar weight in her own eyes. "I'm sorry, Dove. This will all be over soon." Iero pressed a kiss to her forehead, as he had earlier that morning. But this was not sweet or doting. This was the kiss of a father afraid to leave his child. Clinging until the last second. Then he released her and started away. "Don't dawdle too long, you have work to do," he reminded her as he fell in step beside Kail.

"I won't." She watched them leave. Saw the slightest flash of steel beneath Iero's jacket. His daggers tucked safe in their sheaths. But who - she wondered - would see them next?

She dawdled quite a bit. Mindlessly wandering through the woods, head full of murderous thoughts, she tried to think who Iero's target might be. Her biggest clues were that it was a *she* and that she had recently been married. But of course she never really paid much attention to courtly weddings. Whenever guests who *weren't* Twila or Ramar came to the forest, her mind had a tendency to wander during the conversation. And whenever her two dear friends did come to the forest, well, they had better things to do than gossip about engagements.

She gave up on that puzzle as she passed the pixie tree. Usually buzzing with energetic pixies, the whole thing looked empty. Dull. Even they had been pulled into the war effort. Precious and sweet and stuck using their magic for death.

Her mind drifted home to Gaj as she reached the giddenburrow. The fluffy little beasts were fast asleep as she peeked inside. Waiting for night to scamper through the trees. It reminded her of cozy winters in the farmhouse when they would all climb into one bed to keep warm. Just her, Eli, and their parents. Parents now caught between a war zone and a kingdom of rebels. She shook the thought away and focused on spotting as many creatures as she could.

She found a snakelike faerie dragon fluttering above. A few snap rabbits hopped by as she started back towards the gardens. Even Kail's shy little petal bear peeked out of its cave as she passed. Lovely, enchanted beasts that reminded her some things were still right. The forest was still infested by oddities. Her parents were still safe. Her High Emperor and High Empress still needed her. By the time she reached the Emperor's Pavilion, her heart was lighter. More content. Her bare, dirty feet skipped up the steps to find the emperors just where she left them.

"How are the animals today?" Mercury asked.

Rolina froze. "Um, what?"

"You're not as sneaky as you think, Rolina," she teased.

"I don't know what she's talking about." Dimitri lifted his caramel eyes, and Rolina found them full of amusement as he said, "I'm sure my Prayer would never run off to play in the woods when there's work to do."

Rolina smiled, a hint embarrassed as she returned to her seat. "I would never." She picked up the letter she had tossed aside earlier. Three sets of eyes returned to the papers in front of them, and nothing more was said of the matter.

5

Papers and Pixies

Another day of the same. Documents and letters full of fear and desperation. Among the many problems spread before her, Kandston troops were circumventing Onschuld to push into the Southern plains. Rolina - with her limited power - couldn't do much about that, but her heart ached as she read through the report. If Ramar's father took action, he could stop the rebel expansion easily. Cut them off before they could reach the plains. But no. He, like so many others, refused to publicly pick a side.

Duke Cadogan had planted his lies well. Had worked so quietly and so thoroughly that by the time the empire realized there was a problem, he was already at their throats. No one wanted to throw their lot in with either side. Not until they could guess who would win. They'd lost so much trust in the empire without Dimitri or Mercury noticing. Little drips of poisoned words throughout the continent. Small enough to go unnoticed. Large enough to corrode over time.

Rolina forced herself to look away. She placed the report neatly on top of the pile meant for The High Emperors, then scowled as she dug through her paperwork. She worked at her own quiet, lonely desk that morning, set against the wall in her room. The High Emperors had private matters to discuss. Secrets even she couldn't hear. That was fine.

All her life, secrets had been necessary. But they held Rolina's trust so tightly, she never worried what those secrets might mean for her. If she needed to know, they would tell her.

With a sigh, Rolina began another look through the papers strewn across her desk. The enchantment report was due, but unless she'd lost it in the mess, it had never reached her. It was missing. It had to be. Rolina checked and rechecked the stacks of papers on the desk in her room. She found herself scowling at the empty space where it belonged. Searching for it was a waste of time. So was going to the armory to fetch it herself.

On the other hand, fresh air. An actual, real excuse to go outside, rather than her flimsy escape the day before. This wretched rebellion kept her longing for the trees and sky while she spent her days sifting through sorrowful papers. Like a princess trapped up in a tower. Or a tragic heroine cursed to repeat the same day over and over. Except she was only trapped by obligation, not locks or curses or fire-breathing monsters. The missing report was as good an excuse as she was going to get. Rolina stood from her desk, smoothed the wrinkles from her pastel green gown, and marched out her bedroom door.

She took three steps before a door ahead of her swung open. Her lonely heart leapt at the sight of Kail groggily exiting his bedroom. Beautiful, even when half asleep. Perhaps she could catch him, make him come with her and deal with the pixies in the armory. They liked him. Everyone liked him, even if they hated him.

"Late night?" she asked as she neared him.

"Mmm?" He raised an eyebrow as if she'd just spoken through a mile of water.

"Late night?" she repeated, smiling at how perfectly lovely he was, even when he hadn't the slightest idea what was happening.

"Uh, no, I was just very busy while I was sleeping," he said, blinking to shake off the exhaustion.

Now it was Rolina's turn to raise an eyebrow, "Right... You mean you were dreaming?"

"No, silly, I don't dream my own dreams," he said as if she ought to know exactly what he was talking about.

She decided to move on and took him by the arm. "Come to the armory with me."

"Ugh, no." He let her lead him anyway.

"The pixies listen to you," she insisted, dragging him along.

"I need to get to the palace."

"Can't it wait?" she asked, pouting as dramatically as she could.

"No, don't do that face." Kail looked up at the ceiling to avoid meeting her eye. Unfortunately, that made him catch an uneven edge of the stone floor and stumble forward.

Rolina laughed and steadied him. "Come with me," she asked again.

"You didn't come with me yesterday when I asked you," he reminded her as they reached the door.

She frowned dramatically, "I should have known you'd hold that against me."

"I'm petty like that," he agreed, smiling that pixie grin.

"Oh go flirt with nobles already." She gave him a playful shove out the door.

"I don't *flirt*," he laughed, "I charm."

"Off you go then." Rolina pretended to shoo him away.

"Thought you wanted some company?" he noted, falling into step beside her as she started down the path.

"I did. I do," she admitted, her playful attitude fading. "But you are right, you know. We should really get to work."

Kail frowned and it was so utterly heartbreaking she had to do something to fix it. She stooped down and plucked one of the flowers planted alongside the path. "Here." She had to stand on tiptoe, but she managed to tuck the soft purple blossom behind his ear.

He smiled once more and all was right with the world.

"Will I see you at dinner?" she asked, knowing the path would soon split, and he would have to leave her for the palace.

Kail shook his head, "Tomorrow's Tavek, Rolina."

Right. He would be too busy entertaining the nobles and royals of Syytala. Now even Kail didn't have time for her. No one did. "Well," she said, forcing a smile, "at the very least, I'll see you at the party."

He gave her a nod, then started off towards the palace.

Alone, Rolina kept walking. She ran her fingers along the flowers stretching up to greet her. Her only friends in a world torn by conflict. It was selfish of her, she knew. To think about herself and her loneliness when there were soldiers starving and freezing and dying across the continent. Selfish to wish her friends - her family - around her when they were the ones working to set the world right.

Rolina's route through the garden gave her an unobstructed view of the Emperor's Pavilion. She could see straight into the open end of the building, giving her a look at the man pacing inside. She would have waved, but the way he moved warned her not to. Dimitri ran a hand through his ash brown hair. He only touched his hair when he was angry. An effort to divert his desire for physical action into something harmless. Less explosive. It only worked about half the time.

Someone else stood in the pavilion, but it was not Mercury. A man, obscured by one of the tree-like pillars until he stepped forward. Her heart jumped. His stance, his dark hair, so like Eden. But he wasn't. She knew in half a second. Another half second for her heart to sink. She did not know or even recognize the man. An Eldurian, by his similarity to Eden. But on a second glance, his dark skin had a far pinker tone than a typical Eldurian. An Evyan? Whoever the man was, he must have been important. An audience with The High Emperor was no small thing.

Dimitri clenched his fists, his best efforts at restraint near to failing.

Rolina took it as her cue to leave before he caught her spying. Better to wait for him to cool down before risking engagement. She avoided the central courtyard as she continued on. It was too busy that morning, full of servants preparing for the Tavek celebration. Her path brought her to the edge of the gardens. To thick, tangled woods. She did not hesitate to step into the trees. This was her kingdom. Her home. There were easier paths to take, but the woods were shorter. Faster for those who knew their way.

It was not long before the trees broke away to reveal neat, ugly buildings bustling with activity. The military base. Barracks on one side, organized chaos on the other. Training grounds, supply stations, armory, mess hall, and everything else a soldier could need. Less than a year before it housed only a small number of loyal men, though Rolina knew more imperial soldiers were posted throughout the twelve kingdoms of Syytala. The army grew in proportion to the rebel threat, reserves called in, volunteers enlisted. Now their numbers reached the thousands.

She was welcomed with waves and warm smiles. The Lady Evensong Antares, as Rolina was known in public, was a common sight in the military base. Especially recently, as the reports issuing forth from it continued to be her only excuse to escape her room.

Rolina returned their smiles and marched into the center of the chaos. The armory. Several tables were set up inside, two or three pixies flying over each one. They uttered the same spell as soldiers hauled weapons onto the tables for them to enchant, "I grant you strength, a will to defend. Preservation of life, a soldier's friend." And then, spell recited, the soldiers took them away. The enchanted weapons were collected in crates, then either distributed to the men of The Eternal Forest, or prepared for transport to other parts of the continent. The next room over had a similar operation, but they enchanted armor instead of weapons.

She smiled at the efficiency, half expecting the pixies, known for their distracted nature, to be darting around, throwing magic at weapons aimlessly. But they had a system, and a leader. Rolina's eyes fell on a pixie standing in the middle of the room. Most pixies preferred to remain small, but this one took on her human shape and size to make herself more visible to both pixies and humans alike. Rolina recognized the metallic, golden shimmer of her hair.

Marigold.

Far from Rolina's favorite person in the world. But years in the imperial court taught her how to be kind and charming to everyone, no matter how irritating. Slapping on a smile, she made her way through the bustling room, dodging soldiers with sharp objects and concentrating pixies. She was stopped several times along the way by soldiers who wanted to greet her or simply shake her hand. Each time she offered them a gracious smile that was meant to feel like it was just for them, and expressed the deepest pride and appreciation for their hard work. Finally, she broke through the crowd to stand before Marigold. "Good morning!" Rolina greeted, forcing a little sweetness into her voice.

"My Lady!" Marigold smiled and curtsied deeply.

"Your report on the enchanting was due yesterday," Rolina continued, hoping the words sounded like a kind reminder, not a judgment. Sometimes her voice came out harsher than she intended. But she was working on it. No one needed to hear her frustration but herself, that would only add unnecessary tension. "I assumed with everyone so busy preparing for Tavek, it was a simple oversight." There was a question in her voice, a demand for explanation thinly veiled by a gentle tone. Fae were known for their love of parties, and pixies loved none more than Tavek. She would understand if the growing excitement distracted the little creatures.

"Oh that!" Marigold giggled, her voice too full of sugar. Downright inappropriate for a military base preparing for war. "I forgot."

So much for pixies and efficiency.

"But I can assure you, everything is going wonderfully!" she chirped, bouncing on her toes as she spoke.

"That's good," Rolina said, the sweetness draining from her voice despite her best efforts, "I still need a report." Afraid the pixie might write the words *everything is wonderful* on a piece of paper and call it good, Rolina added, "With specifics."

"Of course!" the pixie assured her with a nod that made her golden hair flash in the light.

"Since I'm here," Rolina continued, looking out at the enchanting process, receiving several more adoring smiles as a result, "How are the enchantments holding up? Any issues? Breakages?"

Rolina caught a waver behind Marigold's plastered smile. Her voice dipped low, as though she was sharing a secret, "A small number haven't made it through inspection."

"How small?" Rolina asked, matching the pixie's secretive tone.

"Perhaps... two or three out of every hundred," she guessed, flinching slightly at her own number.

"Three out of a hundred?" Rolina repeated, shock driving out the last remnants of kindness in her voice. Among thousands of weapons, that number reached the upper hundreds. "That's unacceptable."

"We are under more pressure than usual," Marigold excused, pouting like a child. "We've never had to enchant so many weapons at a time before."

"I don't need excuses," Rolina said. A flash of guilt burned in her chest. Marigold was doing her best. She wasn't a soldier. Just a woman using her own gifts to help however she could. Rolina tried to rein in her frustration. Demands wouldn't solve anything. Faulty weapons and enchantments meant death to the soldiers who held them. They needed the enchantments to keep their weapons and armor durable. To protect them on the battlefield. "What will it take to fix this?"

"More hands," Marigold told her, gesturing to the nearest enchanting table. Dozens of weapons lay on the table with only two pixies to enchant them. "They can only do so much, poor things. And the more they have to work, the more mistakes they make."

Watching one of the delicate creatures wipe sweat from her face, Rolina knew Marigold was right. Every available pixie in The Eternal Forest already had an enchantment shift. There was only one place to find more. "I'll write a letter to Kauneus and see if they can spare some enchanters." She thought to have Kail sign it instead of her, knowing his words would mean more to the Fae folk of his homeland.

Marigold's smile brightened, "That would be lovely!"

It sounded like more work to Rolina, but the lives of the imperial soldiers were worth far more than the time it took to write a letter. "I'll get out of your way now, please have that report for me by this evening."

"I'll write it the first chance I have," she promised, crossing her heart with her finger.

Rolina hurried out of the armory and took a deep breath of air free from pixie-sweetness. One job finished, on to the next. As she marched towards the gardens, her mind sorted through the tasks of the day. There were more reports to deal with. As usual. Requests for more weapons or food at this battlefield or that fort. The kinds of things she used to look over with Dimitri or Mercury for a couple of hours, then run off to enjoy her day. Things that used to be easy.

Kandston and Ev provided most of the continent's produce. But with things as they were, Kandston gave to the rebels, Ev to the empire. It should even out, by all the logic Rolina could think of. But somehow, both sides had starving soldiers. Guilt flickered in her chest as she thought of all the food being prepared for Tavek. How could they dance and feast while their men fought and starved?

A sour feeling rose in her gut as she made her way down the line of buildings. A skinny boy rushing from the supply building caught her eye, his arms full of medical supplies. Eli. If she didn't know him, she might think him an uncoordinated thief by the way he scurried across the trampled grass. "Bryer!" she called to him, the twist in her gut subsiding.

The startled boy nearly dropped the supplies. His dark-haired head shot up to look for the person who called. When his wide eyes landed on her, he relaxed. "Evensong," a smile spread across his face. "You're just what I need. Firm hands. Come on," he jerked his head for her to follow then continued on his way. Toward the infirmary.

"What do you need?" she asked, glancing back towards the gardens. She had so much to do, but what were a few minutes? She deserved a moment with Eli, especially if she was being helpful. Rolina hurried after the boy.

"Help with a patient," he replied, allowing Rolina to take some of his load. A box of dried herbs and a coil of bandages.

She threw a doubtful look his way, "I'm not trained for-"

"You don't need training," he assured her as they entered the infirmary.

Rolina balked. Fresh wounds. Blood seeping through bandages. Dread in so many eyes. A nearby healer worked on a patient with an infected wound. Rolina swallowed hard to keep from gagging at the pus-filled gash. She forgot how awful the place was, forgot the stench that hung thickly in the air. Worsened by the war. No longer was this a place for injured workers and servants with colds. It was a house of death. Of pain.

"I need you to hold someone down."

"What?" Rolina's attention snapped back to him, and she hurried to catch up.

"It's not difficult," he promised, though that was hardly her concern. He dropped the supplies on a table along the edge of the room. "Everyone else is busy doing more essential things," he continued, picking through the boxes for ingredients. Mashing them together in a bowl, he sprinkled the substance with a bit of water. Some kind of medicine, Rolina assumed. He scooped it up and started towards a man a few feet away. He lay on a cot, groaning.

"Evensong," she heard her name slip through the lips of a man on another cot, beside the soldier her brother was working on. Her gut twisted into a dozen more knots when she looked at him. His arm mangled and wrapped in blood-stained bandages in need of changing.

Like all the other soldiers, she offered a smile selected just for him. A softer smile. A sadder smile. This one was harder to give than the others, especially as she noticed more bandages peeking up from under his shirt, covering a wound that was awfully close to his young heart. But she gave it all the same, shoving her revulsion at the wounds down deep into her chest. "Hello," she said gently, coming to sit on the edge of his cot. He was one of theirs. One of hers. She could spare a moment for him, she could bite back the nausea from the carnage around her. She could give him a smile that was his alone.

"You're even more beautiful than the stories say," he half-whispered, his voice weak. Even half-dead, this one was flirty. The young ones often were. He couldn't be much older than her, yet he lay there, broken.

"Thank you," she said graciously, taking up his hand on instinct, "Beauty doesn't mean much next to bravery though."

"Trust me," the soldier cracked a weak smile, though his voice continued to come out a whisper, "After spending a few months in a smelly barracks full of other men only to be thrown on a battlefield full of even worse smelling men - half of which want to kill you - beauty means a lot more than you'd think."

Rolina gave him a soft laugh. "I'll have to come by this place more often then, maybe wear some heels." She didn't know if she could though. Even if her presence gave these men hope, she was already reaching her limit of gore and stench.

The soldier grinned, but shook his head, "Do that too often, and nobody will get better because they won't want to leave."

Rolina opened her mouth to say that they'd have to get better so they could pay her back by spending some time in the training grounds with their shirts off, but Eli called softly, "Evensong."

She gave the soldier one last smile, "Excuse me, it was nice talking with you."

"You should come back with those heels to make up for how short our conversation was," he said as she stood and turned towards Eli.

"Or you could catch me in your dreams," she said simply, then froze when she saw Eli's patient. Eli was finishing up rubbing the medicine he made on the man's calf. The leg was swollen and red. Nausea welled up in her throat. Gruesome injuries were not for her. Unlike her brother, she didn't have the compassion to look past her revulsion. Not for long anyway. At least nothing was bleeding.

"Eli," she breathed, forgetting they were in front of strangers.

He shot her a warning look, "I'd be careful what you say in front of this one, *Evensong*." Rolina caught the way he stressed her name. A reminder. Annoyance pushed away some of her disgust. She knew as well as he did, they weren't supposed to use their real names in front of ordinary people. But she *had* slipped up. The irritation dissipated as she watched her brother work. "He's not on our side."

Rolina held back her surprise, keeping her face neutral. Neither side was strict about uniforms. That would cost too much money and time. But the imperial men were required to wear the imperial insignia to identify themselves. Searching the man on the cot, she couldn't find a compass rose anywhere. "Then why help him?"

Eli stood and walked the medicine back to the table. "Because he's hurt," he answered simply. He dug around the supplies until he found some bandages.

Eli had always been kinder than her, but even he had to see what a waste it was. A talented healer like him shouldn't work on an enemy. Not with so many allies in equal or worse pain, like the man behind her, like all the other men in the room. "Hold him down," Eli said it more like a request than an order. Even when he needed something, he didn't demand.

Rolina stood beside the cot, placing a gentle hand on each shoulder. "What are you going to do?"

"Leg's broken, need to set it," he said, feeling the rebel's leg for the correct spot. "It's going to hurt, and he's going to react. Keep him down."

Bracing herself, Rolina looked away from Eli and the broken leg. She couldn't do it if she watched. Not without gagging. The man groaned. "It's alright," she found herself saying. Why, she did not know. He was a rebel. An enemy of the empire. Let him suffer. "It will hurt, but that will make it heal better," she continued, surprising herself. Perhaps a touch of her brother's empathy found its way into her head after all.

Eli snapped the bone into place. The man howled, pushing against her as he tensed. Rolina threw all her weight into pinning him down. It wasn't much, but she managed to keep him on the cot. "It's over now, you'll be alright."

"You can go now, if you need to," Eli told Rolina, practiced hands setting to work making a brace for the rebel's leg.

Rolina stared at her brother. At his mercy. Surrounded by pain every day and he kept going. Kept working. Helping. Saving. Fourteen, and already braver than her. Taller, too, and that vexed her. "See you at dinner?" she asked, breaking from the trance.

"If I have the time," he lifted apologetic eyes to meet hers.

Disappointment rose in her heart. She tried to keep it off her face, but Eli saw through it all the same. The wounded soldiers needed his attention more than she did, but that didn't stop her from missing him. With her own work to return to, she took a step away. She thought about saying *I love you* before she left, but it felt too dramatic, so she turned to the soldier from before and commented, "Imagine doing *that* in heels."

"Oh, I was," he said with a grin.

Rolina smirked and started away without another word.

She did not make it more than a step. An errand boy scurried up to her, doing his best to keep his eyes off the carnage around them. "Lady Evensong Antares, Lord Bryer Antares," he nodded to each of them in turn, "I'm so glad to catch you at the same time."

"What do you need?" Rolina asked, glancing at her brother. One look told her he knew as little as she did.

"The High Emperor sent me to fetch you. Come as soon as you're able," he said, eyes shifting between the siblings.

"Both of us?" Eli questioned, his hands fumbling with the bandages as he spoke.

"That's what he said," the boy confirmed. "If you'll excuse me," he scampered away, all too happy to leave the bloody infirmary.

Rolina looked down at her brother and was met by eyes full of worry. "Both of us."

"That did strike me as strange," Eli noted, looking back down at his patient. "He never asks for me. He doesn't *like* me."

Under ordinary circumstances Rolina would insist Eli was wrong, Dimitri did like him. Just not as much as her. But she hardly heard him, remembering the mood she saw Dimitri in before. This wouldn't be pretty. "Better get it over with."

Eli tied off the last bandage and stood. "Both of us," he muttered under his breath, trying to make sense of it. And that was the thing that worried her. Her mind raced for the reason he would want them both. All of her theories followed one common thread. Bad news.

6

Bookshelves

Rolina stood outside the pavilion with Eli, working up the courage to enter. Inside, Dimitri poured over the maps and documents laid out on the table. The many reports and letters that made it past Rolina's desk and onto his, or skipped her altogether. Occasionally he stopped to mark or note something, too absorbed in his work to notice the siblings lingering just outside.

This was where they stood the day they met, frightened and lost. Haven found them in the woods. Brought them to the pavilion where he had to coax them inside with promises of candy and treats in exchange for good behavior. Power radiated from the building, from the man and woman Rolina saw inside. The emperor and empress she was never meant to meet. Immortal and sovereign and greater than any force Rolina could imagine. Haven walked her and Eli up the steps that day, each one another trespass, a warning to run before it was too late.

She was afraid of him then. Afraid of the chill in Dimitri's caramel eyes. Of the strength in his posture. Of the casual arrogance in his gait. But children are easily bewitched by beautiful things, so she never feared Mercury. An empress turned goddess in Rolina's young eyes. She said something Rolina hadn't heard as they walked up those heavy steps. Something that made her brother laugh.

That was all it took. The sound breaking the tension in the air. Cracking his stone expression. Shattering her fears. The High Emperor wasn't a cruel man. He was a man who could laugh. A man as beautiful as his sister.

He had not laughed in a long time.

Rolina was afraid again. Not of him. Never of him. Of what he had to say. Ever since the rebellion began, since Eden and the others shipped out, she had waited for terror to strike. What if Eden - no.

She would know if something happened to Eden. She would feel it.

Just as she had before.

The night Maddy was injured, she woke up screaming. Not uncommon for the nightmare-plagued girl, but this dream lingered. Images of the wizard being sliced apart, piece by piece, by faceless rebels. And then the news came that he was injured and the dream refused to leave her.

Watching Dimitri between the pillars of the pavilion was not helping her nerves. Rolina tugged Eli by the sleeve and walked up the steps, as heavy as they had been all those years ago. They stopped at the top and Rolina knocked on one of the tree-like pillars.

Dimitri looked up long enough to wave them in before his attention returned to the documents on the table. His brown hair tumbled in front of his eternally young face. The siblings waited, Eli standing a step behind. Rolina stood close enough to steal a glance at the papers, curious if she could find any clue as to why she hadn't been allowed in that morning. She found only the usual. Maps of the twelve kingdoms, marked in two distinct hands. The first, Dimitri's small, careful lettering. The second, Mercury's delicate loops and swirls. Each one tracked different aspects of the war. Supply lines, battle progression, known rebel strongholds. On a map of Ev she found the names *Eden* and *Madara* written beside the town of Bane, though Maddy's name had been scratched out. Her eyes scanned the map for Bolwerk's name. The Montathi warrior was supposed to be somewhere in The Southern Plains, but she didn't know where. Perhaps that was the secret.

Perhaps it was worse.

Dimitri finished writing something on the end of a report, a note to himself or Mercury, before lifting his caramel eyes to study her. Rolina pulled her attention from the maps, smiling at the emperor to soften any remaining temper from the encounter she spied on that morning. "Sorry to keep you waiting, Prayer."

Neither sibling was particularly surprised he forgot to address Eli. He often seemed unaware of the boy when Rolina was in the room. "I don't mind."

"Everything going well on your end?" he asked, stepping around the table to lean against its edge.

"There are still a lot of requests for food and supplies," she told him, though she didn't think he had summoned her for a simple report. "Everything else is easy enough to deal with."

"And how are things in the infirmary?" Dimitri's eyes shifted to Eli.

The boy blinked. Dimitri was stalling. Why else would he bother speaking to him directly? "As good as they can be, Sir."

"I think perhaps the two of you should take the rest of today off," he suggested, crossing his arms in front of his chest. He was trying too hard to be calm, casual.

Rolina's stomach knotted. He was bracing them for bad news. Another guardian injured? No, he didn't call them in like this for Maddy. It was worse. What could be worse? "I couldn't," Rolina said, filling the silence, pushing off the news for as long as possible. "I have to write a letter to Kauneus. And Mercury asked me to look over a proposal to the armor smiths of Elska. Oh, and I want to find someone to clean up Madd's room before he arrives. Then there's-"

"Prayer," Dimitri lifted his hand to halt her. No more stalling on either side. Eli slipped his hand into Rolina's. He sensed it too. The oncoming impact. "We placed a small platoon in Gaj, due to its proximity to Bane," he began, studying their faces with caution. He knew his words were going to hurt.

"Gaj?" Rolina's heart thrummed at the name of her hometown. She hadn't thought about them. Hadn't considered them in her endless guessing of what could be wrong. She should have, knowing the rebellion continued to spread through her home country of Ev.

"I received a report today about rebel activity in the area," he pressed on, speaking with military-like detachment. His words came out flat, but Rolina saw something rare in his eyes. Sorrow. The expression sent ripples of fear down her skin. Were they dead? "Several farms have been raided for supplies."

"No," Rolina shook her head, already in denial of his next sentence.

"Are they..." Eli began, his voice hushed.

"The rebels took several hostages," he paused, searching them for signs his words were too much, that he needed to stop and give them a moment to breathe. Seeing none, he went on, "They included a list of names. I'm sorry, but your-"

"No," Rolina repeated, her voice small. They weren't dead but... no. She refused to hear the words. Hearing them in Dimitri's voice, in the High Emperor's voice, would make them real. Her fingers dug into Eli's hand. If he noticed, if he cared, he showed no signs. Her eyes locked on the emperor, silently praying he wasn't about to say the words she dreaded.

Dimitri began again, "Your parents are among them."

His words turned Rolina's face dark.

"Why?" Eli asked, his knuckles white as he squeezed Rolina's hand. "If they stole the supplies already, what more could they need?"

"Who cares?" Rolina said, voice barely above a whisper. Dimitri and Eli fell silent. "We have to do something," she continued, louder. Her eyes lifted to Dimitri's, "You have to do something."

She understood then, as she looked into his caramel eyes. He was not afraid to tell them their parents were in danger. No, he dreaded telling them he was not planning to help. "We can't waste resources on-"

"Waste resources? *Waste?*" she snapped, pulling her hand away from Eli as she stepped directly in front of the emperor. "These are my parents we're talking about."

"Rolina-" Eli tried to take her hand again, to calm her down before she overstepped.

She jerked her hand away from her brother, eyes glued to Dimitri, "You are the king of *everything*, you can find someone to spare."

"It's not that simple. Or have you forgotten we're at war?" he scolded, unflinching as he held her gaze. She was a child, what right did she have to talk back? What answer did he owe her? Rolina realized he could have kept the information to himself. Could have spared her the burning ache building in her chest. But Dimitri knew she would rather know, that she deserved to know. "The soldiers in Gaj are doing everything they can. That's all I can afford."

"Can they save them?" she asked, bitterness coating her voice. It was cruel. Telling her and doing nothing. Did he understand? Had his heart ached for anything in his long life?

"They will do what they can," he repeated. His voice was steady, but his eyes betrayed him. Doubt. He didn't believe in his own soldiers. He was giving her parents up for dead.

Anger fumed, twisting and screaming in her gut. She searched for the words she needed, but all her thoughts came as shouts and fears. One did not shout at High Emperors, no matter how angry. So they stood, eyes locked. Her breath came in hard. No signs of calming. Watching her, Dimitri's expression softened. He lifted his hand as if to reach for her, but let it fall back to his side.

Rolina spoke through gritted teeth, "I have things to do." Whipping around, she tore out of the pavilion, leaving Dimitri and Eli behind.

"Prayer!" Dimitri called after her, stepping forward as if to follow.

"Don't bother," Eli snapped, unsure where he found the courage to look the man in the eye, let alone speak to him like that. He followed Rolina outside, jogging to catch up. Falling into step beside her, he tried to touch her arm.

"Don't."

Eli's hand retreated to his side. "Do you want to talk?"

"No," she hissed, walking faster to leave him a step or two behind.

"Then let's do something. Distract ourselves," he suggested, already working damage control. Treating her like one of his patients. As though the news didn't hurt him as much as her.

The only thing she wanted to do was flop into her giant bed and wallow. Or perhaps hit something. Dimitri, specifically. Though if she stopped to think about it, she would rather hit a rebel. But distraction wasn't such a bad idea. Like her nightmares, if she could put it out of sight, she could keep it out of mind. Her usual work wouldn't do it. Looking at boring - though vital - reports and requests left too much room for anger to fester. She needed something physical. But all her usual sparring partners were shipped out except for Iero, and he obviously had worse things to think about. "I'm going to clean Maddy's room."

"Shouldn't a servant do that?" Eli asked, making one final attempt to grab her hand. She let him.

"I know how he likes things," she stated, though in truth Eli spent more time with the wizard than she did.

"I'll help," he offered. Rolina didn't know if he wanted a distraction himself, or if he wanted to keep an eye on her. It didn't matter, so she didn't ask. They walked into the guardians' quarters and through the second door on the right. It led to an entryway lined with overburdened, ancient bookshelves with as many splinters as books. Each shelf older than all their living relatives combined. Doors stood on either side and in front of them. Rolina chose the door on the left. Maddy's private library.

If asked to define chaos, Rolina would need only point to this room. In addition to books stacked on all available surfaces, incomprehensible artifacts were crammed in every corner. Her favorite of these contraptions and figures was a theoretical model of the universe, depicting the sun as a golden goddess with six arms, holding the worlds in her hands. As a child, the wizard had shown it to her and described the six worlds, each one sparking her vivid imagination more than the last. Then he told her the model was entirely inaccurate, and the six worlds didn't exist - at least not on their plane - but he kept the model because it was pretty and represented a lovely idea.

The memory softened her mood.

Until she remembered why she was angry in the first place. The danger her parents were in. Scowling, she marched into the sea of books and began sorting through a pile on the table in the center of the room. Each one a mental barrier between her mind and her fears. "*Hiekkem velki*," she swore, just how Eden taught her.

"Your Eldurian is getting better since Eden came back," Eli complimented, joining her at the table. The lack of anger in his voice and actions vexed her. He had every reason to fume and rage as she did. But he went about the room without so much as a frown.

"Only the profanities," she replied, organizing the books into a few neat piles based on where in the room she needed to place them. Eli sifted through loose papers, skimming through the wizard's messy handwriting to determine where each one belonged.

Though she attempted to concentrate on the books, anger flared in her chest again. She wished she hadn't spent so much time in the library as a girl, poking around for faerie tales and legends while pretending to listen to Maddy's latest slice of education. If she was less familiar with it, she would need to search out the place for each book, keeping her mind occupied. Keeping her thoughts far from the danger threatening her parents. But as it was, her thoughts remained on her worries while her hands worked. If only she had something to hit.

Somewhere in Ev, her family was in danger.

Rolina jammed a copy of *Frostlander Traditions* between *The Geography of The Frostlands* and a book about the various ruling dynasties of Iero's homeland.

They could be dead by now.

Skimming through a book with no title, she determined it contained information about Chyddan, Father of Legions, and the creation of Eldur. Rolina squeezed the book into a shelf with other volumes containing useless facts about the volcanic kingdom.

How could Dimitri leave it up to some minuscule platoon to rescue them? And what of the other farmers? How many were suffering at the hands of the rebellion?

Shoving books into shelves, Rolina paid little attention to where they should go.

Dimitri didn't care. Not about a couple of farmers he didn't know. Not when there were bigger problems. Rebels knocking at the gates.

Slamming a book into the bookcase, the old shelf splintered and cracked. Books dumped onto the shelf below and the floor. Helpless, she tried to catch them. There were too many. She dropped the books in her arms as dozens more tumbled off the shelves. A thick volume about famous Viskan wizards landed on her bare foot. "*Hiek*!" she swore.

Tears flooded her eyes as fast as Eli ran to her side. Any hope of distraction vanished as she sank to the floor, sobbing in the middle of the fallen books. Her brother wrapped his arms around her, pulling her close against his chest. "He doesn't care," she cried, burying her face against Eli's shoulder. What were the lives of a few farmers to an immortal High Emperor?

To her, everything. And here she was, crying like a child. Helpless.

No, not helpless. She did not have the power of the emperors, but she had a mind, and plenty of determination. If she wasn't smart, they wouldn't trust her with such important work. Those documents were people's lives. She just needed to think.

Lifting her head, she met her brother's green eyes. "We can save them."

"What are you thinking?" he asked, wiping the tears from her cheeks. He didn't like the scheming undertones of her voice, but he didn't like her crying either. This was an improvement.

"Dimitri won't spare any manpower because Gaj isn't strategically valuable," Rolina stated, standing up and smoothing the wrinkles out of her dress. Dimitri didn't respond well to pleading or whining. Not when she wanted a pet at age ten, not when she wanted that diamond necklace at fourteen. Not now. She needed to convince, not appeal to emotion. "So we make it valuable."

"How?" Eli asked, scooping up a few books as he stood.

Taking them from his hands, she used the motion as an excuse to pause and think. What in Gaj could draw the emperor's gaze? What had drawn the rebels? Food and supplies were the obvious answers. But

Eli was right, it was strange for them to take hostages if that was all they wanted.

"We could talk to Mercury," Eli suggested, moving the pieces of the splintered shelf out of her way. No one had pull with Dimitri like his sister. Or better, they could talk her into authorizing her own soldiers and cut Dimitri out of it altogether. Though, the empress tended to agree with her brother on matters of strategy. It was part of why they worked so well together, managing the twelve kingdoms. Beneath opposing exteriors they had very similar minds. Talking to Mercury would result in her rejecting the request, but in a sweeter, more empathetic manner.

"She'll agree with him," Rolina concluded, shoving books onto the shelf.

"You don't know that," Eli contradicted, handing her more from the floor.

"No, but I don't like the odds," Rolina shot back, stacking books on top of books to make up for the broken shelf. "We need to convince him something vital lies in Gaj."

"You mean, lie?" Eli asked, a nervous edge in his voice. He didn't do well facing down authority. Couldn't even look Dimitri in the eye most of the time.

"If we must," Rolina answered. The words drained the color from her brother's face. A lie would make Eli nervous, but he was always nervous in front of Dimitri, so she didn't think it would hurt their chances.

"He'll see right through it. Mercury too," Eli asserted, moving away to finish sorting through Maddy's papers.

She hadn't thought about him facing Mercury. He'd break the moment she looked him in the eye. "Then we need something real." But nothing worthwhile existed in Gaj. Not to an outsider, especially not to the most powerful man in the world.

"Like what?" Eli asked.

She didn't know. So she thought, and planned, and put books on shelves.

7

Value

Across the entryway, Maddy's office was twice as messy as his library. Rolina and Eli found their work cut out for them if they wanted to sort the room before the wizard returned. Like every room in Maddy's chambers, the back wall was lined with bookshelves. These books were different from those in the library. Mainly spell books and reference books. Several of which lay open on the table, evidence of the wizard's most recent research frenzy before he left for Bane. Most important to the wizard were his histories. Already sitting on their proper shelves before Rolina and Eli arrived. The row of books was broken by several gaps. Missing years the wizard longed to complete.

She remembered endless hours of copying those books. Complaining every minute. Maddy insisted the preservation of history was more important than hand cramps. He believed sharing information was key to the prosperity of all twelve kingdoms. But it was hard to spread what he knew if only one copy of each book existed. And it was an excellent way to improve penmanship and learn history at the same time. He often reminded her she had to learn both anyway, and may as well do them at the same time. That's what usually shut her up. Knowing the sooner she finished, the sooner she could escape his stuffy office and go play.

One history lay open on the large desk in the center of the room. Though Eli worked to clear the desk of clutter, he knew to leave the book alone. The wizard left the unfinished work mid-sentence. A great disappointment to Rolina, who noticed at a glance the sentence was about Eden. But Eli was the one who liked history books, and she was busy sorting through the apothecary cabinet. She let the book lay unread.

"Look at this!" Eli held up an old tome for her to see.

"A book," she grumbled, giving him no more than half a glance, "like the hundreds of others we've sifted through."

"Not just a book!" he walked around the desk to give her a closer look. For a moment, she thought it might be helpful. That it told of some unknown treasure in Gaj. They could show it to Dimitri or Mercury and they would have no choice but to send more soldiers. But the crumbling old thing had a copy of a painting on one page, and some scribblings in another language on the other. Nothing to do with Gaj. "This is a record of post-awakening Viska, written by Toperium himself," Eli said, his voice awestruck as he ran his hand tenderly down the ancient page.

"This helps us how?" she asked, narrowing her eyes at him.

"It doesn't," he confessed, frowning at her reaction.

"Then why should I care?" She moved on from the apothecary cabinet to a shelf where Maddy kept spell components, both common and rare. It needed a good dusting, and it, too, had been invaded by books.

"Because it's fascinating," he said as though it was obvious. Rolina watched her brother's eyes scanning the text as easily as if it were Syytan, not an ancient, dead language. "It's an original copy. Look, this is his handwriting," he held the book towards her.

"Erudite moron," she huffed, gathering the stray books. "I need *ideas*, not useless books." She gave the texts in her arms a solid shake to illustrate.

To Rolina's satisfaction, Eli cringed at the mistreatment of the delicate, old books. He shut the one in his hands tenderly, "You wanted a distraction, forgive me for trying." Marching across the room, he placed the book on its proper shelf.

But she didn't want a distraction anymore, she wanted a plan. "Try something interesting next time," she snipped. She knew Eli didn't deserve her anger. He had to be as frustrated as she was, and he was only trying to help.

The pair fell back into silence. Rolina thought to herself about Gaj. Its secrets and treasures. The more she thought, the more she realized there were none. Her few remaining memories revolved around her family, or her friend from the town proper. Exploring in the caves. Playing with Eli. Helping her mother with the house. Leaving was the most interesting thing she ever did there.

Her heart ached all the more when she thought of the journey. The way her father smiled and joked with them. He must have been worried, leaving their mother alone. No, not alone, she remembered. Their aunt came to stay with her, to care for her while they were gone. He shouldn't have taken them both on a journey like that, Eli was so young. But it was better than leaving them behind to catch the same illness their mother had. And he didn't know he would lose them.

He told them not to wander.

"How about this?" Eli interrupted her thoughts. But this time, the distraction was welcome. She turned to see him leaning over the unfinished history on the desk. "It's about Eden," he teased, knowing she would struggle to resist the bait.

"I noticed his name, but didn't read anything," she said, continuing her work, pretending she didn't care.

"Of course you noticed *Eden's* name," a smile tugged at the corner of his mouth.

"Do you have a point? Because those papers won't sort themselves," she gestured to the desk.

"It's early eighth century," Eli said, flipping back a few pages.

"The Taivan-Krilo war?" she asked, betraying her interest. For a girl who ignored most of the wizard's lectures, she had quite a memory for wars. The way the guardians spoke of them entranced her. Stirring her imagination in shades of red. Especially Eden. The rare moments he was home in the forest, she always tried to pry a story or two from him. Even when she was a child, he spared no details. Haunting her with tales of sating Tasa's blood lust. All with a thrill behind his gray eyes.

She skimmed through the pages, recognizing the story. Eden told it to her himself. Fighting alongside Daingeon and the other Taivans, though he had no wings. An enemy pushed him off the edge of The Loft. He gave himself up for dead. Dain caught him, saving his life.

Eli turned back to the unfinished page, his hand lingering on the smooth surface. "Do you think," he began, voice barely above a whisper, "Do you think he'll write about us? When we're dead. Are we important enough to be history?"

A hush fell over the room. In her heart, she believed the guardians cared for her. Maybe even loved her. But they loved before. How many people walked in and out of their long lives, beloved for a time, then forgotten? She and Eli were a blink. They weren't destined for history books. But maybe that didn't mean they would be forgotten. She knew some people stuck to the guardians and the High Emperors. Long-dead beings kept safe in their hearts. "I suppose that's up to the wizard."

She liked to think she would haunt them. For a decade or two. A specter, but not unwanted. Perhaps she overestimated their love for her. She was only a girl. Mortal and small. But she meant something, didn't she? To Eden. To Dimitri. Perhaps it was delusion, but Rolina did not doubt her value in their eyes.

Her value.

"I know what to do," Rolina realized, a thrum of excitement rippling through her chest. She stood up straighter, spinning to face Eli.

"What?" he asked, a spark in his eye. A small hope hidden behind worry.

"You and I mean something to Mercury and Dimitri," she said, heart pounding as the idea took shape in her mind. "*We* are worth sending more than one tiny platoon."

Eli's eyes widened, shifting to the door as though someone might hear them. "You're not suggesting-"

"It's time to leave the forest, Eli," she whispered. The rebellious, forbidden idea sent a thrill through her body that stifled any notion of fear or consequence.

"We can't." The color drained from his face at the mere thought. "We're not allowed-"

"Do you really think they expect us to stay here forever? They'll forgive us for leaving," her eyes shone with conviction. They had bent the rules for them before by allowing them to stay within the forest. Though they were told never to leave, Rolina knew in her heart they would bend the rules again. Rules that were laid out for them in a rush to cover their mistakes. Rules that needed amending. They weren't the same children who came stumbling into the forest all those years ago. They were a knowledgeable, skilled healer and the most trusted assistant the High Emperors had. They were vital. Loved.

"We should think of something else," Eli said, walking across the room. He picked up a few bottled potions to put away, as though setting back to work would erase the idea.

"There is nothing else," she leaned against the desk, watching him try to ignore her. Pushing into his personal space to make that impossible. "You know as well as I do, there's nothing important in Gaj."

"We can't - I can't," Eli stammered, hands shaking as he placed potions on a rack.

"Don't be such a coward, I can protect us." What was the point of training to fight if she couldn't protect her own brother? If she never left the safety of the forest? "And you're not entirely useless in an emergency." Rolina caught her brother by the arm and took the potions from him, "You're going to drop them with your hands shaking like that." Placing the potions on the rack, she continued, "Our parents need us."

"Our parents?" he stepped back, looking at her as though she was a madwoman, "I don't know them."

Rolina froze.

"I don't remember them, Rolina," he added, dropping his eyes to the floor. "I was three, how could I?"

His words were blameless, but they broke her heart anyway.

"I'm not going to risk you, the *only* family I have, for strangers," he said, taking back the last potion from her hand and placing it in the rack.

He didn't know them.

He didn't love them.

She should have realized sooner. He never talked about their parents aside from occasionally asking her to tell him a story. Something he'd done less and less as they grew up. He never offered any stories of his own, never mentioned missing them. Even the time she told him he had their father's eyes and their mother's nose he only shrugged. She thought then he didn't want the reminder of their separation. Now she understood. He felt nothing more than a shadow of heartache for them.

But they lost him all the same. They lost their son and he didn't remember them.

"I'm sorry," he mumbled, finding something to clean in the corner.

They lost their daughter, and she remembered everything. She remembered a quiet voice singing about raindrops until she fell asleep. Remembered her father coming home with a box of toys the neighbor's boys outgrew. Remembered chasing Eli through the house when he was nothing more than a chubby toddler. She remembered, and her memories would carry her home.

8

Warmth

Rolina did not sleep. Long after she and Eli parted ways, exhausted from cleaning, she lay awake. Her mind reached for an idea. Any path to saving her parents. But her thoughts returned again and again to leaving the forest. She meant more than enough for Dimitri to send soldiers after her. Maybe even one of the guardians. A perfect plan in theory, with or without her brother.

In practicality, it terrified her. Alone on the road. No experience to guide her. Neither she nor Eli had left the forest since the day they arrived, eleven years before. But the image of her parents, abused and starving in some dark cell, pushed away the doubt. All she needed was a bit of food and a blanket to keep warm at night. Ev was a peaceful country. Safe and kind.

Her eyes found their way to the sword mounted on the wall anyway. A thin, delicate blade, but sharp enough to hurt. To kill. Wooden beads embedded into the place where the handle met the pommel. The sight of those beads made her heart ache all the more. Once, they were not part of a sword, but a bracelet. A final gift from her father before he lost them. She wore it until her wrist grew too big. Less than a year before, Iero had snuck in and swiped the bracelet from where she kept it on her desk. He had been enlisted by Eden who was having the sword made special for her. The beads were set into the pommel as carefully as gemstones. The gift, though precious and beautiful, was one she never thought she would have a practical use for.

Rolina could lay in bed no longer. she threw off the covers, touched the wings carved into her headboard for luck, then slid off the bed. Her parents needed her, and she would answer the call. She marched to her wardrobe and threw open the doors. If she prepared for the journey right away, she could leave the following night. Tavek would provide her the perfect cover. Dozens of guests leaving in the dead of night. The guards wouldn't notice their lady among them.

As she dug through ornate dresses and expensive skirts, a new problem arose. Rich clothes, from what she heard, did not go unnoticed on the road. The chances of catching a thief's eye increased with every frill. One item alone passed as inconspicuous. A pair of riding trousers made of rich, dark leather. Taking a moment to examine them, she wondered if most people could tell the difference between quality leather and cheap leather at a glance. Hopefully not. She tossed the trousers on the bed and gave her wardrobe one last sweep. A single pair of trousers was not enough. It had always been a matter of time before her vanity caused real trouble. She shut the wardrobe with a frown.

A problem for later.

She walked to the door, turning the handle slowly. Her next step was to slip into the kitchen and snatch anything that kept well. Though the hallway appeared empty, the bedrooms of several guardians stood between her and the exit. Half of them were shipped out, Kail slept like a rock when he slept at all, and Haven spent most nights in Mercury's room. Leaving only Iero.

She had not seen him since the previous morning, but it wasn't uncommon for the guardian to come and go unnoticed. Light feet and sharp hearing. Once as a child, she sneezed in the middle of the night. Iero appeared seconds later to ask if she was sick. The incident gave her a strong sense of paranoia whenever she was up to something. If she was lucky, the guardian was still out on his ghastly mission.

Steeling her nerves, she stepped into the hall and froze. Her eyes fell on the door across from hers. Eden's. Man of simple taste. Perhaps she could solve her clothing problem after all.

Glancing up and down the dark hallway, Rolina decided she was truly alone. She tried the handle. Locked. Biting her lip to hold in a frustrated growl, she tried again. Locked. Scowling, she tore her hand from the doorknob and started down the hall again. But the sight of Iero's bedroom ahead stopped her. Reminded her of a story he told her a long time ago. About breaking into Eden's room, just to see if he could. The lock. Iero broke the lock. All she needed to do to break in...

Turning back to the door, Rolina yanked the knob awkwardly to the right while turning left. Rather than pushing on the door to open it, she pulled. The door clicked. *Thank you, Iero*, she thought, pushing the door open without resistance. Heat rushed over her skin as she shut it behind her.

Aside from an enchantment providing intense heat like that of his homeland, Eden's room was unextraordinary. If he didn't need something, he didn't have it. Except for one piece of decoration. A large painting of The Frostlands on the right hand wall. The snow and ice discordant in the immense heat. He and Iero had never told her why they had paintings of each other's home countries in their rooms, but she rather enjoyed the reminder of how close the guardians were. They were brothers. All six of them. Bound not by blood, but by the magic that made them immortal. By their duty to The Syytan Empire. By the eras experienced together.

An empty bed sat in the center of the room with its corners tucked in military fashion. Her eyes lingered there.

His presence hung in the air like an afterimage.

But he was not there to comfort her. To go to the emperors on her behalf. To hold her. She had not stepped foot in this room since he left. Hadn't felt his absence quite so strong. The last time he left was different. She had been sad he couldn't train her anymore. Certainly, he had only trained her for about a year, but she liked it. Training with the soldiers at the base hadn't felt the same. Hadn't been as personal. And he had left for so long. Years with only the briefest visits home.

It seemed she had only just got him back, only just realized what he meant to her, and then he was gone once more. Off to war. Her breath caught in her throat.

Best not to think about it.

She tore her eyes away and crossed to a wardrobe against the far wall. Jackets and coats took up half the space in the wardrobe. Many were lavish and expensive. But his other clothes were not much to look at. She selected two shirts, one white, one a dull gray. Like his eyes, but darker. Both simple button downs, long enough to reach her knees. She took a brown belt as well, then reached to shut the wardrobe doors. A piece of tan leather caught her eye, stopping her in her tracks.

Lying at the bottom of the wardrobe, a simple, inexpensive leather jacket. Worn, but well cared for. A hundred memories crashed into her at the sight. Riding on Eden's shoulders during the brief time they had together when she was small, holding onto the collar. Iero enlisting her help as a distraction while he attempted to steal it. Running her fingers along the old leather as he pulled her close. He usually took it with him. But there it was. Just sitting there. A hundred memories burned into a bit of cloth and leather.

Rolina snatched it up, only meaning to hold it for a moment. To feel the familiar texture.

It smelled like him. Years of sitting around campfires to keep his Eldurian blood warm put a permanent scent in the jacket. A scent like embers and smoke. A scent like Eden.

She took the jacket.

Rolina didn't know if it was paranoia or practicality that kept her looking over her shoulder as she slipped into the kitchen. The late-night trip was necessary to outfit her for the journey, but she wished she could skip it. It would be all too easy for one of the guardians to hear her rifling around, no matter how quiet she tried to be. Iero and Kail had eerily sharp hearing.

There were three kitchens in The Eternal Forest. One in the Imperial

Palace that was only kept stocked for guests. One in the military base, meant for making a large amount of meals as fast as possible. And the one she was currently sneaking into. The smallest of the three kitchens, and part of the guardians' quarters.

Rolina cast a glance at the dining room across from the kitchen. She'd been forced to eat alone far too often over the last few months. Alone at a table with eleven mismatched, empty chairs for company. She always sat in the one with a narrow back about the width between a man's shoulder blades. Dain's chair before he passed, meant to allow the Taivan to sit without his wings getting smushed. Rolina had unsympathetically taken it as her own when she was little, not understanding the sentiments likely attached to the wooden chair. High Emperors were replaced when they were killed, but the guardians were not. When they lost one, their place was left empty. A quiet monument to eras of life. Every day she sat in that chair, she was sitting on memories. Thousands of years of life, millions of days seated in that chair, Dain sharing meals with his brothers.

The chair beside it was made of enchanted silver, and always cold to the touch. Iero's chair. Quite the opposite of Eden's, which always seemed to have trails of steam rising off the dark stone. And there was one that absolutely no one sat in. Not Eli, nor the emperors, who preferred to eat with the guardians. Not because it was unstable, or ugly, or reserved, or any kind of normal deterrent, but because the chair was always wet.

Apparently, it had belonged to Ráj, the Valtamerian guardian who died several thousand years before Rolina was even thought of. Though Rolina had never met any members of the aquatic race, she had heard stories of the magically created Valtamerians and seen Ráj's bedroom in the guardians' quarters. It was more of an indoor pond with a few ledges for visitors than a bedroom. She snuck into the room regularly as a child for the novelty of swimming indoors. Usually she was accompanied by a protesting Eli, or her friends, Twila and Ramar, when they came to visit. As an adult, sometimes she still snuck in, though she was vaguely aware it was irreverent to use the dead man's room as a swimming hole. She didn't think she would get in any trouble for it though. Kail often did the same.

She *would* get in trouble for stocking a bag full of food in the middle of the night, clearly preparing to leave. But it couldn't be helped. Rolina slipped into the kitchen and set her empty bag on the counter top. She turned to face the pantry, thinking how lucky she was not to have woken anyone.

Iero leaned against the door frame, blocking her way. "Midnight snack?" He jerked his chin towards the bag on the counter.

Rolina all but jumped out of her skin. "Where did you come from?" she managed to say through the shock.

Iero laughed and pushed off the door frame, "Been here longer than you." Rolina's eyes dropped to the spices in his hands, along with something she didn't quite register before he tucked the items behind his back, grinning. "Secret family recipe, remember? Want some?"

Even as her heart thundered, she forced a smile on her face. "You're making teppen in the middle of the night?"

Iero shrugged, backing away from her so she couldn't see the ingredients as he made his way to the counter by the fireplace. How had she missed the blazing fire warning her that *someone was there?* Or the kettle hanging above it? "Helps me sleep. What brings you to the kitchen at this late hour?" His eyes darted to the bag on the counter before he turned around and started mixing ingredients out of her sight. She did notice him pull a second mug from the cabinet above him.

"Couldn't sleep." But that only explained why she was awake, not what she was doing there. "I thought I'd get a snack," she didn't mention the bag, waiting for him to ask. Giving herself even a single extra second to think of a believable lie.

"And this snack needs to be smuggled out in that bag?"

Rolina laughed, but it came out more nervous than casual. "No. I just started thinking about how when I get hungry while I'm working, it's a waste of time to run over here, and so sometimes I don't even bother, and then I get even more hungry," she shook her head, even though he couldn't see her as he mixed the spices. "I thought I'd grab some snacks for later." Too much. Too many words to excuse away her behavior. Iero always caught when she was acting suspicious, and this was even more suspicious than her usual troublemaking.

"Seems like a good idea," he said, then picked up a thick cloth to grab the kettle from the fire.

Rolina almost raised an eyebrow at him. He couldn't have taken the story at face value. Iero was the one who caught everything. Who called her out if she *blinked* wrong. He was just playing this out, waiting for her to crack. But then -

Rolina's eyes went wide as she watched him pour the warm milk from the kettle into their mugs. A shake. Just the tiniest quiver in his immaculately smooth movements. He wasn't just keeping his back to her to hide his family's secret recipe. He was hiding himself. Hiding a break in his mask. Rolina took a step forward. Her hand on his back, steadying him as he had done a thousand times after her nightmares left her quaking. "What's wrong?"

"Wrong?" he asked, idly stirring the drinks. Watching the milk swirl together with the other ingredients that Rolina didn't let herself look at. "Just tired."

Her eyes followed the movement. There were flecks of blood on his hands. Her chest seized. A quick search told her it wasn't his. But there was more on his shirt. A splash on his neck. It seemed he had completed his mission. She knew he wouldn't tell her whose blood it was, so she skipped the question altogether. "Are they dead?"

He nodded and slid a mug toward her.

She kept one hand on his back as she reached for it. "Did they deserve it?"

"Few people do." He lifted his own mug and took a long sip. Thousands of years of life. Thousands of years of killing. How it still hurt him was a testament to how deep the guardian felt. To how hard he clung to humanity.

Rolina took her own sip of the peppermint drink. Warmth seeped into her chest but it was artificial. External. The teppen did little to soothe the ache she felt for him.

Silence.

Time to change the subject. “Your mother taught you to make this?”

Iero’s eyes met hers and she found the smallest hint of joy in them. A spark buried in the deep. She wanted to touch it, to pull it up to the surface. “Just about every Frostlander knows how to make teppen, but hers was the best. We were poor as dirt, but she used to save every spare penny to buy the ingredients before winter.”

Rolina smiled. The spark in his eye was still buried, but brighter now. Of all the guardians, Iero was the one who liked talking about his family the most. The others were too sad or angry to talk about people who died thousands of years ago. Iero found it more akin to bringing them back to life, if only for a moment. He spoke about them like he’d seen them yesterday, not eons ago. From the stories she gathered, Rolina liked Iero’s mother. A sturdy, loving woman to the end. Even with her illness, she gave every last shred of energy to her family. “I’m glad she taught you, or my life would be lacking in peppermintiness.”

“Don’t let Maddy catch you making up nonsense words,” he said with a small grin before taking another sip.

Rolina returned the smile and held up her mug. An attempt to pull him out of the dark entirely, “To your mother.”

“To mother,” he repeated, tapping his mug against hers, “And warmth in winter.”

9

Faerie-Tales

She was nearly ready. By the time Rolina crawled into bed that night, she had a neat stash of supplies tucked out of sight. There was only one item left to steal. A map. She had seen the perfect one in Maddy's library the day before, small enough not to take up much room in her bag, but detailed enough to guide her straight to Gaj.

Rolina should have gone back for it during the night, but by the time she returned to the guardians' quarters from raiding the kitchen and stealing a spare dagger from the armory, she was exhausted. It was alright to sleep. If anyone saw her sneaking into Maddy's room in the morning, she need only tell them she had a couple things left to clean.

That morning she dressed quickly, the pastel yellow dress swishing around her ankles as she made for the hallway. Empty. Normal, as of late. She glanced around anyway, wary of Iero and his tendency to step out of shadows she did not see. Even with her easy excuse, Iero would know she was up to something. The night before was a fluke. She wouldn't get away with lying to him twice.

Rolina pushed through the door to Maddy's chambers, headed towards the library. She left the door to swing shut on its own, resulting in an unwanted slam. Panic shot through her bones. How could she be so careless? If Iero was nearby, he knew where to find her.

"Hello?" a strained voice called from the bedroom. Rolina jumped. All that sneaking around during the night, only to be caught here.

Wait. She knew that voice. Loved that voice.

Changing course, she threw open the bedroom door, beaming. "Maddy!"

The guardian smiled, half-lying in his bed, propped up by a wall of pillows at his back. A book in his hands. "I was wondering when you would come see me."

Lost in her schemes, she forgot how soon the wizard was due to arrive. The moment wouldn't last though. Her heart sank as fast as it had risen. She was leaving that night. This was all the time she had with him. The time it took to steal a map.

She pushed the ache away, choosing to focus on him. He was home safe, and she was there to see it.

"Why so dark in here?" she asked, crossing towards him. Heavy curtains blocked most of the light. Only a single candle on the nightstand illuminated his face and the book.

"I was sleeping, then I wasn't, and I can't move around much on my own yet, so I thought I'd light this conveniently placed candle instead of hobbling over to open the curtains," he explained in his typical, ambling manner. He pat a spot on the bed beside him, then winced as he moved to give her room.

"I could open the curtains for you," she offered, stopping at the edge of the bed.

He pat the open space again, "Probably sleep again soon. Sit."

She did, looping her arms around his. "I'm glad you're home," she sighed, resting her head against his shoulder.

"As am I," he sighed, leaning his head against the top of hers.

"What was it like?" she murmured. Maddy wasn't like Eden. He wouldn't give her details. Even in his histories, he recorded battles by statistics. How many fought. How many died. Notable events. Who won. Never how it felt. Never what he saw and did and heard. Never how it broke him.

"Bloody, tragic, sad," he listed, his voice low. He stared into the empty space between him and the far wall. "Nothing new."

"Were you afraid?" She squeezed his arm tighter. He may have been a living legend, but he could still hurt. Still break. Each of the guardians were heroes in their own right, but she held the privilege of seeing them as people. They were hers. The idea of them in pain stung her soul. It was silly to worry about the greatest warriors in history. But Maddy's heart was not that of a soldier.

"Always," he replied, his voice just above a whisper.

Rolina fiddled with the folds of his shirtsleeve. She should not have asked. Should not have dug into the wound.

"Oh! I nearly forgot!" he perked up, reaching across her to snatch something off the nightstand. He froze as soon as he sat up again, shutting his eyes. "I should not have moved that fast," he groaned, and Rolina realized his eyes were closed to stop himself from showing her how bad he hurt.

She saw it anyway. Rolina's eyes locked on the left side of his face. In the dim light, she had not seen until he moved. Scars. Fresh and gruesome, cutting jagged lines across his face. One dangerously close to his left eye. Her chest seized. He could have died. She knew it was possible, but the sight of that scar turned it into a visceral fact. Her wizard nearly died. Her teacher. Her friend.

"This is for you," he started to pass her a small envelope, but hesitated when he saw the shock on her face. Maddy smiled. "I know." The words spilled from his mouth like he was discussing something as benign as the weather. "My clean-cut look is ruined." The wizard slipped his arm around her shoulders, pulling her close to press a kiss on her forehead. "I'm fine, I swear."

She nodded, but did not understand. How could he sit there and smile when his face, his beautiful, young face, was so marred?

"Here," he handed her the envelope. "On the other hand, I look far more rugged. You see a man with scars on his face and think, 'that is a *rugged* man,'"

Rolina forced out a chuckle, but laughing at his disfigurement unsettled her. Unsure what else to do, she opened the envelope and removed a slip of paper, smaller than her hand. Scrawled in simple, messy handwriting were the words, *Still alive*, followed by Eden's signature. A laugh escaped her lips. A real, full laugh.

When Eden left them the first time, she was determined to remain his friend. She wrote letter after letter in choppy, childish handwriting. Still learning how to write from Maddy, they were full of misspellings and horrid punctuation. But they had been long and joyful. Full of how she spent her days and how training with Captain North was going. Eden, not particularly interested or even remotely comfortable with children, had written back *Glad all is well back home.* At first it infuriated her. How she could send him dozens of letters and receive only a sentence or two in return. But after a while, she learned to be happy he wrote to her at all. It was thoughtful for an hell born.

And now, this new little letter held so much more in two words than all the others. The sight of his handwriting, the fresh ink, eased her heart. He had taken the time to think of her. To write those two words to comfort her. She was his now. Perhaps this was the first of a new sort of letter. A letter full of love and care rather than obligatory response and tentative friendship. *Still alive*, and that was good enough.

"He tucked that into my pocket while I was lying there, half-dead, and told me to deliver it to you unless I died on the way."

A flicker of joy broke through the fears plaguing her. She still had plenty to worry about, but the slip of paper felt like a promise. *Still alive.* Still fighting. To come home. To see her. To see all of them of course, but she allowed herself some selfishness in her day-dreaming.

It was a sort of half-secret, her and Eden. Dimitri was the only one they made an effort to hide it from, and that meant not telling Mercury either. But the empress, as well as the guardians, had more than a little reason to suspect. They told no one. Everyone knew.

Except, possibly, Dimitri.

"Thank you for not dying on the way home, Maddy," she said, leaning into him once more.

"You're welcome," he flashed her a smile, the sweet one that reminded her of Eli. In fact, she suspected her brother had picked it up from the wizard in their long hours discussing boring, intellectual things.

Rolina still had a map to steal before preparing for Tavek, the celebration that would provide her cover. But she missed the wizard. The man who taught her history and science and all sorts of things she tried not to listen to. Unfortunately, she learned some of it anyway. "What are you reading?" she asked, settling in for a longer stay.

"A collection of old myths and legends," he said, relaxing against the pillows.

Examining it closer, Rolina recognized the worn book. From one of the few shelves in Maddy's library she enjoyed. Legends and fiction were always her favorite. And Maddy was an excellent reader. He used to do different voices for each character. A smile spread across her lips. "Read to me like you used to?" she asked, though she wouldn't blame the exhausted, injured guardian if he told her no.

"Which one?" he flipped back to the book's table of contents and held it up for her to see.

She didn't need to look, "*Alexander and the Apple Tree.*"

Maddy frowned, "The one with all the undead?"

"I like it," she defended. It was one of Iero's favorites too, ever since he was little. "He does the right thing in the end."

"You and your tragic heroes," Maddy grumbled, but there was a playful undertone in his voice.

"Which one do *you* want to read?" She did not care much *what* he read, just that it was his voice reading it. A voice she missed. Would soon miss again.

"I'm in the mood for something happy," he answered, flipping through the pages.

"How about *The Silver Songstress?*" Rolina suggested, shifting on the bed to play with his long, wispy, brown hair.

The wizard didn't notice as she began to braid a strand. "How is that one happy? Three people end up dead."

"They defeat her in the end."

"You have dark taste," he mumbled, then landed on a page he found interesting. "Here, *The Creation of The Loft*. Proper happy."

Rolina groaned, "Proper boring."

"It has a goddess and beautiful people with wings," Maddy protested, "It's delightful. And surprisingly historically accurate."

"Historical accuracy, my favorite part of *fantasy* stories," she rolled her eyes dramatically.

"Do you want me to read to you or not?" he shot her a sharp look, but couldn't hold the expression when he met her eyes. A new smile broke out across his face. "I really am pleased to be home."

"Read, wizard, or I'll have Dimitri send you back," she teased, settling in against his shoulder.

"Maybe I'll have him send *you* back," Maddy retorted.

Rolina's smile faltered. In a way, that was exactly what she wanted. A path home. Yet the idea brought her more guilt than excitement. How could she leave with things as they were? She had responsibilities. Reports and letters and proposals. Who would lighten Dimitri and Mercury's load when she left? Who would stop them from being buried in papers and demands? She knew she wasn't the only person they filtered things through, but even her small portion of the work overwhelmed her. Her family needed her, but so did the emperors.

Closing her eyes, Rolina pushed her thoughts far away. "Tell me a story of your own then," she said quietly.

"Like what?" he asked, and though Rolina's eyes were closed, she felt him looking at her.

"How about..." she tried to think of something happy, something Maddy would find joy in telling. Thousands of years of life to pick from. She chose the beginning. "Tell me about The Making."

Maddy perked up instantly. "Oh it was beautiful," he sighed, his voice washing over Rolina like a salve as he began. "They hadn't told us their plan to make us immortal you know. Only that we were to be trained to protect and advise the High Emperors. We thought it was just some ceremony - like an initiation. But the magic - I could feel something changing in my blood, feel it making me stronger. It was life-giving, powerful. And so, so beautiful."

Rolina imagined it as he spoke, weaving images of the bright, swirling magic that possessed him. That poured life into all twelve of the original guardians, binding them together. The day their names were changed and the Anluan brothers and sisters were born. A similar, imperfect immortality given to the first High Emperors. One that could be passed from emperor to emperor, now resting with Dimitri and Mercury. His words filled her with a familiar awe. Casting their own spell on Rolina's imagination, turning her fretful mind calm. Safe in the world of a time gone by. Safe inside the story. Safe until it ended.

10

Tavek

Waves of soft, blue fabric swished with every step. Lace coated Rolina's arms and torso, from her neck to her hips. The floral pattern perfect for the celebration of spring and new growth. Several layers of semi-translucent fabric added volume to the skirt, but kept it lightweight. Perfect for dancing. Perfect for running away.

A group of arriving guests gaped at her - one hand hoisting the gown over her knees, the other keeping the crown of flowers in place atop her head - bolting through the gardens. Late. She had fallen asleep on Maddy's shoulder. His easy voice and her lack of sleep combined into the perfect lullaby. Though she was pleased to find the dress as easy to run in as she hoped, she wished she had the time to walk. Ladies of her station didn't sprint across the grounds.

The central courtyard, like everywhere in The Eternal Forest, was surrounded by trees. Their gold and silver leaves glittering in the sunlight. The trees provided her cover as she dropped her skirt and slowed to a normal walking pace. Her labored breath gave her away, but she plastered on a smile and attempted to calm her heavy breathing.

Many guests had already arrived, traditional flowers adorning their hair in every shade imaginable. Nobility and royalty gathered in groups to socialize and pretend the world wasn't going to hell. Eli stood in one such group, dressed in a green tailcoat and black trousers. Trees and other plants embroidered on the sleeves and breast, and vines instead of a stripe down each leg, transforming an otherwise nice set of clothing into something stunning. Atop his untamable curls, a discreet and elegant band of golden flowers. Alive in the spirit of springtime. Rolina smiled, noting the majority of Eli's little group were young women. Their coy smiles and gentle laughter not as subtle as they thought.

Eli glanced her way, tilting his head towards the dais ahead of her. A silent warning. He need not have bothered. She knew very well the emperors, waiting on the dais, were not pleased with her tardiness. Custom demanded she present herself to the High Emperors before joining the guests. Ordinarily, she and Eli were the first to do so. Her late arrival forced her to wait while a group of Kaunean elves paid their respects. A stroke of luck, allowing her to fully catch her breath. As soon as they finished, she stepped up to the dais and dipped into a low curtsy.

"You're late," Dimitri said as she rose, the disapproval in his voice disguised by a small smile. Rolina silently praised the Keeper they were in public. He would have a lot more to say otherwise, especially after the way she snapped at him the day before. But Tavek demanded certain appearances, especially that year, with so many eyes searching for guidance, or hoping for a mistake to exploit.

"I'm sorry," she stepped closer, taking one of their hands into each of her own. "I was visiting Maddy and lost track of time." She left out the part about falling asleep. No need to give them a reason to think her lazy.

"That's a good enough reason for me," Mercury squeezed her hand. Half of the High Empress' strawberry blonde hair fell in curls behind her exposed shoulders while the rest was swept up in an elegant twist. Silver hairpins kept it and her own crown of pink flowers in place. She wore a silky white gown that hugged her hips before loosening at mid-thigh, pouring into a sea of fabric. The neckline dipped lower than Rolina could ever feel comfortable in herself, but the empress wore it with ease and elegance. Standing guard a few paces back, the dress was not lost on Haven. The guardian's eyes locked firmly on the High Empress' rear.

Mercury wasn't angry at her tardiness, and Rolina would have been relieved if it weren't for Dimitri furrowing his brow beside her. Only *he* could make a crown of dainty white flowers look threatening, "Tonight is important."

"I know. Tonight promotes peace and unity between the twelve kingdoms," she recited. He had only told her every chance he had in the last few months. It was the only holiday celebrated across all twelve kingdoms, and though it was originally meant to usher in spring, it had become more. A celebration of peace. It was a day when rivals became friends, when petty disputes were put aside, when treaties were signed.

When wars were ended.

"Not if he keeps his eyebrows all scrunched together like that," Mercury commented, smirking at her brother. "You could start a war with those eyebrows alone."

The cold look Dimitri shot her only made her laugh. Choosing to ignore his sister, he turned his focus back to Rolina, "Go mingle with the guests. And be on your best behavior. Tonight you represent the empire, do it well."

Tonight she represented the empire. Tonight she would flee the heart of the empire.

"Don't put so much pressure on the girl," Mercury scolded, running her thumb over the back of Rolina's hand. "People adore you, darling. Just be what you are, and that will reflect well on us."

Rolina nodded and curtsied once more before joining the crowd. This was the part she hated. Waiting. People came from all across the twelve kingdoms, arriving one by one through the course of the day. Many had arrived throughout the week, resting in the Imperial Palace before the day of the party. As a member of the imperial court, her presence was required during the long hours of guests arriving. Chatting about nothing and flashing sweet smiles until the real celebration began. She would rather spend the afternoon listening to one of Madd's lectures.

She waded into the growing crowd, joining a group of young nobles who accepted her gladly.

"Perhaps Lady Evensong can tell us," a woman suggested as Rolina took her place between two young lords.

"Tell you what?" she asked, recognizing the woman as one of the princesses of Elska, but for the life of her, she couldn't remember which one. She recited their names in her head until she came to the one she thought was her age. Zosime, she thought. By the muscles showing through her tight sleeves, Rolina thought she was right. Each of the princesses were taught to find their own place in the Elskan court, and Zosime had chosen the path of a general. According to Mercury, her force was just as strong as the famed Frostlandian Royal Guard.

Her attention drifted to a Taivan in the group as she contemplated if she had indeed identified the princess correctly. Rolina could not take her eyes off the Taivan girl's wings. A dozen shades of glossy brown feathers. By the elegant yet fierce cut of her gown, the muscles revealed by the off-shoulder sleeves, Rolina wondered if she was a noble or a warrior. Perhaps both.

Funny, to casually stand among such powerful warriors and leaders while a war waged just beyond their borders. As if it was all some distant misunderstanding, not a life and death, world-changing event. Shouldn't young women such as these be out there, commanding their soldiers to stand with the empire?

"There are rumors the Duke of Kandston will be here tonight," the lord to her right said. Her attention snapped from the girl to him. She didn't recognize him, but his clothes bore several Viskan qualities, sharp and clean-cut and entirely ordinary in their elegance. An aspiring scholar or apprentice wizard, though the runestone amulet dangling from his neck led her to believe the latter.

"He's not brave enough to show his face here," Zosime insisted, her expression hard, as if holding back her most venomous words.

Rolina expected the back and forth to continue, for the young group to toss around their opinions until he either showed up or didn't, but they fell quiet. Looking to her. Expecting the girl tied so close to the

Syytan Empire to know more, to have some sort of secret knowledge. But she didn't know any better than they did. Her face was too hot with all of them staring, waiting for an answer. Blinking, she tried to determine an appropriate one. One that didn't involve any of the Eldurian profanities she typically used to illustrate her opinion of the duke.

She understood the nervous anticipation in their eyes. Some were outright fearful of the man, knowing all too well the damage he wrought on their kingdoms. Would Duke Cadogan, leader of the rebellion, have the audacity to show his face on this peaceful occasion?

As she glanced around the courtyard, she noted a distinct absence of anyone from Kandston. Were they following their leader's command, or afraid of what the other nobles would do if they came? Though Dimitri and Mercury would never allow harm to befall anyone on Tavek, a holiday of peace. And there she found her answer, "As the only holiday honored across all twelve kingdoms, this is a celebration of peace and unity," she began, trying to sound confident, like Mercury, "if the Duke of Kandston attends, he will be accepted in the spirit of making peace. However, should he show any harmful intention, he should not forget where he stands."

The group remained silent, taking in the words. They were too forceful. Occasionally she spoke like Eden or Dimitri. Putting more of a threat in her voice than she meant. She was supposed to be pretty and charming, not threatening. Her stomach churned. She messed up before the party had even started.

A tall, young woman smiled, a flicker behind her eyes that reminded Rolina of Iero, "If he makes a move against anyone, I'll end him myself."

"Lady Katherine!" the Elskan princess exclaimed. Not in surprise. Amusement.

"I'm sure it won't come to that," the Viskan lord chimed in. "As the Lady said," he nodded towards Rolina, "this is a celebration of peace. He is not stupid enough to break that. If he shows up at all."

The lords and ladies murmured their ascent. She spoke well. They didn't mind the thinly veiled threat in her voice. Though, unlike most of the guests, these were her peers. While they came from all across the continent, there was a unity in that. A vigor of youth that held them together, despite the vast differences in culture. Others might not agree so readily.

Hours passed as Rolina meandered through the growing crowd, sharing in trivial conversation. A few of the more ambitious lords threw flattery her way or asked if she might save a dance for them. To which she smiled and agreed and tried to make them feel important. Not that she cared for their feelings, or for them. She'd rather dance with North and his soldiers, who she knew were holding their own kind of celebration at the base. A rowdier, louder, and probably more fun celebration. But if the young lords thought they had a chance with her, they might be less inclined to side against her, and therefore, against the empire. And if they realized they did not, they would at least remember how good she made them feel. Small, petty things could make all the difference.

As the majority of guests arrived, the celebration could truly begin. But before the musicians could strike up a song, or couples could take to the dance floor, one tradition had to be observed. The guests waited on the outer edges of the courtyard, and the emperors took their seats on the dais. Those who attended the ceremony in previous years murmured in anticipation, while newcomers waited in curiosity. Rolina made her way to the front of the gathered crowd, too short to see from anywhere else. As she broke through the wall of lords and ladies, she found herself standing beside a pair of familiar faces.

Her heart leapt with joy as she dipped into a curtsy, "Your Highness." She lifted her head to meet the dark eyes of Farran, King of Illandia. A hint of a smile on his thin lips. Beside him his daughter, Princess Twila, beamed and bounced on her toes, making the expertly crafted curls in her usually straight brown hair spring up and down.

"Lady Evensong," he offered a respectful nod.

The formal greeting out of the way, Twila pushed her father aside and threw her arms around Rolina, "It's been too long!"

"It has!" Rolina agreed, throwing all her energy into the hug. Their crowns of flowers bopped into each other, causing Twila's crown of red roses to tip back out of place, and Rolina's forget-me-nots to fall off her head entirely. The friends giggled as Rolina struggled to catch the flowers before they hit the ground. She set the crown back atop her head, and Twila straightened it for her. Rolina looked the princess over, taking in the striking red and black of her gown. A gold brooch pinned near her collarbone depicting the head of a ram, the symbol of Illandia. The girls drank each other in, taking a moment to be themselves, to be friends, before both of their smiles faltered. "I wasn't sure you'd be here tonight."

"I insisted Father bring me along even though things are..." *tense, hard, broken,* Rolina imagined a number of words to complete the princess' unfinished sentence. Twila tucked her hair behind her pointed ear, trying to find a way around the uncomfortable topic. It was well known Illandia was taking the side of the rebellion. Well known that the girls ought to break off their friendship entirely. But it was Tavek, and if Rolina couldn't stand side-by-side with her friend on that of all nights, what was the point?

"No Nox and Aurora tonight?" Rolina asked, pushing the conversation along before it became too difficult.

"I didn't want to bring my children through a war zone for a party," Farran commented, casting a pointed look Twila's way, "*Someone* values a night with her friend more than her own safety."

"Don't think of it that way, Father," Twila grinned, all the mischief of her Feinin heritage held in a single smile. "Think of it as a girl braving dangerous lands to show the empire just how important peace is to her. And yes, that includes a night with my friend," she looped her arm around Rolina's.

"It does send a good message," Farran conceded, but Rolina could see the struggle in his face. The fight to remain calm while he - while his daughter - stood in the heart of enemy territory, taking an uncertain step towards peace. It was strange for Rolina to see him so tense. He had always been welcome before the rebellion. Bringing Twila and sometimes his other children along when he had business in the forest.

An excuse for the children to run wild through the gardens. Sometimes he brought Rolina trinkets from Illandia. His way of telling her she was welcome among his family. That he was happy Twila found such a caring friend. Rolina had always been jealous of Twila. Of Farran's children and the way he adored them. Her own father miles away, unaware of what happened to her.

She wondered how such a kind man could ever choose the rebellion. How he could think a man as malicious as Duke Cadogan was right.

"Well I'm happy to see you," Twila whispered in Rolina's ear, "regardless of the message it sends."

She opened her mouth to tell Twila she felt the same, but something glittering caught her eye. She looked towards the trees circling the courtyard.

Dim lights of every different color began to glow in the trees as the sun fell over the horizon. Like a starry canopy hidden in the leaves. Two by two, pixies flew into the courtyard from the entrance opposite the dais. Rolina smiled at the tiny figures. Beautiful, even if she hated working with them. Each wore their finest clothes, bright colors reflecting their unique hair, unnatural hues in nearly every other sentient species. Blues and pinks, golds and greens. And as it was a special occasion, each and every one released their glow, shining the same color as their clothes and hair. They were partnered with a pixie of the same color as they entered, flying in slow and graceful. When the front of the line reached the dais, they split, curving away in opposite directions back towards the entrance. The pixies at the front of each line met each other at the start. The result was a perfect circle, the colors on one half reflecting the other.

Facing inward, the pixies held out their hands, palms upward. One of the leading pixies, a woman with green hair to her knees, spoke. "Come alive, old ancient trees. Wake thee now, refresh thy leaves. Open your petals, flowers all. Spring beckons, answer her call." The spell recited, the pixies closed their eyes. With a single, collective breath, flowers sprouted from their outstretched hands. One flower for every pixie, different kinds, but matching in color. As the flowers reached their full maturity, the pixies closed their palms, then brought their hands close to their lips.

Rolina smiled, her favorite part.

The pixies opened their palms and blew, like a kiss. And from them, thousands of petals flew into the air. They drifted higher, lingering and floating in the air like multicolored raindrops. And there they stayed, blowing back and forth above the courtyard, joining the starry lights in the leaves.

Spring was here.

Their ritual complete, the pixies flew away, two by two as they had come. A silent moment passed as the guests looked up, watching the petals dance in the glow. Mercury waved a hand to the musicians, and the party began.

As was the way of these things, Rolina found herself passed from partner to partner, hardly a moment to catch her breath between dances. If only she could have spent her time with Twila instead. She missed the days of sitting at one of the tables on the far end of the dance floor, too young to join in aside from an occasional dance with Eli in the corner. Just her and her brother instead of dozens of lords and princes vying for her attention. Mercury was right, people liked her. Especially men. And it appeared, from the few times she passed him on the dance floor, Eli was doing just as well with the women. A different lady in his arms each time.

She eyed Dimitri as she and her current dance partner passed the dais. He sat on the throne watching the festivities, but never joining. Not really. Rolina knew he would dance once, with Mercury, and only because she made him. Typically he would sit in his chair and wait for it to be over, but tonight he made an effort to socialize with the guests. He couldn't ease in and out of conversations the way his sister could, and would likely make them uncomfortable if he tried, so he didn't leave his throne. Instead, he smiled and welcomed anyone brave enough to approach. And as others noticed, more came, eager to impress or simply be noticed. One of the princesses of Elska stood by and talked with him for a full twenty minutes before feeling the need to scurry away from his scrutinizing glare. If only he'd asked her to dance. But he wouldn't ask anyone. He would sit in that chair and watch and study, wishing he knew how to step into their world. Most of the time, he watched his sister. Sometimes, he watched Rolina.

The song ended, and Rolina politely excused herself. Her feet needed a break from dancing. She dashed away before any other gentlemen could catch her. Unable to spot Twila in the crowd, she joined another group of young nobles by the edge of the dance floor. Some were the same as before, such as Lady Katherine and the Viskan apprentice. Two prominent young men stood next to each other, an Eldurian hell born from House Malan, and the son of a Montathi chief.

Rolina seized the opportunity to wedge herself between them. A shield against further invitations to dance. Usually, she didn't mind turning men away when her feet started hurting, but that night she represented the empire. And she had a feeling people would like 'the empire' to be accommodating. Neither man seemed to mind the presence of the lovely, petite, lady of the imperial court. In fact, the hell born's gold eyes swept over her from head to toe. Twice. A moment later, Rolina realized he had scooted closer because their fingers brushed. She flashed him a coy smile, though she'd been warned never to trust a hell born. Something wicked flickered in his eyes as he returned the smile. Rolina hid the shudder that rippled down her spine and subtly shifted closer to the Montathi.

"Evensong!" a voice chirped, and Rolina turned to find Twila gliding up to the group. She pushed her way between Rolina and the hell born, a wall between her friend and danger.

A smile tugged at the corners of Rolina's mouth, but vanished as the Montathi beside her commented, "What's a traitor like you doing here?"

The group stilled, waiting for Twila to respond, afraid of an argument getting out-of-hand. Of lines being drawn. Of peaceful hopes ground into dust.

"All are welcome on Tavek," Rolina reminded them before Twila could snap back and get herself into trouble. "Now if you'll excuse us," she added, preferring Twila's company over a group of near-strangers. She guided the princess to the edge of the courtyard, still in sight, but private enough.

"Thanks," Twila said, scowling, "I would have made a mess of things."

"He shouldn't have spoken to you like that," Rolina said, touching her friend's arm gently.

"He's right though," she said bitterly, her brown eyes dropping to the ground. "I just wish I could put my heart into defending myself. In defending my father."

Rolina blinked. This was the first she heard of Twila disagreeing with her Father's decision to side with the rebels. No wonder she was fighting so hard for peace, she didn't believe in her own family's actions. Rolina thought about Farran's earlier words. About their friendship sending a message. If that was true, they needed to stick together all the more.

A selfish thought slipped into Rolina's mind. A way to send a message. A way to keep Twila out of her father's decisions.

"Do you..." Rolina hesitated. This could ruin everything. Twila could run to her father or the emperors and end her plans before they began. But years of friendship urged her to keep going. To trust Twila. "Do you remember what I told you when we were little, about," her voice dropped into a whisper, "my family."

Twila lifted her eyes, confused as to why Rolina would bring it up, but she nodded.

"Yesterday I found out my parents are being held captive by rebels in Gaj," she whispered as quickly as she could, wanting to get the incriminating words out before anyone could hear. "I'm planning to go after them so that Dimitri will have no choice but to send aid."

The princess' eyes were wide, but she didn't say a word, understanding that interruptions would only increase their chances of being overheard.

"I'm leaving tonight, after the party. Come with me," Rolina suggested, praying silently to the Keeper that it wasn't a mistake. That even if Twila refused to come, she wouldn't tell anyone.

"I..." Twila looked across the courtyard. Rolina followed her gaze to

Farran, talking with a group of his own peers. "I shouldn't..." her voice dropped even quieter, "he needs me."

"What for?" Rolina asked, gently turning Twila's chin so their eyes met. "To smile and nod while he sends your people to slaughter? If you want to change his mind, take a stand. It doesn't have to be this," Rolina added, though the more she thought about it, the more she wanted her friend to come with her. Twila's Feinin magic could mean the difference between survival and death in a world largely unknown to Rolina. And her experience would be worth its weight in gold. More than that, her lonely heart *needed* someone. After weeks, months of everyone she loved being too busy to give her more than a few minutes. It wasn't their fault, but it hurt all the same. "You need to show him what he's doing is hurting you."

The princess bit her lip, her eyes shifting back and forth between Rolina and Farran. "I need to think about it. I'll decide before the night is out."

Rolina nodded. Twila even considering it was more than she could hope for. "Let's join the party before anyone wonders what we're up to," Rolina said, relief bubbling in her chest. At the very least, Twila wouldn't tell.

The girls joined hands as they started towards the crowd. They made it no more than a few feet before they felt the change in mood. The quiet. The fear. There was some sort of commotion near the main entrance, opposite the dais. Rolina's heart leapt and she shared a look with Twila before they pushed their way through the crowd, catching murmurs as they went.

It seemed the Duke of Kandston came after all.

11

A Dance

Five months ago Rolina had been sitting across from Dimitri, playing a game of *Bellica*. One of hundreds she had played with the man over the years. Their pieces were locked in a stalemate, but she could take him in three moves. The cards had favored her. She peeked over the top of them to watch Dimitri's caramel eyes search for a way out. He must have known, must have sensed her excitement. So long as he didn't have anything too powerful in those cards of his, she would win.

She had never done that before. As a girl, he would beat her in a few turns, then tell her everything she could have done better. Over the years it had taken him longer. Then longer still until she could play him to a draw. But this was more. A moment of victory, just around the corner. If only he wouldn't sit and think for so long every turn. *That's the advantage of games,* he always told her. *You have all the time you need to make the best decisions.* She thought it was actually the advantage of being immortal. He had the patience to think things through.

At last, Dimitri had played a card. The Dreamer. Rolina smiled. He had nothing if that was the best he could do. The Dreamer wouldn't let him move any game pieces nor capture or destroy any of hers. Nor would he be able to restore any of his lost pieces. The card was nearly useless. It was only beneficial if he played it with-

Oh no. She saw it now. The second card just peeking out from behind The Dreamer. The Ghost. The only card that could turn the useless thing into a devastating blow. "The Nightmare," he said, something wicked behind those caramel eyes. "On your general."

Rolina scowled as he plucked her general off the board, along with the two soldiers beside him. "Not fair."

"I didn't make the rules," he said, smirking as he leaned back in his chair.

That was alright. She could fix this. Even without her general, she could flank his wizard with her other soldiers. Her Assassin card would take him out before he could do anything to foil her evil plot. She started to play the card from her hand when something caught the attention of them both.

Loud voices and pounding footsteps. Dimitri's brow furrowed as if he could see through the wall and into the hallway.

"Is that-"

"Mercury," he said, unable to hide the concern in his voice.

The door swung open and the High Empress strode in, her eyes wide with shock. Haven followed behind her, and Rolina noted that they were both dressed in their nightclothes. Hair mussed and robes hastily thrown over bodies that likely didn't wear much underneath. The little upside down rune tattoo on the side of Mercury's thigh was briefly visible as her robe fluttered. She had never seen Haven's matching tattoo, but she knew where it was. Stamped right on his ass where she hoped to continue to never see it. Behind them, silent as moonlight, came Iero.

"What is it?" Dimitri asked, already on his feet, offering the chair to his sister.

Rolina should have done that. She was the lowest ranking person there. Even if they didn't really care about that sort of thing in private, she still should have been polite.

"Sit back down," the empress ordered her brother, starting a course across the room. As she started to pace, she gestured to Iero, urging him on. "Tell him."

The guardian's face was grim. Rolina studied it. Memorized it. An expression she had never seen upon the thief. "I just received word from my men in Kandston. Last night *every* imperial post in the country was attacked."

"What?" Dimitri's eyes went wide.

Rolina couldn't help the shock that shot through her from showing on her face.

"Everything. Our outposts protecting farms, gone. Our men posted in the capital, dead or captured. They... they've effectively removed all imperial power from the country."

"They've officially declared war." Mercury didn't slow her pacing.

Rolina looked to her, then to Dimitri. Searching for what this meant. For them to say everything would be alright. That they could still solve this with a bit of negotiating and tact. But she knew they couldn't. *Dead or captured.*

"How many are imprisoned?" Dimitri asked, his voice a hard line. Detached. A careful fog over his rage.

Iero shook his head, "Reports are still coming in."

"He's going to start broadening his reach." Mercury said, running a hand through her hair much like her brother often did.

"He?" Rolina dared ask.

"Duke Cadogan." Haven offered her the name, but never tore his eyes from Mercury.

Of course. The Duke of Kandston had been mustering support from his parliament. Spreading lies and rousing them with shining speeches and temptations.

"We need to know where he's going to strike next." Dimitri said, already thinking, already fixing. "Iero, do you have *any* spies left in the capital?"

"I..." Rolina had never seen Iero stammer before. "I don't know. Any communication is a risk right now, even if anyone's left. It could get them killed." He shook his head again, as if still trying to wrap his head around it himself. "My spies are trained well. If anyone's alive, they'll still be gathering intel, even if they can't share it right away."

Dimitri nodded, but it was Mercury who picked up the thread of his thoughts, "You need to get someone new in place just in case. As fast as possible, but carefully." She met Iero's eyes, "I don't wish to risk the lives of your people for naught."

"I'll start organizing care for the wounded and work with Iero's people to smuggle out any survivors we can," Haven offered.

"Get to it. Both of you," Mercury ordered. "My brother and I will see what can be done for now, then work out a plan for the long term."

As the two guardians started to leave, Dimitri added, "Catch one of the servants on your way out and have them fetch the other guardians."

Both gave him an affirming nod, then hurried off.

"What can I do?" Rolina realized she was still holding the cards in her hands. Her grip so tight she had bent them. She set them down on the little table, ignoring the shake in her hands.

"Stay and help us, Prayer," Dimitri said, standing.

The High Emperor and High Empress fell into step beside each other, headed out of Dimitri's quarters towards their offices. Rolina hurried after them as understanding finally began to sink in. War against the empire.

War against the soldiers who welcomed her into their sparring rings and training sessions. War against Captain North, who had taken charge of her combat training when Eden left all those years ago. War against the men and women who lived and worked on the base. War against the healers like her brother who tended to the slightest ailment of the servants and soldiers. War against her family. Against Maddy who taught her stories and science and the most boring, useful things. Kail who rescued animals and loved to paint. Haven who poured his eternal life into healing the sick, the injured, the broken. Bolwerk, who may not have been her favorite person, but she had seen the way cruelty broke his heart. War against Eden, who had only just returned to them a year before. Only months since she had realized what he was to her. And Iero. Iero who stole her useless treasures and never told anyone when he caught her sneaking about, looking for mischief. Iero had already lost so many people in a single day.

Following the emperors to their offices, Rolina knew exactly who was to blame. The Duke of Kandston. In her own heart, in her own silent way, Rolina declared a war of her own. A war against lies. A war against cruelty. A war against evil. A war against Luther Cadogan and his fool's rebellion.

Rolina's heart played a heavy beat. Her eyes trailed the Duke of Kandston as he walked deeper into the courtyard. Dressed in blood red formal attire that seemed to dampen the lights as he passed. His well-groomed hair was tied back from his face, revealing the mild point of the half-elf's ears. Any elegance he may have inherited through his Fae blood did not reveal itself in his face, sharp and rough, with eyes like a hunter.

A band of loyal followers trailed in after him, taking up positions by the exit. Rolina did not recognize any of them, but she judged them as guards for the unwelcome Duke. Weapons were forbidden at Tavek, but she held no doubt they were prepared to punch and claw their way out if necessary. Assuming they hadn't managed to smuggle any weapons inside. Cadogan had connections to plenty of magically inclined individuals, and Rolina could only hope none of them could break the magical wards on the forest.

The dancing stopped. Though with a nod from Mercury, the musicians played on. The guests on the dance floor parted, backing to the edges. Some only wanted room to watch the drama, others were pushed away by genuine fear of the man. The High Empress stepped forward, meeting the duke in the center. Haven, who had been dancing with her, followed, stopping a few paces behind and tucking his hands in his pockets. A deliberate gesture, considering he was a guardian, and therefore allowed a weapon. His sword remained sheathed at his side. Dimitri didn't bother rising from his throne, trusting Mercury to deal with him as well as - or better than - he would.

"My Lady," the duke did not bow, but nodded his head in a mockery of respect. The slight sent a flame of rage through Rolina's chest. Mercury only smiled and nodded in return.

"Cadogan," she greeted him as warm as if he were an old friend, not the man tearing the continent apart. "I hope your presence on this occasion means you want to find a peaceful resolution to this conflict as much as my brother and I do."

"Of course," the duke smiled cruelly as his eyes followed the flow of Mercury's dress, lingering for a moment on her revealing neckline.

The rage in Rolina's chest turned to disgust, watching his slimy gaze on a woman she admired. Beside her, Twila shifted, placing herself in front of Rolina. A gesture she appreciated in the tense situation. Brave as she thought herself, she would rather the duke's eyes fall on the girl he thought an ally than risk becoming a target. Twila's height was a shield, allowing Rolina to peek carefully over her shoulder while blocking the rest of her body from view.

Rolina's eyes passed by the empress and the duke, scanning the crowd for Eli. She found him across the dance floor. The tension in her chest eased ever so slightly when she saw Iero - suspiciously absent from the holiday proceedings until then - skulking in to stand beside her brother. The guardian placed a protective hand on the boy's shoulder, his touch so light Eli didn't appear to notice.

Before her attention could return to Mercury and the duke, her eyes flicked instinctively to Dimitri. Her pounding heart jumped. He was staring back. When he stopped watching Mercury, she didn't know, but he tilted his head subtly. A silent call to his side. Obedient, she faded deeper into the crowd, using them as cover on her way to the dais.

"You and your company are welcome to join the festivities," Mercury continued, though Rolina could no longer see her.

Cadogan laughed, the sound grating against Rolina's ears, "I wouldn't have it any other way, my lady." An unspoken threat lay beneath the words. Rolina's stomach twisted. It was like falling into one of her nightmares. Any second, things were going to crumble.

Slipping onto the dais from behind, she took her place beside Dimitri and his throne. Without looking at her, the emperor took her hand for a second. The slightest reassurance before placing his hand back on the armrest. Watching Mercury face the man whose presence alone pushed the guests to the edge, Rolina's tense chest eased. Why should she fear him? The High Empress certainly did not. Nor did The High Emperor, sitting casually beside her.

Mercury offered the duke her hand, "If you like, we can be enemies again tomorrow. Though I hope you choose otherwise."

The duke took her hand, and they danced. Rolina watched with wide eyes, the guests sharing in her surprise as the two enemies swayed with the music. Though she couldn't see his elven heritage in his face, Rolina saw it in the way he moved. Graceful, light. Almost as lovely as Mercury. The guests stood frozen, eyes locked on the implausible couple.

Dimitri stood, breaking the guests from their trances. "It is a party after all," he said, loud enough for the crowd to hear. He took Rolina's hand and started towards the dance floor. Her heart jumped to her throat. She started to pull away. But it was Dimitri leading her to the floor. She had nothing to fear. She forced herself to follow, one frightening step at a time. Holding her head high, she matched Dimitri's casual expression, veiling her own panic.

It sends a message, she thought to herself. Every tiny action at Tavek did. From standing beside her friend who should be her enemy, to strolling onto the dance floor when she should be running for cover. As they moved, she began to see the story they were telling. High Emperors will not be threatened. High Emperors do not fear. And, most importantly, they were ready, happy, to put everything aside for a chance at peace.

What story would her flight from The Eternal Forest tell?

Eli offered his arm to a woman beside him, following in their footsteps. The woman, a Montathi plains born, didn't hesitate. The present guardians did the same, starting with Kail, then Iero, then Haven. A few of the braver guests took to the floor as well, and soon it appeared almost as though the disruption never happened.

"He's not here for peace," Rolina commented, catching a glimpse of the duke as they danced.

"He's here to be seen," Dimitri agreed, one eye on the dangerous man. Rolina knew the rage in those eyes. The hatred for the man who had lied to and manipulated Dimitri's people. Anger with himself for every sign of discontent he missed before things went too far. Before the first blood was shed.

"Why not kill him here and now?" Rolina asked, imagining a more pleasant world without him. A world where rage and hatred had no place in Dimitri's eyes. They could cut off the head of the rebellion before it grew worse. Before others died. That would be a much easier way to save her parents. Not to mention the entire continent.

"It's Tavek," Dimitri answered, his voice flat. The fire in his eye told her he wouldn't mind killing the duke himself.

"Certainly, but are the traditions of one holiday worth letting that killer leave alive?" she insisted, talking low. It wouldn't do for the guests to overhear the High Emperor discussing murder.

"Yes," Dimitri answered. Taken aback, Rolina turned her gaze to the emperor, "Kill him tonight and we make a martyr out of him and villains of ourselves."

"How? He's an evil man," Rolina contradicted, glancing out at the ring of spectators, "Many of them would applaud you for it." That would send a whole different message. A powerful one. One to stop the rebellion in its tracks.

"And many others would leave telling the story of how he came seeking peace, and we killed him for it." The song came to an end, and Dimitri led her off the dance floor. "Actions are perceived in as many different ways as there are eyes to behold them, and perception is more important than the action itself."

Rolina tried not to scowl as the truth in his words settled in. If sparing the life of an evil man was what it took to stop things from spinning out of control, from causing more bloodshed, she supposed she was alright with it. Not happy, but alright. She looked back at the duke one last time before they reached the dais, "Can we kill him tomorrow?"

Dimitri smiled as he sat on his throne, "Certainly, Prayer, or at least take him captive. Though I suspect he has plans to prevent that."

"He'll leave soon to put some distance between himself and here before midnight," Rolina agreed, sitting on the armrest. "Can we send Iero to track him, or do we have to wait for that too?"

"We're merciful, not stupid," Dimitri answered, and as Rolina scanned the crowd, she noticed Iero had vanished again. Already snooping around for information on the duke's plan of escape.

Rolina's gut twisted tighter, tying knots upon knots in her stomach. The duke's appearance, unwelcome as it had been, would aid in her own flight. Pulling the attention of Iero and the other eyes hidden throughout the forest. Somehow, that made the guilt worse. As though taking Iero out of the equation made it unfair. Too easy.

On the other hand, perhaps fate was intervening in her favor. Opening her path. Encouraging her to leave, to save her family. But she didn't think the Keeper liked to fiddle with people's plans so directly, so she shrugged it off as chance.

"Well then, tomorrow ought to be a lovely day," she looked down at Dimitri from her perch on his armrest. His caramel eyes lifted to meet hers. She nearly tumbled off at the expression she found there. Gentle. Warm. Searching. As though he wasn't certain she was as alright as she was trying to act. As though he knew she would vanish any moment. And as they sat regarding each other, as her fears dissipated and she wondered if she could ever leave him, if perhaps she should just ask him, one more time, for his help, his actions finally sank in. "You danced with me."

"And?"

"You've never done that before," there was a question in her voice.

"I needed to keep the party going," he said. She knew that already, but she found her heart sinking at the admission. Any girl would have worked out the same. Not to mention, she wasted her only dance with Dimitri by talking about murder. "That's why I called you over," he continued, surprising Rolina. Dimitri's explanations for his actions didn't usually last more than a sentence. "With Mercury taking care of the duke, there was no one else left."

"What about that Elskan princess?" Rolina said, pushing her luck.

They never talked about all the pretty girls he stayed away from. She forced a little casualness into the question by reaching for the necklace he wore. Straightening out the carved, yellow jadestone that had snagged on his shirt. As though she cared more about it than the answer to her question.

"Dancing is too nerve wracking to share with a stranger," he said, fiddling idly with the lace on Rolina's sleeve. Another thing he didn't do often. Touch idly. The gesture too familiar and warm for anyone but her and his sister.

"Don't tell me you, The High Emperor of Syytala, are afraid of dancing," she said, a smile tugging at the corner of her mouth.

Dimitri's voice dropped to a whisper, "Tell no one."

Rolina laughed louder than she meant to, drawing the eyes of several nearby guests. She didn't care. Not as a smile cracked across Dimitri's face. The same smile that shattered her fears of him the day they met. She could only hope any of the guests who saw it felt the same warmth. The same trust and desire to know him that she felt eleven years ago. To her, even a glimpse of that smile was worth the fate of all twelve kingdoms.

Dimitri pulled his hand away from her sleeve, "Go on then, have fun."

She held back a frown. Talking with him was the most fun she'd had all evening. Dutifully, she stood and smoothed the wrinkles from her gown before starting away.

"Prayer," Dimitri called softly. She paused, "keep away from the duke."

"I know," she nodded, then walked into the crowd.

Her eyes scanned the dancers first, where she spotted Twila dancing with her Father. They were talking as they danced, Twila's sharp features tight with concern. Farran's dark eyes outright fearful. Out of place on the dance floor, though many wore similar expressions after the duke's arrival. Twila found Rolina's eye from across the dance floor, a frown etched on her face. Farran's gaze followed. The knots in her stomach pulled taunt. They were talking about her. About her plans to leave.

Rolina shoved the thought away. Twila would never betray her trust. They were just talking. Afraid as everyone else was those days.

She moved on, searching for her brother. This was her last chance. The party wouldn't last much longer after the damage Duke Cadogan had done. It was time to say goodbye without saying it. She found Eli surrounded by young women again, and she joined them with a polite smile.

Relief flashed across his face, "It's only just occurred to me that I haven't danced with my sister yet." He hurried away from the girls, catching Rolina by the arm as he went.

"You're welcome," she whispered in his ear as they stepped onto the floor.

"Can you believe he actually came?" Eli muttered, ignoring her comment.

"I wouldn't worry about it," Rolina said, dismissing her own concerns. It was up to Iero now. "Do you actually like any of those girls?"

"Not the way they'd like me to," he answered, glancing at the group waiting for him by the edge of the dance floor. Half of them were ready to swoon at the quick, polite smile he tossed their way.

"Why not?" she asked. Each of them rich, young, and beautiful. And the ones Rolina knew seemed nice enough. Not that she was eager for him to have a girl in his life besides her, but sometimes she wondered if he closed himself off to the idea for her sake. As though he thought having another girl around would hurt or threaten her. If anything, Rolina thought it would freshen the place up.

"Why do you always turn down the men who show an interest in you? You know Ramar would-"

"You know exactly why," she whispered, the closest she had come to admitting anything about her and Eden. Time to change the subject before he asked any more, before he made her say it. He already suspected her and Eden, she knew by the way he teased her. Better to throw in a little doubt to cancel out her near-admission. "Have you seen Kail tonight? He looks delicious in teal."

"He does," Eli agreed, "The seamstresses really outdid themselves this year," he went on, completely missing his sister's point, "Have you seen the detail on my sleeves? And Keeper above, now that I'm looking at it close, the lace on your gown must have taken ages."

Rolina chuckled, the tension in her chest vanishing as they danced.

"What's so funny?" he raised an eyebrow.

"I was commenting on the man, not the clothes."

"Oh. *Oh*," realization dawned on Eli's face, then confusion, "But I thought you... never mind. He, uh, looks nice."

She almost snorted trying to keep her laughter in check. "Shall we talk about something else?" Eli's shoulders slumped in relief.

A tinge of pain pulsed through her chest, remembering this would be her last moment with Eli for weeks. In the past eleven years, they never spent a day apart. But she refused to waste those last moments on sorrow. So they talked about the warmth of spring. About swimming in the river that cut through the forest as soon as the winter chill gave way. About how happy they were Maddy was home. About the twirling of ballgowns and the growth of wildflowers. About hope and spring and peace.

Not about war. Not about loneliness or the upcoming separation Eli knew nothing about.

Eli lulled her into the sway of the music and she shut her eyes. It was settled. And no doubt, no enemies, no fears could stop her from enjoying their last evening together.

12

Out of the Forest

The duke and his company left before the hour was up. Relief spread through the attending guests, but the party had been irreparably damaged. Tavek tapered off earlier than in years past. The guests either made their way to the Imperial Palace to stay the night, or sent servants to prepare their carriages and horses.

Rolina found her way to the dais to excuse herself. *Off to bed*, she told the emperors, her heart aching with the lie. She told Dimitri and Mercury few lies in her time with them. Half of her hoped they would call her on it, ask what was wrong. Stop her from leaving. She wanted to hug them. But the familial gesture in the formal setting would tip them off. It was one thing to fiddle with Dimitri's necklace and sit on his armrest. Another to throw her arms around him. She left them with a smile and a goodnight.

Turning to leave, she caught Twila's eye. The princess fulfilled her promise, answering Rolina's earlier question with a single, deliberate nod.

Rolina's heart jumped in her chest. She wouldn't be alone.

But they couldn't leave together. As sly as she could manage, Rolina pointed west, the direction of the road leading directly to Ev from the forest. She could only hope the princess understood the signal. *We'll meet on the road.*

Rolina continued on her way. At first, she walked at a slow, sleepy pace, heading towards the guardians' quarters. Once out of sight, she veered off, darting towards the guardians' stables. She fetched her horse, a brown Illicy, from the adjoining pasture and saddled him quickly. Usually, a stable boy or a servant helped her, and the saddle proved difficult alone. But with the help of a stepladder, she managed. Panting from the effort, she made a mental note to learn how to ride bareback, like Iero, so she never had to lift a saddle again.

Before mounting the large horse, she removed Eden's jacket from her bag, stowed away in the stables before the celebration. She held it close to her chest for a moment, then pulled it over her lace-covered arms. "It's now or never, Tovi," she whispered, stroking the white stripe down his face. Rolina mounted the horse, then adjusted her voluminous skirt so it didn't entangle her legs. It fell over Tovi's sides like a rich, shimmering blanket, fluttering in the breeze as she urged him forward.

Her heart thrummed as she joined the guests on the northwest road. Coaches and horses ambled along, carrying nobility and their companies back to their homelands. Rolina kept her head down, wishing Eden's jacket had a hood. She rode as far as she could from the other travelers, counting on their exhausted eyes to miss her. All the while searching, scanning, for Twila.

A black carriage rolled up beside her, filling her with hope as Twila's voice called, "Evensong, hop in, tie your horse to the back."

She did as instructed, then hurried inside. "You stole your father's carriage?" Rolina said, gaping at Twila as the princess stretched out on the seat.

The princess grinned her Feinin smile, "I *stole* nothing. Our driver may be under the impression that Father decided to stay in the forest in an attempt at negotiating peace, but in case things go wrong, I'm going to Un to keep out of the way until he's finished. That's also how I convinced him to leave without the guards. Guards attract attention and all that."

Rolina beamed, "I can't believe you're doing all this for me."

"Not entirely for you," she noted, but her answering smile made it clear Rolina was her priority. "Think about what Father said at the party."

"It sends a good message, us working together," Rolina agreed, "except that we're doing it without permission."

Twila straightened, "Father will understand. As soon as he learns rebels in Gaj are taking farmers hostage for no reason, he'll be livid. Think about it Rolina, Illandia is just north of Ev, and Gaj is near the border. Whose soldiers do you think those are?"

Rolina's eyes widened. Illandian soldiers. Farran's soldiers.

"We don't allow this sort of conduct among our ranks, and I've a mind to put them straight," Twila continued, bitterness growing with every word. "It's bad enough we have them deployed at all without them mistreating the locals for no damn reason."

"Do you think you should ask your father why they're there before you go?" If it was a simple abuse of power, they were hurting the farmers for the fun of it. They would do whatever they felt like to them. But if there was a reason, the farmers might still be unharmed. Rolina prayed there was a reason, that they weren't torturing them for sport.

"I know why they're there," Twila met Rolina's fearful eyes. "I shouldn't say."

"Twila!" Rolina smacked her friend's arm.

The princess frowned and rubbed her arm. "Supplies and recruits. They ask for recruits and take whoever they can get. Then they raid the farms and they take the supplies. The farmers starve, they beg for food. The rebels tell them they'll get food if they enlist," Twila explained, anger coating every word.

"That's horrible," Rolina shuddered.

"It's stupid," Twila shook her head, "A recipe for disloyal soldiers."

They weren't supposed to hurt the farmers. Manipulate and starve them, yes, but not kidnap them. Not abuse them. The rebels took them without orders. Without reason.

Rolina's chest seized.

"You alright? You look pale," Twila sat forward in her seat.

"I... I'm just afraid for them." Something inside her eased as she spoke. Twila was the first to listen. Really listen. Eli was busy working damage control on her and Dimitri didn't care at all. But with Twila, she could say anything.

"Remind me," Twila said gently, "I know your parents are from Gaj, and the emperors took you in, I don't remember why." She had only told Twila the story once. Whispered it to her in the cover of thick woods at night. The only light from the glow of Kail's faerie stoats sleeping nearby. Her deepest secret, revealed to the first friend she made after coming to the forest. Twila had dutifully kept that secret ever since, even from her own family.

"It was an accident really," Rolina said, uncertain if telling the story would help or hurt. But Twila was willing to risk herself for their safety. She deserved to know more. "My father would sometimes travel to Un to sell surplus crops if we had any. The market there was worth the journey. My mother fell ill just before the trip that year, so he decided to take Eli and I along so we wouldn't catch it. Our aunt came to care for my mother." Rolina forced the story out like a list of facts. None of the emotion. None of the sorrow and hurt from losing her parents.

"Eli... is Bryer? Your brother?" Rolina had only spoken their real names to Twila once, when she first told her the story. Even after learning the name, Twila never called her Rolina, only Evensong. The name Mercury gave her.

Rolina nodded and continued, her words clipped as she forced out the details, "Father told us not to wander off. He asked me to keep an eye on Eli, but it was busy and he was distracted. Eli ran off, and I tried to get Father's attention, but Eli was getting farther away, and I decided to run after him. Into the forest."

Understanding dawned on Twila. The last time she heard the story, she was a child. Naive to the laws of the forest, as Rolina and Eli had been. Now she saw the whole picture. Anyone who entered the forest uninvited was sentenced to death in order to preserve the secrets and safety of the empire. "They kept you to spare you."

Again, Rolina nodded, "It was a compromise I didn't understand. Father came to the entrance of the forest and begged for us to be returned if we were found. They told him we had already been executed, so he wouldn't come looking again."

The princess' eyes widened. Rolina hadn't told her that part before. She herself hadn't known until years later, until the guardians were tired of lying when she asked why her father hadn't come for them. "What a horrible thing, to think your children dead."

"We weren't allowed to leave, but they treated us well," Rolina said, wondering how it sounded to someone on the outside of it. To her, it was mercy. Her freedom for her life. A good, happy life. But as she laid out the facts, it began to sound like cruelty. Like stolen children locked away for a single act of foolishness. Like parents whose grief could be ended with a whisper of truth.

At the time, the decision broke her little heart. She tried again and again to escape with Eli when they were small. She didn't remember when she stopped. When the decision turned into a fair one. When she forgot to grieve the fact that her parents thought her dead. She never stopped missing them, but at some point, she forgot to hurt about it.

Sometimes the pain came back to her. When she looked at the wooden beads embedded into her sword. The remains of the last gift her father gave her. When she saw her mother in Eli's smile. The same gentle kindness in his mannerisms. When she told the guardians stories about exploring Blackburn Pass with her friend, Tovi. When she thought about her horse, named after the boy. Then the ache would return for a moment. Until she turned her thoughts away.

The pain should have lasted.

"I suppose it doesn't hurt to be the daughter of the most powerful man in the world," Twila commented, trying to lighten the mood.

"Daughter?" Rolina raised an eyebrow.

"Didn't you know? Everyone thinks you're Dimitri's daughter," Twila answered, smirking. "It's the only theory about you and Bryer that has managed to last."

"Why would anyone think I'm his daughter?" Why would they make up theories in the first place? Rolina shook her head, dumbfounded by the foolishness of it. "We look nothing alike."

"It doesn't matter. You and Bryer showed up out of nowhere, people are going to speculate," she answered with an innocent shrug, "and gossip."

Rolina chuckled. Noble gossips were the worst, though she had to commend their creativity. They could transform a look into a scandal. A mistake into a travesty. And apparently, lost little girls into imperial daughters. "Why not say we're Mercury's children?"

"Because she's nice to everyone, but Dimitri is only nice to *you*," Twila said, grinning.

"Of all the foolish things," Rolina rolled her eyes and ran a hand through her hair.

"There!" Twila straitened, pointing at Rolina as though she'd caught her, "That's one of his mannerisms."

"Everyone touches their hair," Rolina denied, pushing Twila's finger away.

"Not like that."

The girls continued chatting as the carriage rolled on, their conversation drifting farther and farther from anything serious. At some point in the night, Rolina drifted to sleep, curled up on the seat opposite Twila. The princess watched her friend, the moonlight staining her blonde curls silver. She watched her and knew her role in this journey wasn't to save any farmers, or stop the evil of corrupt soldiers, or even to have time away from her father. It was to protect Rolina. To keep the inexperienced, moonlit girl safe. To protect an innocence Twila herself had long since lost.

Rolina had been to the edge of The Eternal Forest twice in her life. Once when she first stumbled in, chasing after Eli, and once when Eden brought her to see the border she must never cross. She had cried and decided to hate Eden forever, though he was blameless in the decision to wall her within the forest. Her hatred lasted no more than a month, but the border remained closed. Where the trees ended, so did her freedom.

The morning after Tavek, Rolina passed the border without noticing. Fast asleep, nestled on the soft seat cushions. Twila drifted to sleep in the night as well, slumped against the wall of the carriage. A bump in the road jolted the pair awake. Unfamiliar surroundings disoriented Rolina until she saw Twila sitting across from her, rubbing the sleep from her eyes. Memories of the previous night rushed into her head. Of what she had done. Where she had gone.

Rolina peered out the window. Open plains stretched before her in hues of green, dotted with pastel flowers swaying in the breeze. Eleven years surrounded by trees, Rolina forgot what a horizon looked like. Dividing the earth and sky in one distinct stroke. Her breath caught in her throat, awestruck. She imagined throwing the door open and darting out of the carriage. Running through the field, diving into the wildflowers without a care in the world. But she did have cares.

Rolina remained in her seat.

Twila slid closer, looking over her shoulder at the scenery, "It is only grass." As she said the words, her eyes moved from the view outside to the girl beside her. Her eyes wide, wondrous. Mystified by the world she had never seen.

"It's beautiful," she sighed, taking in a deep breath. Nectar and grass and earth filled her senses. A different sort of fresh than the forest. A calm surrender.

The view disappeared as quickly as it came. The city of Un pressed as close to The Eternal Forest as it was allowed. The carriage paused at an imposing gate, and Rolina watched their driver pay the toll for their passage. Her cheeks went pink, she had not thought about tolls or how much they would cost. She brought only the handful of doubles she kept in a box on her vanity. Rolina glanced at Twila, once again thankful the princess agreed to come along.

Driving the carriage through the streets proved slow. Dozens of people pressed in, calling out and holding various items above the crowd. The poor attempting to sell their wares to the rich personage within. Some had nothing to sell, but clamored for attention in the hopes of earning a spare double. Rolina had only been to Un once, a decade before, but she did not recall so many beggars. Had the war done this to them? Or was it always like this, and time erased it from her mind? She turned away. How could she look them in the eye while riding in a carriage fit for a king? The driver made his way through the people gently, until they broke through to the central marketplace.

Rolina risked another look outside. She found busy, yet open streets. Shop boys and girls stood outside decorated storefronts ushering potential customers inside. Shouting things like "best prices for all your household needs," with deliberate smiles on their faces. Traders manned colorful market stalls, their wares spread in eye-catching displays. Vivid fabrics and sparkling jewelry. Entertainers played and danced in the streets, boxes and hats on the ground for passersby to toss them a few doubles. Sometimes traders visited The Eternal Forest, but never had she seen such a vibrant, booming marketplace.

Not never, she corrected herself, *once.* This very city. A three-year-old Eli by her side, staring in wonder as their father drove their produce cart towards the market. A somber expression as he repeated, one final time, *Don't wander off.*

A warning ignored.

The carriage rolled to a stop before a simple, clean building. Taller than most buildings in The Eternal Forest, rising at least three stories. Wide and long with a stable attached to one end. "This is where we're staying."

"Staying? Shouldn't we keep going?" They needed to put as much distance between themselves and The Eternal Forest as possible before someone noticed them missing.

"We may have slept through the night, but our horses will be tired," Twila reminded her, throwing the carriage door open. "Besides, it's best if we leave here at night so we're not spotted."

Rolina was about to ask who might spot them besides their driver when she noticed a familiar face outside the carriage. Several. The same Kaunean elves she had stood behind while waiting to present herself to the emperors were climbing out of a similar carriage, and a pair of Eldurian guards flanked another rolling in behind them. It seemed this was a popular spot for nobility on their way home. Rolina froze in the doorway of the carriage, "They'll recognize me. I can't have anyone asking what I'm doing here, they might-"

"No one will recognize you," Twila assured her with her Feinin grin, "or have you forgotten who you're traveling with?"

Relief flooded through Rolina as she remembered days playing hide-and-seek in the gardens. Remembered accusing Twila of cheating when she used her Fae abilities to turn herself into part of a tree. The half-Feinin girl could alter things, *glamour* them. The word stroked Rolina's memory, giving her confidence as she stepped out of the carriage. Twila had given her a new face. And, when she looked down at herself, she realized her ballgown had been transformed into a simple dress, more befitting of a handmaiden than a lady.

The elves greeted Twila cheerily and ignored Rolina altogether.

Twila flashed Rolina an I-told-you-so grin as they entered the building.

Rolina tossed her a playful scowl as they were directed to a room down the hall.

"Admit it," Twila said, "You're happy I'm here."

Rolina flipped her hair out from her stolen shirt, cinching it around her waist with the belt she found in Eden's wardrobe. Considerably smaller than the guardian, she had to stab an extra hole through the leather for it to stay in place. She snatched up Eden's jacket from where she tossed it on the floor, then stepped from behind the dressing screen. Twirling once for Twila, who sat on the edge of the bed across the room, she flashed a girlish smile. The white shirt fell to just above her knees, and she pinched the edges like a skirt, "Lovely, aren't I?" she chuckled, dipping into a curtsy.

Twila looked up from lacing her green dress, a simple thing, aside from the expertly embroidered design on the sleeves. "You would look stunning in a burlap sack."

"As would you," Rolina replied, walking across the room to a table with three chairs around it. She plopped down into the one nearest the room's narrow window and tossed Eden's jacket on the table.

Finished with her dress, Twila stood and joined her. Her eyes dropped to the jacket, noticing a compass rose pressed and burned into the leather. A checkered pattern on the northwest point. "This is Eden's," she noted, not quite a question.

"I needed plain clothes," she shrugged, pretending the jacket meant no more than a bit of warmth.

"And why, may I ask, did a slip of a girl like you decide to steal from the second biggest guardian there is?" Twila's grin returned as she ran her fingers along the leather. "Iero would have been a better fit."

"His clothes are too nice," Rolina excused, fiddling with her hair to keep herself from touching the jacket.

"I see," Twila didn't sound convinced as she took her hand off the jacket, but mercifully let it be. "Shall we discuss our plan?"

Rolina nodded, but she didn't have a plan. A part of her never believed she would make it out of the forest. She wouldn't have without Twila. "Once we arrive in Gaj, I'll join the imperial soldiers stationed there and aid them with my local knowledge." The quality of the improvised plan surprised her, though her local knowledge had faded over the last decade. She kept that part to herself.

"And as for tonight, we'll slip away around, oh, midnight perhaps?" Twila suggested.

She agreed, though part of her feared it would be too late. If their absence was already detected, if Dimitri had already sent someone her way, the delay would end their journey before it began. But the day after Tavek was busy, especially this year. Rolina knew it was more than a party, that allegiances were pledged and allies gained. The emperors and the remaining guardians would have their hands full with the guests at the palace and bargains being made. Iero would be off pursuing the duke. She wondered if he would catch him. If he would end the war right then and there.

"Enough of that," Twila interrupted her thoughts, "You're overthinking again, I can see it on your face." She leaned forward and put her hands on each of Rolina's cheeks, forcing her to meet her eye, "What will be, will be, no use worrying about it."

"Can you blame me?" Rolina gave Twila her most pitiful pout.

Twila scowled and took her hands away. "This won't do," she slammed her hands on the table as she stood, "Come on, we're not going to gloom about until midnight. We're going out."

"Out?" Rolina's chest seized. She couldn't risk being seen, couldn't leave that room until late in the night. And if she really thought about it, it would make her guilt deeper. If she went off to have a good time, knowing she had disobeyed. Had left the forest, broke the rules, ignored the compromise keeping her alive. Leaving was necessary, she knew, but how could she have fun with the guilt weighing on her? It wasn't a vacation, it was a mission. A duty to be taken seriously.

"Stop," Twila commanded, grabbing Rolina's hand, "You're doing it again already." She pulled Rolina out of the chair and towards the door. "This is not up for debate. I'm going, and we're safer together, so you're coming with me."

"I don't think this is a good idea," Rolina got out before Twila pulled her through the door.

13

Playing With Fire

Rolina kept close to Twila, afraid of what might happen if she stepped out of sight. This was the town her father lost her in just over a decade before. How easy would it be to get lost again?

Twila strode through the streets with a noble confidence. She had been to this place many times on her way to and from the forest. She knew its streets and hollows. Had no cause for fear as she led Rolina to the marketplace she glimpsed earlier. "There's this little stall across the way that sells the best apple tartlets, but they'll be gone if we don't get there soon," she explained, pulling Rolina into the throng of people. "You *have* to try them."

Rolina had no choice but to yield to the wave of Twila's excitement. It was foolishness, buying sweets when they were on the run. Any moment, Rolina expected Iero to appear from the shadows and drag her back to The Eternal Forest. But they couldn't leave until evening. Not with *him* to deal with.

Rolina glanced over her shoulder at the man who had driven the carriage, the man now tailing their every step. Rolina would have appreciated his dutifulness if it weren't so inconvenient.

The scent of the market stall hit Rolina before she realized they had arrived. Pies and sticky buns and dozens of sweet treats awaited, curls of steam drifting from their welcoming cores. Hunger struck Rolina hard at the sight of them. Her will to protest sapped from her. As they waited in a surprisingly long line, Rolina watched the people behind the counter.

A family. A gangly boy in his teens delivered a basketful of treats from inside the building behind the stall. Twila explained they usually had too many customers to efficiently serve inside the tiny baker's shop, so they had built the stall as an extension. Rolina barely heard as she watched a girl, no more than eleven, carrying a pie to a waiting customer. At the wooden counter sat the oldest woman Rolina had ever seen - at least, the oldest woman Rolina had seen who *looked* her age. She took the customers' doubles with a smile and waved directions to the family behind her, who dutifully appeared with whatever treats were requested.

"They're delightful, aren't they," Twila commented, noticing Rolina's attention fixed on the bakers.

Rolina nodded, but she didn't feel delight. A jealous ache twisted in her heart. What would her life have been like if she remained with her parents? Would she be happier in the simple life of a farmer's daughter? Helping around the house and farm, destined to marry some local boy - probably Tovi - and have a few children. The idea half pleased and half terrified her. Her life would have been easier that way, but she wouldn't know the guardians, wouldn't know the emperors. Wouldn't know Eden. She could only imagine the hole they would have left. The longing for something she couldn't quite name.

Half a dozen tartlets cost Twila three smolders, and she handed over the coal doubles happily. "One for you," she handed Rolina a tartlet as they walked away, "and one for you," she added, offering another to the Illandian man still tailing them.

He thanked the princess with a humble nod before eagerly accepting the treat.

"And one for me," she said, then tucked the other three away for later in a satchel hanging at her hip.

Heat prickled Rolina's fingers as she lifted the tartlet to her lips.

Love at first bite. Sticky filling oozed onto her fingers and lips as warmth spread through her soul. The sugary-apple flavor stirred something in her. A memory. Had her father bought her the same treat on her original journey?

"Father says I inherited a Fae pallet," Twila said, leading Rolina somewhere new. She followed with a more ambitious step than before. "Fae food is much more flavorful than human food, and he thinks that's why I like sweets and spicy things. They're more potent."

"Everyone likes sweets," Rolina commented, licking her fingers clean. Perhaps a quick jaunt away from the inn before they left wasn't such a bad idea. "Where to next?"

"I've no idea," Twila admitted, "but the market's always good for meandering."

And so it was. The glimpse Rolina caught before was only a taste. Music filled the air as a group of street performers danced. Their Elven elegance drew attention from all directions. Rolina paused to watch, but Twila marched on, and Rolina had no choice but to hurry and catch up.

"Never trust an elf," Twila muttered quietly.

Rolina nodded, knowing better than to delve into the intricacies of the rivalry between Elves and Feinin.

Twila pointed ahead, her gait turning purposeful, "There's a shop that sells the most peculiar-"

A shout cut her off.

Her body went rigid, scanning the area for danger. The way their Illandian escort jumped, Rolina knew he was useless as a guard. She reached for the dagger tucked in her belt, stolen from the armory two nights before. Rolina preferred her sword, but it was harder to conceal than a dagger, so it remained in their room.

There were no thugs or soldiers headed their way. Only a boy in the street, down on his knees before a family of nobles Rolina nearly didn't recognize. Until her eyes landed on the Viskan apprentice she had spoken with at Tavek, a sorrowful expression on his face. His eyes locked on the boy in the street as though he wanted to rush to his side, but couldn't. Couldn't, because his parents were shouting for their guards to take the boy away.

"Please," the boy begged, desperation cracking his voice, "I just need someone to listen."

"Get away, you dirty beast!" the Viskan boy's father hissed, pulling his wife away, towards the shelter of a storefront behind them.

Rolina's feet started moving before her mind could process. Instinct drove her, an instinct to protect, to defend. Beside her, Twila began to follow, but the Illandian man caught her by the arm. Rolina hardly noticed. "What's going on here?" she demanded, walking between the boy and the Viskan family.

"This fiend accosted us as we exited the shop," the lady answered, pointing an accusatory finger down at the boy in the street. Their guards moved closer, weapons at the ready.

"I only asked for you to listen!" the boy defended, his voice sharp. Rolina looked over her shoulder, noticing for the first time the sharp point of his ears. Fae. She thought perhaps Elven or Feinin. His clothes were dirty and worn, a tear in the seam of his left shoulder. Strange, as both elves and Feinin tended towards vanity. And the more she looked, she saw light bruises and scratches mottling his skin. "Please, just give me a moment. Why doesn't anyone ever *listen!*" His last word sounded more like a growl than the squeaking plea of before, and a sliver of flame flickered on one shoulder, growing fast.

Feinin then, and losing control.

"You stay away from us!" the lord spat, then directed his attention to Rolina, "You best get away from it as well, it's half-mad." Beside him, the apprentice flinched, embarrassed by his father's words. He didn't seem to recognize Rolina, and she thanked the Keeper that Twila's glamour held.

"You stay away from *him*!" Rolina snapped back, hoping the rage on her face wasn't veiled by the glamour as she glared at each of their guards in turn. Before a single one of them could make a move, she swept around and snatched both of the Feinin's hands, "Come with us, we'll listen." With a gentle tug, he was on his feet and the flame extinguished.

"Can you help?" he asked, the anger vanished from his voice.

"I don't know, but I'll listen," she promised, her eyes darted to the nobles as she led the Feinin further away. Towards Twila and the Illandian man.

The Viskan lord pushed his family back, "Don't say I didn't warn you when he burns you to a pile of ash." With that, they scurried away.

The Feinin didn't notice, his full attention on Rolina. Her heart thundered, knowing he was easily as dangerous as the nobleman believed. Even the least among them held enough power to tear her apart. She wasn't certain she had met a Feinin before, not a full-blooded one. Rumor said their emotions easily seized control of their magic, often to catastrophic levels. Best to keep him calm, lest rumor prove true. "What do you need to tell us?" she asked, opening her hands as she reached Twila.

He didn't let her take her hands away, his grip on them soft, but firm. His eyes darted to Twila, "You're half Feinin," there was a question in his voice, but understanding quickly dawned in his eyes. "Princess," he nodded respectfully. His hands slipped away from Rolina's at last, stepping closer to Twila. He dropped to his knees as a small sob broke through him, "To think that fate would guide me to you."

"What do you need?" Twila asked, stepping back.

"They're hunting us," he breathed, lifting teary eyes to meet hers.

"Who?" the princess asked, her jaw tight as she fought to keep calm. What reason could Twila have to fear him? Rolina would have thought the princess eager to help one of her mother's people.

"They come at night," he said, his shaking voice almost a whisper. "They take us from our homes. Bleed us dry. They know our tricks, our power. We need help. Can you help us?"

Rolina waited for Twila to answer, but she stood, frozen, her eyes wide with some horror Rolina did not understand. After a pause that made Rolina's heart race, Twila asked, "How did you get out of Kauneus?"

"Out?" Rolina raised an eyebrow.

"Please," the Feinin begged, but whether his avoidance of the question was deliberate, Rolina could not tell. "We're dying."

"Here," Rolina took his hands once more and helped him to his feet, "come get yourself cleaned up. You'll feel better, and you can explain yourself more clearly."

The Feinin stopped, "You aren't listening."

"I'm listening," Rolina said calmly, afraid to push the volatile Feinin over the edge, "I'm not understanding. If you come with me, you'll have plenty of time to explain, to make me understand."

The Feinin let Rolina lead him away.

Twila was quick to catch up, squeezing in close to whisper, "This is a terrible idea."

"He needs help," Rolina replied, though Twila's warning rang in her ears. Some forgotten human instinct in her whispering *run, run, run!*

"If you're going to do this... Keep. Him. Calm," Twila hissed, then moved away to put some distance between herself and the Feinin. If Twila was afraid of what would happen if he lost his calm, then the rumors had to be true. The boy could burn them to dust.

Rolina kept her chin up and led the group to the inn, the Feinin's hand clinging to hers. Warm and soft and welcoming, even as it shook. Perhaps that warmth came from the fire lurking beneath his skin. "It's alright," she promised, taking in the panic on his face. Beyond the scratches and grime, he was elegant and beautiful. She knew better than to trust his youth, Feinin lived long enough that he was likely near a century old. Old enough to remember a time before the rebellion was even a thought.

A few heads turned their way as they walked through the inn to their room. People who had never seen a Feinin before, fearful or curious. She hurried him along lest the staring upset him. And as they reached the door to their room, Rolina was almost surprised that Twila made their Illandian escort stay outside.

She offered the Feinin one of the chairs on the far side of the room, then began rifling through a desk nearby, hoping it held what she needed. "Twila, would you mind getting some water so we can clean him up?"

The princess hesitated, wary of leaving Rolina alone with the stranger. She must have decided the Feinin boy was calm enough, because she left.

"What's your name?" Rolina asked, retrieving some loose paper from the desk, along with a pen and ink.

The Feinin's expression tightened.

"Oh, that's right, Feinin don't give their names to just anyone," Rolina said, keeping her voice light and pleasant. She was unsure if she remembered the detail from one of Maddy's lessons or if Twila had told her. "Humans do though. I'm Evensong," she came to join him at the table.

Some of the fog in his eyes lifted at the sound of the name, the way it had when he first recognized Twila. "The High Emperor's daughter?"

Annoyance ticked in her chest at the assumption, but she pushed it aside, "No, that's just a rumor, but I do know him." She laid the items down on the table. "If someone is really hunting the Feinin, he'll want to know. Tell me everything, and I'll write it down in a letter for you to carry to The Eternal Forest. That's why you're here, isn't it? You're on your way to tell the emperors?"

He nodded. "I went to Illandia first. The others told me not to bother, that King Farran hates the Feinin, but I didn't think it could be true."

"It's not," the words came out harsher than she intended. Calm. This boy needed her to be calm. She took a breath and said, "His children are half Feinin."

"That's what I said, but they say after the queen passed he felt betrayed. Feinin are supposed to live so much longer than humans, and yet, he lost her," the boy said, sorrow lacing the words. Though she had left Kauneus for Illandia, the Feinin still regarded her as their own. A Feinin queen beloved in both countries. "I didn't believe he hated us - I still don't - but I think some of his people do."

"Why?" Rolina asked with more than a passing interest. Illandia was Twila's country. Enemy territory and the home of the only girl she called a true friend.

"They told me the king wasn't there and threw me out. They didn't listen to me. Or let me leave a message for him, or... or anything," the Feinin boy continued, shaking his head. "So I moved on. Even if the emperors wouldn't hear me, I would have a chance to catch King Farran on his return journey. Or any of the nobility that would pass this way." Like the Viskan nobles he begged to listen.

Rolina took his hand, "I'm sorry no one has heard you, but I promise you will make it into The Eternal Forest. Even if the emperors can't see you, someone will, and your message will reach the right hands." As she spoke the words, she realized she was usually that someone. All those pleas and requests written by people with as much desperation as the boy before her. His was the first face to go along with them. The first to look her in the eye. The usually impersonal task transformed into raw emotion at the sight of them. A cry for help in silvery blue.

"The king does not accompany the princess?" he asked, cocking his head slightly.

"Not at the moment."

"That's alright," he said more to himself than Rolina. "I'll go to the forest. I'll get help. I- You're certain you can get me into the forest?"

"Absolutely," she lied.

"I owe you for this," he said, his jaw quivering.

Rolina shook her head, "It's my job."

The door swung open and Twila came to join them at the table, a basin of water in her hands. "You ought to look presentable if you're going to see the High Emperors," she said flatly, then wrung out a cloth over the basin and began dabbing at the dirt on his cheek.

His eyes locked on the princess as she worked, "I... appreciate you doing this. To think the daughter of Queen Aine would be so humble and... kind."

"It's nothing," Twila disregarded his statement with a harsh edge in her voice. She wanted him gone. Getting him cleaned up and ready was her way of pushing him out the door. "I sent my man to buy you some clothes less... touched by the road."

"Tell me your story," Rolina said, deciding it best to get him out before Twila snapped.

"Feinin have vanished from the forest for several years - something that should be impossible. But the last few months, it's been worse. There are hunters in the forest. Perhaps a dozen of them. Humans, we think. A dozen humans shouldn't be much of a problem, but they know how to fight us. How to conceal themselves and break through our magic. They come and they take us to their hidden places and bleed us dry."

"Bleed you?" Rolina recoiled at the image. Even Twila froze before wringing out the cloth and continuing her work.

He nodded solemnly. "They change their hideouts, and we've found some of their old ones. They... they don't bother to remove the bodies."

"How often does this happen?" Rolina asked, writing every detail.

"Sometimes they come every night, taking one Feinin at a time. Other times they wait and prepare themselves for a larger raid. They've taken up to thirteen of us at a time," he said, and though he was still broken and sorrowful, Rolina noted the relief in his eyes. Heard at last.

"Give me any details you can, where their hideouts have been, patterns, anything," Rolina said. It didn't take him long to tell her all he could. The hunters left few clues behind aside from the bodies, and that told them more about how they killed than anything else. Twila finished cleaning up his face and soon the Illandian man returned with the clothes. The Feinin dressed behind the screen and appeared looking like a new man.

"That's more like it," Twila muttered, then turned to Rolina, "You've finished your letter?"

She nodded and stepped closer to the Feinin, holding out a letter, "This one is in case you get flustered again, all the details are here, and you don't need to worry about forgetting anything." Rolina held out a second letter, "This one is for the guards at the gate. No one enters the forest without permission, and a word from me will get you inside." She hoped. She didn't actually have the authority to let anyone in or out.

"You have my thanks," he said, taking the letters. "Both of you," he added, nodding to Twila. "I owe you." Again, Rolina began to tell him he didn't, when he perked up and asked, "Do you happen to have a bottle?"

"A bottle?" Rolina raised an eyebrow.

Beside her, Twila straightened, a spark of excitement in her eyes, "I'm sure we could scrounge one up," she waved a hand to the Illandian man and he darted away to find one. He returned surprisingly fast, a small bottle in hand.

The Feinin took it and pulled out the cork before holding his hand above the opening. His brow furrowed with concentration and he bit his bottom lip. A spark shot from his hand into the bottle. Then another, and another, then a stream of fire. Rolina watched with awe as he corked the bottle up and held it out to her, a small flame flickering inside though it had no air or kindling to feed it.

She took the bottle gingerly in her hands, staring at the magical flame.

"Fire is my clan's gift. That won't go out, so you can use it to light your way. Or, if you're in danger, pull out the stopper and it'll burn anything you aim at, or you can throw it, and it will explode when the glass shatters. But once it's open, that's it. You can only use it once," he explained, taking one of Rolina's hands as he added, "I know it's not much to repay what you've done, but I hope you'll accept it."

Rolina lifted her gaze from the bottle to his silvery blue eyes, "It's more than enough." A bit of bottled magic, just for her.

He smiled for the first time in the hours Rolina had known him, then took his hand away from hers, saying, "I'll be on my way then."

Rolina said goodbye, but Twila only stood, watching with near-predatory stillness as he exited. As the door shut behind him she whipped around to face Rolina, "You could have gotten us killed."

The Illandian man took that as his cue to leave.

"He needed help," Rolina contradicted.

"He's Feinin, he's dangerous. *Never* trust a Feinin you don't know," Twila spat, and Rolina wondered if they were her words, or her mother, Queen Aine's.

"I'm sorry," Rolina said, though she wasn't in the least. Helping that boy was her job. Her duty. Just because she left The Eternal Forest didn't mean she would forget the people who needed her.

"At least something good came of it," Twila looked down at the bottle in Rolina's hands. "Fire from the Gean clan is potent, to say the least."

"You know his clan?"

"I knew the moment I saw those flames on his shoulder," Twila muttered, marching back to the chairs and plopping into one.

"What are they like?" Rolina asked, wishing she had more of a chance to ask the Feinin about his people.

"Like all Feinin clans," Twila said with a scowl, "dangerous."

14

Hunter's Eyes

The back door to the guardians' quarters cracked open. Slow. Quiet. Iero slipped inside, footsteps falling silent on the hard stone floor. Even without a reason to sneak or hide, stealth came as second nature. The art of thievery and remaining undetected so ingrained in him he made no noise. If he put a little effort into it, there would be no finding him. A shadow like any other.

Iero whistled on his way to his bedroom. A habit picked up after the many occasions he startled someone who didn't hear him coming. His whistle came as a warning. Stop talking, stop what you're doing, if you don't want the thief to know. A courtesy he did not offer everyone. Though the other guardians could sense him. Always. The magic inside them played the same song, connected them beyond sight and sound. When he entered a room, they knew.

He yawned and stretched his arms above his head, wishing he had time for a nap. But as things were, he could only take a moment to clean himself up before reporting to the emperors. During the night, he stalked after Duke Cadogan, watching and waiting for an opportunity to strike. But, to his eternal shame and frustration, he lost the man a few miles into the Southern Plains. He blamed the blunder on lack of sleep and ordered his scouts to track the duke and his guards. To find and deal with them before they reached their own country, or any of the more problematic rebel strongholds. Then he turned himself around and made the long trek home.

His tired eyes nearly missed the anomaly. Most humans would. But Iero was not most humans, nor entirely certain he was human anymore. His eyes fell on the handle of Eden's bedroom door.

Iero liked locks. Especially locked doors and finding his way through them. He knew the locks in the guardians' quarters like the back of his hand. Had centuries to memorize every fine detail. Eden's door knob sat askew, further to the right than usual. Someone had taken advantage of the broken lock. The lock he broke when he was bored and a little bit drunk all those years ago.

Iero pressed his forefinger against the wooden door. It gave way, spilling heat into the hall. Swearing, he stepped back, the Eldurian heat searing his Frostlander blood. He glanced down the hall, considering finding someone else to investigate the sweltering room. But, like many spies and thieves before him, curiosity got the better of Iero, and he stepped inside.

The thief spent little time in Eden's room due to the inhospitable temperature, but as far as he could tell, nothing was out of place. Humble furnishings left neat and tidy. The large painting of The Glacial Plains hung on the wall, as it had for several thousand years. Iero smiled at the painting, a reminder of his home, his humble start in the most desolate region of The Frostlands.

His eye caught on the wardrobe against the wall, on a disturbance so minute most would miss it. Even the other guardians. But Iero had hunter's eyes, trained and honed in the harsh winters on the plains. He crossed the room for a closer look.

Dust.

Four months since Eden shipped out. Four months without anyone entering or leaving this room. Four months for dust to settle. The wardrobe's handles were smudged, and the dust at the bottom had scrapes from someone opening the doors. Iero tugged them open, searching for other discrepancies. He assumed something was missing, but as he didn't make a habit of digging through Eden's stuff, he couldn't guess what. Clothes, he supposed. A strange thing to steal. Especially Eden's plain, almost ugly attire. Unless it was a coat, the only finery the Eldurian kept despite selecting the same ugly brown jacket every day.

Iero hated that jacket. Had even taken to underhanded tricks to stop Eden from wearing it. He made an error in telling Eden it could get torn or ruined if he took it with him to Bane, prompting the Eldurian to leave it behind. Sure, it got him out of that ugly jacket for a few months, but he'd only put it on the moment he came home. Perhaps he should steal it again before Eden returned. And burn it. He searched through all the beautiful coats and jackets the Eldurian left behind. The brown jacket was not there. Iero looked again, then ducked down to check the bottom of the wardrobe. Gone.

Wiping sweat from his forehead, Iero shut the wardrobe doors and swept his eyes across the room. His vision blurred and his head spun. Time to leave before he melted into a sweaty pile of nothing. Not even his pixie-enchanted clothing could fight against the Eldurian heat. He scurried out of the room, all too happy to shut the door behind him and seal away the furnace-like temperature. Leaning against the door to breathe cool air, his eyes landed on the door opposite him. Rolina's.

Rolina loved that ugly brown jacket. Said Eden wouldn't quite be the same without it. Iero heard more, knew more, than he let on in front of the girl. Knew how hard Eden's departure struck her. Knew of stolen kisses that weren't quite as stealthy as they thought. Of her family's plight in Gaj. If she took the jacket - a small measure of comfort - he couldn't blame her. The poor thing was only a child.

Iero pushed off Eden's door, stepping forward to knock on Rolina's.

No answer. She could be off at the palace, entertaining the remaining guests from Tavek. Princess Twila had been there, and the two were often found together. But this late in the day, Twila and many of the guests would have left. If Iero knew Rolina as well as he thought, she would have returned to catch up on missing sleep. A luxury he wished he could indulge in.

"It's only me, Dove," he called. It felt remarkably like talking to air. "Rolina?" Iero tried the handle, a small, instinctual panic rising in his gut. Locked. But locked doors were never a problem. Strapped to his upper thigh, where many a rogue would keep a spare weapon, Iero kept a set of lock picks. He needn't worry about keeping the tools of his trade in so visible a place, marking him as a thief. In order to see them, one would have to see *him*.

Iero had broken into this room before, as he had all the others in the hall. Admittedly, this one more than most. In all the years he ran to her rescue when the nightmares woke her screaming, she never connected his arrival with her locked door. And long before her nightmares, before she was born or even imagined, he used to break into the room every so often when it belonged to Dain. Part of a running bet that he could never pluck a feather from Dain's wings. Each failed attempt cost him a punch in the face or arm, but he kept trying. A feat he never achieved before the Taivan's death.

Skilled hands made quick work of the lock. Iero cracked the door open, calling her name one last time before entering. His heart seized in his chest at the sight of her empty room. *Don't jump to conclusions*, he warned himself. But he tended to worry more over Rolina and Eli than the others. He couldn't help the way they reawakened the fatherly instincts long tossed aside. Her room appeared as it always did, bed unmade, desk covered in papers and trinkets, a few dresses slung over a chair. But he knew in his heart something was wrong.

Her sword. The pretty little blade Eden had made for her was not in its place on the wall. She would not take it if she wasn't planning to use it. The girl was gone. Vanished in the night.

She stole the jacket too. He took some small relief in her purposeful actions, indicating the duke had nothing to do with it. Though he wouldn't rule out Cadogan's involvement without proof. He could have used himself as bait to lure Iero away while his men worked, snatching up Rolina and planting evidence to hide it. Possible, but unlikely. She ran away, and given the alternative, he decided that was good.

Taking Eden's jacket - and possibly other clothes - could be more than a sentimental action. She needed plain clothes to go unnoticed. A disguise. She wouldn't need one of those if she'd been taken.

The food. Iero froze, confounded by his own stupidity. She wasn't stealing snacks but provisions. "Stupid, *stupid*," he muttered to himself as he darted back out into the hall. What an obvious, idiotic thing to miss. Sure, he had other things on his mind. Blood to wash from his clothes and his memories, but that was no excuse. He was the one who *noticed* things. He should have known, should have stopped her.

He veered sharply to the left, pushing into Maddy's room without knocking, tossing the inner door to the wizard's bedroom open as he asked forcefully, "Have you seen Rolina today?"

Maddy, lying in bed half asleep scowled at him, "No, why?"

"Oh, nothing," Iero dismissed, shoving the concern from his voice. "I need to ask her something." The wizard was too weak to help, why worry him?

"Iero," Maddy narrowed his eyes at the thief, "Why don't I believe you?"

"Because I'm not a trustworthy individual," Iero answered with a smile he didn't feel, "It's nothing." The thief dashed from the room before the wizard could ask more questions.

Iero burst outside, darting between buildings and around the back of the guardians' armory until he reached the stables. He counted the horses, *Hades, Dusk, Blaze, Moondust, Cow, Archimedes, Kala...* No Tovi.

Iero's feet flew, carrying him across the gardens to the military base. He checked a few more places, asked his spies. No one had seen Lady Evensong that day... Or Princess Twila.

Out of the base, back through the gardens, to the Emperor's Pavilion. Mercury and Dimitri would not take the news well. He hoped to find Mercury alone, the news wouldn't hurt her the same way, and perhaps Iero could get out of telling Dimitri himself. He had to tell them about losing the duke as well, but he didn't care about that anymore, his head filled with dreadful images of Rolina in danger. Dread mixed with ancient memories, blurring the lines between Rolina and another girl Iero had lost. A girl he would dig through time itself to save.

Both emperors stood inside the pavilion, discussing something at the war table. Iero wanted to leap up the steps and tell them the news, but even in his urgency he knew better. Slowing his pace, he whistled as he neared the pavilion, alerting them to his presence. They did not notice, leaving Iero to stand and wait and wonder how far she might have gone by then. She would have traveled northwest, towards Gaj. Towards her family.

Shit, Eli... He hadn't checked the boy's room. They could have left together. Eli wasn't exactly bold, but his sister had dragged him into trouble before. If he was with her, good. She was not alone. If he was not... Iero swallowed hard. He did not want to be the one to tell the boy his sister was gone.

He tried not to watch the exchange between the emperors as he waited, but he was, at his core, a snoop, and found his eyes couldn't resist the scene in front of him. They poured over the maps and papers on the table, working together to find an end to the mess. Where to incorporate the allies gained from Tavek, how to minimize loss of life on both sides, where to fight, what to leave alone. Tired eyes searching for answers.

Iero watched them, their beautiful faces worn, drawn out. Dark circles under once vibrant eyes. They looked old. Their long lifetimes catching up to them.

Will this break them?

He shook the thought away. Dimitri and Mercury were too precious, too important to lose. He would not let them fade.

Footsteps sounded behind Iero. Before he could turn his head to see, he heard a commanding voice demand, "You, thief, you know everything that goes on in this forest. Tell me you know where my daughter's gone off to." King Farran stopped beside Iero, just outside the pavilion.

Panic rose in Iero's chest, remembering what his spies had told him. No one had seen Princess Twila that day. They were together. *Of course* they were together. How long had they been planning this? Was it more than a desperate attempt to save Rolina's family? If the princess was with her, it could mean so many other things. Iero forced the nerves from his voice as he answered, "I believe she is with Lady Evensong."

"And where is Lady Evensong?" Farran snapped, an intensity in his voice Iero recognized. A father's fear, teetering on the edge of explosive.

Iero tried to think of an answer that would appease the king. Something honest, but calming. An assurance the girls were safe. But Iero didn't know if they were, so he opened his mouth, hoping the right words would come pouring out on their own.

"What's going on?" came a gentle voice from within the pavilion. Mercury. Iero and Farran looked her way, and she beckoned them inside. She stepped around the table, folding her hands together in front of her. Regal, shining, perfect.

Iero bounded up the steps, Farran not far behind. "His Majesty and I have some concerns," he told her, eyes darting to Dimitri as he, too, strode around the table. Blocking it from Farran's view. A rebel king, standing in the heart of the empire. "It would seem no one has seen either Lady Evensong or Princess Twila today," Iero hesitated as he said the next words, dreading the reactions of both other men in the room, "Not even my spies."

Dimitri tensed. No one talked about it in front of him, but they all knew Rolina was his girl. The one he looked after while pretending she annoyed him. The one he shaped and molded into a woman to admire and respect. Daughter of the Emperor.

"Is there anywhere they could have missed?" Farran asked, desperation leaking through his regal mask. "Evensong knows The Eternal Forest better than most, does she not?"

"Not better than my men," Iero stated.

"Then where the hell are they?" Farran growled, taking a step closer to Iero.

"Gaj," Dimitri said, surprisingly calm, "On their way to it, at least."

"Why?" Farran's attention snapped to the High Emperor, fury in his dark eyes.

Iero wondered what lie Dimitri would offer the man. What reason could he give without revealing Rolina's identity. He gave an answer Iero did not expect. The truth, "Her parents were taken hostage by rebels there. *Your* men, if I'm not mistaken," the emperor added, his caramel eyes boring into the king. "She left to force my hand and make me send my men there to help them. I'm guessing she asked Twila to come along so she wouldn't be alone."

Farran nodded, a muscle in his jaw flickering as he fought for control of himself, "Twila could never tell her no, not if her family's involved. She... family means everything to her, and Evensong is like another sister." There was more. Iero saw it on the king's lips, words he wanted to say, but held back.

"I can go after them," Iero volunteered, eager to have Rolina safe and sound, tucked away in her room where nothing and no one could touch her. "They left sometime last night, they can't be much farther than Un. If I ride fast-"

"No," Mercury cut him off, surprising all three men in the room. "We need you for..." her eyes flicked to Farran, wary, "something else."

"Kail then," Iero said, though he was loath to leave the task to the other guardian.

"No," Mercury repeated.

"Are you seriously planning to do nothing while *both* of our girls are in danger?" Farran took a step towards the empress.

"Let her speak," Dimitri said, on the verge of a growl.

"Do you have anything of Twila's with you?" Mercury asked Farran without so much as a twitch of concern. She crossed the room to stand before him.

"I can check. Why?" he asked, wary of the powerful woman before him. But he understood this was about more than what side they were on. This was about their children, and that made them allies, at least for the moment.

"Maddy can use it to contact her. You can speak to her, make sure she's alright while we decide on a plan," she turned to Dimitri, "And you'll speak with Evensong."

He didn't question his sister. Iero knew how they operated, knew when one's emotions were overpowering, the other took charge. In fact, Iero was surprised she didn't offer to talk to Rolina for him.

"I'll have someone escort you to the guardians' quarters," Mercury said to Farran, waving at a servant standing patiently outside the pavilion.

The servant girl hurried up the steps and received her orders, the trepidation clear on her round face as she stepped up to Farran and said, "Right this way."

"Do you think I'm just going to leave when we still don't have a plan to go after them? That I'll let you scheme up some way to turn this to your advantage behind my back?" he hissed, not moving an inch as the servant backed away.

Mercury frowned, "I merely hoped for a chance to speak with Iero about last night, and as far as Lady Evensong and your daughter are concerned, neither one is a pawn to be sacrificed. I'd rather work together to save them than let our differences lead them to harm." She stepped up to the king, taking one of his hands in her own, "You have my word I will treat Twila with as much concern and respect as our Evensong until long after they are both safe and sound."

Farran studied the empress, cautious as he said, "I suppose I have no choice but to trust you in this." With that, he took his hand away and turned to the servant girl, "Lead on."

Silence fell until he was far out of sight.

"What was she thinking?" Dimitri hissed, running a hand through his hair.

Half a smile spread across Mercury's face as she stepped closer to Dimitri, "She was thinking that you love her very much, and would do anything to protect her."

Dimitri scowled. "What's your plan then? If you're not sending Iero or Kail, you have something in mind, don't you?"

A flash of guilt across her face, "They're needed elsewhere." She turned toward Iero, deciding the rest of the conversation needed to be in private, "We're sending you to Valtameri."

Iero's stomach dropped. "Why the hell would you send me there?"

"We need you to get a message to Hel. Last we heard, his armies were growing, and his ties beyond Syytala could bring in more support. He's been reported sailing in The Drowning Sea," Mercury explained, speaking gently to ease the growing fear in Iero's chest. "I know how much you hate the sea, and we don't ask this of you lightly."

The knots in Iero's stomach multiplied at the thought of the undersea kingdom. He missed when Ráj was alive and there was never any question of who to send to Valtameri. "Could you send Kail instead?" His head spun. He was made for stealth, for quick escapes and silent footsteps. In the sea, he couldn't move the same, couldn't sneak around or slip into shadows. And there were other reasons he avoided the place. Nauseating, panic-inducing reasons.

"We're sending Kail to Kauneus," Dimitri stated, pushing his emotions further aside, returning to the calm, collected leader Iero was accustomed to.

"I could go to Kauneus," Iero offered weakly, but he knew exactly why they chose Kail over him.

"They're Kail's people, not yours."

"Well, exactly," Iero said, perking up a bit, "I should be going to The Frostlands. The Aleksandrovs are still undecided and their military is-"

"Hel's armies are stronger," Dimitri interrupted.

"But also less guaranteed," Iero argued. Getting that man to help them would be like trying to pull teeth from a snow leopard. And though The Frostlands were vulnerable at the moment, dealing with the recent death of their king, Iero had no doubt his son, King Daniel Aleksandrov would keep the country loyal to the empire. To do otherwise would leave their already weakened kingdom all the more vulnerable. And, from the few times Iero had met the boy, he seemed like the good sort.

"Exactly, Iero. It won't take much to get their support," Mercury said gently, "Even last night, Lady Katherine promised to keep us updated about their situation at the border." Their weakest point at the moment. The line between them and the rebel kingdom of Kandston. "We can handle The Frostlands for now. And I know you can do this," Mercury assured him, squeezing his hand.

"I..." he tried to conjure another excuse, an escape from facing a fear he had long tried to overcome. He had none. It was a long shot, but if Hel finally caved in, they could win the war in an instant.

"Use the Valtamerians to track Hel down, then tell him about the war," Dimitri ordered, ignoring the sick look on Iero's face.

"Get him to return, if you can. Or at least send his armies." Before Mercury spoke her next sentence, a darkness settled over her face, "There are... other rumors as well. About who Hel has sailing with him."

Iero raised an eyebrow.

"A man with a beautiful face, ruined with scars," Mercury continued.

The heart in Iero's chest stopped and the air was sucked from the room, despite being open to the forest outside. He managed to rein in his panic long enough to breathe, "Sikker?"

"We believe so," Dimitri answered.

"You can see why we need *you* to be the one to find them," Mercury said, and though she spoke gently, Iero couldn't help but find the words cruel.

"I... I'll be ready to leave by morning," Iero said. There was no way out. He started to leave the pavilion, but stopped when he remembered an earlier concern, "Have either of you seen Eli today?"

"He came by earlier," Mercury said, a tightness in her voice. Eli was hers as much as Rolina was her brother's, and she was coming to the same conclusion as Iero. He had to be told.

"What do we tell him?"

Mercury's face dropped, but she pressed on. "Give him the day. He's busy. He won't notice she's gone."

"And then?" Iero asked, frowning.

"I'll tell him myself," she said, looking down at the table to hide her face. But she could not hide the sorrow lacing her voice.

Iero wanted to tell her it would be alright, but he didn't know if it would, and he was angry with her for sending him to the place he hated most, to find someone he wasn't certain he wanted to face. "The duke got away from me," he told them as he turned to leave.

Neither emperor nor empress were surprised.

Iero had to trust them, had to follow orders. Though he couldn't help but wonder what they would do about the girl. It was enough to keep his mind off his own dire situation. Or perhaps he chose to worry about her, rather than himself. Trying to calculate her odds of survival without training. Even in a peaceful country like Ev, it was not likely. Not during wartime. Maybe something stuck with her, some tidbit of information from the stories they told her. Enough to keep her alive.

He doubted it.

Why hadn't they taught her of the world? The real world beyond her faerie-tale existence. She could fight, but not much better than the average thug. Chances were the numbers would be against her if she found herself in a fight. She couldn't hunt, or make a fire, or navigate. And what did Twila really know of life on the road?

Arrogance. Pride. Their own hubris stopped them from arming her with wisdom or skill. Why bother teaching some mortal girl how to take care of herself when surrounded by the most powerful men in history? They could take care of her. They were Imperial Guardians for heaven's sake, older than history, stronger than steel. Egos the size of mountain ranges.

Rage burned in Iero's stomach. He was as much to blame as the others. How much time would it have taken to hand her a lock pick and show her how to use it? Haven could have shown her to heal, like he did with Eli. Madd could have contributed a spell or two, instead of useless facts and bits of history. Even Kail could have... well, Kail was an idiot, but he knew how to charm his way out of trouble. A skill Rolina might benefit from. It didn't matter. They didn't teach her. All of them knew, in the back of their minds, she would return to her family one day. All of them. But instead of showing her how to stand on her own two feet, they taught her to lean on them. All but Eden, who taught her a bit of swordplay when she was small. Perhaps if he hadn't been gone for so much of her life in the forest, he would have shown her enough of the world to make up for the mistakes of the rest of them.

Arrogant bastards.

At least they taught her one thing, through their stories and actions.

How to be brave.

Marching to the guardians' quarters, anger fumed inside his chest as hot as the Chyddan. He strode down the hall to his ice cold bedroom, mind racing.

Iero, trained for perfect silence, slammed the door behind him.

15

Out the Window

Iero once told Rolina of a girl with the soul of a goddess forced to serve in the household of a demon. A girl who hummed while scrubbing muddy floors and imagined feather dusters were princesses in frilly ballgowns. A girl who was beaten raw and bloody any time the demon found imperfection in her work, real or imagined. A girl who never lost her smile, no matter what was done to steal it. He told her about rescuing the girl from the demon's home, only to have her snatched away again and taken to a stronghold deep in the mountains.

This was the part she was reminded of as she leaned out the window of her and Twila's second-story room. The part when Iero climbed the mountain and scaled the stronghold's mighty wall to reach her. The dashing, heroic part that always sounded a bit exaggerated even though it came from an immortal guardian. A part of her had always wondered why the girl didn't climb out on her own instead of making Iero come all that way.

Now she understood. It was only the second story of an inn, not the towering walls of a mountain fortress, but Rolina felt a bit woozy looking down. She imagined multiplying that height several dozen times, and replacing the nice, soft bushes below with jagged, threatening rocks and knew with absolute certainty she would have waited to be rescued too.

"Are you *sure* you don't want to try sneaking out the front?" Twila said, joining her at the windowsill.

"It could be worse," Rolina commented, smiling out at the empty night, "We could be on the *third* floor." There was still plenty of light over the rooftops a few blocks away, where Twila said there were parlors and taverns bustling with people. But in their corner of Un, the citizens were fast asleep. The inn itself was silent as death, the nobility housed within resting in comfort before their long journeys home.

"We could *walk* down to the first floor," Twila said, frowning at the faraway ground.

"Come on, it'll be easy," Rolina said, walking away from the window at last. It wasn't a scary mountain fortress, and she had always been a climber. Even the time she broke her leg falling from one of the trees of The Eternal Forest hadn't stopped her from trying again once she was healed. She hadn't brought any rope, but the bedclothes had been easy enough to tie together. Rolina gave them a few testing tugs before anchoring them around the bedpost. "You go first."

"Me?" Twila's head whipped around to face her.

"So I can hold onto the blankets while you climb. If you go second, you won't have anything but the bed to hold you up," Rolina tossed the free end of her homemade rope out the window. "I'm lighter than you, so I'll be safer on my own." And she knew what it was like to fall, and did not fear it.

Twila let out a whimper, "Do I have to?"

"Yes," Rolina said, positioning herself to hold Twila's weight on the rope. "Go on," she waved a hand towards the window.

The princess turned back to the window, scowling down at the world, "You're sure this is safe?"

"Safe enough," Rolina replied.

Twila threw one final scowl Rolina's way before sitting on the windowsill and pulling her legs over the edge. She gave the homemade rope a testing tug.

"I've got you," Rolina assured her.

The princess let out another whine then grabbed hold of the rope and started down the side of the building. The blankets strained in Rolina's hands, but between her and the bed, it was more than enough support to see Twila safely to the ground.

"I'm alive," she heard the princess sigh.

Rolina smiled and reeled the rope back up before securing their supplies to the other end. "Ready?" Rolina called, and when Twila said she was, she lowered the supplies down to the princess. And then it was her turn. She sat on the edge of the windowsill, dizziness creeping at the edges of her mind. It was practice, she told herself. In case she was ever trapped in a scary fortress and didn't want to inconvenience any immortals. She took the blankets in hand and slowly lowered herself off the ledge.

There wasn't much in the way of footholds on the smooth wall. She mumbled a few curses for not training her upper body strength as much as Captain North wanted her to. When Eden left the forest all those years ago, he'd turned her training over to the man. North had been determined to make her a real soldier. Even had her marching and doing drills alongside them at first. But she kept wandering off towards whatever caught her eye, or challenging soldiers who were quite a bit bigger than her to duels. Captain North had arranged a more individualized training regime after that, incorporating some advice from Iero to teach her as if it was an adventure. She stuck to the new routine as best as her flighty mind could, but clearly it wasn't enough to build the muscles she needed for this wall.

At least she was climbing down. Down was easy, gravity did half the work. The trick was not letting it work too fast. After a few angry grunts and a bit of contemplation as to whether Eldur had an appropriate profanity for her situation - something about cursing walls that were too slick for climbing - her feet touched the ground and she released the blanket rope.

"There now," she sighed, out of breath, "easy."

Twila rolled her eyes then jabbed her thumb towards the stables, "Come on, let's get our boys."

They left their supplies on the ground for the moment, then started towards the stables. Carrying bags full of supplies would only arouse suspicion. "Evening," Rolina greeted a guard by the entrance. She selected one of her warmest smiles to give him.

"What brings you ladies here so late?" he asked, furrowing his brow.

The pre-planned lie slipped through Twila's lips easily, "I couldn't sleep, so my girl suggested a ride to calm my nerves."

The guard frowned, "You might try a cup of tea."

"We did," Rolina sighed, shaking her head. Then she leaned in close to the guard and whispered, "Only Feinin tea works on the poor girl, and we're fresh out. Haven't been able to get any since the war started. And she has *such* insomnia." That lie wasn't part of the plan, and she didn't know where it came from. Perhaps she had spent too much time with Iero since Eden and Maddy left for Bane. The guard's eyes flicked to Twila's pointed ears before he stood aside.

Twila flashed Rolina a wide grin as they entered the stables. Soon Tovi and one of the horses that pulled their carriage the night before were saddled and ready. Twila had to steal the riding tack for hers because it was being used as a carriage horse until then. There was no alternative unless they wanted to alert someone of their escape by offering to buy it, but the theft bothered Rolina. Perhaps Iero hadn't rubbed off on her as much as she thought.

The girls rode out into the street, stopping briefly to claim their supplies before continuing out of Un. Every minute burned away the fear in Rolina's heart. They were out of The Eternal Forest's shadow, and no one had come for them yet. Perhaps with everything that happened the night before, no one had noticed her missing. She shook the thought away. Farran would have noticed Twila gone by then, she was everything to him.

"Night riding always calms the soul," Twila sighed, tilting her head back to look at the stars.

Rolina smiled. It was important, in times like these, to celebrate every victory, no matter how small. Even if it was soon to end, even if Iero - or whoever Dimitri sent - was seconds away, she had left the forest. She had done something real, something strong. So Rolina lifted her eyes to the stars and let out a deep breath of midnight air. The trees of The Eternal Forest were ancient and strong, their branches obscuring the sky from view even in the most open places. Rolina had not seen stars so clear in years. Not even when she climbed as high as the thick branches would let her. She could barely remember the true, swirling majesty of them. Her breath caught in her throat. Tears pricked the corners of her eyes. This was what she had been missing all those years. The stars of her homeland.

"Do you think," Rolina said, hope and fear and awe swirling in her chest at the sight of those stars, "Do you think Tavek made a difference? Do you think they'll stand with us?"

The princess shrugged, though Rolina didn't see it as she stared at the stars. The Duke had done his work well. He had poisoned the minds of the people across the continent, all without the High Emperors noticing anything was amiss. Not even Iero or his spies knew the extent of discontent among the people. The hatred bred through lies. Several of the twelve kingdoms had been reluctant to choose a side as a result, knowing their own people were split. Choose wrong and they could end up with their own civil war to deal with. It was easier for them to walk the line, to let their people choose a side for themselves and publicly remain neutral.

Dimitri and Mercury refused to force anyone to fight, refused to demand support from the twelve kingdoms for fear of becoming the tyrants Cadogan's lies proclaimed them to be. That left them with good old fashioned diplomacy to fight against the fear and apathy of the ruling class. "I think people are starting to realize they can't keep twiddling their thumbs and hoping this goes away. I think-" Twila gave a yelp of surprise, pulling Rolina's attention away from the stars.

"What is it? What's wrong?" Aside from the shock on her face, Twila appeared fine to Rolina, so her eyes darted to their surroundings, searching for whatever danger Twila had spotted.

"It's my father," Twila said, eyes wide.

"What about him?" Rolina looked over her shoulder, half-expecting the man to be riding up to catch them.

"He's... talking to me in my head," her voice shifted and Rolina raised an eyebrow as she said to the air, "Yes, I'm talking to Evensong." Her attention snapped back to Rolina, "He says the wizard cast a spell to let him speak to me."

"You mean Maddy?" Rolina asked, wondering if them working together was a good sign.

Twila nodded, but her words were no longer directed at Rolina as she said, "Of course we're safe, I'm not an idiot." A pause. Rolina watched the sour expression on Twila's face as she listened to whatever her father had to say. "No, we will not be turning back. We left for. A. Reason." Another pause in which Twila's face turned from sour to defiant, "No. She. Is. Not." The pause lasted only a second, "No, *you* don't understand. I'm doing this because she needs me. Just because *you've* never had a friend you weren't willing to stab in the back doesn't mean-"

Whatever Farran said bit the words right out of Twila's mouth. Rolina stared at her friend, looking for any clue as to what he was telling her. Twila's face darkened. "It is." After a pause so long that Rolina began wondering if Twila had decided to shut her father out entirely, the princess' face softened. "Don't you see, Father? This is an opportunity. Stay with the emperors. Find a common ground and use it."

Rolina imagined what it must be like, having a father she could be so open with. If she tried to tell Dimitri what he should do or what she felt was right, he would never take her seriously. She was a girl in his eyes. A nineteen-year-old child next to his over seven-hundred years of life. No wonder he could sweep her emotions aside like dirt, he had centuries to practice how not to care.

That wasn't fair. She knew it wasn't. He was thinking of the whole situation, not just her parents. He wasn't doing it to hurt her.

It hurt her all the same.

"Of course," Twila said, then bitterly added, "I love you, too," before turning back to Rolina. "He's gone. I think he's going to stay in the forest."

Rolina smiled, though it was equal parts hopeful and doubtful, "Do you think us leaving... do you think it will make them hear each other out?" How many lives would be saved if Illandia could be turned for the empire?

Twila returned the grin, but it didn't last, "There are things you don't know, Evensong. Things happening in Illandia that even I can't tell you. I don't know if he'll be able to see past them."

"I understand," Rolina said, but she didn't. What could possibly be so big and overwhelming that Farran would send his soldiers to die? That he would refuse to hear out the emperors, who had done nothing but welcome him until he sided with the rebellion.

Rolina focused on the road ahead. Even if she didn't agree with him, Twila's loyalty was first to her father, then to her people. Rolina felt the same about Dimitri. Even if she was defying him by leaving, it took the threat of her parents' lives before she even thought to. And if she could help the empire on her way, if she could learn from Twila about the rebels or help people like that Feinin boy, was it truly a betrayal? She could only hope Dimitri saw it as she did. That he understood her actions weren't merely for the sake of defying him.

She was done fighting battles with paper and ink alone. For her family, it was time to offer body and blood to the cause.

Dimitri strode through the doors of Maddy's chambers, twirling a silver hairpin in his fingers. An item taken from Rolina's room so he might speak to her. An item he bought for her from one of the traders who came to the forest. He didn't have a reason, he just thought she might like it. It was the first thing he saw when he walked into her room, and therefore the thing he took. But now the memory of it irritated him. A worthless thing turned precious the moment he put it in her hands. The shadow of her smile laughing in his head.

"I've been expecting you, Sir," Maddy nodded politely and would have stood if not for his injured leg. He set aside a book in his hands and straightened up as much as his weak body could.

"I brought this for the spell," Dimitri held out the silver hairpin, shaped like a feather. The girl had always liked feathers and wings. It was the reason Dimitri gave her Dain's old room. The Taivan's bed had wings carved into the headboard. Wings she touched whenever she thought she needed a bit of luck. Dimitri wanted the hairpin out of his hands. Wanted to stop thinking about her like she was his and be angry she defied him.

But he wasn't angry. Annoyed, yes, but he understood her better than she thought. And she, him. He would have done the same for his family, for his sister. Had done far worse. He was more afraid for her than angry. But Twila was with her, and as much as he disdained the princess' father, he knew she would do anything for Rolina. They were... good together. Complementary. If one fell, the other would be there to catch her.

Maddy took the hairpin from Dimitri and rolled it in his fingers, "There's something you should know before we try this."

"What?" Dimitri lined the single syllable with enough agitation that Maddy's eyes darted away, eager to find something new to look at.

"Nothing, really," Maddy assured him, "except one, small thing," the wizard dared a quick peek before looking back down at the hairpin in his hand. "Generally with telepathy, the target only receives the message if they are receptive to the sender."

Dimitri's jaw tightened, taking the hint with as much dignity as he could, "You think she won't talk to me."

Maddy offered a well-meaning shrug. "She ran away for a reason." He meant it in an observational way, but the moment it came out of his mouth, he knew it was the wrong thing to say.

"Meaning, she ran away because of me," Dimitri interpreted, eyes drifting toward the curtained window. His turn to look away, to hide.

"No," Maddy shook his head, wincing as the motion sent fresh pain shooting through his injured face and neck. He shut his eyes, pushing away the sting. "No," he repeated, opening his eyes to find Dimitri watching him with more than a little concern, "of course not."

The emperor refrained from commenting on Maddy's condition. "If I sent more soldiers, or one of you, she wouldn't have run away," his matter-of-fact tone helped him detach from the emotion, to separate mind from heart. A strategy learned long ago that he now struggled to implement. "She won't talk with me because I did nothing."

Words came easy to Madd when writing them on a page, or when discussing scholarly things like history or magic. But when it came to speaking to someone in pain, he never quite found the way of it. Emotions weren't like facts and science, where everything had an answer if he looked hard and long enough. He did not know how to comfort a man who would not admit he hurt.

He kept silent.

"Nevertheless, I would like to try. Even if she won't hear me," Dimitri concluded, meeting the wizard's eye.

Maddy nodded, "Come close."

There was a chair beside Maddy's bed, no doubt used by Farran only moments before. Dimitri sat.

"Take my hand."

Dimitri did as told.

A candle on the bedside table flickered, and Maddy held the hairpin up for Dimitri to see, "She doesn't *love* this, does she?"

Dimitri did. "Why?"

"I'm going to light it on fire," Maddy said, a spark in his eye.

The emperor's gut twisted, but he pushed the pointless emotion aside, "I can always buy her another."

"Perfect," Maddy squeezed Dimitri's hand and held Rolina's hairpin over the candle's flame. His smooth voice dropped into a chant. The Ancient Viskan words almost soothing the way he spoke them. So natural on his tongue. He had lived when the dead language was still in use. When it was *his* language, not just the words spoken to call to the earth, to summon its magic. Sometimes Dimitri forgot how much older the guardians were than him, he was so old. It felt like he had lived forever. But High Emperors had lived and died dozens of times over - their imperfect immortality passing from one to the next - while the guardians lived on.

The wizard's chant ended and his eyes flicked up to Dimitri, "Say something to her."

"Rolina?" Dimitri said to the air.

Not a sound in response.

Maddy frowned. "It would seem our spell has failed."

It would seem she didn't want to talk to him.

Dimitri was on his feet in an instant, headed for the door, "I knew this was a bad idea. I'll tell Iero not to go to Valtameri and have him go get her."

"No," Maddy called after him. "I can find another way. When Farran spoke to Twila, she said they were safe. We have time," he promised.

Dimitri hesitated, "How long will it take you to find another way?"

"A day, maybe two," Maddy told him, "I just need to think, I'll figure it out, I always do."

The emperor scowled, "Something could happen while I'm waiting on you. Someone needs to go after her. Now."

"She'll be fine," Maddy said, and Dimitri could see in his eyes that he meant it. "She was raised by you, taught by me, and trained by our best. Now's her chance to use what she's learned. Dangerous or not, don't take that chance from her. She won't forgive you, even if she tries."

Dimitri's jaw tightened, his mind recalling a time a similar chance came to him. The gates thrown wide. The world in peril. He would have killed anyone who tried to stop him. Rolina wouldn't react quite so violently, but that didn't make it mean any less. He understood the need for freedom, no matter how dangerous the times. "You have two days." With that, the High Emperor swept out of the room.

16

Zey

For the first time in her life, Rolina wished she listened to Maddy's lectures about plants. Wildflowers danced in the open meadows beside the road. Yellows and purples and blues. It would make the wizard proud if she came home and told him exactly what kinds of flowers they were, even if she couldn't say what they symbolized or which ones could be used for magic. At the very least, she wished she had the words to describe the place. The guardians had so many stories to tell her and this was her chance to give one back. What was the point if she couldn't get the details right? If she couldn't tell them what kinds of flowers she saw.

"How long has it been since you were here?"

Rolina turned to find Twila watching her as she rode, more than simple curiosity on her face. Concern. They had ridden through the night and into the morning in relative silence, their minds occupied by their surroundings and the potential dangers of the night. Even when they stopped to let the horses rest, they kept close together, staying quiet. Now it was deep into the day, and neither girl was the sort to shy away from conversation. Not with each other. Twila had made a few attempts to start one, but they exhausted quickly. She never meant to ignore her friend, but Rolina couldn't keep her eyes off the landscape.

New and remembered all at once. Her mind clinging to shreds of memory from her original journey.

"Eleven years," she answered.

"So you were... eight when you came to the forest?" Twila asked, pausing to count on her fingers.

"And Eli was three," she added with a nod. They hadn't spoken about Rolina's life before The Eternal Forest since she originally confessed who she was to Twila. Neither of them brought it up again, but Rolina had always been relieved she didn't have to keep the secret from her friend. She and Ramar were the only people outside the forest she cared for. Aside from her family of course.

"Is it strange? Seeing it again?" Twila asked, and Rolina knew she was trying to help. Trying to provide Rolina an opportunity to talk about what was bothering her.

But she wasn't bothered. She had plenty to worry about. The safety of their journey and her parents in danger were at the top of the list, but she didn't feel the fear or panic she assumed would follow her. Rolina may not have remembered much about the flowering meadows surrounding her, but that didn't stop them from feeling like home. Like a safe, warm place. Like a mug of teppen in the winter.

They were only at the start of their two-week journey, but they were moving. That alone eased the creeping fears that first caught her when Dimitri told her about her parents. More than that. She'd been standing still for a while. Sifting through papers and waiting for the guardians, for her friends, to come home. Waiting for their safety instead of *making* them safe. Her actions now were deliberate. Foolish. The best choice she made in a long time.

"It's a little weird that I don't remember as much as I thought I would, but I only came this way once," Rolina said, staring out at the open meadows. A breeze rippled through the tall grass and flowers, catching her and Twila's hair on its way.

"I suppose you wouldn't recognize much. You've been living with the emperors longer than your own parents," Twila said, then bit her lip as though she could swallow the words.

But Rolina already realized that. Had thought about it the moment she turned sixteen. Even though she couldn't remember the exact date she came to the forest, it was enough of a marker for her to realize how long it had been. Of course, she didn't remember her birthday either. Maddy asked her when she was little, and all she could remember was it was in the summer, and Eli's was in the winter.

They picked a day for each of them. That would be another thing to ask her parents when she found them. When was she born? "All the more reason I'm excited to see them," Rolina smiled broadly at Twila.

The princess' shoulders slumped with relief. "What are they like?"

"Who knows?" Rolina laughed, "I'm starting to question the quality of my own memory." She may not have known who they were anymore, but she knew they were good. Worth saving. Every tiny scrap of remaining memory screamed at her they were loving, warm, playful, strong. They were her shelter until the end. Until they all made mistakes. Her mother got sick. Her father looked away. Eli bolted. She chased. And then they were lost.

And then they were found.

Faded memory or not, that day was burned into her mind.

Haven's red hair tied back out of his face except for one escaped strand. One of his rare, mournful looks on his freckled face that vanished the moment he laid eyes on them. *And who might you be?* An offered hand and a promise of sweets and next thing Rolina knew, they were marching up the steps of the emperor's pavilion. Mercury spoke. Dimitri laughed.

Caramel eyes found their way to hers.

"They're good people," Rolina said, shaking away the memory before she killed another conversation.

"Then I'm happy to rescue them," Twila said cheerfully. "Since you're being *unusually* open about your past, but don't remember much *before* the forest," she continued, forcing a playful lilt into her voice as she cautiously approached the new question, "Do you know why they kept you?"

Rolina raised an eyebrow, "I told you already, they kept us instead of following the law that outsiders who enter the forest uninvited are executed."

"I know," Twila paused to think of a better way to ask, "I meant, do you know why *they* kept you? As in the emperors. Why not pass you off to the servants or something?"

"They did." Rolina laughed at the confusion on Twila's face. "I didn't let them pass me off for long." Rolina wouldn't normally share the story, but something about leaving the forest was opening her up. They were on their way to rescue a pair of unknown farmers in the middle of nowhere. With parents like that, Rolina knew she never should have met the High Emperors. There was no point in pretending a girl like her having a connection to the most powerful people in Syytala wasn't strange.

"You know how I get nightmares?" That had been an easier secret to share. It was more of a warning than anything, confessed on the night Farran convinced the emperors to let Twila stay the night in Rolina's room. The first of many nights lying awake, sharing secrets and giggling about nothing in particular. She always slept better when Twila was visiting. Hardly a nightmare at all.

Twila nodded.

"They had Eli and I staying in the palace, away from the emperors and the guardians. I got a nightmare and ran barefoot across the grounds, in my nightdress, in the cold, to the Emperor's Pavilion. To find Dimitri."

"You weren't afraid of him when you were little?" Twila asked. He wasn't exactly the warmest person, and Rolina knew he had scared Twila until she was in her teen years.

"I was," Rolina said, grinning at her own, stupid, childhood logic. "I thought he was scarier than the monsters in my nightmares, so maybe he would scare them off."

The princess laughed, revealing her bright, Feinin smile.

"I did that every night for a month until finally they moved Eli and I into the guardians quarters so I wouldn't freeze or ruin my nightgowns." She remembered many horrified looks from the servants when

Dimitri brought her back to them in the mornings, covered in dirt and little scratches from darting through the trees and brush. "After that it was easy to get in their business. I followed all of them around, started going to whoever was home for my nightmares, and eventually I was just part of the place.

"Kail loves kids, so he was easy to wrap around my finger. Haven had pretty hair, so I used to ask him if I could play with it while he mixed medicines." She had worked many a tangled braid into Haven's thick, red hair. Once she messed it up so horribly, he'd chosen to cut it rather than try and work the tangles out. The first and only time she had seen him wear it short. "And once I said something or other about not knowing how to read in front of Maddy. It had him cursing the quality of Evyan education. I mean *cursing. Maddy.*" She shared a grin with Twila as she went on. "That's why he started teaching us. Then Eden started teaching me to fight. He honestly couldn't get rid of me until he left for Eldur, because I wanted to learn *everything*. And Iero, well, I think I remind him of..." *Petra.* She nearly said the name of Iero's daughter aloud. But that wasn't her secret to share. "Home," she said instead. "It was easy, really." Not that she had been trying.

"And the emperors?" Twila asked, smiling faintly at the story.

"Haven's always with Mercury, so I got to her through him. Plus she thought Eli was the cutest little boy in the world. He had such chubby cheeks," Rolina puffed out her cheeks, but could only hold it a second before she burst into laughter.

Twila chuckled before adding, "And I assume Dimitri liked you because Mercury did. Who knew it was so easy to get into the good graces of the most powerful people in the world. Eight-year-old you was a manipulative mastermind."

Rolina nodded, smiling, though that wasn't entirely true. Dimitri had been harder. She never *tried* to make the others like her. Befriending even one of them was more than she expected. Even as a little girl she knew they were too important to be bothered. That didn't stop her from following them around though. But Dimitri... she felt something the moment those caramel eyes met hers. A jolt. A connection. It made her far too curious to leave him alone. There was something in him that needed puzzling out, and eleven years later, she didn't think she had found it yet.

"I'm sure you would have done the same," Rolina said with a grin. Another gust of wind cut through the meadow. Rolina pulled Eden's jacket tighter around her body.

"Alright, since I've been pushing my luck today, and it's been working, I'm going to ask," Twila said, a feline grin on her lips, "Are you and Eden... you know," she raised an eyebrow suggestively.

Rolina's stomach dropped. "I don't know what you mean," the words came out more defensive than she meant them to.

Twila only grinned, "You used to talk about him all the time when he was away in Eldur. But you've talked about him less and less since he came back. Almost as though you have something to hide." She tossed Rolina a playful look before turning her eyes back to the road.

A city lay before them, still several miles out. Zey. Rolina had seen the place on her stolen map. She knew little about it, but Twila had scrunched her face up in disgust when Rolina mentioned it.

"And you stole his jacket."

Rolina shrugged, trying too hard to look like she didn't care, "I already told you, I needed plain clothes."

Twila shot her a look that demanded a better explanation, "Interesting that you close up when I mention Eden of all things. If it weren't true, you'd have more to say."

It was the one thing she absolutely could not tell Twila. Eden wouldn't like it. He didn't want to hide their relationship. That had been Rolina's choice. The compromise was they wouldn't deny it if the other guardians asked, but they wouldn't tell. And Dimitri *absolutely* could not know. It would only upset Eden if she told Twila and *still* wouldn't let him tell the others. The guardians were brothers through their magic, and Eden didn't keep secrets from his brothers.

But there was more to consider than simple attraction. They both knew it couldn't last. The math didn't add up. She was mortal. He was forever. Somewhere down the road they would crack. She should, by all logic, let Eden go before it hurt. If the others knew, they would try and get between them. Try and gently separate them before they were so tangled up the only way apart was shattering. She knew this inside and out. Had thought and considered and tortured herself with what-ifs and inevitables. The problem was her heart.

It couldn't release Eden.

"Eden's my best friend."

The princess' expression turned incredulous.

"Aside from you of course," Rolina added before continuing, "I miss him, so I took his jacket."

"You didn't steal from him last time, and he was gone for years," the princess pointed out.

"I didn't know him like I know him now," Rolina admitted. Certainly, he had been the one to originally spark her interest in swordplay, and she had written him letters and tried to get closer to him whenever he came home to visit, but it was difficult work. His replies to her multi-page, overly flowery letters were paragraphs at most. And when he came back to the forest, it was usually for events like Tavek or important meetings. Leaving her only the tiniest windows to befriend him. He wasn't like the others, who she wrapped around her finger simply by being around. She had to put effort into Eden, and even then she only really came to call him a friend perhaps a year before his return.

And then he did return. A friend who taught her dirty words in a foreign tongue and pushed her into taking up her sword once more. A man who people feared, but would never, ever harm her. Like Dimitri. Like, well, most of the guardians.

Twila tried a new angle, still unconvinced. "You miss the others too, don't you?"

"They're all home except Bolwerk, and he..." Rolina hesitated, knowing she shouldn't speak ill of a guardian, "I don't miss him as much."

Twila snorted, "What a nice way of saying you hate him."

"I don't hate him!" Rolina tried not to look too pleased the conversation was drifting away from Eden. She didn't like lying to Twila. No wonder keeping secrets from his brothers was so hard for Eden.

"You do," Twila laughed.

"I don't. He's just a bit..." She couldn't think of a soft way to say what she thought of him, though she knew *hate* was too harsh. They lived in The Eternal Forest together, just like the others, their bedrooms only a few doors apart, existing in the same space separately. After several childhood attempts to get along, she learned not to bother.

"Mean. The word you're looking for is mean," Twila said, and that was that. "I can't imagine living with that many men. The smell must be terrible."

"I have Mercury."

They fell into their conversation, keeping away from any important topics from then on. Only when they found themselves before the gates of Zey did the conversation drop, crushed under the weight of the city.

Tall spires and impressive towers rose above the city's wide stone wall, stretching towards the sky like the ancient trees of The Eternal Forest. Rolina knew little of cities. Somewhere, buried deep in her memory, she recalled staring up at the seemingly endless towers. She, Eli, and their father would have passed through the city on their way to Un a decade ago. But a few scattered recollections of the towers were all she had.

She heard whispers though. Stories of depravity and filth. Of crimes unseen or ignored by those capable of helping. They had to be exaggerations. No one was that indifferent. People, in her experience, were good. They could be rude or even cold, but they did as they believed right. No one could see the acts described in those tales and think them good. No one could let them happen.

"Father and I usually try to make it past Zey before we have to stop, but I think the horses need to rest," Twila said, frowning. It wasn't just the horses that needed a break. Though Rolina spent many a day riding through the forest, this was more than she was used to. Her body was stiff and beginning to ache. "We'll be safe enough together," Twila said, casting a glance over her shoulder at the open road behind them.

Evening fast approached, and though Rolina did not like the idea of staying the night in a town with such a reputation, she knew other criminally inclined individuals would camp outside the city waiting to prey on those who did not make it inside before the gates closed. Better to gamble a night at an inn full of criminals than a night in the wilds with them. At least she would have a door to lock.

Rolina paid the toll at the gate, aware of the way the man taking tolls studied her and the princess. His eyes rolling over them, savoring every curve. Noticing they were alone and seemingly unarmed. Rolina's stomach rose and she hurried on as soon as her doubles were counted and deemed enough. She rode close to Twila, wishing she could reach out and take the princess' hand.

"There's a place my father and I have stayed at once or twice, it should be safe enough," Twila said, taking the lead as they rode deeper. Rolina didn't say a word. Her eyes darted from shadow to shadow. Heart thundering at each person that so much as glanced her way. Where Un had been vibrant and colorful, this place was shadows and shifty gazes. Instinct told her to flee. Reason told her that running would only send her to the arms of thieves and bandits outside the gate.

They passed several inns and taverns, none appeared particularly inviting. Dilapidated buildings, beggars, thugs. When Twila stopped and said they had arrived, Rolina's stomach tied itself into knots. It was old and in disrepair with several windows on the top floor boarded up. A place she could never imagine the king of Illandia staying in, let alone allowing his children to. It must have been the best inn in Zey, and that only made her fear the others. Perhaps it wasn't as bad on the inside.

They paid a stable hand to take their horses. Rolina struggled handing Tovi's reins to the man, afraid he might take advantage of having such a well-bred horse in his stable. The brown Illicy could fetch quite a sum to the right buyer. Horses from Onschuld weren't often found beyond the desert kingdom's borders. Not without an Onschuldan warrior like Ramar riding atop it, deterring anyone who might think to steal one.

Heart aching from leaving the horse, she entered the inn, Twila at her side. Eyes roved over them as they strode up to the counter. Rolina ignored the scoundrels drinking and watching her and greeted a gruff man behind the counter, "Hello." He looked at her, but offered no other response.

"How much for a room?" Twila asked, skipping the pleasantries.

The man looked them over, assessing their worth, "Five flickers."

"Five?" Even Rolina knew the place couldn't be worth that many doubles.

"*Five*," the man repeated, a malicious undertone in his voice.

Rolina narrowed her eyes, "I think we'll take our business elsewhere."

"I don't think you will."

The girls turned to leave, but Rolina crashed into a large man who wasn't there a moment ago. Stepping back, she saw three men blocking their path to the door. Her hand went to the dagger tucked under her shirt. One of the men took a step closer. "See," the man behind the counter continued, "two's for the room, three's for protection." She stepped back, only to find herself pinned between the man and the counter. Another man had Twila by the hair. The princess yelped as he shoved her against the counter beside Rolina. "Wouldn't want anything to happen to pretty things like yourselves."

Rolina shot a panicked look Twila's way. Perhaps the princess had inherited more Feinin magic than glamours, though she had never shown any to Rolina. She couldn't fight three of them on her own, she needed Twila to do something. Anything. The other men crowded in close. Mercury always told her only to fight as a last resort, "Alright, I'll pay, make them leave us alone."

The man behind the counter considered for a moment, then announced, "Price has gone up," before nodding to the man in front of her.

He grabbed her by the arm and started reaching for her belt. Rolina drew her dagger, slicing it across the man's exposed wrist. He yelped and let her go, but as she started towards the door, hoping Twila was right behind her, a second man caught her by the waist and threw her onto the counter. Pain wracked through her head at the impact. He pried the dagger from her hand as she struggled and kicked, screaming for the indifferent patrons to help her. They sat and drank, ignoring the terrified girl.

Twila bit the one holding her, deep enough to draw blood. The man hardly winced, and Rolina wondered for a fleeting moment how much alcohol one had to consume to go that numb. Then the thought was gone as she fought to free herself from the man pinning her on the counter.

"The bottle!" Rolina cried, remembering the gift the Feinin boy gave her. A fireball would certainly be enough to get them off her. She strained against the man to reach her belt. The bottle wasn't there. She left it in Tovi's saddlebag.

But the cry was enough to give Twila an idea. The princess released an angry scream and fire erupted from her fists. The man holding her jumped back, scrambling to get away from the flames. Twila turned to face the man pinning Rolina, who had already loosened his grip. "Let. Her. Go."

"We don't want any trouble from your kind," the man behind the counter stammered, giving a sharp nod to the one pinning Rolina. He released her, putting a few paces between them. She slid off the counter and scooped up her fallen dagger.

Twila took her by the arm. "As she said, we'll be taking our business elsewhere." She swirled around, pulling Rolina with her as she swept from the building.

Rolina concentrated on reclaiming her frantic breath, on steadying her equally panicked friend. "Since when can you create flames?" she managed to huff as they stepped out into the street.

"Can't," Twila said, her eyes wide as a cornered animal's, "They weren't real."

A glamour. It seemed the illusions could do more than Rolina realized. Now that she thought about it, she didn't feel any heat despite being so close to the flames.

"Come on, I know another place," Twila said, biting back the panic in her voice.

"I'm sorry I wasn't any help." If it weren't for Twila... she didn't let herself think too long about what she would have done.

Twila shook her head, "I wouldn't have thought to do that if you hadn't mentioned the bottle." The girls fell silent as they walked the darkened streets, clinging to each other like children afraid of the dark.

"Maybe show off a bit of magic sooner this time?" Rolina suggested as they walked up to the door of another nearby inn.

Twila forced a chuckle and reached for the door. "I miss traveling with Father. All those guards."

Rolina nodded in agreement, chuckling though it wasn't funny. She finally realized just how protected she was within The Eternal Forest. Magical wards and barriers against all kinds of threats. Guards posted discreetly in the trees. A thousand trusted soldiers a five minute walk from her bedroom. The guardians themselves, never too far. This world was different. Brutal. And all she had to keep her safe were her unimpressive skills with a blade and a friend with a bit of illusion magic.

She looked at the princess beside her as they entered the inn. A girl who hardly hesitated to throw herself into danger and come with Rolina. All for a pair of farmers she didn't know. All for Rolina. "Thank you."

Twila flashed her Feinin grin, "All in a day's work."

17

Sweet Dreams

Rolina knew it was a dream. Sometimes she could retain a bit of lucidity and push away the nightmares. But it wasn't a nightmare. It was dinner. King Farran sat across from her, Twila seated at his right hand. At his left, his other two children. Nox and Aurora. But the girl - she was blindfolded. The thick, black fabric cutting a line through her red-brown hair and across her eyes. She ate with a smile, silent, as they all were silent.

Her attention drifted away from Aurora, seeking out her friend's eyes for some explanation. But Twila ate without a word, a grim expression etched on her face. Beside her, Farran wore the same face. Finally, Rolina's eyes landed on Nox. The boy did not eat. He stared at a glass of wine he swirled in his hand.

He was different than his sisters. Not only in the dream. His Feinin blood did little to slow his own aging. Nineteen, but he looked only a touch younger. Twila looked the same, younger even, though she was the oldest sibling. Aurora, the youngest, still looked like a child, perhaps thirteen, though she was a year younger than Rolina. The girls inherited bits of their mother's magic. Glamours for Twila and truth for Aurora. Nox had nothing.

"They are mine." Farran's voice snapped Rolina from her thoughts.

She turned her gaze to find his dark eyes locked on hers. "As are you, if you want to be."

Twila and Aurora took her hands, smiling at her. Rolina gaped at Aurora, blindly looking her way. Twila took Farran's hand as well, and he and Aurora reached for Nox's. The young man took Aurora's hand, then set his glass of wine down to take his Father's. Their hands never met. Nox stilled. His eyes wide and distant.

Then they bled.

Rolina screamed. Helpless as dozens of cuts opened on the boy's skin, one after the other. She snatched up a napkin and darted around the table, pressing it against one of the bigger wounds. "Help! Help him!" Rolina screamed, grabbing another napkin from the table. She only had two hands and there were so many wounds.

His family sat and watched.

"Help," Rolina whimpered, forgetting it was a dream. Forgetting the blood drenching her hands was not real. Forgetting everything but the boy and his pain.

Then he was still. No breath in his lungs. No light in his bloodied eyes.

"Nox?" She took a step away. "Nox!"

Her eyes jolted open. There was no body. No blood. Only the ceiling of an unfamiliar room. The princess sleeping soundly beside her. Rolina took a moment to calm her breath. She had dreamed worse things. Dreamed of devils and beasts and bodies unrecognizably broken. This was nothing to fear, even in the dark of a faraway night. Rolina rolled onto her side and looped her arms around Twila's body. Her warmth radiated peace into Rolina's heart. It was only a dream, like so many others.

Rolina eyed Twila as they led their horses from the stable. If the princess noticed the way Rolina clung to her the night before - the barely controlled breath, the fear - she did not show it. She appeared well-rested and ready to get back on the road. Not a hint of the terror that followed them after their encounter at the first inn.

The girls mounted their horses and rode out of the city. They watched their surroundings as they went, wary. The full depravity of the city laid bare to them the previous night. When Zey finally faded from view, Twila loosed a sigh of relief. Rolina thought she would feel the same. Safe with miles between her and that dark place. But something followed. Images replaying in her head.

Haven usually pushed her to talk about her nightmares. She never really thought it helped, but this one clung to her. And he was a healer after all, the *best* healer. If Haven said to do something, it couldn't hurt. "Twila," she began, voice lacking the confidence she hoped for.

The princess turned her way, the sunlight casting a halo of gold on her dark hair.

"I haven't seen your siblings in a long time," Rolina said, uncertain if she should really tell Twila. If the dream bothered Rolina, she couldn't imagine how much worse it would be for Twila. She was their sister. Dream or not, it could worry her. "How are they?"

"Fine, last I saw them," Twila said, smiling. But there was something hard in the smile. Something forced. "Father's been keeping us close to home since all this started."

"But he brought you to Tavek," Rolina pointed out.

"I begged him to," she said as though it was unimportant. But Rolina knew her well. Saw something hidden in the way her eyes shifted back to the road.

"I had this dream last night," Rolina said, wondering if it would prompt Twila to tell whatever she was hiding. "Dinner with your family."

"That sounds nice," Twila said, something far away in her voice. Wistful. Longing. When was the last time she had a chance to sit and be a family?

"Not exactly," Rolina confessed, "Aurora had this weird blindfold and Nox -" She wasn't sure if she should tell Twila about the gruesome image.

"Nox?" Twila prompted, almost too eager, too concerned.

"He started bleeding out from his eyes and then cuts started opening all over his body," Rolina said, flat, cool. Better to get it out in one burst than stumble through it.

Twila's eyes went wide, "That's horrible!"

"I know it was just a dream but it made me worry," Rolina hoped Twila would understand why she brought it up. She wasn't trying to torment her by putting the images of the dream in her head. She just wanted to know they were alright.

"They're... fine," Twila repeated without confidence. That hidden thing on the edge of her lips.

"Are you?" Rolina asked, watching her friend carefully.

"Me? Of course," Twila replied, the words too forced and she knew it. "I'm worried about us, this journey, that's all."

Rolina nodded, but that hidden thing was still there, waiting to be uncovered. She opened her mouth to keep pushing, but Twila didn't let her.

"Do you think they've sent anyone after us yet?"

"I don't think Dimitri or your father are the kind of people to wait. Not when it comes to us," Rolina replied, though she had more than enough doubts telling her otherwise. About Dimitri. Not Farran. The king had spoken to Twila through magic as soon as he realized she was gone.

Rolina hadn't heard a word from Dimitri. She wasn't sure she wanted to. He was the one who refused to help her family in the first place. What if she wasn't enough to change his mind? He treated her differently than other people, but she didn't actually know if that meant he loved her. And if it did, that didn't mean he loved her enough to *waste resources* bringing her home.

"You're right. They'll be coming," Twila said, and like Rolina, she didn't seem to know if it was a good thing.

The circle was nearly complete. Maddy sat on the floor of his bedroom, his good leg bent inward and his injured one laying out in front of him. Chalk covered his hands as he scribbled runes across the floorboards. The rug that normally covered them tossed aside in his frenzy. Maddy's eyes flashed wildly, the familiar buzz of magic thrummed in his chest. Eras had come and gone, but magic excited him as much then as it had when he was a boy. It called to him, tugged on something within him, something not quite sane. An obsessive delight. A joyful temptation. The heartbeat of the earth in his blood.

"Aren't you supposed to be in bed?"

Dimitri's voice broke Maddy's concentration. He hadn't heard the emperor come in, totally absorbed by the circle. The wizard flashed a twitchy smile, then turned to look at a clock on one of his shelves. "Already so late?"

"You said midnight," Dimitri reminded the wizard. "You're ready, aren't you?"

"Nearly, I just need -" Maddy braced his hands behind him, preparing to push himself up.

"Don't," Dimitri raised a hand and the wizard froze. "You're still injured, and I need you to heal fast. Staying off your leg is not a request," he glared at the wizard until Maddy sank back onto the floor. "What do you need?"

Maddy returned his attention to his work, picking up a candle and knife sitting on the floor beside him. "Pillow," he gestured with the knife to the mound of pillows on his bed, then set to work carving runes in the candle.

Dimitri snatched the pillow off the bed, "What do you need with this?"

"Set it there," Maddy pointed with the knife to just beyond the border of the chalk circle.

"Here?" Dimitri asked, tossing the pillow on the floor.

"Little further," Maddy answered, finishing the candle by carving Rolina's name down its length. He placed the candle in the center of the circle before picking up a sheet of parchment with both Rolina's names written over and over. *Rolina Cotter. Evensong Antares.* The name of a farmer's daughter beside a lady of the empire. Several herbs had been crushed and placed in the center of the parchment.

Dimitri nudged the pillow further away with his foot. "What is this for?"

"Don't worry about it. Sit at the edge of the circle," Maddy instructed.

The emperor did as told.

Maddy plucked his last ingredient from beside him. Another item of Rolina's, a necklace with a blue stone. He placed it with the herbs and crumpled the paper around it. "Rolina has always been susceptible to dreams," Maddy spoke faster with each syllable, excited by the spell, "We can use that."

"How?" Dimitri looked down at the runes on the floor and felt a bit like a child pretending to conduct a seance.

"You want her to hear you, whether she is receptive or not," Maddy lit the candle with a wave of his hand. "If you speak to her through a dream, she won't be able to push you away like regular telepathy."

"Like a nightmare." Dimitri's caramel eyes flickered as he watched the flame.

Maddy nodded at the dreary comparison. "Close your eyes."

Dimitri obeyed as Maddy began a chant. Holding the paper above the flame, the items caught fire. Maddy placed the flaming ingredients on his palm, seemingly immune to the burn. Holding the smoldering pile up to his lips, Maddy blew gently on the smoke, towards Dimitri.

The emperor fell unconscious onto the pillow behind him.

One last flicker of light, and the items in Maddy's hand extinguished. Smoke curled in the air. The wizard did not move, holding the smoldering ashes in his hands.

He continued chanting.

The day grew old. Rolina and Twila rode through the countryside. Her heart heavy, thoughts caught between the guilt of leaving the forest and the duty of saving her parents. It was all for them. All for a good, worthy reason. But the guilt stayed with her. Riding alongside her, expanding her fears. Her mind a repeating circle of concern.

Dimitri would send someone for her as soon as he discovered her missing. If he hadn't already. She imagined Iero stepping out of the shadows as she slept, scooping her up to ride home without waking her. Better to keep moving.

When at last night grew too dense, they decided to stop and camp rather than risk losing their path in the dark. Rolina spotted a grove of trees by the road, providing minimal cover from prying eyes. Protection made all the more important by her experience in Zey.

Rolina didn't know the first thing about making camp. In the guardians' stories, they tended to skip over that bit. Sometimes they mentioned sitting around a fire. Other times fire was dangerous. How they decided when it was safe, she didn't know, and chose to err on the side of caution. No fire. Not to mention, neither she nor Twila knew how to make one. She did pull her bottle of Feinin fire out of Tovi's saddlebag to light the night as they made themselves as comfortable as they could.

She cleared a place for herself on the ground, and bundled herself in her blanket next to Twila. "Should we sleep in shifts?" Rolina suggested.

Twila nodded, "You go ahead and sleep. I'll wake you in a few hours."

Too tired to protest, she settled on the ground, keeping her sword and dagger close, running her fingers over the wooden beads embedded into the handle. In the open night, far from home, she forced her eyes shut. Every noise, every whisper of wind, made her jump. What sort of fool was she, to lie all but alone, exposed to every creature and wicked thing in the night? Rolina assumed sleep impossible, but lying down might restore some small amount of energy. Eventually, exhaustion took her all the same.

At first, Rolina's mind lay quiet as she slept, too exhausted for dreams. Then a sound came creeping into her head. Waves. A long distance away. She had never seen nor heard the ocean save for her dreams, but she knew the sound. Hearing turned to sight, and she found herself standing on rocky ground, high pillars of stone blocked her from seeing more than a few yards, but she knew the ocean lay beyond them.

The ocean, or a nightmare. She would not know until she looked, and the ocean waves called to her, *come and play*. Perhaps she could find a way around.

Rolina turned and her heart stopped. Her eyes fell on a slender figure with his hands in his pockets. Dusty brown hair falling in front of one eye. "Dimitri," she took a step back, praying it wasn't some nightmare-distorted version of the man. Sometimes she could fight the nightmares before they came. Other times... she hoped it was not like other times.

"Hello, Prayer," he pushed the hair from his face, examining her with his caramel eyes, assessing the damage. "This is not an ordinary dream," he pressed on, never one to waste time, "Maddy is working a spell so I can talk to you."

She took another step back, "It's really you standing there?" Either it was a nightmare waiting to turn on her, or it was time to discover how angry he was. She hoped it was a nightmare. Nightmares didn't have consequences.

"In a way," he watched her carefully. Searching, she realized, for any sign of how she felt to see him. "Are you safe?" he asked after a pause, a flicker of concern breaking through his practiced indifference. "And Twila?"

"So far," she answered, lifting her chin in confidence. Hiding her fear in her heart.

"Good," he said, more relief in his voice than she expected.

"Is that all?" The words came out dismissive, even rude.

He did not seem to notice, or if he did, he didn't care. "I'd like to know your plan." Before she could reply, he continued, "Are you going to ride all the way there? Sleeping on the side of the road or in dirty inns? No one to watch over you." His voice never raised, but grew more tense with every sentence. "What will you do when you arrive in Gaj? Where will you stay? Did you bring any money? Do you think my soldiers will shelter you? Because unless you can prove you are, in fact, Lady Evensong, they have no reason to. So tell me, Rolina, what is the plan?"

Her chest tightened, each word strangling her with doubt. But she would not let him talk to her like a misbehaving child. She was not a little girl anymore, and she was not his. No matter what she felt for the man or what people thought. Her real father waited in chains and she would not let a little doubt stop her from reaching him. "It doesn't matter how I get there, or if they believe I am who I claim to be. I can't stand idly by when my parents are in danger. Unlike you, I can't disregard my feelings for the sake of strategy."

"Unlike me?" He laughed. The kind of overtired, joyless laugh that surfaced when he was at his limit. "If I could do that, your plan wouldn't work, would it?" It was the closest thing to an admission of love Rolina had ever heard from him. "Look," he began, his voice soft, a hint of desperation leaking through, "you've made your point. I'll send aid to Gaj, I'll save your parents. Just come home." Rolina almost wondered if it was a dream after all, his voice sounded so human. As though the piece of him she'd been searching for since they first met eyes was just below the surface, trying to break through. "I need you safe." She watched in awe as he extended his hand to her. A question. "Prayer?"

At the sound of the nickname, spoken in such a pleading whisper, she nearly ran into his arms. Arms that could shield her from cruel cities and nights in the dark. Arms that had kept her from the filth of the world for so long. A shelter. A prison. She didn't know which. She loved him, but could she trust him? As much as she wanted to, she couldn't risk returning to discover he had not sent anyone. He was fighting a war, the lie would be worth it. Nor would it be the first lie he told her, only the worst. No, she couldn't run to him, couldn't take his outstretched hand. Not until her family - her real family - was safe.

"I'm sorry," she breathed, taking a step away.

"You don't trust me?" he asked, sorrow slipping through his voice.

She didn't answer, didn't know how.

"Alright," he dropped his hand to his side, jaw tightening as he regained his composure. "Be safe, my Prayer." He said it with kindness, despite the anger, the fear, bleeding through his air of indifference.

"I will," she promised, stepping forward, fighting the urge to reach for him.

Dimitri faded with the dream as Rolina opened her eyes, her breath catching in the cool night air.

Dimitri woke on the floor of Maddy's bedroom and sat up with a scowl. "You didn't tell me I would lose consciousness."

"It's dream magic, what were you expecting?" Maddy gave him an innocent shrug before asking, "How did it go?"

The emperor met Maddy's eye and said, "I need you to contact someone else."

"Who?"

"Eden," Dimitri replied, running a hand through his hair.

18

A Bit of Blood

Every day, every night, the same. Eden's muscles ached, his bones burned. Cutting, slicing, ripping through every enemy that dared cross his path. Fighting until he couldn't stand. Dragging his tired body back to camp, killing as he went. Collapsing on the tent floor for a few short hours of rest. The clamor of battle lulled him to sleep and woke him when he was ready.

Time eluded Eden while at war. He often fought for days, ignorant of the hunger and exhaustion looming over him. His hell born magic sustained him longer than an average man. The battle fueled him, drove him. All he needed was Tasa in his hand, ready to slice into body after body. The cursed sword begging for more blood, constant in its wicked desires.

But there were other days. Other times when he wanted nothing more than to burrow under a dozen blankets and sleep for a week. When dreams of hot meals and warm baths fluttered through his head, draining his lust for the fight. On those days, Tasa's desire for blood taxed him. A nuisance he struggled to satisfy. Each soldier felled was less a step towards victory, but a step towards sleep, towards the rest he needed for basic functioning.

On those days, he fought for show, each swing of his sword a burden.

Every moment, soldiers looked to him, expecting the war-loving monster. His men bristled with confidence knowing Eden the Brutal fought at their side. Enemies fled. One sign of weakness, one break from the myth he had become would dispel the illusion. Eden killed with ice in his gray eyes. Unflinching. Unwavering. An instrument of death.

Eden's limbs grew heavy. His body slow. Slow got men killed. Slicing through another enemy, he turned toward their camp in the hills. With a sigh, he adjusted his grip on Tasa and began cutting a path back to camp. Tasa thrummed with every drop of blood, craving the kill. Soldiers fled when they beheld his merciless eyes. Tired, he would have let them go, if it weren't for the legend he needed to maintain. No signs of exhaustion, no weakness in front of the soldiers.

Men died at his feet.

Eden slipped away into the surrounding hills. From the valley, the imperial camp appeared small. A neat group of tents atop a hill. In reality, it spanned miles, tucked in the spaces between the hills like veins reaching towards the valley. Spread wide and hidden to prevent spies from determining their true number. The visible portion of the camp housed the general and other leaders. A center of command where orders issued forth in impersonal waves.

Eden marched past the other people in the camp, and they knew to leave him alone. Let the guardian sleep. He ducked into a small tent on the far side of the hill. Enough room for two. Him and Maddy. Now just him. Eden tossed Tasa on the floor like an old sock and crashed onto his cot. Before, when Maddy was there, sleep found him easier. He could rest in the knowledge Maddy was out fighting, giving the soldiers a hero to look to while he slept. Now, he alone carried the burden, the responsibility of inspiration. Every moment he spent off the battlefield, a moment without a legend to rally behind.

But at his core, he was just a man. And men needed rest.

Eyes heavy, unconsciousness danced at the edges of his mind. Teasing him as he lay there, exhausted. He only needed a few hours of rest before returning to the frenzy. Was it too much to ask? His breath slowed. He thought it good to have Tasa out of his hand, to stop hearing the incessant begging. Good to step away, if only for a moment.

"Eden," called a voice out of place. His mind felt a sturdy tug towards alertness. The voice did not belong in a war camp far away from home. Perhaps he had already drifted to sleep. "Eden!" the voice repeated, more urgent this time.

The guardian opened his eyes, but found himself alone.

"Eden, can you hear me?" The voice was unmistakable. Dimitri.

"Yes," he groaned, then buried his face in the blankets, "how?"

"I had Maddy cast a spell," his voice replied from nowhere.

"*Heikkem velki*," Eden swore, hoping the wizard could hear the profanity directed his way. "Say what you need to say." He wanted to add, *Then get out of my head*, but held his tongue. High Emperors deserved some form of respect, even from him.

"I'm reassigning you," he continued, and Eden thought he detected a waver in his master's voice.

Having already lost one guardian in Bane, Eden didn't like the idea of leaving. Especially then, with Bane at a tipping point. Victory would be decided soon, Eden wanted to ensure it was theirs. But Dimitri wouldn't speak to him directly if it wasn't important. It was easier to have Maddy pass messages along with his own, inherent magic than cast telepathy spells. "What's the job?" he asked, frowning into the blankets.

After a deep, hesitant breath, Dimitri said, "Rolina ran away."

"She what?" Eden sat upright.

"Her family was taken hostage during a raid on Gaj," Dimitri explained.

Careful to keep his voice calm over his pounding heart, Eden asked, "Do the rebels know who they are?"

"Doubtful."

Some small good news, at least. "She went after them? Alone?" Another question hid beneath the words. *Why?*

Dimitri must have caught the question, because he explained, "I told her I couldn't waste any resources to rescue them. And no, she's not alone. Princess Twila went with her."

"She ran away so you would have to send someone to Gaj," Eden reasoned aloud, a smile tugging at the corners of his mouth despite the dire news. It wasn't just anyone who could manipulate Dimitri like that. And as he was stationed the closest to Gaj, it would be easy for Eden to catch her there and return her home. Though he didn't care for Twila, he knew the potential complications if the enemy princess was harmed. And at least Rolina wasn't alone.

Though he feared for her safety, a small thrill pulsed through his veins. In his battle-distorted view of time, he wasn't sure how long it had been since he last laid eyes on the girl. Months at the least. He didn't often let himself think of home while away at war, but when he did, he thought of Rolina and the way her skin felt against his fingertips. "When did she leave?"

"Three nights ago."

Gaj was a mere two day's ride from Bane, but a full two weeks from the forest. He couldn't justify leaving Bane now, only to wait around. Wasting time. Nor could he go after her on the road. There were several paths to Gaj from the forest. If he chose the wrong one, he would miss her. "My lord, do I have your permission to stay here and see the battle through first? We're close to winning. A week at most."

Silence. Eden waited, and for a moment he thought the spell snapped, ending the conversation prematurely. Until Dimitri's voice answered, "Permission granted. Unless the battle lasts longer than expected."

"Yes, Sir," Eden replied, lying back down on the cot.

Dimitri said no more, and Eden assumed the connection broken.

A week of fighting, maybe a little more, and he would see Rolina again. As long as she made it to Gaj safe. Laying there, dreaming of her face when they saw each other again, he never doubted she would. She was strong, stronger than even she knew. Nothing would stop her from reaching her parents. Nothing ever stopped Rolina when she had a cause worth fighting for. Though a little assurance couldn't hurt.

Eden rolled onto his back, watching the cloth ceiling quiver in the breeze as he prayed quietly, "Chyddan, curse those who would harm her. Wreck those who stand in her way. Place your wicked protection upon her. Guide her safe to Gaj." He ended the prayer by making a hell-sign with his fingers. He shut his eyes and nestled into the blankets, satisfied that the prayer would be enough. Though he had to stay and see the battle through, his thoughts were with Rolina as unconsciousness took him.

"Did he say anything about my father?" Twila asked, studying Rolina with anticipation. The countryside had turned from hilly meadows to thick with trees that lined either side of the road.

Rolina shook her head, "Only that he wanted me home safe. You too," she added, though she didn't think Dimitri cared about Twila beyond the political complications if anything happened to her.

Twila shook her head in disbelief, "I thought hearing Father's voice in my head was strange, I can't imagine him appearing to me in my dreams."

"It wasn't that strange," Rolina told Twila. She was used to vivid dreams. Part of her wondered if she really had seen Dimitri, or if her mind made it up

"He's sending someone after us?" Twila asked, shifting nervously in her saddle.

Rolina nodded. She left out the part when he promised to send someone even if she returned. How could she explain to Twila that she didn't quite believe it without painting Dimitri in a bad light? It wasn't that she thought him heartless, but she knew he had priorities. Her family wasn't one of them.

"Did he say who? Is it one of the guardians?" Twila asked, urgency in her voice. She knew as well as Rolina their lead would only get shorter if he sent a guardian. Fast. Efficient. And likely with orders to take them home, not to help her family.

"He didn't say," Rolina admitted, the uncertainty itching under her skin.

"And is my father-"

"He didn't say anything about your father," Rolina snapped, her frustration pushing the words out of her before she could think. Twila didn't deserve her anger. Rolina softened her voice, "If you're really that worried about him," she hesitated, afraid to say her next words, "I'll understand if you want to turn back."

Twila blinked, surprised. "I've come this far, haven't I?"

Relief flooded Rolina. She didn't know what she would do without her. She opened her mouth to tell her how much she appreciated her when a cry broke through the air.

Rolina liked trees. The ones lining the side of the road were younger and smaller than those in The Eternal Forest, but they made her feel safe. A taste of home. Walls to protect her. But the cry that sounded from within gave her a new perspective. What monsters hid inside the trees? Wolves and bears and men. A thousand enemies assaulted her mind. Her hand dropped to her dagger. Heart thundering. Eyes darting. Searching the trees. Hunting.

Beside her, Twila straightened, her attention snapping toward the sound.

"Help!" The cry made Rolina's heart jump. It was closer now. A figure stumbled from the trees. A woman. Her hand pressed against her gut. Red streams oozed between her fingers, staining her clothes. Rolina squirmed. Blood and guts were Eli's job. The woman looked up. "Help!" she repeated, her voice turning weak. She collapsed. From the ground, she stretched her hand towards them. Red smeared on her palm.

"It could be a trap," Twila warned.

Rolina was already climbing off her horse. Trap or not, she couldn't leave the woman to die. "You'll only lose more blood moving around like that," she said, panic wavering in her voice. Twila dismounted and joined Rolina, bracing the woman. Rolina caught sight of a long gash along the woman's leg. Pumping blood onto the dirt like a leaky bucket. Rolina swallowed hard. The last thing she needed was to vomit. Save now, be sick later.

"There's no time," the woman gasped, reaching her shaking hand towards Rolina. "Bandits... Coming this way."

Rolina's heart leapt to her throat. Her eyes shot to Twila. The princess held her chin steady, even as her eyes betrayed her panic. Rolina jumped to her feet and ran to Tovi's saddlebag. She used her dagger to tear away a piece of her blanket, then rushed back to bandage the woman's wounds. Even without the knowledge, experience, or stomach Eli had, she knew pressure would help.

"Let's get her on the horse," Twila ordered. The pair lifted the woman to her feet.

Voices. The bandits, searching for the woman. Trees obscuring them from view. Preventing any assessment of their number or when they would break from the trees.

"Hurry!" the woman gasped as they approached Twila's horse. "They'll take you too!"

The bandits rushed from the trees as they hoisted her up. Rolina swore, darting towards Tovi. Three bandits had horses of their own. They could easily chase her down if she fled. She pulled her sword from where it lay hidden in Tovi's saddlebag. Beside her, Twila braced herself, standing before the woman on the horse protectively.

They closed in, surrounding them in a dense circle. "Would you look at that," one of the men on horseback taunted. "Two more perfectly good marks."

Marks. This was beginning to make a twisted kind of sense to Rolina. She'd heard of bandits snatching people up. Of underground slave markets that Dimitri and Mercury usually had the time and manpower to weed out. But with war turning their gaze elsewhere, these criminals could run rampant. Could snatch up anyone who looked strong enough for labor, but not strong enough to fight back.

Only fight if absolutely necessary. Mercury's warning, told to her a dozen times. "We don't want any trouble," she said, lowering her sword. Now was not the time to act rash. A real fight was different than training with Iero or the soldiers. It was unfair and dangerous and terrifying. It was men throwing her around like a sack of grain and pinning her to countertops.

"Neither do we," the man said with a malicious sort of friendliness. "So why don't you come quietly, and you won't end up like our friend here," he nodded towards the wounded woman.

Like the men Rolina encountered in Zey, words would not work on these creatures. Rolina readied her sword and shot a glance Twila's way, needing to know she was beside her. The princess did not blink, standing tall like a warrior. Rolina wrapped her free hand around the bottle of Feinin fire, stowed on her belt after their previous encounter. It would be easy. Throw the bottle, flee in the ensuing panic.

Something invisible stayed her hand. Was this the right moment? With wood and grass and all sorts of things that could catch a little too easily. She didn't want to burn down the entire countryside. And what if she needed it later? She couldn't waste it and leave herself vulnerable to worse enemies.

The leader signaled his companions. They pressed in. Rolina moved first, releasing her grip on the bottle to charge toward the oncoming bandits. She drew her blade across a bandit's chest. Blood sliced into the air. Rolina forgot to move. Her eyes locked on the violent red.

A bandit swung his sword at her, breaking her from the trance. She jumped back, barely escaping the sharp point. *Fight or die.* She scrambled to block a second blow from the man, aware of several other bandits closing in. *Fight or die!* She cut her sword to his left. An obvious, easy to block move. But as he maneuvered to block the blade, she swung her leg around, slamming it into his exposed side. He stumbled back. More from surprise than pain. Rolina drew her blade across his sword arm, near the wrist. He dropped the blade. It was as close to taking him out of the fight as Rolina could. Unwilling - unable - to kill the man.

She turned her attention to a pair of bandits on her left. Two at once. Could she fight two men at once? Not if she fought fair. Rolina crouched low and scooped up a fistful of dirt. As she rose, she lunged forward. Ducking beneath a dagger to get close. She slammed the fistful of dirt into his eyes and lifted her knee to connect with his groin. No time to watch him double over. The second bandit stabbed a dagger towards her. She blocked it. Easier than she expected.

But he did not fight fair either. A second dagger in his other hand, he lashed out. Rolina reacted too slow. It sliced a thin line into her side. Pain stung at her skin. But pain was for later. Gritting her teeth, she twisted her sword around and cut him across the chest. Not too deep. Not enough to kill.

Weren't there more bandits coming after her? She dared a look past her enemy. At Twila. But she wasn't Twila anymore. A beast stood in her place. Huge. Wild. Vicious. Some kind of mythical feline thing Rolina couldn't name. Fangs flashed as she bit towards the nearest bandit, bigger than any Rolina had ever seen, even on any of Kail's magical beasts. The man screamed like a child and ran. He wasn't alone as Twila stepped a great, clawed paw forward and released a roar that shook the trees. Her glamour had half the bandits scurrying back the way they came. But what happened when one of them dared touch her? When their swords swept through the illusion?

Taking advantage of her distraction, Rolina's opponent charged in, daggers flashing. Rolina yelped, jumping back in a last minute effort to dodge. His dagger dug into her arm. She screamed.

Calm down.

North and the guardians taught her better than this. Her scream turned into a cry of anger. She dove in, sword flying. He caught the blade with one of his daggers and brought the other around toward her exposed side. With one hand, she caught his wrist. Twisted it back. Brought it up to her mouth and bit. The man cried out, dropping the dagger. "Two weapons is cheating," she hissed. Releasing him, she slammed her free hand into his face, digging her nails in. A waste of the perfectly good manicure she'd gotten for Tavek. He stumbled backward. She turned her sword, cutting a deep gash along his arm. He dropped the second dagger.

Releasing his face, she readied herself for another attack. From him or the next bandit. It never came. He bolted away from her, shouting profanities. The beast was breathing fire. The bandits ran for the trees.

The fight was over.

She looked to Twila, the glamour already dispelled as she returned to the horses, panting. "We should keep moving... there could be more."

Rolina's eyes darted past her. To the woman on the horse. "She needs a healer," Rolina agreed. They had to move. Had to get this woman help. As Rolina mounted Tovi, she wished her brother was with her. His touch would save the woman. Rolina couldn't help, couldn't see past all the blood to the problem beneath. And Twila was not a healer. No, as Rolina turned her eyes back to her friend, she realized she was barely holding it together.

Out of breath. Out of energy. Sweat dripped from her body. Pulling herself onto the horse beside the woman took her last drop of energy. A glamour that big was too much for a half-blood. She was sapped. Drained. Leaving nothing to protect them but Rolina herself.

Rolina tightened her grip on her sword and took up Tovi's reins with her free hand. Twila had yet to fail her, now it was her turn. If a threat appeared, she would be ready. A bit of blood wouldn't stop her again. She would not fail again.

They rode late into the night. Rolina insisted from time to time they could make it to the next town. They could find her a doctor. The woman fell in and out of delirious sleep. With the moon high above them, Twila finally spoke up. "We need to rest. The endless riding will only make her worse."

Heart aching, Rolina knew she was right. They stopped and made camp. Rolina gave the woman a blanket. Twila cleaned her wounds. Bandaging them with scraps of another blanket. Rolina held the bottle of Feinin fire up to give Twila a light to work under.

They attempted to settle into camp, all the while watching over the woman. Her breath labored and broken. Sweat on her sickly skin. Rolina did not know for sure, but she guessed the feverish symptoms meant one or both of the wounds were infected. She needed help, but they could only sit and watch until morning.

"Why would they do that to her?" Rolina asked, her voice low, strained.

"Because she tried to escape. Because cruelty is fun if there are no consequences," Twila answered, lying a few feet away. Too relaxed. Too calm. The anger roiling just beneath the surface. Invisible save for the tension in her clenched jaw.

"Even though it hurts other people?" She could never desire to harm a living being. Could never understand those who did.

"*Especially* because it hurts other people," she said, rage leaking through her deliberate calm. "If you don't look at them beyond profit and personal gain, if no one stands in your way, why not hurt them?"

The woman gasped in her sleep. Rolina darted to her side, watching her ragged breath. "Something's wrong."

"She is injured, of course something is wrong," Twila snapped, sitting up.

"We need to help her. What if she... what if..."

"She was always going to die, Evensong," Twila said, the anger giving way to sorrow. She moved to join Rolina beside the woman. Tearful eyes watching her in pain.

"We have to try-"

"We did all we can. There are no doctors or healers out here," she said, her voice gentle, on the verge of breaking. She placed a hand on Rolina's back.

Rolina was too occupied by the woman to notice the comforting touch. Her mind raced for a way to save her. Some small hint from time spent with Eli and Haven. Her vision filled by the ghastly wounds, Rolina did not realize at first. The woman had stopped breathing. "Is she-" her breath caught on the lump in her throat. "Is she-"

"Yes," Twila said quietly, pulling Rolina into her shoulder.

They clung to each other. Twila held her for a long while. Until she cried herself out. Longer. Until she fell asleep. Then Twila lowered her to the ground, laid a blanket over her, and went to deal with the body.

19

A Visit to the Library

Blood streamed from Eden's face. His head slumped downward. Kneeling in the mud. Rain poured from the heavens, soaking his dark hair. Mixing with blood as it streaked down his body. He wore only a pair of wool trousers, his other clothes and shoes removed. Cuts and bruises decorated his muscled form, his back a twisted pattern of criss-crossing lash marks. Eden shivered. A body built for hellfire exposed to the chill of night.

From behind, a man in a dark hood grabbed him by the hair, jerking his head upward. Surrounding them in a dense circle, other men laughed and heckled. Rolina watched in silence from the edge of the circle, willing her feet toward him, begging them to run to the guardian's aid, but her body would not move. Her hand stretched outward, trying, pleading, to reach him.

A second man stepped out from the jeering crowd to stand before Eden, a casual arrogance in his gait. Rolina caught a hint of a cruel smile from beneath his low hood as he sneered, "Is this the great Eden the Brutal? Most feared of all the Imperial Guardians?"

Laughter peeled through the crowd.

She knew the smile, even as it twisted knots in her stomach. The Duke of Kandston. "Look at you," he paced in front of Eden, working the crowd as he mocked, "beaten, bloody, down on your knees where you belong."

A wicked grin twisted across Eden's beaten face, a feral glint in his gray eyes. The ache in Rolina's chest expanded, burned, until Eden spoke, "*Silkautan ku tei, ora-lim.*" Rolina smiled. Though she knew little of the language overall, Eden wasted a great deal of time teaching her Eldurian curses and profanities since his return. More than enough to understand the guardian's malicious words. *Still prettier than you, dog-face.*

The insult lost on the crowd, the duke continued, "You think you're some kind of hero, boy? Some legend we should bow down to. You are *nothing.*" He smiled then, twisted and dark beneath his hood, "Just a dog to be whipped." He nodded to the man behind Eden, holding his head by the hair. In response to the silent order, the man shoved Eden's head down and raised his hand. Terror shot through Rolina's aching chest as she realized his hand wasn't empty. A whip. Heart screaming, she averted her eyes. Nothing saved her from the sound. The horrible snap. Eden's cry.

"Again," the duke ordered.

"No!" Rolina screamed, reaching for Eden.

The whip descended. Rolina did not look away in time. The grimace on his face as the whip cut another line across his back crushed her. "Eden!" If her legs would only move - why wouldn't they move?

Eden lifted his eyes as the whip came down again, unbreakable gaze locked on Duke Cadogan. He did not flinch as the whip rended his flesh. "*Kuole ne tei!*" Rolina did not recognize the words this time, but by the tone of his voice, the calm fury as another lash sliced, it was not pleasant. As blood poured from fresh wounds, mingling with the rain, he spat, the saliva splattering on the duke's boot. Eden smiled.

Cadogan looked down at the spit, scowling. He let out a low growl, then slammed his boot into Eden's face. Coughing blood, Eden didn't have a chance to recover before the duke ordered, "Again."

"No!" Rolina screamed, helpless.

Hands from behind gripped her by the waist, pulling her backwards, away from the scene. “Eden!” she shrieked, struggling to free herself, reaching for the guardian as he fell into the mud.

The whip came down hard. Rolina flinched, shutting her eyes. Trying to pry the hands from her body. If she could only move, break free, she could stand between Eden and the whip. Or cause a commotion, distract them long enough for Eden to escape. But she couldn’t. She could only struggle and witness as the hands pulled her away.

“Rolina!” a voice behind her called. “Stop struggling, it’s only me.”

Tearing her eyes from the crowd, she dared a look at the man dragging her away. “Maddy?” Confused, she turned back to Eden and his captors. Gone. In their place a wall of books, lined up in neat rows.

The wizard released her, “Is that really what you dream about? No wonder you always wake up screaming.”

“Dream?” Relief flooded her heart, easing her aching chest. Of course it was a dream, Eden couldn’t be taken so easily. Rolina turned around to face him, surprised to find she was in a large library. “Where...”

“I took you out of your dream and into mine,” Maddy said, surveying the peaceful library with pride in his eyes, “I made this place.”

“It’s really you? Like the dream with Dimitri last night?” she asked, still a bit shaken.

“It is,” he answered with a wide smile, opening his arms to her.

She dove into the embrace. Few things felt more like home than a hug from The Mad Wizard. And she needed a bit of home. The moment his arms were around her, she crumbled. A sob broke from deep in her chest. Weak legs buckled.

Maddy’s grip tightened, “Something’s wrong. In the real world.”

She nodded into his chest as he scooped up her legs and carried her to a couch a few rows of books away.

“Are you safe? Did something happen?” He moved to lay her on the soft cushions, but she only clung to him tighter. Instead, he sat down with her still in his arms. She curled her legs closer to her body and collapsed into heaving sobs. Small and helpless like the child they all saw her as. The wizard ran a hand through her hair, the gesture a blend of fidgety and comforting. “Are you safe?” he repeated.

Rolina nodded again.

His grip on her relaxed slightly. "And Twila?"

Another nod.

"Tell me... when you're ready."

Rolina fractured in the security of Maddy's arms. A teacher. A friend. Someone who would never hurt her. Never let anyone touch her. "There was a woman," she said, her voice so soft Maddy pulled her closer against him to hear. "And there were bandits. We tried to help her."

Against her, she felt the wizard tense, "They didn't touch you, did they?"

She shook her head, "Didn't let them. But the woman. She..." *Died.* Rolina couldn't bring herself to say the word aloud.

"You tried to help her?"

"She was running from them. We got her away, but she was already hurt," Rolina whimpered. "Her wounds were... too much."

"She died free. And she didn't die alone," Maddy said, then couldn't stand the dark topic any longer. "I'm glad Twila's with you. She's very good at glamours for a half-blood."

"Wish we had a wizard," Rolina said, rubbing her eyes on her sleeve. "Wizards can do more than illusions."

Maddy shook his head, "You know how I feel about wizards. They're dangerous. Wrong."

"You *are* a wizard," Rolina reminded him, her eyes lingered on his face. Something was off, but she couldn't figure out what.

"Not just any wizard, a natural, earth born wizard. Not one of those selfish abominations running about nowadays. When *I* was young, people respected that some people are born with magic, and the rest just have to deal with it. Now they take magic for themselves. It's not natural, and I for one-" Rolina realized she needed to stop him before it became a full rant. But it had done the trick of distracting her. She found herself smiling.

"You're right, Twila's better," she pulled away from him and swung her legs around to sit beside him instead of curled in his lap like a little girl.

"She's a tough one," Maddy agreed. His brown hair fell in front of his young, unblemished face.

"Your scar," she murmured before she could stop herself. It was a sensitive topic after all, and Maddy hated those. But she had already begun, so she may as well finish the thought, "What happened to it?"

"My scar? Oh," he touched his left cheek tenderly. "You manifest as your own self-concept in dreams," he explained, and as he ran his fingers down his face, the scar reappeared. "I forgot about the scar, so it was gone."

She blinked at him, afraid to look at the scar. Too gruesome. "Sorry for reminding you."

Maddy shrugged, "You're about two inches shorter in real life. I wasn't going to mention it, but..."

Her brows knit together. "I'm always this tall."

The wizard laughed, full and delighted. Rolina didn't find it as amusing. "Back to the matter at hand," he said upon seeing her scowl, "I just wanted to check in on you. I can leave you alone to sleep now, dream and nightmare free. Unless, perhaps, I can help?"

"You already have," Rolina told him with a melancholy smile.

"No, I meant *really* help," he said, waving one hand in the air dismissively.

Rolina perked up, "How?"

Maddy shrugged, "I'm not physically there, so I can't cast any spells for you, but I can answer questions. Give advice. You tell me."

Her first thought was to ask about the flowers, but that was a waste of an opportunity. "Can you tell me how to make a proper camp?"

"That's an easy one."

Before he could begin, another thought crashed into her mind, "Did Dimitri send someone after me?"

"Yes," a smile danced at the corner of his mouth.

"Who?" she asked, expecting the obvious. Iero and Kail were the only guardians available, and a little, selfish part of her knew Dimitri would send a guardian.

A playful glint in his eyes, Maddy answered, "Eden."

Rolina's heart leapt. "I thought he was still in Bane." She looked at a nearby bookshelf, pretending it made no difference to her. But it did. It made all the difference in her little world.

"The battle is almost over. He's going to meet you in Gaj and help you sort things out," the wizard told her, grinning.

"Why are you smiling?" she asked, forcing a frown on her lips, fighting the excitement building in her chest.

"Iero said you stole Eden's jacket," Maddy teased.

Blood rushed to her cheeks and she tried to turn away before Maddy noticed. "I needed something plain to pass by unnoticed," she excused, but the jovial expression on the wizard's face told her he didn't believe it.

"Sure," he nodded, a wicked sparkle in his eye.

"It's nothing," she added, more forceful than she intended.

"Well," he let the word hang in the air a little too long. His own personal torment for her. Then released her by changing the subject, "I'm awfully bored around here, so I've decided to check in on you every night. If you need help with anything else, just ask."

She nodded, though she hardly heard him. Eden was coming. *Eden.* Her heart beat faster at the thought. She imagined looking up to see him riding in from the distance. Running to meet him. His arms around her after months apart.

Maddy's gentle laugh broke her from her thoughts. "I was going to tell you all about making camp, but perhaps I should leave you to your dreams."

Embarrassed, Rolina opened her mouth to tell him to stay, but with a snap of his fingers, the wizard was gone.

20

The Trouble With Feinin

Cold gripped Rolina. She clung to the blanket, shuddering as her eyes opened. The sun on her face provided no warmth that day. The chill came from deeper. Her eyes drifted to the sound of Twila moving nearby, preparing the horses for the journey. The princess had already packed up their humble camp aside from the blanket wrapped around Rolina's shoulders. Her dreams had been an escape that night, her wizard rescuing her from the dark of the world. Now she remembered. Rolina scanned the camp, bracing herself for a sight that never came. The dead woman was gone.

"Where is she?" Rolina stared at the empty space where the woman had been. Her blanket was gone as well. She hoped Twila buried her with it. She didn't want it back.

"I took care of it," Twila answered gently, stroking Tovi's side idly. Watching Rolina. Wary. A fragile thing on the edge of a shelf. One shake, one tremor, and she would fall and shatter. When Rolina said nothing else, Twila added, "We still have a long way to travel." A cautious push. They needed to move on before it broke them. Broke Rolina. Before new dangers crept from the trees. Before life caught up to them.

"We didn't ask her name," Rolina ignored the hint, unable to tear her eyes from that terrible empty place. "Or if she had a family. What if she does? What if they're waiting for her to come home?"

"Evensong," she left the horses to join her, crouching down to her level, "there was nothing more we could do." The princess brushed her thumb along Rolina's chin, lifting her eyes away from the empty place. She let the touch soothe her. Made herself forget the cold images of the dying woman. There was only warmth, love, in her friend's touch. "Come. No point standing still." She took Rolina's hands in hers and lifted her to her feet.

The scenery passed her by as they rode. Her mind too numb to take in the trees and sky. No reason to wonder what the flowers were called, they were all the same. Markers for the woman's grave.

She needed to shake it. To wake up. Twila made some attempts to talk with her, but she barely heard over the sounds of her own memory. The fight with the bandits replayed in her head. If they had been faster, smarter - no. The woman was wounded before they arrived. There was nothing she could change to save her. Still she wondered. Imagined herself saving the woman, racing to a doctor, or finding a traveling healer along the road. Her vivid imagination turned against her, reminded her she was not a hero. She couldn't save even one person.

Perhaps the woman's death, tragic as it was, was not the reason she couldn't snap out of it. Perhaps she was afraid of her own failure to do what was necessary. The shallow wounds in her arm and side were proof enough. Without Twila, she would have died for her mercy. For her unwillingness to strike the bandits down, despite the cruelty they inflicted.

Her hand went to the collar of her jacket. Eden's jacket. Her fingers traced the familiar leather. So much colder without the Eldurian warrior's heat. Rolina missed him from the moment he left the forest, but this was the first time his absence burned. He told her a hundred stories of war and death, but she never saw it as cruel. He fought to defend, not to harm. A stalwart hero, putting innocents at his back and evil in his path. A wall between the wicked and the good. So different from the grinning bandits, heartless and greedy, delighting in the woman's pain.

A new town rose before them. Smaller than either Zey or Un. The town she saw on her map the night before. The one she begged Twila to keep riding towards. To find a doctor. To save the woman. A cold reminder of her own uselessness. Twila was right. It was too far to reach that night. Already, the sun was setting.

The woman was always going to die.

"We'll stop here," Twila said, taking charge as Rolina withdrew into herself. She followed the princess blindly. Twila guided her to an inn on the opposite side of town. Close to the gate they would exit through the next day. It was cleaner than Zey. Safer too, Rolina hoped. They paid for a room with two beds.

"We couldn't have saved her," Twila said again, sitting beside Rolina on one of the beds.

Rolina counted the walls. Four, like there should be. Four walls sealing her from bandits and death. Safe. Or as close as she could get on the road. Twila had taken a chair and wedged it under the door handle as an extra precaution. Something Rolina should have thought of - would have thought of - if she wasn't so distracted. "Maddy said it was good she didn't die alone."

"Maddy?" Twila raised an eyebrow.

"I forgot to tell you," she looked up at her friend. The princess' eyes were full of concern. A look that drew Rolina back towards reality. She was not alone, and her friend, her brave, wonderful friend, didn't need anything else to worry over. "He came to see me in my dreams last night."

Twila shook her head, some of the dark in her eyes lightening, "First the High Emperor, now The Mad Wizard. Your mind is a busy place."

Rolina half-smiled, though the expression was heavier than she expected. "I suppose so." She was so used to vivid dreams, she almost forgot it was strange. They fell silent as Rolina rested her head on Twila's shoulder. The princess leaned into the touch and took Rolina's hand. So much stronger than Rolina. Smart and quick. Not only standing after the fight, but carrying Rolina along with her. "Why doesn't it affect you like me?" Rolina asked. Knowing might help her be strong like her friend.

"It used to," Twila said quietly, her hand tensing in Rolina's.

"You've seen death before?" Rolina lifted her head to look at Twila. A new weight pressed on the princess. A memory. Why hadn't she told her?

"I was in the room when Mother died," she confessed, staring at the empty space in front of her.

Rolina squeezed Twila's hand. Alive. Alive again now that her friend needed her. Needed her to listen. All these years and Twila hadn't said a word. Then again, she always avoided talking about her mother after she passed away. Even when it was fresh. Especially when it was fresh. "I'm sorry."

"Don't be," Twila said, a sad smile on her lips. "It was a privilege."

Rolina studied her face, but didn't speak, sensing Twila had more to say.

"Mother only had power through Father. He was the natural born king, and she was a foreigner and a Feinin, but she did so much for our country. She advised Father on *every* decision, and she was someone the people could look to. A symbol. The face of the monarchy when Father was buried under the weight of running a kingdom."

"I remember her," Rolina said quietly. The Feinin queen was hard to forget. Sharp, yet kind features and a grace that poured from her soul into the world around her. A grace Rolina sometimes caught in Twila's stride. She fell ill when Rolina was nine. Died a year later. She never saw the queen's suffering, save for its reflection in Twila's face when she came to visit.

"When she died, it nearly killed Father. I don't know if you remember, but-"

"You didn't come visit the forest for over a year," Rolina said, finishing her friend's thought. At the time, she wondered if she would ever see the princess again. She and Ramar were the only friends Rolina had near her age, and the thought of losing one broke her heart. A selfish desire, she always knew. Twila's family needed her more than Rolina did. Still, it filled her with relief and joy when the princess at last returned to the forest.

She nodded, "He didn't know what to do with us. He was too busy grieving to be a father. Or a king. There's this woman back home, a maid from Taivas who used to be our nurse. She's the one who made him realize he couldn't do it all alone. She helped him raise us after that. And I... I took Mother's place." It wasn't until Twila rubbed her sleeve against her cheek that Rolina realized she was crying. Her voice never wavered. "I became the face of our kingdom, the one who walked among the people. That's where I *really* saw death, Evensong."

Rolina released Twila's hand to wrap her arm around the princess.

"Bringing food to the poor and raising funds for sickhouses. People I couldn't help, happy to see me all the same. Happy to lay their eyes on a princess before breathing their last breath," her voice wavered. "So yes, I've seen death before. Again and again. And I think... I think it's why father and I see things differently. He sees what's written on pages and told to him in meetings. I see what's in the world. I see when our people prosper, and I see when they die. But I can't do anything. Can't change his mind." Her breath caught in her throat before she choked out, "He would have listened to Mother."

"I'm sorry," Rolina breathed. Her own problems shrank in light of Twila's circumstances. She was so young, yet she had the weight of a kingdom on her shoulders.

"No," Twila wiped her tears away and straightened, "It's not his fault. There are other factors... I'm sorry, I can't talk about that."

Rolina didn't want to risk Twila closing up, but she needed to know what the princess was keeping from her. What reasons Farran had for siding with the rebellion. Especially if it could help the empire. Help Mercury and Dimitri end the bloodshed. She kept her voice gentle as she said, "When you were out of the room, that Feinin boy said something that didn't make sense to me."

"He was half-mad, I'm sure he said plenty that made no sense," Twila said, the humor in her voice too stiff.

"He said people think your father hates the Feinin," Rolina watched her friend's reaction carefully.

There was no shock on her face. Only anger. "*That* is a lie."

"I know," Rolina agreed, Farran could never hate his wife's people, "But rumors start for a reason. Where do you think this one comes from?"

"Me," her voice cracked and she pulled her knees closer to her chest.

Rolina's eyes widened, but she reined in her shock, afraid the princess would mistake it for judgment. She hadn't heard the full story yet, she couldn't jump to conclusions.

"My parents did so much for the Feinin people. They were cut off from the world, but Mother organized trade lines and negotiations and treated them like they were an extension of our kingdom," Twila paused to wipe a tear on her sleeve. "And Father gave her whatever she needed to do it. When she died, it all ended."

"What does that have to do with you?" Rolina asked, pulling her friend even closer.

"I told you. After she died, I became the face of our kingdom. The voice of our people. I took over everything she used to do," Twila looked away, shame flickering in her eyes, "Everything but maintaining that relationship with the Feinin. I didn't even try. I just cut them off. And Father didn't push it. He knew I was doing so much already, and he was busy with twice as much. I abandoned them, and people blamed Father. They started saying he couldn't stand the Feinin because they reminded him of Mother. It's not true. It was *my* fault."

Rolina shook her head, Twila put too much responsibility on herself, "Negotiations take more than one side. The Feinin could have sent someone to continue working with Illandia. It sounds to me like your mother put all the work in, and they couldn't be bothered to lift a finger."

Twila lifted her face, confused, "You don't know, do you?"

"Don't know what?" Rolina furrowed her brow.

"Feinin can't leave Kauneus. That's why mother wanted to help them. She wanted to bring the world to them, since they couldn't go to it," Twila explained, a hint of the sorrow draining from her voice.

How did you get out of Kauneus? Twila had asked the Feinin boy the moment she laid eyes on him. Rolina forgot the peculiar question in her urgency to help him. Now she wondered just as much as Twila had. "Then how did we meet that Feinin boy in Un? How did your mother leave to live in Illandia?"

"I suppose I have to start at the beginning," Twila said, half a smile on her face. A vast improvement from the tears. "I thought that wizard of yours taught you everything."

"He did. I just didn't listen," Rolina admitted with a grin.

Twila's smile grew, almost reaching her eyes before she asked, "You at least know the Fae didn't originally come from here?"

Rolina nodded. That particular lecture was more of a story than a lesson, so it stuck in her mind. The Fae were banished from their home continent and came to find a new place on Syytala. Pixies, Feinin, elves, and all number of faeries arrived to take whatever land they could, shaping it with their magic until it fit their needs. It was the reason Syytala had such varied climates and landscapes. Why lush farmland could rest between a desert and a kingdom of ice. Why the trees of The Eternal Forest grew so tall and their leaves glimmered in the sunlight.

They didn't care how it affected others. What did it matter if they pushed a few fragile humans from their homes, if it meant they could live as they pleased? Even when the magic began infecting humans, physically changing them, they didn't care. Eventually, the humans learned how to fight back. How to use their new, magical gifts against the Fae. People were hurt - killed - on both sides.

"When the Fae realized they needed to put aside their pride and find a way to live peacefully with humans, the Feinin refused. Even when all other Fae gave in, they held onto their hatred of the humans. They even started separating themselves from other Fae, claiming they were better.

"A few thousand years ago - I don't know exactly when - there was this Feinin queen. I've forgotten her name, sorry. She tried to finally break through their pride and get them to live in peace, but they refused. So she cursed them."

Rolina raised her eyebrows, "She cursed her own people?"

Twila nodded, "She told them if they refused to live with the humans, then she would keep them apart. Permanently. They can't leave Kauneus until the curse is broken."

"How can they break it?" Rolina asked, a familiar thrill building in her veins. It was so like one of her faerie tales - complete with Faeries. But this one was real and present.

"Mother made me memorize it, hold on," Twila paused to think, then her eyes lit up as she quoted, "'When Human and Feinin entwine their fate, a vow made in love will break your hate.' There's more... I don't remember it right now."

"A vow made in love?"

"Very Fae," Twila said with a grin. "Basically, one day a human and a Feinin are going to fall in love, and the moment they say their wedding vows, the curse is broken."

Rolina couldn't help but smile, "Romantic. Not that I'm happy they're cursed or anything." Her smile faded at her next thought, "Why wasn't the curse broken when your parents were married?" Embarrassment flooded her cheeks. She should have kept the question to herself. Her friend was in tears a moment ago and now she was poking a stick into the wound.

Now it was time for Twila's grin to falter, "Because they weren't in love."

Rolina's eyes went wide. It was too late to take the question back, so she kept going, "But everything you've told me about them..." In her own sparse memories of the couple, they were doting and affectionate. Unashamed of the many eyes that turned their way whenever they entered a room, jealous of them, of their bond. The power in it.

"It... took some time for me to understand," Twila said carefully, afraid she might reopen the wound herself. But she looked Rolina in the eye, placing her trust in the girl who had shared so many of her own secrets, "They loved each other, but not at first. And it was only ever a love like friendship." A hint of a smile played on her lips as she added, "A love like you and me."

"I don't know about that," Rolina shook her head, but she was smiling, "Friends don't usually have three children together."

"Not *exactly* like you and me," Twila chuckled.

"How was she able to leave Kauneus?" Rolina asked, realizing the weight had finally left her and Twila. It could return any moment, she knew, but that only made her want to drink in Twila's smile all the more.

"She married him. They weren't in love, so it didn't break the curse, but it was enough to earn her own freedom," Twila explained, happy to talk about her parents' history. Her own history.

"Is that why she did it?" Rolina asked, then bit her lip. She was asking insensitive question after insensitive question. She wished someone else was there to shut her up. Like Ramar. He'd slap his hand over her mouth and she'd probably bite him, and the whole thing would devolve into a wrestling match which he would win. But by then they would've forgotten what started it, and she wouldn't be so embarrassed.

Twila didn't seem to mind the question. "No, well, not entirely. She did it because she liked Father, and Father wanted a powerful queen. Because she could do more good as a queen than some common Feinin. Because it was an opportunity."

"She sounds like a brave woman," Rolina said. She had been walled within a forest of her own for eleven years, and she had been terrified to leave it, even for the few weeks it would take to save her parents. Queen Aine left for good. She must have been ten times as frightened.

"I think she would have liked us being friends, even after all this time."

Rolina smiled and rested her head on Twila's shoulder. "I like us being friends."

Maddy made good on his promise to teach Rolina how to make a proper camp. He pulled her through his carefully constructed dream world to several different landscapes, teaching her how to utilize the resources around her in an emergency. They started with the kinds of places she would find in Ev, meadows, glades, and rocky hills, with a promise he would show her more in the future.

Then they were back in his dream library where Rolina collapsed onto a couch that was more comfortable than a dream construct had a right to be. Maddy sat across from her, sipping tea. "Are you feeling better than last night?" he asked as though she had experienced something as ordinary as a cold. Something to overcome in a day.

Rolina didn't begrudge him for acting casual about it. Maddy had never been one to delve into painful topics. She was happy he asked her about it at all. "I am." Talking with Twila helped, as well as spending time with the wizard. It was a small thing, and yet learning how to make camp gave her a sense she was in control.

"An interesting thing happened today," Maddy went on, closing off the topic altogether. "A boy showed up a couple days ago, and today he had a meeting with Mercury. A Feinin boy."

Rolina stiffened. As happy as she was that the boy had the opportunity to share what was happening to his people, she was afraid they would be angry with her for sending him their way. Most requests for aid that weren't vital to the war went into her ever-growing *save for later* pile. But she couldn't look into that boy's eyes and tell him his problem wasn't important. People were dying, and she hoped it was enough of a problem that she wasn't in trouble.

Days and miles away, she still worried about what they thought.

"He had a letter from Lady Evensong Antares herself," Maddy waved a hand over his cup of tea and it refilled itself.

"Are they upset?" Rolina asked sheepishly.

"Upset?" Maddy raised an eyebrow. "Mercury was beaming and going on about how you 'always were the sweetest thing,' and how proud she was that you took time to help someone else when you have your own problems to worry about and all that sort of thing."

The tightness in Rolina's chest eased. Proud. The High Empress of Syytala was proud of her. *Mercury* was proud of her.

"And Dimitri, well, he doesn't *beam*, but I detected a distinct smirk."

"I got a smirk?" A smile broke across Rolina's lips. "A whole smirk?"

"A whole smirk," Maddy confirmed before pausing to sip his tea. "Couldn't hide it when he came by earlier."

"Came by? Did he need you to work some magic?" Rolina asked, a lightness in her chest she hadn't felt in months. It was strange hearing about the emperors and forest from so far away, but good. She was free but still connected. Things weren't broken between them.

"Just divvying up orders," Maddy answered, frowning despite his casual tone of voice. "Seems I'm going home for a while."

"Home?"

"Viska," Maddy's voice was dripping with venom. "The wizard's council has been a bit wishy-washy when it comes to picking a side. Sending in the most famous wizard in history ought to light a fire under them." Maddy wasn't bragging, and that bothered Rolina. Normally when he gave himself a compliment like that, it was accompanied by a boyish smile or mischievous spark in his eye. This was flat, factual.

"You don't want to go to Viska?" Maddy always had such dreadful things to say about wizards, but he loved his homeland. A center of knowledge and learning, a country founded on education and discovery. Maddy's favorite things.

"It's not the same place it used to be," Maddy said, reading the questions beneath the one she asked. "But that's a problem for another day," he waved the topic away, some of the cheer returning to his voice. "I'm not leaving until I can walk a little better."

"As much as I'm wishing for a fast recovery, I hope I get the chance to see you before you leave," Rolina gave him a warm smile.

Maddy took one, long sip of tea, "I'll be sure to hobble until you get home."

Until you get home. No *if*. No question. Rolina sat back in her seat, feeling as cozy as if she was in his real library digging around for faerie tales.

"Why are you looking at me like that?" Maddy asked her.

She wasn't aware she was staring. The corner of her mouth quirked up, "You don't have even the slightest doubt that I'll make it, do you?"

"Why should I?" Maddy asked her, propping his feet on a low table between them. "You're one of us."

21

Boys and Bridges

The trees were still dense around Rolina and Twila as they continued their journey. Rolina watched them carefully, fearful of another ambush. She listened for screams. Planned for injuries. The trees that once felt welcoming turned into a cage.

"It's beautiful today, don't you think?" Twila said, music in her voice.

"I suppose," Rolina hadn't really looked at her surroundings beyond the dangers that might lay hidden behind them.

Twila shook her head, "Where did you go, Evensong?"

Rolina's attention snapped to Twila, "What do you mean?"

"You're usually the one commenting on how beautiful things are and taking in the day," Twila pointed out. "Aren't you always saying we need to notice what's good, especially when everything else is bad?"

Rolina smiled, thankful yet again that Twila was by her side. Pulling her out of her own head. She looked at the trees once more. A dozen shades of green danced above her, golden light breaking through to rest on her shoulders. "It is beautiful," she agreed, a calm serenity settling over her. Things were far from perfect, but she was doing what she could to fix them. Why worry about the rest?

Twila opened her mouth to comment, but froze. Her eyes locked on something ahead of them.

Rolina followed her gaze. Their path led to a bridge. The only crossing for The Hunting River in days. She saw it on the map she stole from Maddy, knew it was coming. But what she did not expect were the rough-looking men gathered in the middle, blocking the path.

"Is that... normal?" she asked, already knowing the answer.

Twila shook her head, her expression deathly calm.

"Is there another crossing?" she asked. The map was old, perhaps something new had been built since it was created. She did not want another fight. No more confrontation. No more trying to escape.

"Not unless you want an extra week on the road," she answered, eyes darting from thug to thug. Assessing. They harassed a group of travelers from the opposite side of the river. Blocked their path. Rifled through their things. "This happens all the time lately, thugs taking advantage of the war. They've never come near me before, but I've never traveled without Father or his company." Her eyes shifted to Rolina, concern plain on her face.

Their night in Zey flashed through Rolina's memory. The thugs closing in on them, throwing them around like dolls. They couldn't fall into that trap again. There was no time to find another path, and even if they did, other crossings could be blocked as well. Rolina couldn't fight them alone, and the last glamour had taken so much out of Twila. Rolina couldn't rely on the princess using that much magic. But perhaps she could do something smaller, more sustainable. "Can you glamour us to look like men?" The thugs, occupied with the other group, had not seen them yet. And certainly, they may have only been concerned with robbing passersby, nothing more. But she didn't want to take the risk that they might be after other things. Not after Zey. At the very least, they might offer some twisted version of respect to a pair of men that they wouldn't give to the girls.

"I- I'm not sure," Twila admitted as Rolina rode off into the trees. The princess followed, "Creating that beast illusion wiped me out. I don't usually glamour anything bigger than myself."

"Can you glamour one of us?" Rolina suggested as she dismounted.

"I think so," Twila said, doubt lacing her voice. "But we need to get by them fast. The longer I hold the glamour, the harder it is."

Rolina nodded, "Glamour yourself at the last minute."

"What about you?" Twila asked, watching as Rolina pulled her dagger from her belt.

Rolina rummaged through her supplies for Eden's other shirt. "Keep watch."

Mercury told her not to fight unless she needed to, but she decided looking weak wasn't her style. Nor was she like Eden. Big and scary and willing to fight, to kill. She was somewhere in the middle. She could almost hear Dimitri's voice as she ripped Eden's shirt to pieces. *Use your brain.* She slipped behind a tree, out of Twila's view. *Use everything you have.*

She reappeared with the strips of Eden's shirt wrapped tight around her chest. Understanding dawned on Twila's face. A disguise. "Tie this for me," she ordered, her arm twisted at an awkward angle to pinch the ends of the fabric together. She pulled her hair out of the way with her free hand.

Twila dismounted and did as told, cinching Rolina's chest flat. Not that there was much to flatten.

She retrieved her shirt and dagger from behind the tree. Lifting the dagger to her hair.

Twila gasped, "No, don't-"

"I'm tired of thugs trying to take advantage of me for being a girl," she shot, then sliced off a chunk of her hair.

"It was so pretty." Twila, nearly as vain as Rolina, groaned mournfully as she chopped another piece. Lock after lock hacked away, Twila flinched with each cut. "Let me do it. You're going to cut off an ear or something," she took the dagger from her hand. Rolina let her, standing perfectly still as she continued her work.

"Make it short," she emphasized, "Like a boy."

The princess let out a whiny sound as she cut her hair, careful and precise. Watching it fall to the ground, Rolina's stomach twisted. It was only hair, it didn't mean anything.

What would Iero say when he saw it?

"Alright," grumbled Twila, "You look perfectly boyish."

She touched her head. Gone. All of it. Her fingers explored, finding it cut close to her scalp, a couple inches at its thickest. "Right," she said, biting back the panic. There on the ground, the golden curls Lady Evensong was known for. "I'm your little brother."

"Alright, 'brother,' do you have a name?" she asked, brushing hair off her dress.

"Um, Eli," she answered, tearing her eyes from the loose hair on the ground.

"Eli... Elian, that's Bryer's real name, isn't it?" Twila asked, something sparked behind her eyes.

Rolina nodded.

"That's a great idea!" a smile spread across Twila's face. "You be your brother, I'll be mine. It'll be easier to hold the glamour if it's someone I know."

Rolina flashed a smile. Anything that added to their chance of success sounded good to her. "Perfect!"

"Leave the talking to me, *Eli*," she said, starting towards the horses.

Rolina raised an eyebrow at her before pulling Eden's shirt over her shoulders. "Why?"

"Change your hair and your looks all you like, you can't change your voice," she explained, offering her the dagger before mounting her horse.

She tucked in Eden's shirt, then stowed the dagger in her belt. "Your magic can do that? Make you sound like him?" she asked, mounting Tovi.

Twila nodded as they rode back out onto the road. "I can only mimic voices and sounds I've heard before, but you should hear Aurora. She can make up anything." Just before they broke through the trees and into view, Twila let out a deep breath, her body transforming with the exhale. Her curves smoothed out into a lithe, muscled chest. Her long hair replaced by short, dark waves. Tight, black pants instead of her green skirt. Sharp ears rounded down as Nox was the only one of the three to take after their father in that area.

"Handsome, aren't I?" Twila flashed her brother's smile at Rolina.

"Your voice is still yours," Rolina would have laughed at the feminine voice coming from Nox's lips if she wasn't so nervous.

"I'm saving that until I need it," Twila explained, then fell silent as they approached the bridge. The other group had been allowed to pass while Rolina disguised herself. The men watched their approach, sizing them up, evaluating their worth.

A tall, confident man flashed a malicious smile, "Afternoon, boys."

Boys. He bought it.

"We don't want any trouble," Twila assured them, switching seamlessly into her brother's voice. The sound of it startled Rolina's nerves. She wondered if she could tell the difference between Nox and Twila's glamour if they were standing side-by-side.

"Neither do we." The other men on the bridge chuckled, then their leader nodded toward Rolina, "Away from the horses."

Before she could protest or dismount, a man grabbed her by the arm, pulling her off of Tovi and to one side of the bridge. The sudden movement sent a bolt of pain through the shallow wounds on her shoulder and side. Another thug yanked Twila to the opposite edge of the bridge. They dug through the supplies strapped onto the horses' saddles. Thankfully, she only brought Eden's clothes. Men's clothes. And Twila didn't have anything but the clothes on her back. Nothing to give them away. They ignored most of the supplies, but took their remaining doubles.

To Rolina's horror, the men who pulled her and Twila apart began searching them. Patting down their bodies for hidden valuables. She locked eyes with Twila. In seconds, they would be discovered. What then? She wasn't exactly the most curvy woman, so she prayed to the Keeper he wouldn't realize. Her heart pounded as the man searched for valuables hidden on her person. Felt right through the deceptive bagginess of her clothes. Confusion spread across his face. He knew. Or at least, he suspected. The man patting down Twila appeared equally confused, his hands feeling a very different body than he saw. He opened his mouth, studying her face as though trying to determine if she was, in fact, a woman. The one searching Rolina began to say something, but Rolina looked him in the eye and whispered, "Please."

The man hesitated. Glancing over his shoulder at the other thugs gleefully sorting through their stolen spoils. Then back to her. He started to take his hands away. Relief sparked in Rolina's heart.

Then was extinguished entirely as the man searching Twila announced, "I think this one's a girl."

"A girl?" This caught the leader's attention, and he turned to look Twila over. "No way that's a girl."

Good. His interest seemed more curious than malicious.

"I dunno," the man who was searching her said with a shrug. "Just seems weird. Like I'm seeing something different than-"

As the man reached to touch Twila again, Rolina made her move. She started towards the left, an attempt to dash away, but found the limit of her captor's mercy there. Next thing she knew, her arms were pinned behind her and others were pushing in to help restrain her. Great. All she'd done was get herself into worse trouble.

"Get off her," Twila growled, her glamour flickering in her anger.

"The hell?" their leader gaped, along with several of the thugs who had been gathering near Rolina. Taking advantage of the distraction, Rolina reached for her dagger, but barely brushed it with her fingertips. The man pinning her arms hadn't loosened his grip. Rolina twisted around violently, biting the man in the shoulder. He growled and pushed her head away.

Twila wrenched one arm free from the stunned thug holding her. She shot her hand towards his eye, but he ducked. Instead, she grabbed him by the hair and yanked his head down into her knee. She yelped, the move hurting her almost as much as him. But she was free. The princess bolted for the horses, darting between the thugs. One caught her skirt and sent her tumbling to the wooden planks of the bridge.

She clawed at the uneven wood, trying to pull herself out of his grasp. But he was bigger, stronger. With one, solid tug, he dragged her back, catching splinters as she went.

Rolina swore, anger surging through her at the sight. She was tired of being useless. Of relying on other people to save her. Twila needed her. She couldn't fail.

With a scream, Rolina twisted her arm around to her dagger and pulled it across the arm of the man holding her. He recoiled as she brought it in for another strike, slicing across his shoulder. Then she was moving, diving between the men trying to catch her.

They were stronger.

She was faster.

Rolina swung her leg around and kicked the man dragging Twila in the face, then dipped low and sliced the edge of Twila's skirt, tearing her free. The princess scrambled to her feet and bolted for the horses. This time she made it, but Rolina was still in the middle of the fight.

Her eyes searched for an opening. Frantic, her heart thundered dangerously in her chest. There were too many of them. Perhaps if she hadn't fought they would have robbed them and let them go. Perhaps her fear had pushed her into further danger. But after Zey, she couldn't risk it. Couldn't wait to be certain of their intentions and find herself in deep trouble.

She ducked and dodged, but soon one caught her by the back of her shirt. She brought her dagger around, slicing blindly at her captor. The attack missed, but put the man off balance. She kicked backward, connecting with his leg. He fell, crashing into another man behind him and carrying Rolina with him. She scrambled from his grasp and onto her feet, then charged after Twila. The princess had led the horses clear of the bridge before mounting hers. Rolina dove between a pair of bandits, breaking into the open. And before they could follow, before they could catch her and break her, she ripped the bottle of Feinin fire from her belt and threw it behind her.

Heat blasted into her, propelling her forward. Singed the back of her neck. She dared a look over her shoulder. Red. The whole bridge consumed by flame. The men shouted and threw themselves into the water below. She didn't think the little bottle would be so powerful. So destructive. As far as she could tell, no one was dead, but guilt still stung at her heart as she hauled herself onto Tovi's saddle. They were cruel, violent men, who deserved a cruel, violent fate, but the hellish flames burned regret into Rolina's chest.

"Come on!" Twila shouted, kicking her horse into a gallop.

Rolina tore herself away and galloped after the princess. Feeling the heat on her skin long after the flames died.

22

Valtameri

There were no open bodies of water in The Frostlands. None that had not frozen over ages ago when the Fae came and shaped the land into snowy plains and mountains. Frostlanders drank melted snow. Bathed in it, cleaned with it. They did not swim.

Iero did not swim.

Not until years, centuries after becoming a guardian, did he learn how. Fleeing in the night with Eden by his side after a mission gone wrong, nowhere to go but the river. He hesitated. Eden threw him in. Sink or swim. He swam.

Almost.

Eden had to drag him out on the other side, coughing and choking. Every time he faced the water since, he couldn't help but think of that night. Of splashing and floundering. Of nearly drowning before Eden gripped him by the arm and swam for the both of them, the river crashing, rushing, threatening.

When he arrived at the Valtamerian shoreline, he prayed to the Keeper he would not need to touch the water. Little huts and haphazard buildings dotted the beach. The Valtamerians' only settlement on land and sole contact with the rest of the continent. A group of Valtamerians, busy repairing a roof on one of the unstable huts, noticed him riding their way. They scrambled. The Valtamerians darted in and out of huts and soon the whole settlement was clustered together. Inhuman eyes watching. Cautious of the stranger. After a moment of discussion, two Valtamerians broke away from the group to meet him.

First, a man with soft blue skin and scales coating his neck and shoulders. Hairless, as all Valtamerians, his head had an angular protrusion jutting from the back. Almost fin-like as it sloped into his forehead.

Second, a girl. Young. A child perhaps. Iero couldn't always tell when it came to the fish-like creatures. They weren't always the same height as humans. Her skin was blue and yellow. Striped like an angel fish. Scales shimmered under her eyes and along her cheekbones. A long, pointed fin grew from her head in lieu of hair.

The scales, the strange skin, their wide, fish-like eyes twisted knots in his stomach. So gross. So disturbing. Guilt bubbled in his stomach, he shouldn't think like that. They were people, same as him, just... different. Scaly and drippy. Human once, and not so different in heart. Magic polluted the blood of their ancestors when the Fae came, changing them into something not quite human, not quite faerie. Like Taivans and Eldurians, magically adapted to the Fae-altered environment. Like him, and the faerie ice in his Frostlander blood. Valtamerians took the brunt of the physical changes. Instead of simply growing some gills or fins, their whole bodies became fish-like.

Iero swallowed hard, forcing the revulsion down. Why couldn't they have turned out like the mermaids? "Hello," he smiled, dismounting Hades as they met.

They returned the smile, revealing rows of sharp teeth, the man's like a shark, the girl's like an angler fish.

Iero's courage sapped away, but he carried on all the same. "I'm Iero Anluan, and-"

"You're a guardian?" the girl cocked her head to the side.

Iero nearly flinched at the disturbing movement. He took a steadying breath, then continued, "Yes, I am. I came to-"

"Come, you must rest," the man said, gesturing for Iero to follow. "It's a long journey from The Eternal Forest."

"It is," Iero agreed, though the Valtamerian shore lay only a few days ride away. The Valtamerians weren't known for traveling much on land. Just about everywhere on the continent was far for them. He followed, eyeing the ocean ahead. "You're very gracious," he added, his voice almost shrill in his discomfort.

"Thank you," the man took the false compliment with a smile. Iero kept his eyes forward, avoiding the temptation to look at the Valtamerian's shark teeth.

"I came because I need someone found," Iero explained, trying to push things along. If he could get what he needed from the people in the shoreline village, he need not travel to the heart of the kingdom. Down in the depths of the sea. Though he had doubts as to the quality of help the villagers could offer.

"Who?" the girl asked as they entered the village. Others crowded in. Asking questions, looking at him like he was as strange to them as they were to him. They appeared to have a particular fascination with his hair. And his horse, Hades. One of them took her reins, leading her away to tend to her needs. A few, interested Valtamerians followed, curious about the land animal. Iero's heart pounded as he watched her walk away. Could fish take care of a horse? He couldn't refuse their hospitality. And if he did need to travel to the heart of Valtameri, he would be forced to leave the horse in their care anyway. That didn't mean he had to like it.

"I'm looking for a man named Hel. A human man," Iero answered, though his eyes remained on Hades until he could no longer see her. "I need to send him a message." He didn't mention Sikker. Couldn't mention Sikker. Couldn't let himself hope he really was traveling with Hel. No, not hope. Dread. No, both. Something in his blood hummed when he pictured Sikker's scarred face.

The last time he saw it he was wiping blood off Sikker's porcelain skin. Usually Haven took care of them when they were hurt, but Haven had been too angry. Iero was angry too, but he put it aside. He washed away the blood, most of it someone else's, and bandaged Sikker's hands. He bit his tongue until it bled that day, all the words in his heart too cruel. Sikker stared at the wall, silent and pale as death. Nothing behind those indigo eyes.

"Who is he?"

"Huh?" Iero snapped back into reality and found himself still surrounded by Valtamerians. He shook off his own thoughts, "Hel was spotted south of here, in the Drowning Sea."

"Dangerous waters," an old fish-woman said, shaking her scaled head ominously.

"I'm aware," Iero said, blinking as he studied her face. Her wrinkled skin sagged in a human way, despite the fish-like texture. Gross. "Can you help me?"

"We can find your man," the shark-like one declared, confidence brimming in his voice. Iero's relief vanished when he added, "But it sounds like business for the mainland." Only Valtamerians could describe an underwater kingdom as *the mainland.*

"Are you certain you can't help me yourselves?" Iero asked, a mix of hope and desperation in his voice.

The fish-people agreed. The answer was no.

"Traveling to such a dangerous sea has to be permitted by the elders," the little girl explained.

"Alright then," Iero's voice cracked as he said the words, pitchy in his defeat, "to the mainland." He stared at his feet, unable to will them into motion. "Can one of you guide me?" he asked quietly, dreading the water, the oppressive force surrounding him.

"I will!" the angel fish girl volunteered.

"Perfect," he said, devoid of enthusiasm. "You'll take care of Hades? The horse," he asked the Valtamerians, uncertain he should trust them with the precious animal.

Several fish assured him they would.

Out of excuses, Iero trudged toward the ocean, stopping about a foot from the water. The angel fish girl dove in, splashing in the shallow water playfully. Iero swallowed, stiff and anxious, then reached for his satchel. Inside, ingredients for a water-breathing spell Maddy gave him. The satchel itself was enchanted for waterproofing, and cinched up tight to stop its contents from drifting away once submerged. Iero unfastened the buckles and removed the ingredients one by one. He mixed and crushed them in the palm of his hand, creating a flaky powder. Then, he leaned down as a wave stretched up the sand toward him, scooping a bit of saltwater in his other hand. He combined the water and the ingredients, creating a repulsive, greenish, purple-flecked paste. Closing his eyes, Iero popped it into his mouth.

Iero forced the slimy substance down, despite its valiant efforts to come back up. He stood frozen, waiting to see if he would gag as the water splashed against his boots. When he didn't, he checked the buckles on his satchel and walked into the ocean. "I can do this," he whispered, the water up to his waist. Water hadn't killed him yet, there was no need to fear.

"This way," the angel fish took Iero's hand. Instinct told him to pull away from the scaly touch, but he resisted, allowing her to pull him deeper into the water. She dove into the sea, releasing his hand. Expecting him to follow.

"I hope this works," he whined, then dove under. He expected the salt water to sting when he opened his eyes. It didn't. In fact, he could see quite well, though the water distorted and magnified his surroundings. The angel fish swam circles around him, waiting for the guardian to adjust to the water. In the sea, where she belonged, the girl looked more natural, more beautiful. A different creature than the disturbing thing he met on the shore.

Her beauty did little to distract Iero from the next task. From the moment he dreaded. Against every instinct, Iero breathed in.

Water rushed into his lungs, but did not burn or choke him. The weight of it strange in his chest. Foreign, heavy. But he didn't die, and that was all he could ask for. "So wrong," he shuddered, then his eyes widened, stunned by the sound of his own voice. He reached a hand to his throat. The sound came out so clear, so natural. "How does my voice sound like this?" he asked the angel fish. "The water- why doesn't it distort the sound?" Maddy's spells had improved since the last time he went to Valtameri. He had a distinct memory of garbled, difficult to understand voices.

She laughed, flashing her angler fish teeth, "I think your enchantment makes you more like us than you expected."

"That's not really an answer," Iero pointed out, but the girl did not respond as she swam ahead.

"This way!" she called, stopping to wave him on.

"I don't swim as fast as you," he shouted to her, already falling behind.

She waited for him to catch up with a dramatic pout. From then on, she paced herself, checking frequently if he was still there. After a miserable swim she stopped. "Here it is."

Iero followed her eyes to an empty expanse of ocean. "I don't see anything." He had been to Valtameri once several hundred years before, and though he hated every second, he thought the city unmistakably beautiful. He wouldn't miss it.

"The Kara Storm," she explained, awe in her voice. "This current will take you directly to the mainland."

He still couldn't see it, but trusted her oceanic senses. The girl pulled him through the water. Invisible or not, he felt the moment his body passed into the current. The water tugged and pushed. He could not fight the pull if he wanted to. His body stiffened. He had no control, no power there. Like drifting seaweed, he flew helpless through the water.

It felt remarkably like drowning in a river.

By the time the current spat Iero out, his body shook. His mind trapped in memory. He had enough of currents pulling him down for one lifetime. When he managed to get ahold of himself, to push the memory into the back of his mind, he realized where they were.

Valtameri lay before him like a dream.

Rocky spires rose from the depths of the sea. Glowing lights cut through the murky shadows of the ocean. Valtameri's capital city, Syvanin. Despite his hatred for the place, he could not deny its beauty. Beauty like a haunted forest, or a cemetery at night. A beauty Iero could not trust. Strange bio-luminescent lights set the place aglow, and yet it still felt dark to Iero. Like anything could be lurking just out of sight. Ordinarily he liked shadows. Ordinarily, he *was* the thing in the dark.

The angel fish girl swam lazy circles, waiting for Iero to regain his bearings. "Ready?"

He nodded, wishing he could swim back to the surface. A surface he couldn't see from the depths.

The girl started off again, her blue and yellow fins pushing her through the water with ease. She guided him between the rocky spires. They passed other Valtamerians and water faeries, shocked by the sight of a human swimming behind her. Arms stinging, Iero kept going, eager to reach their destination and have it done with. She led him to the largest of the kingdom's spires, through an opening in one side. Valtamerians did not construct buildings as humans did. In Syvanin they hollowed out its many natural spires to create a city. The room within the spire was lit by bio-luminescent coral lining the ceiling, giving the room an uncomfortable, half-glow. The floor - if it could be called a floor - was covered in a layer of sand, drifting back and forth in the ocean's flow. The walls were carved with shapes Iero did not recognize, and he didn't know if they were decorative, or if they meant something.

Ushering him deeper inside, the angel fish swam halfway up the wall to a round door. She tugged it open and gestured for Iero to follow. The next room was larger than the last, though similar in style. Several Valtamerians and aquatic faeries floated, drifted, and swam within. The elder's council. They turned to see the newcomers, a wave of surprise rippling through them.

"Human!" a Valtamerian with red skin cried, "You must swim up to the air!"

"You'll drown," another agreed, swimming to help.

Choosing not to point out he never would have reached Valtameri if he couldn't breathe, Iero told them, "It's fine, I'm under an enchantment."

"What brings you here, ground-walker?" a woman asked, her voice projecting an intelligence rarely found in a Valtamerian. Her pale green body coated in scales, her skin translucent. Her face narrow, elegant, with two fins on top of her head that joined at the nape of her neck, continuing down her back beneath her clothes. Her silvery, watery eyes unblinking.

"I'm Iero Anluan, Imperial Guardian, come to seek your aid," he announced, sending a wave of chatter through the group of Valtamerians. Questions and theories of why a guardian would travel all the way into their sea.

"How do we know you are telling the truth?" the intelligent one asked. The first to question his identity.

Iero caught the fabric of his shirt as it floated around his body, pulling it taunt to display the compass rose embroidered on the breast. The eastern point stitched red to stand out above the others. The green woman swam close - closer than Iero liked - to examine the symbol.

"It is the imperial insignia," she told the others, approval in her voice. "But anyone could sew that on a shirt," she poked the red point of the compass rose.

Iero frowned, faced with another thing he hoped to avoid. With a sigh, he handed his satchel to the angel fish girl and peeled off his shirt, holding it close to his body as he turned his left shoulder to face the woman. The enchanted tattoo shifted with the movement. Ink sliding beneath his skin to point east. If the water didn't frighten him, it would have felt good on his Frostlander skin. The chill of the depths was akin to a crisp, fall day in the Frostlands.

The woman traced a slippery finger along his shoulder, sending a chill through Iero. "It really moves," she said, awe lacing her voice as the stroke of her fingers continued down Iero's arm. She must have felt Iero's muscles tense at the touch, because she backed away with a few flicks of her fins. "What would you ask of us, guardian?"

"I need you to track down a man sailing in the Drowning Sea," he announced as he pulled his shirt back over his head.

Another murmur traveled through the group. A wave of distress and curiosity.

"What man?" the green-skinned elder-woman asked, ignoring the fears of her comrades.

Sikker. The name nearly slipped through Iero's lips, but he wasn't the one Iero was sent to find. "His name is Hel. It is of the utmost importance that I reach him," he stressed, securing his satchel at his side once more.

"What you ask will be done," she assured him, looking to the other elders for approval. They nodded their heads and murmured assent. "Many a creature lurks in those waters. Pirates and sharks are the least of your worries there. But a few, well-trained scouts should be safe enough."

"Thank you," Iero sighed, relieved. The Valtamerians had a history of cooperation with the empire, in part because they left the oceanic kingdom alone as much as possible. But he feared complications when asking about The Drowning Sea. Guardians rarely stepped foot off Syytala, and Iero himself had never traveled the waters south of the continent. Had never seen the fearful, pirate-infested place with his own eyes.

"Rest now, you've had a long journey. Then tell us all you know of this man and how we might find him. You are welcome to stay here in the city," she offered, sending a shiver down Iero's spine.

"Perhaps it's best if I stay on the shore," he suggested, eager to breathe air. Maddy provided more than enough spell components for a prolonged stay, but Iero preferred not to use them. Not to stay on the bottom of the sea, miles of water pressing down on him.

"It's a long journey to the shore," a reddish fish-man said, shaking his finned head.

"Don't you want to stay and oversee the mission?" the green fish asked, making an expression Iero assumed was similar to raising an eyebrow, except she had none.

"The shore isn't that far, I could travel back and forth," Iero said, ready to put the issue to rest and return to dry land. He wondered what the salt water would do to his hair.

"You rode the storm," the woman sighed, "no current is as strong as the storm."

Iero's chest tightened, "Then how long does it take to return?"

"Close to a day for a ground-walker," the angel fish girl piped in.

Hope vanished. He needed to oversee the mission. For the sake of the empire, the war. Though convincing the man would be difficult, Hel's army was only growing the last time Iero encountered him. If he joined in the fight, the war would be over in no time. And if Sikker was really with him... that alone was enough to make the mission vital. Not to the empire, but to Iero. He wanted to see him. All the feelings warring inside him demanded it. Whether to hug him or stab him Iero didn't know, but he needed a new memory to replace the image of those empty, indigo eyes.

Valtamerians had a tendency for distraction. If he didn't stay on top of them, near them, the mission would falter. His shoulders sank and he drifted closer to the silty floor. "It seems I'm staying."

"We'll have someone show you to a guest room," the elder woman said, pleased at ensnaring such a renowned guest. Valtamerians did not often play host. When the opportunity came, they relished it. Waving her webbed hand, another fish swam to his side from the edges of the room. Some sort of servant or attendant.

"Right this way, Sir," the fish said with a genuine smile.

Iero's stomach clenched and his jaw tightened. His mind and body screamed at him to leave, to swim toward the surface, to get out. Huffing a heavy, resigned sigh, Iero shoved his instincts down and followed the Valtamerian out of the elder's council room. Swimming on sore arms. They arrived at a small, bare room. Another sand-covered, uneven floor, and a cupboard set into the wall. In one rocky wall to his right, a window looked out on the city. Though windows in Valtameri were more like glorified holes. No glass or shutters to block out the world.

The attendant left him to his own devices. He swam closer to snoop in the cupboard, finding it empty. May as well keep his satchel there. It could drift away if unsecured. He tucked it inside and double checked the latch was properly locked. Then, nothing else to do, Iero let himself sink to the bottom, the heavy water in his lungs pushing him down. Sitting on the silty floor, his hair waved above his head. "I hate it here," he said. No one heard him in the deep, endless ocean.

23

Bonfire Night

One week. One week since Tavek. One week since she stole away in the night, the Princess of Illandia by her side. Halfway to Gaj. Rolina counted every day. Each one a day closer to her parents. A day closer to returning to the brother left behind. The home left behind. A day closer to Eden. But this day meant more than the others.

They managed to get some flint in a town they passed through a day before. Their doubles had been stolen by the thugs on the bridge, so they traded some wild blackberries they had picked along the way. Rolina sat on her knees, striking away with her dagger, trying for a spark. It should have been easy. Maddy taught her how. She had done it again and again while practicing in his dreams. She was beginning to think the wizard had made it easy for her.

"*Heikkem Velki*," she swore, tossing the flint and dagger on the ground. "I give up."

Twila frowned, tying up the horses after taking them to a stream to drink. "Are you going to tell me what's wrong, or should I guess?"

Rolina turned to the princess, "Excuse me?"

"You've been grumpy all day," Twila pointed out, coming to sit beside Rolina on the dirt.

"It's nothing," Rolina huffed, then picked up the flint and dagger once more, if only to give her something to do other than talk.

"It's not," Twila said simply.

Rolina knew her friend wouldn't let it drop, so she said, "Tavek."

"What about it? Did something happen?" Twila asked, trying to catch Rolina's eye, but she refused to look up from her work.

"No," she didn't want to say more, but it was better than having Twila prod at her with questions. "We have this tradition. Since we have to throw a big party every year, there's not enough time to spend with each other on Tavek. So a week after, we celebrate on our own."

Twila's face softened, "It's tonight."

"It was going to be disappointing this year anyway," Rolina grumbled. Half the guardians were gone and everyone was on edge. But missing it stung. It was her chance to have even a moment with everyone, with Eli, with the emperors. Everyone who she missed spending time with. Well, not everyone. Not Eden. Not Bolwerk either, but she didn't care as much about him. Still, it would be strange having him gone. It was all strange and horrible and she wanted everyone safe and together and all the bloodshed over. "It shouldn't matter."

"It should," Twila countered, hooking a finger under Rolina's chin to lift it. "It's everything you're fighting for, isn't it? For your family. For peace that allows you to be together and celebrate."

Rolina didn't realize her shoulders were so tight until she let the tension go. Twila understood. Of course she understood.

"What do you usually do to celebrate?" she asked, letting Rolina's chin go.

She turned back to the pile of kindling in front of her, yet to be ignited. "Bonfire."

Twila smiled wistfully, "I've never been to a bonfire."

"Really?" Rolina's head shot back up and she looked aghast at Twila. "But they're so fun."

The princess shrugged. "It's not something we do in Illandia."

Rolina turned back to the kindling and began striking away with renewed vigor. "Then we'll just have to have one." She doubted her skills could make much more than a small, temporary blaze, let alone the huge, raging flames of a real bonfire. And if she did, she couldn't control it. Still, fire was now a necessity.

Twila laughed beside her, "By all means. But what do you *do* at a bonfire?"

"Have fun," Rolina answered. She thought of years past. Of riding on Haven's shoulders. Of dancing with Iero. Of laughter and heat and staying up well beyond midnight.

"Ah, have fun, why didn't I think of that?"

A smile tugged at the corner of Rolina's mouth. "You can tell stories," she offered, remembering tales of daring escapes and wild lands. The guardians had thousands of years to choose from, and they always picked the best parts of their lives. Mercury liked talking about the day she first saw The Eternal Forest, full of spring blossoms. Even Dimitri usually contributed a story or two, and that hidden thing behind his eyes would spark and flare. So close to the surface Rolina wondered if she might see it at last.

"Or dance." She liked dancing, but especially on bonfire night. Formal parties had rules. Bonfire night did not. If she wanted to twirl and twirl and twirl she could. She did. Until she was so dizzy she dropped. Usually, Haven was the one to catch her.

"Or drink," she said, picturing Iero gulping down the potent, ice cold alcohol he had imported from Frostlands. Snowfire, he said it was called, and he promised to let her try it when she was eighteen. A promise the other guardians had objected to, claiming the liquid was the most disgusting, backwater swill the Glacial Plains had ever created, and one sip would have her shivering all night. Haven called it Frostlander Moonshine.

They had been absolutely right. Still, it was worth it.

This last year, before Iero had offered her the promised taste of snowfire, Dimitri let her steal a sip of his wine. It made her feel important and grown up and a little bit sleepy. None of the guardians bothered to mention that they had been letting her and Eli sneak sips of their drinks for years, and it was really nothing new. But it *was* new. It meant Dimitri realized she was growing up.

He wasn't the only one. She hadn't noticed Eden's eyes on her as she twirled and laughed and listened to an exceptionally drunk Iero attempt to tell them about the time he stole an entire twelve-foot tall statue. She only noticed Eden was quieter than he usually was on nights with his brothers. She thought it had to do with the rumors she'd been hearing. The first whispers of the coming rebellion.

Eden told her, months later, after that first kiss, that was the night he first realized he found her attractive. He'd wrestled with feeling guilty over it, with trying to squash the attraction before it grew. She was younger than him. Thousands of years younger, but Eden was immortalized at twenty-one. It wouldn't be long before she caught up. Before she passed him. Kept going. Kept aging.

They didn't talk about that part very often. When they did, it often turned into an argument. Rolina would tell him she didn't care. Their life together would be strange, but it would be theirs. Eden would tell her he did care. That she would realize one day she wanted someone who could go through life with her, and by then she may have missed her chance.

"Stories, dancing, drinking, and fire," Twila counted each one on her fingers. "It has the potential for disaster, but I like it."

Rolina smiled, her thoughts returning to the present. To the task in front of her. "There's food too."

"Sweets?" Twila asked eagerly.

"The sweetest," Rolina confirmed. She struck the dagger against the flint and at last a spark managed to hop to the kindling. With a gasp, Rolina's heart leapt in her chest. "Can't let it go out, can't let it go out!" She worked quickly. Blowing on the spark until it became a flame. Feeding the flame more kindling until it caught the structure of wood carefully constructed around it.

Then she sat back, staring at the growing flames. "I did it," she breathed, unable to tear her eyes away.

"Evensong," Twila said beside her, pride lacing her voice, "You can make fire."

Rolina grinned. "I can make fire."

They sat in silence, the light flickering and dancing before them. Until Rolina stood and offered a hand to Twila. "Dance with me?"

Twila laughed, but took Rolina's hand, "There's no music."

"We don't need any," Rolina pulled the princess to her feet. Then she tilted back her head, threw out her arms, and twirled.

The girls danced wildly, with no sense of rhythm or beat. No rules or restrictions. Just movement and fire and earth under their feet. They laughed and giggled and sang out-of-tune. Twirled and jumped. Spun thoughts of war and danger right out of their heads. And then they collapsed, breathless under the stars.

Rolina's chest rose and fell as the cold, clean air filled her. Exhausted. Happy.

Twila's hand slipped into hers. "Do you remember the first time I came to visit after Mother died?"

"Yes," she managed to say, her breath still elusive.

"That day in the trees?"

"Yes." They decided to see how high they could climb on one of the towering trees of The Eternal Forest. This was long after Rolina broke her leg attempting the same stunt on another tree, but she hadn't learned her lesson. Together they went higher and higher, giving each other boosts or pulling each other up to the same branch. They weren't even halfway, but it felt like they had climbed miles. And then, as Rolina was helping Twila up, the branch cracked.

The girls went hurtling towards the earth. Twigs snapping and scratching their skin. Even as she tried to catch hold of another branch, Rolina hadn't let go of Twila's hand. Twila held on just as tight. They would fall as they had climbed. Together.

Then everything slowed. *They* slowed. Stopped. They were floating. Drifting on air like feathers. The confusion lasted only a moment before they spotted Kail, who had been walking by at the perfect moment. His faerie magic stopped them from crashing into the earth. From cracking bones and breaking skin. The guardian had very little control over his own magic, but in his panic at seeing their fall, he managed to tap into the right power.

The guardian helped them to their feet and looked them over to see if they were hurt beyond minor scratches. And when he was satisfied they were alright, and about to tell them not to climb so high, the girls looked at each other and grinned.

Do it again.

Rolina didn't remember which of them asked Kail, or how they convinced him, but soon they were drifting on air again. Laughing and flipping. Trying to swim through the sky. Seeing if they could spin faster if they tried tipping each other over. Giggling at the way their hair looked when they were upside down. And when Kail's volatile magic flickered out, and he barely managed to catch them before they hit the dirt, they laughed all the same.

"That was the first time I laughed since she died," Twila muttered. A year. It was nearly a year after her mother passed away. A year without laughter. Her voice wasn't sad though, or longing, but peaceful. Content. "You have this way about you, Evensong. A way of fixing things you can't even see."

"I'm not the only one," Rolina replied, looking up at the stars. The stars of her homeland. Of Ev. Without Twila, the journey would have crushed her. Without Twila, she would be lying awake and afraid every night. Without Twila, the peace spreading through her body would have been impossible. How long Rolina watched the stars shine, she did not know. Twila's breathing shifted, telling her the princess was fast asleep. She soon followed, the soft crackle of the fire her lullaby.

24

Ruin and Earth

The closer Rolina and Twila came to their destination, the more soldiers they passed. Rebels and imperials alike. The imperial soldiers were always satisfied with a quick flash of the insignia on Rolina's stolen jacket. The rebels were trickier. She had to hide the insignia deep in its folds, concentrating so she didn't reveal it with a wrong movement while Twila used her Illandian influence to get them by.

Their disguises didn't hurt. No one tried to take advantage of the two young men. They held no value beyond what money they might have, and they were dressed poor enough that anyone who spotted them wouldn't bother. Unless they saw Twila without her glamour. It was difficult to maintain all day, so she only put it on when they saw someone approaching in the distance.

Except for one morning when Rolina caught Twila doing something odd. A few days earlier Rolina woke in the bed of the inn they were staying at to find the princess already awake, staring in a little square mirror hung on the wall. She had glamoured herself into Nox again, though there were no prying eyes to catch her as herself. The princess lifted one of her hands and ran it along her - Nox's - chin. Then she heard Rolina move and instantly let the glamour go. Rolina hadn't mentioned it. Twila missed her brother, and that was something Rolina could understand.

Rolina spread her map out on her lap as they rode. Three days left until Gaj. Rolina counted each one. Excitement and dread mingling in her stomach. Soon she would be with Eden and her family. Soon it would be done. Her eyes drifted to Bane, marked an inch away from Gaj. Two days apart. Eden had probably already left the valley. Already saved her family. Unless... What if the battle delayed him?

"How close are we?" Twila asked, referring to a town that lay along their route. The last one between them and Gaj.

"Not far," she answered, studying the area for any sort of landmark that matched the map. Nothing. "I think." She looked up at Twila, "Does any of this look familiar to you?"

Twila shrugged, "Vaguely. I'm usually cooped up in a carriage when we make this journey."

Rolina folded the map and tucked it away. "It's getting late," she looked up at the sky, the sun painting it with pinks and yellows. "I hope we make it before-"

The town lay before them, half obscured in the dim light. Instead of the quaint, rural, farm town she anticipated, she found a ruin. Humble buildings falling apart. Some no more than a pile of sticks. Devastated.

They moved toward the town in silence. A pair of armed men walked out to meet them. Rolina thanked the Keeper for Tovi. Putting a few feet of separation between her and the men.

"What's your business here," one of them demanded. He was middle aged, with tired eyes, and carried himself in a way that warned not to cross him.

Rolina opened her mouth to answer, then remembered her disguise. Her voice would reveal her as a woman. Instead, she cast a pointed look at Twila, who had glamoured herself to look like Nox the moment the town came into view. "Just passing through," she told them in her brother's voice.

"Why?" the man continued, studying each of them in turn. Behind him, the other man stood ready, hand on his weapon. He was younger than the first, perhaps in his thirties, but his eyes were just as wary, just as exhausted.

"Come on now, no need to hassle them," came a voice from behind the men. Rolina looked up to see a woman walking their way, a crossbow slung over her shoulder. "They're only travelers."

"We don't know that," the older man began, casting a glare at the woman.

She ignored him. "It's getting late, you should talk to Danner if you want a place to stay," she told the girls. "We aren't exactly equipped for visitors at the moment, but we won't turn you away."

The man glared at her, "You can't be serious. They're strangers."

"Not another word from you," she ordered the man, then gestured for Rolina and Twila to follow. They did, eyes scanning their surroundings as they went. Searching for signs of danger.

"What happened here?" Twila asked as they passed a burned out building. Around them, every capable person worked to clear away rubble or make repairs. Others stood watch throughout the town, cautious eyes following them. Even children helped where they could. Working or looking after younger siblings.

"Bandits," the woman explained. "Been taking advantage of the war. We don't have the resources to defend ourselves, and the empire can't bother protecting a little town like ours at the moment."

Rolina's chest tightened. Bandits. Like the ones who killed the woman they tried to save. How many places were left vulnerable because of the war? Homes destroyed and crops stolen. Bandits and rebels alike, tearing a hole in the world. If only she had the strength of a guardian. She would make things right. Fight away the bandits. Clean up the town.

The woman led them to a house with a blacksmith workshop attached to one end. For the most part, it appeared intact. A few wobbly beams held up the shop ceiling. Inside, a man pounded away at the metal on his anvil, and the woman had to maneuver through the crowded shop to stand in front of him before he realized they were there. He looked up, catching his breath as he took in the visitors. "Evenin', Danner. Got a few travelers that need a place to stay. You got room?"

"Only if they don't mind a tight squeeze," he answered, smiling good-naturedly. Rolina glanced down. He was working on a weapon. A sword, by the look of it. Shouldn't he be making beams and nails and tools to help them rebuild?

"We don't mind," Twila told him, then offered her hand to shake, "My name's Nox, this is my brother Elian."

Rolina smiled awkwardly and shook the man's hand after Twila.

"Come on in and we'll get you sorted," Danner started towards the house, gesturing at a tree near the workshop as he moved. "You can tie your horses up there. The stables are under repair and the fence 'round Old Mav's pasture came down."

Rolina shot a glance toward Twila. Perhaps they should leave these people alone. They had enough to worry about without hosting guests. The princess didn't catch the look. They tied up their horses and removed their heavy load, then met the blacksmith inside.

People everywhere.

Rolina stiffened in the doorway. Despite the warning, she had not imagined it this tight. Mostly children, too young to go out and help with the repairs, and women, busy in the kitchen cooking food for what may have been the whole town, or looking after the kids. A few men dotted the crowd, and as Rolina peered closer, she realized they were injured. Incapable of contributing.

"I have one of the only functioning kitchens in town at the moment," Danner mentioned, "Most of these young ladies are only here for the cooking." The tightness in Rolina's chest loosened. There would be more space soon. She didn't know why the crowd bothered her. She had attended plenty of crowded events in the forest. But there were no walls caging her in there.

"Some families have been staying here until their houses are rebuilt, so I can't say it will get much better once the others come back from work, but there should be some room for you." Any relief Rolina had about the crowd thinning vanished. He led them down a hallway to a room deep in the back. "Here's where the men have been sleeping," he cracked the door open for them to see dozens of blankets scattered across the room. Most lay on the floor, even though there was a bed in the center of the room.

As he shut the door, Rolina waited for him to show them the women's room, then remembered their disguises. It looked like she was in for a night surrounded by strange men. But these weren't hardened thugs or merciless bandits. They were just men. Farmers and workers and fathers and brothers. Practically refugees in their own town. So what did it matter as long as she remained near Twila?

"Can you hold the glamour through the night?" Rolina whispered doubtfully.

Twila shook her head, "I'll sleep with the blanket over my face."

"Are you sure? We could keep going. Leave them alone," Rolina whispered, feeling deeply intrusive. The last thing these people needed were two more bodies taking up space.

"It's cold out there, we're staying," she insisted.

Rolina frowned but said no more. They found a spot in the corner and settled in as men returned from working on the village. The room grew more packed. More stuffy. Rolina wanted to bolt outside and gulp down the fresh air. But Twila was already settled in, her blanket hiding her face and body. Rolina pressed in beside Twila. The closer, the safer. The princess hardly noticed, already fast asleep.

"Have there ever been any High Emperors from Viska?"

"First of all," Maddy grumbled, scowling at Rolina as they walked through the shelves of his library, "if you *ever* listened to what I taught you, you would know the answer. Second, *must* we talk about Viska?"

"I guess it's been on my mind since you told me you're going," Rolina said, slipping her hand into his. He had forgotten his scar again, but she didn't want to remind him. It was nice to see his face as she remembered it. Untouched by war.

"There have been several High Emperors from Viska. Some excellent, some horrendously evil, and some in between," he answered, running his free hand along the spines of the books they passed. "And before you ask, not all of them were wizards. Viska is about more than magic, but people always forget that. The wizard's council included."

Rolina didn't miss the bitterness in his voice when he said *wizard's council*. "I take it they're the reason you don't want to go?"

"Did you get that from the angry face, or from the angry voice?" Maddy asked, the corner of his mouth quirking up in half a smile.

"Voice," she answered, "I was too busy looking at these very old books to see your face."

"Old books are my favorite," Maddy said, one of his smoother topic changes. "Even new books are old books in this library, because I like them better that way."

"The old book smell is very realistic for a dream construct," Rolina agreed, then tugged the conversation back on course, "Why don't you like the wizard's council?"

Maddy sighed and stopped walking, "Why so curious all of a sudden? You usually ignore this kind of stuff."

"Normally this stuff is politics, and that's boring. But now it's about *you*, and *you* are interesting," Rolina answered, tugging his arm to keep him walking.

"I'm interesting? I thought I was boring."

"You're that too. Answer the question, wizard," she demanded with a dramatic flick of her wrist.

"I could throw you right out of this dream, you know," he threatened half-heartedly.

She glared him, daring him to do just that.

He sighed again, defeated. "I don't like the wizard's council because they all think they know best. But *I* know best. I'm not just bragging either. I'm smart and I'm old and I know a hell of a lot more than them."

Rolina gasped theatrically, "Hell? Maddy, did you just *swear?*"

"It doesn't count, I'm dreaming," he excused, then pressed on before she could say more, "They like to pretend they're 'seeking my wisdom' or 'come to learn at the feet of the master' - and yes, some of them have actually called me master - but they never listen to the *one thing* I care most about."

"Preservation of history?" Rolina guessed, smiling like a teacher's pet.

"Preservation of magic," Maddy corrected.

She should have known. "The earth borns." Beings, like humans and dwarves, who weren't ordinarily born with magic were occasionally blessed with it. A natural ability to command the magic of the earth itself. It was one of his lectures she remembered. Partially because he repeated it so often, and partially because she found it so romantically tragic. Poor Maddy was the only one left.

In ancient days, even before Maddy and the guardians, jealous humans watched the way the earth borns commanded magic and began to emulate them. Their actions forced the magic out of the earth, unlike the easy way the earth borns commanded it. Earth borns could do spectacular, potent magic at a very early age, but the unnatural wizards had to work for decades to wield an inkling of that power. And the more power they took from the earth, the more it was drained. It took millennia, but eventually the earth was too empty to bless the people. There were no more new earth borns, and without the same life-giving magic of the guardians, all but Maddy died out over time.

But they could return. If the wizards let go of their power, or simply stopped training new wizards and let themselves fade out, the earth could grow strong again. And when it had enough magic, it would share it with someone. And then someone else. And then another and another until earth borns were common as cows.

"I keep telling them, magic is stronger if you let the earth choose who wields it," Maddy grumbled. "Even I used to be stronger," he admitted, sounding every bit as old as he was, "But my magic comes from the earth, and they're killing her."

"The earth is a her?" Rolina asked with a smile.

"Of course the earth is a her," Maddy replied as though thinking otherwise was the most ridiculous thing he'd ever heard.

"It's difficult giving up power, I would imagine," Rolina said, though she didn't agree with the wizard's council choosing to keep it. To steal magic from those who were meant to wield it.

"I suppose it doesn't look fair," Maddy admitted. "Asking them to give up the scraps of magic they have just so I can keep mine. But it's more important than that."

"It's for everyone," Rolina finished his thought. "The earth's magic sustains all creatures, not just those with magic."

"You *do* listen sometimes," Maddy smiled down at her.

"Like I said, I listen to the stuff that's *you*," she said, then turned to look at the books. "Are these accurate? Do you have them all memorized or something?"

"A few. Well, a lot. Some of them are decorative," he admitted. "A packed library is just more impressive."

"Who are you trying to impress inside your own head?" she asked with a grin.

Maddy paused, blinking as if he'd never thought about it before. "No one I suppose."

Rolina woke to the sound of metal on metal. Pounding. Crashing. The sound of a blacksmith at work just outside. She groaned and sat up, finding the room near-empty. Two injured men were sprawled out on blankets, unable to join the work. Beside her, Twila woke, pulling off her blanket to reveal her glamour already in place.

"What's all the noise?" she moaned, forgetting to use her brother's voice.

Rolina's eyes widened, but if the men in the room noticed, they didn't show it. "Voice," she whispered.

Embarrassment flashed across Twila's - Nox's - face. "Sorry," she said, sounding like the boy whose face she wore.

She shrugged, trying not to speak more than she had to. Then she stood and gestured for Twila to follow. The sooner they left these people alone, the better. The girls exited the house and started towards their horses, but Twila caught Rolina by the arm and said above the crashing metal, "We should thank him before we go."

Rolina nodded and followed Twila towards the blacksmith. But before they arrived, Rolina caught sight of a group of soldiers headed their way. Her eyes scanned them from head to toe. Not an imperial insignia anywhere. Rolina held out an arm, stopping Twila in her tracks just as the soldiers stepped into the shop. Danner set down his tools and looked up at the closest one.

"We're here for the weapons," the soldier said, not an ounce of sympathy in his voice.

Rolina's jaw tightened. How could they walk through this broken place and demand anything?

"Give us what we came for and we'll be on our way," a second rebel demanded.

"You can take what I have," Danner gestured to a stack of weapons laying on a nearby table. "As I said before, you didn't give me enough time to make everything."

The first rebel spoke again, "You don't have everything?"

"I said as much when you put in the order," Danner reminded them, his mouth a stern line.

"We came for enough weapons to resupply the whole outfit, and you're sayin' you don't have 'em?" the rebel snapped, inching closer to the blacksmith. His hand rested on a sword on his belt.

"If you were listening the first time, you wouldn't have to ask," Danner snapped.

"This isn't going to end well," Rolina whispered to Twila.

"We should get out of here before we get caught in it," Twila whispered, taking a step back.

Rolina shot her a surprised look, "We can't let them hurt him."

"We can't let them hurt *us*," Twila countered.

"You helped me try and save that woman on the road, how is this different?" Rolina snapped, horrified that the brave princess wanted to run.

"I thought we had a chance to get her to safety before the bandits arrived, I never wanted to fight," Twila confessed, taking another step back towards the horses.

"*I'm* going to help him whether you stand with me or run," Rolina said, anger lacing the whisper of her voice.

"Give us our weapons, old man," a rebel shoved the blacksmith back a few steps.

"I can't give what I don't have," Danner said, fighting to keep his patience.

"And if we let that slide? What does that say to our other suppliers?" the rebel continued, stepping closer to Danner. "They can be lazy? They don't need to give us what we need?"

They hadn't so much as glanced at Rolina and Twila, so she took a moment to retrieve her sword from Tovi's saddlebag and strap it to her belt. The wooden beads in the handle reminded her who she fought for. Innocents like her parents. Like the people struggling to defend and restore this town. She reached for her dagger, slow and subtle, as the two of them stepped forward, flanking Danner.

Twila let out a quiet snarl and marched right up to a soldier, "Leave," she hissed. Pride flickered through Rolina's chest. The princess couldn't leave him undefended any more than Rolina could.

The rebel laughed and took a step back, "Who do you think you are?"

"Danner's right," Rolina said, done keeping her mouth shut, "you don't listen well."

He squinted at her, "Are you a girl?"

She stepped up to him and pulled her dagger from hiding, pressing it against his throat, "I'm a *Lady*."

He started to laugh again, but she pressed the dagger harder against his throat, drawing a trickle of blood. She was tired of people pushing each other around. Tired of bandits and rebels and the abuses of corrupt men. All that frustration in the tip of her knife, ready to strike, to slash down all the evil in the world.

An image cut through her rage. Eli healing the man with the broken leg. Helping an enemy. Eli would not want her to harm this man. A man who believed the lies spread by the Duke of Kandston. Like so many others.

From days and miles away, Eli stayed her hand.

"This is none of your business," the rebel snapped, slapping her hand away. He stepped forward, grabbing her by the collar. Her mercy set her off guard, off balance. The rebel caught her too easily. She was trained for this, her emotions should not overpower her training.

With a growl, she swung her knee up between his legs. He let her go with a yelp, doubling over. Riding her momentum, she swung her dagger, nicking the arm of the rebel to her right. The motion sent a slight burn through her shoulder. The wound was nearly healed, the pain almost nothing. But it reminded her. She had to be careful. Had to be better than last time.

She ducked low as he moved to retaliate, taking the opportunity to stab her dagger into his leg. Deep. Deeper than she intended. He screamed. Blood pulsed from the wound. She tried to pull the dagger free of his flesh. Too deep. She drew her sword. A second rebel closed in. Panic swelled in her chest as familiar doubt crept in. What if she crippled the man for life? What if he bled to death? Her dagger doomed him.

No.

She was done. No more pity for those who chose abuse and harm. Never would she find joy in harming another human, but she snuffed out the part of her that chose mercy for the wicked. Cruelty for cruelty. Pain for pain. She slashed her sword across his chest - not too deep this time - and kicked him in the gut. Off balance and disoriented, the kick knocked the rebel to the ground.

When she looked up, she found the rebels scrambling. Two of them dragged the man she wounded away, her dagger still sticking out of his leg. Their leader helped her most recent victim to his feet and they ran to catch up to their fleeing allies.

"That was easy," she said, huffing, though as she stared at the trail of blood left behind, she didn't believe the words. With each fight, something inside her was hardening. Something she wasn't sure she liked.

"They just don't make men like they used to," Twila laughed.

"You shouldn't have done that," Danner said as their attention turned back to him. "They'll be after you now."

They wouldn't be around long enough for that. "Why would you give weapons to the rebels?" Rolina asked, but there was no anger in her voice. She was beginning to understand things weren't as black and white. Rebel and imperial. Good and evil.

"It's better that way. They've been keeping the bandits away after what happened. In exchange, we give them what they want. Food, clothes, weapons. Otherwise, they might let the bandits back through."

Tribute or death.

"Thanks for getting 'em off my back for a day or so, though," Danner added, shaking his head. "Gives me some time to finish making what they want."

Rolina looked the way the rebels came from, a tinge of guilt in her chest. Had she caused another problem? Made things worse for these poor people? "Will they be angry?" She already knew the answer, but she wanted to know if they would come back with a stronger force. If she should try to find a way to help.

"Course," Danner said, but scoffed, "I wouldn't be too worried though. They aren't as big and tough as they seem. There's maybe ten of 'em in their whole group. It's more the *idea* of rebels around that keeps the bandits away. If they knew what they were really up against they'd have torn this place down the rest of the way by now."

"Then, you'll be alright?"

Danner waved a hand dismissively, "So long as I have what they want by then."

"We should leave you to it then," Twila said, grabbing Rolina by the arm to pull her away.

But she couldn't just leave them. Sure, the nearby rebels may not have been as big of a problem as she feared, but their town. Their broken, burned out town. She couldn't stand aside while people were suffering. "How long do you think it will be before they return?"

"Couple days. They're camped out in the woods," Danner explained.

"Then we'll stay an extra day," Rolina announced. Twila shot her a sharp look, but didn't protest. "We'll help with some repairs to repay you for letting us stay."

"Do as you please," Danner said gruffly, but Rolina caught the slightest smile before he turned back to his work.

Rolina took Twila's hand and marched off to find someone who needed extra help. It sent a message. A Lady of the Syytan Empire working side by side with the Princess of Illandia. Their own hands rebuilding a town broken by the war. That was the reason Twila left, to show her father what they could do if they worked together. If they threw down their weapons and saw what was important. The people.

It didn't take long before they were put to work. Carrying away wheelbarrows full of rubble. Hammering new support beams in place. Even helping move a family back into their newly rebuilt house - a task that delighted Rolina. And when they dropped to the floor, exhausted in their corner of Danner's crowded house, it was with a sense of satisfaction Rolina had not felt since long before she left.

25

End

"Are you sure we can't just... keep going?" Rolina asked sweetly as she tethered Tovi to a tree.

Twila secured her own horse to another before setting to work removing its gear. "Gaj will still be there tomorrow."

Tomorrow. The word hummed through Rolina's bones. One day until the end of her journey. Until she saw her family again. "We can't be *that* far," Rolina insisted, even as she began taking her horse's gear off. Eden was likely already there, her parents safe. There was no longer a need to rush.

"Tovi deserves a rest, don't you think?" Twila replied, flashing a knowing smile at Rolina.

She sighed and brushed her fingers along the horse's side. With success only a few hours away, Rolina's mind drifted far from worry and into memory. "I have a friend named Tovi... Had. I suppose I wouldn't recognize him if I saw him now," she admitted, then braced herself to heave Tovi's heavy saddle off.

"From Gaj?" Twila asked. Already finished with her horse, she began unpacking her blanket.

Rolina set the saddle on the ground and huffed, "From when I was little."

"You named a horse after your friend from home? That's sweet," Twila said with a soft smile.

"They had the same color hair," Rolina said, finding her own blanket and laying it on the ground beside Twila.

"Adorable," the princess said, settling down on the ground.

"Oh he was. My parents didn't like him. Well, they didn't like his parents. They owned the local tavern and they didn't want me around that sort of environment." A wide grin spread across her face, "He used to sing the dirtiest songs, but neither of us knew what they meant."

Twila chuckled, listening, but relaxed.

"And we used to sneak off and play in these caves that were just outside of town," she said, remembering hours chasing him down dark tunnels. Scaring themselves at every turn. It was a miracle they never lost their way for good. "And we used to practice wheelbarrow jousting together."

"What the hell is wheelbarrow jousting?" Twila propped herself up on an elbow, interested.

Rolina laughed, "It's exactly what it sounds like. We weren't old enough to compete, but we were certain we'd be champions." She remembered the wheelbarrow was too heavy for either of them to lift, so instead they just ran at each other with sticks and called it 'training.' "I wonder... I hope I have a chance to see him. Before Eden marches me back to the forest." It was the first time she allowed herself to look beyond her mission. To think of the home left behind, and not just the people she needed to save. To dream of a friend once lost.

Twila scrunched up her face, "If Eden tries to take you home before you get the chance, don't let him. I want to see this 'wheelbarrow jousting.'"

Rolina chuckled, "Easier said than done." Eden was a soldier first, and he had orders to follow. Still, if she asked him, he would at least try to drag his feet long enough for her to see her old friend. She lay against the earth, beside Twila. "Thank you for coming with me."

Twila waved her hand dismissively, "I needed to get away, even for a few weeks."

"I hope your Father does what you asked him to," Rolina said, slipping her hand into Twila's. "That he finds a common ground with the empire. Even if it's tiny, it's a start."

"Me too," she replied, her voice going quiet.

"Are you worried about him?" Rolina asked, sensing the shift in her friend's tone. "Or are you afraid he'll be angry with you?"

"Both," she answered honestly, "and more."

"Like what?" Rolina prompted, once again reaching for that unspoken thing hidden beneath Twila's words.

"Nothing really." She changed the subject, "We should rest. I'm sure tomorrow is going to be an exciting day."

Rolina nodded, but how could she sleep? Tomorrow would find her home and with her family. With Eden. As close to a perfect moment as she could imagine. Eli would have to be there too, to make it really perfect, but this was enough. What would they think of her? A farmer's daughter turned Lady of Syytan Empire. Their girl transformed into a woman. A smile tugged at the corner of her lips. She imagined warm embraces and awestruck eyes. And pride. Pride for the woman who risked everything to save them. Pride for their daughter.

Pride from another set of eyes.

Cold gray ones.

The end came. Eden sensed it. The desperation in the air. The hopelessness in the rebels' eyes. They could not win. And now, they knew. Their lines worn down to a broken remnant of soldiers. Tasa pulsed, sending a thrill from her blade into Eden's hand. More soldiers chose to flee than to face him. The reaper who took the souls of those before them. Eden the Brutal, The Blessed of Chyddan.

Killer of Men.

His own soldiers stood strong, riding the tide of battle towards victory. Brave beside his legend, willing to die for it. For him. For the families they left behind. For the world in need of salvation. They fought for deeper things than Eden, who relished the act of war itself. Their lives worth more, cherished by wives, children, brothers, sisters.

Eden the Brutal, Cherished by None.

He tightened his grip on Tasa, swinging the blade up to cut across a rebel's chest. The man fell. Eden continued on. Beyond the pathetic remains of the rebel defenses, he could see their camp. Months he spent working towards this moment. Pushing them back. Breaking through line after line. If he took the camp, he took the battle. The rebels would see it fall and scramble. Their hope lost.

He marched on, cutting down soldiers as he went. A group of rebels saw him on course for the camp. They steeled themselves and charged in to stop him. Fools. Eden ran at them, a fiery glint in his eyes. He came in close then dropped, sliding over the bloody grass to cut low. Tasa caught two across the legs, dropping them to the earth. The others scrambled out of the way, losing their momentum.

Eden finished the maneuver with a roll, landing in a crouch. One of the remaining three thought to take advantage of his position on the ground. Running in with a growl, sword lifting to strike. Eden's sword met the soldier's as he stood, pushing the rebel's blade to throw the man off balance. Eden shoved him hard, knocking the soldier backwards as he prepared Tasa for a killing blow.

The other two ran in, but not before Eden drew Tasa across their ally's neck. One darted left, the other right, flanking him. But Eden knew they were slow. Saw it in their earlier reactions. When they came close enough to attack him, he dropped to the ground again. The men cried out, having cut each other instead of their enemy. From his place below them, Eden drove Tasa up under the chest plate of the man to his right. He fell beside the guardian. Eden jumped to his feet, facing the last soldier. The rebel took a step back, clutching his wound with his free hand. Eden glared at him with dead gray eyes.

He chose to run.

Eden smirked as he marched into the rebel camp. The handful of remaining soldiers between him and the camp put up little resistance.

They knew they were done, there was no hope of victory left for them. Eden's men kept the rebels at his back occupied as he marched into the camp. At its center, he kicked down the hastily made flagpole. The rebel flag dropped to the ground with a thud. It was the Kandston flag, deep blue with a field of wheat embroidered in gold, but with the words *New Empire* painted over it in red. A waste of paint.

He moved on, searching the camp until he found what he sought. A figure who had been absent on the battlefield. The coward general of Bane. Eden found him hiding in a tent behind a table. He gripped the terrified man by the shoulder and dragged him out into the open.

"It's over!" he shouted, pointing Tasa casually towards the squirming man. "Throw down your weapons!" The rebels, tired and defeated, obeyed without much resistance. Those who did put up a fight were quickly dealt with by the imperial soldiers. Eden relished the victory. After months of fighting, it almost felt too easy. But easy was good. Easy meant more survivors. Less soldiers trying to be heroes and dying for it.

Eden's men rounded up the rebels as he marched the general across the field. Dragging him towards the imperial camp. As he passed, many of his soldiers cheered or clasped him on the shoulder. He took their praise well, though refrained from any celebration of his own. It was just another battle in eras of warfare. But he understood the importance of recognizing his soldiers' mirth. Encouraging it. The victory would spur them on, push them to fight better with every success.

Eden marched the general to the main camp and through the entrance of a large tent. The command center. He found three high ranking soldiers within, discussing their next move. Their own general remained on the field, rounding up rebels, but these men would do. "Take care of him," Eden commanded, shoving the enemy general their way. "I'm leaving, you're in charge of wrapping things up," he said to one of them, a lieutenant, he thought, but wasn't certain. Eden stopped bothering with names and ranks centuries ago. If they looked important, they probably were.

The soldier began to stammer in protest, but Eden left without another word. Striding away down the hill. Through the hidden portion of the camp. It would be wiser to rest, but the battle had stretched longer than he expected. Longer than he told Dimitri it would. Even so, he would have found it difficult to wait another moment before following his next orders. To go after Rolina. Partly, he worried about her. Mostly, he missed her.

On the north side, he found their makeshift corral. Eden whistled. Not a shrill, commanding whistle, but a light, constant, musical note. A beautiful, big palomino mare lifted her head, trotting towards him.

"*Kier*, Alice," he purred, his voice soft, kinder than he used with people. "*Iha puell*," he cooed in his native Eldurian, stroking her nose. It took only a few minutes for him to prepare her for the journey. Speaking to her in Eldurian as he did, explaining their mission, even though he knew she couldn't understand. When he finished, he climbed atop her back. His fierce severity in sharp contrast to the beautiful, delicate horse.

"Come, Alice," he said, then clicked his tongue. Alice surged into motion. "Let's bring Rolina home."

26

Home

Home. A town in the distance, surrounded by lush, hilly farmland. Rolina's heart jumped. *Home.* The word reverberated deep in her chest. Somewhere within her, she remembered the view. The decade hadn't stolen it from her, only buried it. The peaceful houses woke her memory, stirred up images of bright summer days and cozy winter nights. Gaj lay unchanged after a decade.

She fought the urge to kick Tovi into a gallop. To leave Twila behind, heartbeat quickening as the distance faded and she was there. *Home.* Her family waited. Eden waited.

What if he did not? A familiar doubt crept into her mind. The battle in Bane had already stretched longer than the emperors anticipated. Evidence of how well Kandston had spread their misinformation and manipulated people across the continent. What if the battle continued to delay him? Dimitri warned her, the soldiers in Gaj would not believe she was who she said. All the more true now that her famed golden curls lay rotting in a forest, miles away. Unlike the guardians, she didn't have an enchanted tattoo or even the imposing presence to prove her identity. She needed a back up plan.

Rolina turned to Twila. She hadn't needed to wear Nox's face more than a few minutes in the last couple days. Perhaps she was rested enough to maintain a glamour of someone she didn't know quite as well.

"Why are you looking at me like that?" Twila asked, raising an eyebrow.

"Because I have an idea," Rolina grinned. "In case Eden isn't here yet, I need a back-up guardian."

Twila went pale, "You want me to glamour myself into Eden?"

"No," Rolina laughed, "If he *is* here, having two of him would only cause confusion. And trouble." Before Twila could start looking relieved, Rolina said, "I want you to turn into Iero."

"I don't want to impersonate a guardian," Twila hissed, her voice low as if someone might hear them in the empty, wide open roadway. "That's how you get executed."

"Oh please," Rolina waved the thought away, "If we get caught, I just need to tell Eden it was my idea. He'll understand."

"Eden the *Brutal* has never struck me as the understanding type," Twila pressed.

"He's more reasonable than you think." Seeing a familiar teasing spark light in Twila's eyes, she pressed on, "How do you think a camp full of *imperial* soldiers are going to react to the princess of a rebel kingdom? You need a disguise anyway, it may as well be a useful one."

"I don't have to tell them my name," Twila pointed out.

"Twila," Rolina fixed her with a stare that said, *you know I'm right*. "They're not going to believe I'm Lady Evensong if Eden's not there. And..." she pressed on before Twila could protest, "they'll know exactly who you are as soon as they see your ears. If Feinin really can't leave Kauneus, that kind of leaves you as the only possible option."

"Then we wait for Eden and tell them I'm an elf, not a Feinin." Twila turned her attention to the town ahead of them, attempting to end the conversation.

Rolina wouldn't allow it, "If it was your family, would *you* wait?" Perhaps the guilt tactic was a little much, given the tension between Twila and her father at the moment. But Rolina didn't want anything to go wrong. Not when her own family was at stake.

Twila's confidence faltered. "I… no." She rolled her eyes dramatically, "You promise you'll stand up for me if I'm caught? And that Eden will listen?"

"Of course."

"Fine," Twila conceded with a scowl, "I'll do it."

"You're a good friend," Rolina said, a smug grin on her lips.

"You're a terrible one," Twila said with a smirk that only grew as she continued, "First you drag me off on some adventure then you make me impersonate one of the second-highest ranking men on the continent."

"You're happy to be here," Rolina's smile turned to a knowing one.

Twila rolled her eyes again and said nothing more against it.

They rode into town, drawing the eyes of several citizens going about their daily business. Perhaps it was the Onschuldan horse. People from Ev had likely never seen a horse from so far away. She dismounted the horse, then hurried to the marketplace, hoping to find someone who knew where the soldiers were camped. Her feet knew the way. Days spent exploring her little kingdom, remembered after a decade. She passed faces that seemed oddly familiar. People she must have known once. For the second time she wished Eden's jacket had a hood. The last thing she needed was some person recognizing her and stirring up the town. She was only a child when last they saw her, impossible to recognize, but she worried all the same.

Darting through the marketplace, she was pleased to find it nearly empty in the late afternoon. Fewer eyes on her, but still someone to direct her. She was told they were on the western edge of town, and her instinctual knowledge of the town's layout carried her there. Twila followed, stopping only to shift into Iero's skin.

"Don't forget the tattoo," Rolina reminded her, "That's how the guardians prove their identity."

"I know," Twila huffed, her voice still feminine. "But I've never actually seen it."

Rolina almost snorted at the voice coming from Iero's lips. She reined in her amusement to assure her friend, "Neither have they. Just make sure the eastern point is at the top, and that it moves to always point East." She paused to readjust her simple, stolen clothes. To make some attempt at looking more feminine. The result was marginal at best, but Rolina could only hope it helped.

Twila furrowed her brow, and said sarcastically, "Simple."

"You only have to hold it long enough to show whoever's in charge, then you can let that part of the glamour go," Rolina assured her.

Frowning, Twila nodded. "Let's get this over with. Hopefully Eden's here so I can turn back into *me*." She marched toward the camp, and Rolina hurried to catch up.

Dimitri told Rolina the platoon was small, but she expected more than the few, sparse tents before her. "State your name and business," a soldier asked as they approached, laziness in his Evyan drawl.

"Iero Anluan. Fighting rebels," Twila answered in a perfect Frostlander accent, though not quite an accurate match to the guardian's voice. Her tone was too... fancy. Like she came from Eira or some other nice, Frostlandian city, not the middle of nowhere.

The soldier couldn't tell the difference. He straightened, eyes going wide as they flicked to the insignia on Twila's glamoured shirt.

"Lady Evensong Antares," Rolina offered, "Also here to fight rebels."

This time the soldier's brow furrowed, and she noticed his eyes shift to her hair. She already knew she didn't look like much without her golden curls, but the glance irritated her. No, she didn't match the descriptions and rumors this man had probably heard of the beautiful, elegant lady. Her hair was hacked short and her clothes - men's clothes - were oversized and dirty. Her current style was more along the lines of grimy vagabond than imperial beauty.

"I, uh, Lieutenant Darragh's that way," he pointed over his shoulder to a tent, slightly larger than the others.

"Thank you," Rolina mustered whatever charm her looks allowed and flashed a sweet smile at the soldier. "Take the horses," she handed him Tovi's reins. Lazy or not, the men of Gaj knew their way around horses. Twila took the cue, passing the soldier the reins to her dark horse as they started towards the tent.

"I see the emperors sent their best and brightest," Twila whispered.

Rolina chuckled, but smacked Twila's arm, "Be nice, he's probably my cousin or something."

A grin flashed across Twila's stolen face.

They stood in front of the tent, and Rolina knocked on one of the wooden posts holding it upright.

"Who's there?" came a gruff voice.

"Iero Anluan, Imperial Guardian," Twila answered. Her smile told Rolina she had warmed up to the idea of lying through her teeth. A new challenge for the princess.

"What? Get in here!" the man snapped.

Pulling open the tent flap, Rolina let Twila step inside before her. A man in his forties sat behind a flimsy desk, built to be carried from camp to camp, lightweight and collapsible. He rose to his feet, nearly knocking the desk over as he barreled around it, waving his finger. "I don't know who you kids think you are, but-"

Twila casually opened her glamoured shirt and slid the left sleeve off her shoulder.

The man's eyes dropped to the tattoo, different than Iero's real one, simpler, and the ink was black instead of a deep blue, but convincing enough as the glamoured ink shifted with her movement. The man stepped back, "Apologies, sir, you'd be surprised the pranks the kids around here try to pull."

Twila looked ready to burst with laughter as she slid the shirt back on her shoulder and began buttoning the front, "Of course. You can never be too careful."

Rolina stepped up, impatient to know her parents' fate, "What can you tell us about the situation with the rebels?"

"And you are?" he scowled.

"Lady Evensong Antares," she answered as though it was obvious.

The man's brow furrowed. He looked back at Twila, then to Rolina again. A question formed on his face.

"Has Eden arrived yet?" Twila stepped in before Lieutenant Darragh could ask it.

"Eden?" the man's eyes widened in terror, "Eden the Brutal is coming? Here?"

Rolina's heart sank. Eden was not there after all. That meant her family wasn't safe. A tinge of guilt flicked through her. She had dawdled in that last town, helping them rebuild. That meant an extra day when she could have helped her parents. But then, could she really have left those poor townspeople to their misfortune? At least she thought of a back-up plan to prove her identity.

Twila pressed on, mumbling, "Typical," under her breath. "Communication's been a mess since this whole thing started."

"So, the hostages," Rolina pulled the conversation back on track.

"My scouts are searching the area, but no luck so far," he stated, shaking his head. "We'll be following a rebel, and the next thing you know, he's up and vanished in the hills!"

"The hills? You mean Blackburn Pass?" She knew the place well. At least, she did as a child. She used to play there with her friend. Tovi. Telling her ghost stories as they ventured deeper into its dangerous maw. Whispering about monsters in the caves.

The caves!

"I know where they are," she announced, almost surprised at herself. Standing in her childhood home, the memories came back, fast and clear. "There's a system of caves. The entrance is sort of squished under a rock. I can take you there."

"We've searched every inch of that pass," The man said, dismissing her.

"It's easy to miss," she snapped back. She'd traveled across a country widely unknown to her, pushed through fears and defended herself against bandits and scoundrels. A prideful lieutenant wasn't going to stop her now. "Check again."

The man shrugged, "You sure you know the way?"

"Yes."

"Come with us tonight then. They won't see us coming in the dark."

Rolina hated the idea of waiting, but the man was right. Stealth could be the difference between success and failure. And perhaps Eden would arrive by then. "See you at nightfall." Another doubt came to her as she spoke the words. What if she couldn't find the place in the dark?

"I'll prepare the men."

"We should prepare as well," Twila tugged Rolina's sleeve, guiding her out of the tent. "What do we do until then?"

"Reconnaissance," she announced. Tovi likely still lived in this town, probably worked in his family's tavern. Her memories were over a decade old, but his were fresh. He could help them find the caves. Even if he hadn't been to the caves in years, even if he couldn't help, she *wanted* to see him. He was one of few people she missed from Gaj. One of few she remembered.

Like earlier, her feet remembered the way as she set out toward the tavern. She was not allowed in as a girl, but she spent many an hour waiting outside for Tovi before they set off on a new adventure.

As they turned a corner, the tavern came into view. Rolina opened her mouth to tell Twila where they were going. The words never passed her lips. She took a breath, and a step, and a hand clamped down over her mouth.

Twila, walking beside her, reacted first. Starting towards her assailant with nothing more than gut instinct. Something sharp and deadly whistled through the air. An arrow. It thudded into her shoulder. The impact had her falling. Rolina reached a helpless hand her way.

Her assailant wrapped an arm around her waist. Rolina screamed. The sound never touched the air, muffled by the hand around her mouth. He pulled her away from the injured princess.

What was she doing? She needed to free herself before she could help Twila. Rolina jerked around, tearing and clawing to break free. She thought to bite her captor's hand, release a scream, bring help running. The way he held her, she could not get her mouth around his hand. She kicked and scratched. Tried to slam her foot down on his instep. The attacker lifted her higher. Her little legs fell short of their mark. She attempted a kick between his legs. Wrong angle.

Everything failed.

Rolina twisted her arm around to beat against the man's head. Ripping at his hair, clawing like an animal. Something hot and wet dripped down her fingers. Blood. She kept it up, though it hardly seemed to affect the man. A memory slipped into her mind. A single sentence muttered in a deep, Eldurian accent. *It only takes about seven or eight pounds of pressure to rip off an ear.*

She felt around the man's head for his ear and pulled. Her squeamish instincts resisted the violence. *Fight or die.* She pulled harder. From her angle, she couldn't see if it worked, but as her fingernails dug into his flesh, the man swore and pulled his hand away from her mouth. Wrenching her hand from his ear. She screamed. Drawing people into the street.

The people of Gaj were fighters, she was living proof. Already, she saw several of them snatching up things to use as impromptu weapons. But the threat of the townspeople only pushed her captor on. Pulling her down an alley as his hand slapped over her mouth again. Out of sight. Away from the princess.

A second man waited in the alley. He shoved something in her mouth and threw a sack over her head. Blind. She felt them binding her wrists and ankles. She tried to keep a little space between her wrists, so she could slip out later, but the man pressed them hard together. Hard enough to cut off blood flow. They hoisted her up over something. A horse, she realized as they bound her body to the animal.

Her breath came shallow and stuffy through the bag. The horse lurched into motion. Twila, bleeding in the dirt, could not protect her. Her heart pounded in time to the horse's hoof beats. Tears streaked down her face.

Eden will come.

It did not stop the tears, but her mind focused. The Eldurian would come, smiling like a dragon as he cut them down. No sooner would they toss her in some wretched prison than Eden would break the lock.

Her body shook. Helpless as if in one of her nightmares. Gagged. Bound. She could do nothing but focus on that image. Not a whimper could escape her lips. Swept away on the back of a horse. Her vision black. Eden would come. A greater threat than Twila or Iero or the worthless soldiers of Gaj. She saw the men who took her, who took her family, in her mind's eye.

Saw Eden cutting off their heads.

27

Blackburn Pass

Rolina's muscles burned. Her stomach lurched as the horse came to a stop. Someone pulled at the ropes binding her to the animal. They slid away as strong hands lifted her off the horse. She wanted to fight, but she could hardly keep her feet under her. Her captors pushed her over uneven ground. They spoke, their voices distorted through the sack on her head. A pause. She yelped, unheard through the gag. Startled as one of the men grabbed her legs, pulling them off the ground. She did not fall. Her second captor held her up by the shoulders. They moved on. The crunch of loose rocks under feet. After a bit of shuffling and scraping, they lowered her to the ground. Dragging her across the rocky earth. She squirmed and tried to kick the captor holding her legs. After a moment, the dragging stopped, and they placed her on her feet again.

She stumbled as they pulled her along. If she could keep track of the path, perhaps she could find her way out later. After a few sharp turns and meandering passages, Rolina lost all sense of direction.

So much for that idea.

A door creaked. The men threw her forward. Arms bound, she could not brace herself. Her chin slammed into hard stone floor. Pain shot through her face and head, trailing back into her spine. An alarmed cry sounded in time with her own. More hands were on her.

But they were soft. Caring.

Her bonds loosened. The sack came flying off her head. Dim light accosted her eyes, and Rolina blinked rapidly. "Poor thing," a gentle voice breathed as the gag was removed. Sorrow laced the words. As Rolina's eyes adjusted, she saw the figure of a boy sitting before her, examining her bruises. "What have they done to you?"

She pulled away from the stranger's touch, only to send a jolt of pain through her body. The ride and the impact left her aching.

He lifted his hands in a disarming gesture, "I'm not going to hurt you. I'm a prisoner here as well."

Rolina blinked, her vision began to adjust to the dim light. They were in a cave. With rough, dark walls. Unchanged by human hands, save for an oddly shaped door jammed into the entrance. A handful of furnishings graced the room. Four cots against the far wall. A splintery table with matching chairs. Blackburn pass. Rolina found the enemy hideout, just not the way she planned.

"What's your name?" the boy asked. His voice timid, careful.

"Evensong," she answered, studying him. Skinny. Small. Patches of dried blood and day old bruises on his skin. Young, maybe fourteen. Eli's age.

"Lady Evensong?" he blinked in surprise.

She nodded.

He shook off his shock and continued, "Well, Lady Evensong, that doesn't look good," he gestured to the rapidly developing bruise on her chin. "I can help, if that's alright?"

"How?" she asked, pulling further away.

"I can do a little magic," he explained, reaching tentatively toward her.

Rolina let him touch her. "What's your name?"

"Spirit."

"What do they want with you?"

"My magic," he answered, then muttered to himself, "I can fix this," before pulling his hand away. He shook it out in the air, then touched her chin again. The warm touch soothed. She hardly saw him before.

But the gentle stroke of his fingers on her chin filled her. His hazel eyes focused on his task. His face gaunt, starved. His body frail. How long had he been here, alone in the dim?

"Thank you," Rolina said as Spirit took his hand away. Her bruise vanished, the headache along with it. "What's special about your magic?" As far as she could tell, he was human, and with an accent like Haven's, he was from the Kandston countryside. That eliminated all possibilities but wizard magic. An apprentice. Nothing special.

Spirit shrugged.

She opened her mouth to ask him how long he'd been there when the door swung open behind her. Spirit's eyes went wide and he darted to his feet, skittering away to the edge of the cell. Two men stepped inside. Guards. Followed by two more, carrying something between them. A person on a stretcher.

"Twila!" Rolina jumped to her feet.

"Against the wall," one of the guards ordered.

Rolina didn't budge.

"It's best to do what they say," Spirit squeaked from behind her.

Anger thrumming in her chest, she stood aside.

They carried Twila across the cave and unceremoniously dumped her on one of the cots there. Rolina took a step towards the princess, but the guard repeated, "Against the wall." She remained where she was until the rebels walked out and shut the door behind them. Then she bolted across the room and dropped beside Twila.

The princess groaned, "Evensong, where are we?"

"Blackburn Pass," Rolina answered, studying the hastily wrapped bandage on Twila's shoulder. The red of fresh blood oozing through it. She turned to Spirit, lingering a few paces away, "Can you help her?"

"I… I can try," he crouched beside the cot and began studying the wound.

"Why would they hurt you?" Rolina breathed, taking her friend by the hand, "Did you tell them who you are?" She could understand it, if they thought she was imperial. But if they knew she was the princess of Illandia, it made no sense.

The princess nodded, then winced as Spirit tore away the bandage. "They don't care."

Confusion mingled with the rage in Rolina's gut. She heard the men speak, heard by their accents they were a mix of local Evyans and Illandian men. "But your father-"

Twila let out a bitter laugh. "He's powerless."

Rolina froze.

"It's Nox," Twila said, her voice dropping to a broken whisper. "They have him."

Pressure ached in Rolina's chest, squeezing her heart to the verge of popping. "What?"

"Cadogan had him kidnapped *months* ago," the princess trembled as her voice cracked, "Evensong, they said if Father didn't do what they wanted, they'd *kill* him."

Rolina opened her mouth to speak, but no words came out. Her dream returned to her. Cut after cut on Nox's body, blood pouring from his eyes. If they treated Twila so poorly in a matter of hours, what tortures had they inflicted on Nox? "You hardly had to think before you volunteered to come with me - to rescue my family - and you didn't think you could tell me yours was in danger?" She said the words softly as she brushed tousled dark hair from Twila's face.

Twila shuddered with a sob and gripped Rolina's hand tighter, "They said not to tell anyone. If they find out I told you-"

"I won't tell anyone," she swore, but her eyes darted to Spirit, carefully examining Twila's wounds. The princess wasn't thinking straight, wasn't seeing straight, if she was letting this tumble from her mouth in front of a stranger. The pain distorted her reasoning, and by the way her eyes locked on Rolina, she wondered if the princess even noticed the boy was there.

"I decided to come because it would give Father a chance," Twila explained through her shallow, broken breath. "The rebels couldn't blame him for staying in The Eternal Forest if it was to get *me* back. It would look suspicious if he didn't. And for a few weeks, he'll be safe. And perhaps, if he's lucky, he'll find a way to tell the emperors without *telling* them. And now I've ruined it. Got myself caught. I've given them more power to use against him."

Rolina finally understood the decision she had been trying to make sense of. The loving man who always treated her like a daughter hadn't fallen to the lies of the rebellion. He was trapped by them. Forced to give up control for the sake of his son. "After we save my family, we'll save yours," Rolina promised, though she didn't know where to start.

Twila shook her head, "We can't. We're trapped."

"Not for long," Rolina assured her. "Eden's coming."

A sad smile flashed across Twila's face. "And when he does, you can't tell him what I just told you."

"But he could-"

"If he finds out - if the emperors find out - Nox dies," Twila's grip on her hand tightened, desperate.

"What about Aurora?" Rolina asked, remembering the blindfolded girl in her dream. She hadn't seen her for as long as she hadn't seen Nox.

"We got her out. Remember that maid I told you about? The Taivan who helped father raise us after mother... after," her voice broke, but she pressed on, "She fled with Aurora to Taivas. Don't tell anyone that either. Only her, Father, and I know where Aurora is. And now you," Twila said, her voice flat. Tired. The panic was beginning to subside, but the exhausted despair settling in wasn't any better.

"I'm glad she's safe."

"*If* they made it," Twila said, her voice shifting into resigned sorrow.

"I'm sure they did," Rolina said, squeezing Twila's hand back. A comfort. A reminder she wasn't alone.

"Promise me you won't tell," Twila pleaded.

"I promise," Rolina said, watching the tears slide down Twila's cheeks. Feinin promises were sacred. More than that, *Twila* was sacred. This was a promise she could never break.

Her eyes drifted from Twila's face to her shoulder. The blood was gone. The wound healed. Entirely. Her eyes widened and she looked up at Spirit. He gave her a shrug and skittered away, sitting on one of the other cots. She needed to feel him out, see if he would tell what he'd just heard. If he did, would it be so bad? *She* promised not to, but if Spirit told the empire of Illandia's plight they could help, and she wouldn't have to break her promise.

"She'll be tired for a while," he mumbled, tucking his knees close to his chest.

"Thank you," Rolina said, awestruck as she looked back down at the nonexistent wounds. How could a boy like him heal so completely? Then again, Twila was half Feinin. Her own blood likely aided his magic. Otherwise, Rolina's own aches should have vanished entirely as well.

"Don't tell the wizard either. It still counts as telling, even in a dream," Twila said, pulling her attention back to the princess.

"I won't," she promised, though mentioning Maddy put another thought into Rolina's head. It was late afternoon when the rebels took her. She was not sure how long she was on the horse or being led through the tunnels, but it had to be late. Late enough to catch Maddy in her dreams. To tell him their situation and ask for help. "I should rest as well," Rolina announced. As she spoke the words, she realized how true they were. Spirit's magic helped, but her body ached from her ride on the back of the horse. Exhausted from a day of travel, topped by a kidnapping. She stood up and dragged one of the cots along the wall to sit beside Twila's. Then she plopped herself down, put a hand on Twila's face and promised, "Everything will be alright."

Blinded by a sack over her head, Rolina stumbled over uneven ground. Two firm hands pushed her along, rough and unfeeling. Her leg slammed into something made of wood, and she yelped in pain. Whoever guided her huffed, then grabbed her leg, lifting it onto the wood. Stairs. Awkward, blind, she climbed up each step as her captor continued pushing. Her bare foot fell hard over the air as she took one last step that wasn't there. Laughter rose from every direction.

Something brushed her face, though she couldn't make out any details through the sack. It came to rest around her shoulders, then tightened. She felt it then, against her throat, scratchy and raw.

Rope.

Light and color burst in the sky as the sack lifted free. Blinking in sudden daylight, she gasped in the fresh air. She stood on high, looking down at a crowd. Jeers and laughter threatened her on all sides. Beneath her, the splintered trap door of a gallows. An execution - her execution - but she didn't understand.

"I haven't done anything!" she shouted to the crowd, hoping for a sympathetic ear. Rolina made to remove the noose from her neck, only to find her hands bound. "This is a mistake!" she continued, struggling to pull her wrists free of the cords.

"There's no mistake, Rolina."

Her body stiffened at the voice, her eyes falling on the man seated before the platform. "Dimitri!" she cried, every instinct in her body to run to him, halted by a single length of rope.

"You left," he continued, voice casual. Bored. "You broke the law."

"We should have executed her the moment she stepped into The Eternal Forest," said Mercury, seated beside him. Rolina could've swore she wasn't there a moment ago. Her pale blue dress shifted and shimmered as she crossed her legs at the knee. Soft beauty out of place in the harsh crowd. She shared a look with her brother, amused, cold.

"I'm sorry!" Rolina's breath caught as she pleaded. Panic rose in her stomach. She was on the other side of the line. Something unfamiliar, unloved. She left and wasn't theirs anymore, nothing more than a problem. "I'll come back! Please!"

Dimitri waved his hand, dismissive as he leaned back in his chair, stretching his legs on a stool. "My sister speaks true. We're simply correcting our mistake."

"Mistake?" her voice cracked, seeing strangers in their eyes, "You love me."

The High Emperors laughed. Discordant, wicked laughter. "Did you really think so?" Mercury asked, her laughter subsiding.

"Why would we ever love *you*?" A cruel smile spread across Dimitri's face, "We are immortal, forever. You... you're just a blink in our lives. A speck of dust to brush away."

Tears streaked down Rolina's face, her throat tight as she whimpered, "How can you say that?"

"Because it's true," he said, and as he saw the words break her, he laughed. "What are you waiting for?" he asked, addressing the person behind her, the one who pushed her up the steps.

"Do it," Mercury agreed, a smile tugging at the corner of her mouth.

"No!" Rolina screamed, knowing it wouldn't mean a thing to these distortions.

She heard her executioner's footsteps come around from behind. Saw his face. Hesitation in every step as he walked to the lever that meant her doom.

"Eden?" she squeaked through the tears.

Looking down at her, he froze, jaw tight. Afraid to speak.

"Eden!" she begged, his own eyes looking back at her, not like the twisted abominations of Mercury and Dimitri below. "Don't do this, don't let them kill me!"

Pain flickered across his face, and he stepped towards her, away from the lever. Leaning down to her eye level, he murmured in his deep, Eldurian voice, "I'm sorry." The guardian pressed a quick kiss against her lips.

"Eden," she breathed, wishing she could reach for him, touch him, but he stepped away, "please."

The guardian turned his back to her.

"Eden!" she screamed.

He pulled the lever.

28

Lungs

Days came and went beneath the oppressive weight of the sea. Iero could not say how many. The passing of day and night occurred in a distant sky, above his ceiling of waves. He rested when he could. Though lying on the silty floor of his room for a few hours of fitful, inconsistent sleep could hardly be considered replenishing.

The sand and salt scratched at his skin, tainted it. Little particles coating his body and hair like some disgusting exoskeleton. Each passing second a trial. His heart pounded. Every tiny thing set him on edge. Iero considered himself a brave man, but fighting against his Frostlandian instinct to stay far away from open bodies of water was maddening.

He faced his time in Valtameri like a prisoner facing his sentence, counting each day until freedom. Until then, he spent his time among the elders of Valtameri, sitting in on their meetings, giving them an occasional push to find Hel faster. Trying not to think about Sikker, and what he would do when he saw him. Which was, of course, all he thought about.

The elder woman with green skin remained the only one to strike Iero as having any semblance of intelligent thought. The other elders must have felt the same, as she turned out to be their leader. Her name was Vi, and she led her people with a less-than-firm-hand. But she was kind, and Iero liked kind people. They were the ones who forgave him when he vanished for hours at a time, when he learned their secrets - kind people had secrets of an entirely different sort - or when he was simply rude, as he had a tendency to be when made to wait.

He had been waiting since he arrived in Valtameri. As the council members droned on about the recent discovery of a breed of fish not seen in the area for some years, Iero felt awfully tempted to say something rude. Not just rude, scathing. Something mean-spirited that would break through their thick skulls and force them to understand that his problem was far more important than a school of fish. But he couldn't settle on a satisfying enough insult, and Vi - unlike the others - did not deserve a single unkind word. He kept his mouth shut.

Iero floated about halfway up the room as he listened, fighting to remain upright. The Valtamerians had fins all over their bodies capable of stabilizing them with an occasional flick, but Iero had to kick or stroke or flail in awkward attempts at balance. He would have let himself settle onto the floor, but the elders tended to gather high up in the room for some unfathomable reason.

After a long, miserable wait, the elders called in a scout. The most recent to report on the mission to find Hel. They liked to spend a great deal of time and far too many words to say there was no progress at all. Each time, he nodded along and tried to find a nice way to tell them to try harder. Kail would know what to say.

Today was different.

Iero almost missed it as the scout driveled on about some dolphins she saw at the surface. He tried to listen, but the words were so dull he began daydreaming about the sun on his skin and crisp, dry air. And then, as she neared the conclusion that should've been something about optimistically finding absolutely nothing, she said, "He's on a ship called *The Eternity*."

Iero perked up, stunned and delighted by the prospect of real, actionable information. "Where is this ship?"

"It was last seen docked at Draven's Cove," she announced with a smile.

His heart lifted. The ocean's overwhelming pressure lightened. His way out revealed. "We should leave for the cove right away," he said, veiling the giddy feeling in his chest with a commanding voice he'd perfected over the centuries. "What means of travel is available to me?"

At this, Vi joined the conversation, "I had the liberty of having our ship lifted."

"Lifted?" Iero raised an eyebrow at her.

"We have only the one ship, and we store it here in Syvanin," her voice revealed a hint of excitement at the opportunity to use it. "When human allies need it, we lift it to the surface."

He did not know what to expect, but lifting a ship from the bottom of the sea took him by surprise anyway. How could such a thing be seaworthy after years marinating in saltwater? "Is there a crew?" Could creatures who spent their lives under the sea pilot a craft meant to glide above it? He couldn't sail himself.

"We'll be ready by morning," the scout assured him, and Iero found her cheerful tone of voice aggravating.

But he would be gone by morning. Sooner. The ship would leave by morning but, to Iero's delight, he could leave for the shore that moment. "Thank you," he told Vi and the elders, forcing the excitement from his voice. If he sounded too eager to leave, he might offend them. "I'll get my things, then I need a guide to shore."

"I will take you," the scout offered.

Iero was so pleased, he might have kissed her if the thought of touching her scaly skin didn't repulse him. The scout, his avenue to freedom, agreed to meet him outside the central spire after he collected his things. Iero thanked her again, then left to fetch the satchel stored in his room. He wished he had taken it with him, then he could leave from the council room. But he was afraid it, or it's life-giving contents, would drift away without his noticing. So he stuffed it in the cabinet in his room because it had a door with a latch.

He felt the eyes of the elders on him as he swam away. A slow and pathetic sight compared to the aquatic race. The constant swimming only served to solidify his hatred of the water. Feet were meant to be on the ground. As he swam through the uneven halls and passageways, he imagined breathing air again. The taste, the ease of it. Water in his lungs only weighed him down.

Halfway through the hall to his room, his gut lurched. Different than his usual unease. The water in his throat choked him. Choked him? Iero touched his throat. His body began to burn. No, not his body. His lungs.

The spell was wearing off.

Iero swam as fast as he could. The burning strengthened with every second. He was going to drown. Reaching the guest room door, he yanked it open, swimming for the cabinet in the wall. Strength giving way with every stroke. Body breaking from inside out. Centuries of life ending at the bottom of the sea. He always knew the water would get him.

Wrenching the cabinet open, he grabbed the satchel. His body shook, convulsed. He forced his hands into cooperation, digging for the ingredients. Already soggy with saltwater, he squished and ground them together in his palms. Unseen tears poured from his eyes as the burning peaked. Life was leaving him. Water poisoning him from the inside out. Iero shoved the repulsive substance in his mouth, swallowing it down through a mouthful of water.

The guardian gasped, water flowing through his lungs like air once more. Pouring in and out in deep, panting breaths. Floating limp in the water, his body shook. Half from pain, half from brutal, heaving sobs.

"I hate this place," he said quietly. Again, louder, "I hate this place!" He felt a strong desire to punch something, but there was no furniture in the room. So he slammed his hand against the floor. The water slowed the impact into an unsatisfactory pat that scattered the silt around his hand.

Giving up, he let his body settle against the scratchy sand floor. He didn't move for some time, staring at the room he hated. A fish swam in through the window, darting around curiously. Dozens of them had done the same since he arrived. Pests. His eyes followed the little thing as his breath stabilized. "I want to go home," he whined. He knew at least he would be out of the water soon, but on a ship full of fish-people, hurtling through the sea. "I want to go back to the forest with solid ground under me and air in my lungs. And sneak around and pick locks and sleep in my bed. Or any bed."

The fish ignored him, swimming to investigate his satchel as it drifted back and forth on the silty floor. It poked its face against the bag, curious.

Iero sat up and shooed the fish away. The remaining ingredients floated idly in the water, sinking toward the floor. Iero collected them and returned them to the satchel before slinging it over his shoulder. His breath restored, it was time to leave.

Iero had always been fit. Perhaps a bit malnourished during the winter months of his childhood on the Glacial Plains, but not since the day he first stepped into the snow, hungry and desperate. Not since the day he became the hunter. Even so, he had always been more lithe than muscular. Not like Eden or Bolwerk, who prided themselves on their strength and ferocity, or Kail, who liked the way people noticed his muscles through his tight clothes.

Iero was beginning to understand why. The days of swimming through Valtameri's undersea passages and halls had toned and sculpted his arms beyond anything they had ever been. And though he would never admit it, he liked the way they looked. Tough and attractive. It may have been worth the constant burn tearing through him with every stroke.

It was his sole consolation as he swam out of the central spire of Valtameri to meet his guide. He followed the scout through the deep waters, trusting her to detect currents he could not. The invisible roads leading back to shore. They told him it would take a day for a human to return to the surface, and though he dreaded every minute, he could see the end to his torment.

He did his best to keep up with the scout. Difficult, even as she made an obvious effort to swim slow for him. If this agonizing pace was slow to her, Iero could only imagine her full underwater speed. He was not a strong swimmer, and if he stopped to consider it, he would realize he was slow compared to other humans as well.

Determination made up for his poor swimming ability. The scout asked several times if he wanted to stop and take a rest, but he always said no. A few miles of water all that stood between him and fresh air. Even as his breath grew labored and his arms progressed from burning to screaming he did not stop. Hatred kept him going. Like Eden on the battlefield, his mind found a place where it couldn't feel the burn in his muscles or the exhaustion in his soul. But every man had his limits, and he was finding his.

Light shimmered above.

Iero's heart lifted. The surface. Still some distance above, but visible. Real. More beautiful than the daydreams that kept him going beneath the waves. Urgency surged through his body. He swam like a madman, muscles screaming to stop. The air and sky and sun just above him. Iero broke through the water line with a gasp. Coughing and gagging as the water left his lungs, replaced by light, refreshing air.

Breath.

The guardian laughed as he waded on the surface. Laughed at the open air and sky. He saw the shore, nearer than he realized. A smile spread across his face, pure and joyful. The scout broke the surface a moment later, her scales glistening in the sunlight. He saw the Valtamerian ship floating by the village. The bustling Valtamerians prepared it for the journey.

Iero turned to face the shore, forcing his aching muscles onward. Though the spell still worked in his body, he refused to dive back under the water. It would have been faster, but the thought of submerging himself again for even a moment repulsed Iero. Head above water, he breathed in the miracle of air, paddling like a child toward the earth. When he reached the shallows, he put his feet under him, walking through the sloshing waves. The Valtamerians ran to meet him.

As the laugh of a madman ripped from his lungs and the last of his strength gave out, he caught a final glimpse of the ship. The vessel that would take him across the sea to find Hel and his army. To find Sikker. A pulse of dread and excitement shot through his chest.

Then he was empty.

Iero collapsed on the soft, yet solid, sand.

29

Local Boys

Rolina did not tell Twila of her dream. She wanted to. Wanted to hear her friend's voice reassure her. It was only a dream. But how could she add any more sorrow to this place? When she woke, she did not know what time it was, or how long she slept. Only that she missed Maddy. Her timing off. No news to share, good or otherwise.

Across the room, Twila and Spirit sat against the cave wall talking quietly. The boy so thin and frail he looked like a skeleton. The least they could do was feed him. Rebel bastards.

As Rolina sat up, intending to join them, she heard the door clank, pulling her attention away from them. In stepped a pair of rebels. Tall. Rough. Armed. "You're coming with us," one of them announced, fixing his glare on Rolina.

"Am I?" Rolina made no move from the cot. Why, she did not know. They were bigger than her. Uninjured. On their own turf. Resistance was stupid.

One man stayed by the door while the other walked towards her.

"Evensong," Spirit warned, eyes wide, "Don't fight them, they'll only hurt you."

Rolina took in the bruises on his arms, the dried blood staining his clothes. She did not doubt it. "Fine." She stood, holding her head up with as much dignity as she could. "But cooperation goes both ways," she strode past the man walking towards her, "I go with you, you don't touch me." The men gave no protest as they led her out into the cave tunnels. One man behind her, the other ahead.

They did not blindfold her. Idiots. She took in the caves. The long tunnel leading from her cell into the dark. A light ahead. A torch. They followed it. The farther they went, the more light she found. They passed other tunnels. Other odd-shaped doors, adapted to fit the natural cave. Were her parents behind one of them? She noted which doors had guards and which did not. She would check every one if she had to. But she was smarter than that.

She listened.

"I don't see what we need with all these folks," one of the guards complained to another. A local boy, by his accent. Had she known him once? Or was he from some other corner of Ev?

"Did you see they took the Seelys? Kids and all," the second replied.

Seely. She almost remembered the name.

"No," the first shook his head in disbelief, "Even little Blaire? She's not even four!"

"Saw 'em throw her in with the other prisoners," he continued.

They were too far away to hear anymore, beyond vague mutters. Rolina did not miss the way he said *other* prisoners. As if they were guarding some of their own. She knew the first door to check.

Her guards led her through another strange door. A table and chairs sat in the small room. A man waited, his legs propped on the table. His eyes closed. They indicated for her to sit across from the man, then left the room. A plate of food and a cup of water waited for her. The man lifted his head as she sat, resting his tired, apathetic eyes on her.

"Thought you were supposed to be beautiful," he muttered, his Evyan accent just as thick as the guards they passed. Another local boy. Good. She had a hard time believing a boy from Gaj would hurt her. And he was young. Close to her age, no more than a year older. She hoped that meant he hadn't had time for life to harden him. To push him to acts of violence.

"Ever heard of a disguise?" she asked, using the fork they left for her to pick at the relatively tolerable food. Some sort of seasoned meat. Fresher than the stale bread she ate on her journey, but somehow worse.

"So, you're Dimitri's daughter," he continued, ignoring her comment.

Rolina tried not to scowl. How far did that rumor reach? No point in correcting him, she was valuable either way.

"I want to know what he's told you. Tell me, and you'll be treated well here," he promised.

Mercury always told her appearing weak and submissive had its advantages. Cowering before those who think themselves powerful blinded them to the coming dagger. Good advice if she had a dagger, but she lost it in her last fight and her sword was with Tovi and his gear. She chose to heed Eden's words instead. *Cowards will run from the strength in your eyes.* Lacking Eden's over six feet of height and muscular build, Rolina mustered up as much intimidation as her five feet and half an inch could, and lifted her eyes to meet his. "If I don't?" Not a question, a challenge.

"I'll let you know if and when we reach that point," he leaned back in his chair again, resting his head in one hand before continuing, "Let's not reach that point."

"Ask your questions," she said it like an order. The way she imagined Eden would. No one controlled the situation but him. She could do that too.

"Let's start small. Where are the guardians currently posted?"

Rolina snorted. "You consider *that* small?"

"We already know where to find most of them. What's one or two more?" A taunt. Meant to scare her. To make her think they knew more than they did. If he knew Eden was practically on their doorstep, he wouldn't act so calm.

"I'm not important enough to know things like that. I'm a pretty face they use to gain favor at parties," she said, dismissing the question.

"I suppose you aren't hideous," he said, tired eyes studying her face. "People like to tell pretty women things."

"Maybe boys like you," she replied with half a smile, sweeping her eyes over him as well. Not half bad. A bit disheveled and dirty. Undeniably a country boy. Strong arms and lazy eyes.

He returned the smile, and there was something sarcastic in it, something cold, "May I remind you, cooperation is in your best interest."

"How about a name, first?" she asked, leaning back in her chair as though it were comfortable.

With a scoff and an eye roll, he answered, "Tovi."

Rolina nearly tipped out of her chair.

Here sat the boy who brought her to the caves all those years ago. No wonder the rebels found the place. They had the same guide. How did she miss it before? It was all she could see now, the little boy she once knew. Written all over his face. Even in his sleepy eyes. "Tovi." The name slipped breathless through her lips.

He squinted at her, "You have a problem with my name?"

"No," she scrambled to recover, "You have the same name as my horse." She named it after him. After the boy she spent hours exploring the limits of their town with. Darting through dark tunnels and bright avenues.

"Your horse?" he rolled his eyes. "Stop wasting my time and answer the question."

She should tell him. He would remember her, remember the bond they once had. It would make him sympathetic. He would help her.

Unless he used it against her the way she wished to use it against him. She wanted to tell him, but if he knew her parents were locked up somewhere in those caves and didn't care, he wouldn't have sympathy for her either. Anger flared in her chest. Tovi allowed her parents to rot in a dirty cave. Tovi, the one she missed.

"I told you not to be difficult," he warned after her long pause.

"A threat, how frightful," she said, flat and sarcastic. Anger clawed under her skin, trying to break through to the surface. Leaning forward, she trapped him under her glare and hissed, "Tell me this, Tovi, how can you lock up your own people?" It was a stupid thing to say. She hoped he assumed she meant the people of Ev in general. Lady Evensong had no way of knowing Gaj was his hometown.

"How about this, then," he continued, ignoring her accusation. All business. A far cry from the adventurous, lighthearted boy she once knew. "Have any of the guardians, or emperors, mentioned anything about a stone? Where it might be?"

If the rebels wanted it, it was something powerful. Magical.

"No," she answered honestly, though her mind couldn't help but drift to her conversation with Dimitri and Mercury mere weeks earlier. About the nonsensical spread of Cadogan's troops. *He's looking for something.* Was it this stone?

Tovi leaned forward, their faces inches apart, studying her, "You're lying."

"I'm not." But a memory of yellow flashed through her mind. Dimitri's jade. The one he always wore. He never told her why it was important to him. Perhaps it was enchanted.

"What are you thinking?" Tovi asked, seeing the realization dawn on her face.

She should have hidden it better. She was smarter than this, she just needed to think. "I'm thinking you're a slimy, traitorous, pawn with breath like a dog's."

"I should have known better than to try and reason with the emperor's daughter," he rolled his eyes, then stood up suddenly. Rolina recoiled. "Next time you'll be dealing with someone a bit less nice than me. Back to your cell." He reached across the table and grabbed her arm.

"Don't touch me!" she ripped her arm away. Skin crawling. The backstabber had no right to touch her. "I'll walk on my own." Even in her rage, she had the foresight to slip the fork off the table and into her sleeve.

"You'll do as told," he barked, snatching her arm. Yanking her to her feet. He marched her out the door. The guards were gone. He was going to take her himself.

"Let go! You traitorous bastard!" she screamed, his touch toxic in her anger. Struggling and pulling, she could not escape, but she slowed him down.

"That's it!" he snapped. Taking her by the hips, he hoisted her over his shoulder and kept walking.

"Put me down!" she shrieked, kicking and hitting. Blind rage taking control. He did not slow. "Tovi David Tavner, put me down!"

He stopped.

A mistake. She let it slip by without thinking.

He set her down, turning her to face him, "How do you know my full name?" Gone was the uncaring, indifferent interrogator. Here was a question he *needed* to know the answer to.

"You're hearing things," she shot, using her anger as a poor attempt to cover her error. The damage was done. She hadn't even realized she remembered the name until it came spilling from her mouth. "Have you been drinking? You look like the sort to drink." His parents did own the local tavern. Not that she was supposed to know that.

"How do you know me?" he demanded.

"I don't," the conviction slipped from her voice.

"Tell me," he shook her once, on the edge of snapping.

Iero would know a lie worth believing. Something simple and half-true. She couldn't think like Iero. So she did the last thing she wanted to do. Told the truth. "I am not Dimitri's daughter, and I was not born in The Eternal Forest. I came from here. You used to know me."

"I would remember if I knew Lady Evensong," he snipped, his grip on her shoulders sending pain through her half-healed wound.

"That wasn't always my name," she confessed. No turning back. Her only hope lay in memory. In some spark of empathy hidden there.

Tovi studied her face again. Her eyes. Then he saw it. Saw her. "Rolina?" the name came out a whisper. His expression softened into wonder. "I thought you died."

This might work. Old memories held power. And there she was, a memory incarnate. His hold on her weakened. "I know the rebels have my family. Are they alright?"

He stepped back. "More or less."

They were alive! Alive meant they could be saved. "Where are they?"

"Why would I tell you?" he snapped. The shock worn off. The memory shattered. "I don't care who you *used* to be. You're Lady Evensong. An enemy."

"Do you really think what the rebels are doing is right?" she stepped closer so he had nowhere to look but her eyes. "This war is based on lies. Lies spread by Duke Cadogan and-"

"It's the emperors who are to blame," Tovi shot back. "They sit in their palace issuing orders without a care to who it impacts. And they use their guardians to crush any dissenting voice-"

"Lies," she interrupted, the anger reasserting itself in her chest. "Dimitri and Mercury work to end oppression and poverty in every corner of the continent. Cadogan twists their laws into restrictions, but-"

"Duke Cadogan is the only man brave enough to call them out," Tovi said, she could see in his face he believed it. "You may have been raised on their lies while they groomed you to be their little princess, but some of us had to go on living in the real world." With that final remark, he grabbed her by the arm, pulling her down the tunnel. "If I were you, I'd think long and hard about telling us what you know. We *used* to be friends. I'd like that to mean something, but it can't. Not if you keep defending them. Not if you stay blind to their lies." They arrived at her cell, a guard waiting beside the door.

As he unlocked the door, Rolina hissed, "It *does* mean something, Tovi." She thought about Twila, about the rebel princess staying by her side through it all. About the message it sent. "It means there's a link between our sides, a bridge. You and me, we can meet in the middle. We can fight to end this, together."

"There is no middle, Rolina. Not without one of us breaking." Tovi threw her into the cell without another word.

Rolina's heart shattered with the impact.

30

Healing

"Did they hurt you?" Spirit asked. He sat on one of the cots, his legs pulled tight against his chest. Defensive. Small. Rolina pulled herself off the floor and wiped the dirt from her clothes.

That bastard actually threw her into the cave. Where had the boy she once knew gone? Lost and twisted by lies. Duke Cadogan's lies. If only they could have killed Cadogan at Tavek and had it over with. "I'm fine," she huffed, marching across the cave toward Spirit. She slumped onto the cot beside the boy, resting her back against the rough wall, looking out at the cave. It was just the two of them. "Where's Twila?"

"They came for her a few minutes after you," Spirit answered, staring up at the dark ceiling. "What did they ask you about? They always ask me about magic. I guess I'm good at it."

Rolina's stomach twisted. Twila was twice as defiant as her. That combined with a less restrained interrogator could lead to trouble. Her eyes drifted to the bruises and cuts dotting Spirit's skin. Some old, some new. All brutal. Best not to think about it until they brought Twila back. "They wanted to know about a stone I've never heard of. And where the guardians are posted."

"A magic stone?" By his voice, Rolina thought the question was more to fill the silence than for clarification. Good. She was not in the mood for silence. Silence meant worry. Eden could not arrive soon enough.

"I don't know. Maddy taught my brother and I about magic artifacts and things, but I only paid attention to the legendary weapons." Like Tasa. She could not wait to see that nasty old blade and the man who went with it. "I doubt I would remember if he said anything about a stone." Perhaps she should ask him, if she could time her sleep better than before. No, then she would know things. Better to learn after she was free.

"And you don't know about the guardians either?" he mumbled, peering out from behind his knees. How could a person become so timid? So afraid. If she could, she would lend him her courage.

"Maybe," she shrugged, "I've been gone for a few weeks and things change fast, but I knew where a few of them were. Though I never know where Iero is unless I have my eyes on him." She knew exactly where Maddy was headed. Just as soon as his leg healed more substantially.

"That's for the best," Spirit said, "They can tell when you're lying. That's probably why they didn't bother hurting you."

Rolina bit her lip. It was only a matter of time before they asked her a question she *did* know the answer to. Before they asked Twila. She could only hope Eden arrived before then.

"What are they like?" Spirit asked, breaking Rolina from her thoughts.

"Who?"

"The guardians," Spirit said, a hint of genuine interest in his voice. Rolina didn't blame him. Commoners knew little of the guardians beyond their legends. Even the nobility only knew the surface. The faces they put on at parties and negotiations. Rolina knew more. Saw glimpses of their hearts.

An impossible question. Each one was full of life and memory, and for some unfathomable reason, they cared for her. "Old," she answered, she could see it in their eyes, "but, awake." She smiled, picturing their faces in her mind's eye. Memories of vivid days and kind, perfect nights. "Iero's tricky, everyone knows that, but people seem to think they can outsmart him. They can't. Maddy - sorry, Madara - is brilliant and won't shut up about it." This drew a chuckle out of her before she continued, "Kail's not the brightest, but he's smarter than people think. He knows how to charm." Her mind skipped over Bolwerk and Haven, jumping to Eden. He made her think of the sun on her skin. Of laying out in the garden after training. Of old stories and hidden evils. He made her want to stand up and punch her way out of the caves right then and there.

Spirit didn't push her to tell him about the other three. He was too timid for that. "What about the emperors?" he asked instead. At some point as he listened, his body loosened up. No longer using his knees as a shield.

"I'm not Dimitri's daughter," the words came out more forceful than she expected.

Spirit pulled back, mumbling, "I didn't think you were."

"Sorry," she flashed him an awkward smile, "people tend to assume."

"It's strange, from what I hear, he's sort of... harsh. But he likes you. What's that like?" Spirit asked, easing up again.

"What do you mean?" Rolina almost smiled at Spirit calling Dimitri harsh. A boy as timid as Spirit probably thought everyone was harsh.

"He can't exactly be warm, can he?" Spirit's words came out soft, almost inaudible. As if afraid his questions would upset her.

"He's not exactly cold either," Rolina defended. A shield wrapped itself around her heart. Instinct told her not to talk about The High Emperor in a personal way. The word 'warm' sounded too similar to the word 'weak' in her ears.

No, that wasn't it. Her reluctance came from somewhere deeper. More personal. Dimitri was *hers.* She knew by the way he treated her. Different than the guardians, than the nobility, than Eli. Different than Mercury, the only person she knew with certainty he loved. His warmth belonged to her.

"Exactly," Spirit continued as though he hadn't noticed her defensive tone. "It's strange he cares for you. At least to someone like me who doesn't know him."

Rolina smiled sadly, "I suppose it is peculiar." She offered him a shrug then changed the subject, "What about you, Spirit? How did you end up here?"

The boy shifted, uncomfortable. But he offered up a slice of information, as if testing he could trust her, "I've been a captive of Kandston most of my life."

She gaped at him. "They took you away as a child?" The cruelties of Kandston and the rebels never seemed to stop shocking her.

He nodded, tucking his knees up close to his chest again. "They heard about my powers and thought it could be useful." His voice dropped to a whisper as he added, "I don't think I'm very useful though."

By the bruises decorating his skin, Rolina assumed the rebels didn't think him particularly useful either. "What makes your magic special, Spirit?" As far as she could tell, he was an apprentice wizard. Except, he'd called them *powers.* As though the magic came from within him. Not from dedicated training like a wizard. Impossible. He couldn't be an earth born. They were gone. Except for Maddy.

Weren't they?

"I don't know. I guess I'm good at it or something." He shrugged in a defeated sort of way. "At least I'm decent with healing."

"Um, Spirit, have they ever called you anything in particular?" she prodded, hoping to learn the truth. If earth borns were returning, Maddy would be beside himself with joy. "A wizard? A magician? Or perhaps something to do with the earth?"

At her last question, he tucked his knees in closer, a suspicious glint in his eyes, "Why?"

Rolina dropped her voice to a whisper, "Spirit, are you an earth born?"

"No," he answered too quickly, his eyes wide as he studied her. Clearly the rebels hadn't taught him how to lie. "I don't even know what that is," he added, brow furrowed with fear.

"It's alright," she whispered, excitement growing in her chest. "I know someone who can help you."

Some of the fear broke to a sorrowful sort of hope, "You do?"

"I'm Lady Evensong, remember? I'm friends with the most powerful earth born wizard in history." She chose a smile just for him, one full of hope, gentleness, and just a touch of sympathy. "When we get out of here, you can come with me. It'll be safe for you in The Eternal Forest, and Maddy can teach you how to use and control your magic."

"You would do that? Take me to your home?" he asked. In the dim, she almost missed the tears lining his eyes.

"Yes," she promised, daring to reach for his hand. The boy let her take it, though he didn't stop hiding behind his knees. "It's time to bring you out of the dark, Spirit."

In the last fourteen thousand years, the town of Gaj changed very little. As the world cycled through hard times and good times, Gaj remained resilient against the dark. Correcting itself to the same sleepy farm town.

Eden saw the humble place in a new light. This was the town where Rolina was born. These were the streets she haunted as a child. The place that provided her to him. It didn't suit her. The dull, backwater burg fit dull, backwater people. Not the lady he knew. As he rode through the town, he decided it was never meant for her. Just a stopping point on her way home. On her way to The Eternal Forest. To him. A place springing with life, not sleeping it away.

More than a few eyes followed him. The attention of strangers was nothing new. The dried blood and other traces of Bane hardly made a difference. His disheveled hair and beard - grown far past their usual length - didn't matter either.

They would know him by his eyes no matter how he appeared.

The dull, silver eyes of a hell born. Empty. Cold. Unwelcome. Mothers herded children indoors as he passed. Men wrapped protective arms around their wives. Old and young watched him with wary faces.

"*Heikkem ihmsi*," Eden swore under his breath. Alice snorted as though she agreed. The guardian gave the horse an appreciative pat before dismounting. Walking put him on the same ground as the people who feared him, instead of towering above. A small thing, but a step towards trust.

He walked among them, searching for a familiar bundle of golden curls. He was not surprised when he made it all the way across town without spotting her. She was either under the care of the soldiers there, or at her family's farmhouse.

Eden entered the encampment at the edge of town. Unimpressive after several months in Bane, where their camp functioned as a fully-operational battle station. He walked on, assessing the level of incompetence he was dealing with. They let him closer than he liked before a pair of soldiers noticed and came to speak with him. Quite the oversight to let an armed hell born into camp.

The pair glanced nervously at one another, silently deciding which of them had the misfortune of speaking to the imposing hell born.

Eden spoke first. "Direct me to your commanding officer."

"Excuse me for asking, uh, sir, but what's your business here?" one of the soldiers stammered in a thick, Evyan accent. Eden could barely understand the man. It was hard enough to understand Syytan when it was spoken properly.

"I am Eden Anluan, Imperial Guardian. I will discuss my business with your commanding officer," Eden stated, watching the soldiers go pale.

"Lieutenant Darragh is that way," the second soldier pointed, all too happy to pass the hell born on to someone else.

Eden shoved Alice's reins into the soldier's hand and ordered, "Take care of her." At least these backwater idiots knew their way around horses. Eden marched on, following the soldier's directions to a small tent near the center of camp.

Lieutenant Darragh stood outside, talking with a man in civilian clothes. Their voices low. Eden's keen ears picked up every word, even at a distance.

"How are the villagers?" the Lieutenant asked.

"Recovering," the civilian said, "Their injuries weren't terrible. The rebels left as soon as they had what they wanted."

The Lieutenant shook his head, "I should've sent some guards with them."

Eden's presence stole their attention as he approached. "Lieutenant Darragh?" Eden offered the soldier his hand to shake in an effort to be polite. Politeness was always an effort for him. "Eden Anluan."

The civilian shrank back.

Darragh took in the violence decorating Eden's body. The blood and filth. "Sir," the soldier shook his hand. "We didn't know you were coming until yesterday, so I apologize if we're a little unprepared."

He knew he was coming. Good. Rolina must be there. Right on time. If only he had come sooner. If the battle ended a week ago, he could have greeted her with her parents at his side. Free and safe. "I assume Lady Evensong and the princess arrived?"

"The princess?" Darragh raised an eyebrow, "I don't know about any princess. She was with Iero Anluan.

"Iero?" Why send another guardian without informing him? And what of Twila? Understanding dawned on Eden as he remembered Twila's glamour abilities. She wouldn't be welcome in an imperial camp as herself, and a bit of authority couldn't hurt their chances of being taken seriously. Still, he didn't like the idea of anyone parading around in Iero's skin. "Where are they now?"

Something between shame and embarrassment flashed across the lieutenant's face, "There was an incident in town. They were taken."

Daggers shot through his heart at the thought of Rolina in danger. In pain. He masked the panic, pretending to care no more than duty required. Eden learned long ago to suppress his immediate reaction. Especially when it meant displaying any weakness. Or attachment. Watching over her was his job, nothing more.

The image of Maddy with blood leaking into his eye flashed through Eden's mind.

He shook it off. He wouldn't let them harm her. "What are you doing to resolve the situation?" They shouldn't have let her out of their sight.

"We haven't been able to locate their hideout," Darragh explained, voice small. "We know it's somewhere in Blackburn Pass."

"If you know it's in the pass, why haven't you found it?" Eden demanded.

"There are too many enemies, we don't want to act until we're certain where to-"

"You could ask one of the rebels." The way Eden said 'ask' held the vague implications of ripping someone's throat out. Nothing left to say, Eden started towards the hills.

"Sir, may I ask where you're going?" Darragh called after him.

"To clean up your mess."

31

Tovi

Eden crouched behind a pile of rocks in Blackburn Pass, peering through a break in the stones. Stealth may have been Iero's specialty, but Eden knew how to keep quiet when needed. Rebel soldiers patrolled the area, and Eden had his eye on a specific one. The soldier in question was tall, burly, and in the unfortunate position of being the closest. Growing closer by the minute.

Gravel and dirt crunched under the man's boots, and Eden smiled. Just a few more steps, it would be all too easy.

The man stopped.

A dozen curses shot through Eden's mind, but he managed to hold his tongue. Eden watched the man scan the area for enemies just like him. Watched and wished he would take another step, even just one.

Too much to wish for. As far as he could see from his limited perspective, there were only three other soldiers in the area. One up on the far side of the pass, surveying the rocks and brush. Two others in the middle, blocking the way of any would-be passersby, claiming the area as the rebellion's. If he was quiet, careful, they might not notice.

The man turned his back. Eden didn't hesitate, lunging out of hiding to grab the man around the mouth and pin his arms behind him. "Not a word or you're dead," Eden hissed, pulling the struggling man behind the rocks. Eden peered between them, checking if any others had seen them. They made no moves to indicate they noticed, but the rebel across the pass was turning to look in their direction.

Time to leave.

Eden heaved the unwilling man toward a glade of trees breaking through the rocks. The move took seconds, even with resistance, but it was enough time for the rebel to notice his ally's absence. He shouted across the pass, alerting the others. Eden had no time to waste.

He pushed onward, dragging the struggling man with him like he was no more than a child throwing a tantrum. The rebels were moments from searching the area, from catching up, outnumbering him. Even as he hurried away, he felt Tasa thrumming in her sheath, pleading with him to stop, turn, fight. Now was not the time. Eden flew across the rocky earth, never slowing to look back. Rolina needed him, and the man squirming in his arms was his path to her.

Try as she might, Rolina couldn't catch Maddy in her dreams. Whether she had timed it wrong or there was some sort of magical blockade in the caves, she didn't know. She woke at what may or may not have been the next morning to find Twila still fast asleep beside her. When she returned from her interrogation, Twila told her they wanted to know if the empire knew anything about their plans. If she or father had betrayed them. They must have believed her answers, as there were no new bruises to be found on the princess' tan skin.

Spirit slept on the furthest cot from the girls, curled up tight. As if he felt pressed to defend himself even in sleep. His cot had a single, scratchy blanket with a few holes. Pathetic as it was, he had it pulled up over his head as if it could protect him. Poor thing. She could only hope his dreams were happier than his life.

Rolina stood, thinking to stretch her legs and try to come up with a plan of action. As confident as she was that Eden would come for her, she couldn't wait around for rescue. If Eden wasn't already there, then the battle held him up. She had no way of knowing for how long.

Before she made it more than three steps, she heard the tell-tale clink of the door.

She froze. Spirit jumped awake and sat up sharply. The two of them watched the door as Twila continued to slumber. It swung open, but rather than big, intimidating guards, there was only a boy. A boy Rolina knew.

"Tovi," she said flatly.

"With me," he ordered her, then turned and started away.

Rolina scowled, but wasn't about to miss a chance to learn more of the layout of the caves. She hurried after him, shooting glares at the guards posted just outside the doorway. They locked Twila and Spirit back up as Tovi led her away.

Rolina hurried to walk beside him instead of behind him. "Where are we going?"

"Shut it."

Rolina bit back the words, *aren't you just a bundle of joy,* and lied instead, "I'm sorry I was so upset before." The traitor deserved every last vicious word.

Tovi paused to study her in the torchlight. "I'm glad to hear you say that." He kept walking. Did that mean he believed her? Those apathetic eyes shielded his intentions.

They passed the room she had been taken to before. Rolina stifled a smile. Tovi was showing her more of their hideout, whether he meant to or not. She did her best to memorize the turns and splits in the cave. There was no way of knowing if he was leading her deeper in or further out, but knowing the path was better than nothing.

A few more turns and they stepped out into a large cavern. Rolina balked. The place was crawling with rebels. Weapon racks lined much of one wall and soldiers trained nearby. Across the cavern more soldiers ate and socialized, the area set up like a mess hall. This had to be the heart of their operation in Gaj. If Dimitri knew just how many rebels were holed up there, he wouldn't have hesitated to send in his soldiers.

"Come on." Tovi started to reach for her arm, but she jerked it away.

"I can walk on my own," she hissed, then kept going. Eyes turned her way as they passed, headed towards another tunnel branching away. News of her identity must have spread by then. Lady Evensong, powerful, knowledgeable, and excellent bait. They looked at her like a trophy. Like a sign. If they could catch the High Emperor's so-called daughter, they could do anything.

Her stomach twisted, but she kept her chin high. Let them see she was yet to be defeated. So long as Mercury and Dimitri ruled, she never would be.

At last they reached the tunnel and Rolina's shoulders slumped with relief. No more eyes following her. All but his, of course. She looked into Tovi's face, searching for a clue of his intentions. For any shred of the boy she once knew. He was blank. Empty. Eyes ahead as if he couldn't care less who was walking beside him.

Neither said a word until the sounds of the soldiers in the cavern had at last faded. Torchlight became scarce, as if this part of the caves wasn't used very often. The perfect place to kill her, if he chose to. "I kept coming here after you died."

Rolina studied him, but his stone expression hadn't changed.

"I kept exploring on my own. As if you were only lost, and I would stumble upon you at any moment." The smallest hint of a smile appeared on his lips, but he didn't look at her. "I used to imagine you laughing at me for taking so long to find you. But that part of the dream was always impossible. It could only happen if we had never changed. If we had never been separated. Never grown up."

At last, his eyes turned to her. He reached a hand towards hers, but she pulled away. "Can we forget, for just a moment, that we're different people now?" His hand remind outstretched between them, waiting, hoping. "Can you stop being Lady Evensong, and just be Rolina Cotter?"

"Can you stop being a rebel asshole and just be Tovi Tavner?" she replied, watching him carefully.

"Yes," he promised, "for a little while."

Slowly, cautiously, she took Tovi's outstretched hand.

And then he tugged her closer. Pulled her tight against him as his voice broke, "You're alive." Rolina blinked, stunned as she felt him shudder. A sob shattering everything between them. Tears pricked her own eyes as she returned the embrace. "You're home."

"I missed you," she mumbled, afraid to speak out loud lest she would break. But then, this was not one of the guardians. Not an immortal who thought her childish for laying her emotions bare. It was Tovi. Her Tovi. She spoke again, louder, even as the quiver in her voice fought to choke the words, "I missed you."

"Not half as much as I missed you," he replied, pulling away to look at her face. Tears streaked his cheeks. Clean trails through the dust and dirt from the caves. A wide smile bloomed on his lips. "Come on." He tugged her further down the tunnel. Rolina let him, her fingers laced with his as they had been so many times. Funny, how they still seemed to fit perfectly.

"Where are we going?" she asked, wary of the fading torchlight.

"Exploring."

She looked back over her shoulder. How far had they gone from the cavern? From her way out? "Are you sure it's safe?" The idea of wandering through a maze of dark caverns was much less appealing as an adult. Now that she understood she was far from invincible.

"It'll be fine. I've been this way loads of times." He crossed his heart the way he always had when they were kids, and the familiar gesture eased something inside her. No, she didn't trust him, but perhaps hope wasn't lost entirely. "There's something I want to show you."

Lady Evensong knew better than to let a rebel lead her into dark tunnels, but Rolina Cotter would follow her friend anywhere. She tightened her grip, trusting his experience to guide them through the dark.

"Did you know that these tunnels stretch all the way up into Eldur?" Tovi asked her, a bright smile on his face.

"No, I didn't," she answered, raising an eyebrow. She knew the mountain range grew larger the closer it got to Eldur. That the rocky, volcanic kingdom held mysteries of a grimmer kind. Perhaps it wasn't so strange to learn the tunnels ran that far.

"The further North you go, the more you'll find artifacts left behind from Eldurian attempts at conquering Ev," he told her excitedly. "I don't think they even know this stuff is here." He came to a stop suddenly. Rolina squinted in the dark tunnel to try and make out what had caused him to stop. Was something out there? Some dark cave creature ready to eat them? All she saw was black.

"I'll give you a boost, shorty."

"Boost?" she looked up and could just make out some sort of ledge. How Tovi had ever found it was beyond her. He helped her up and Rolina found herself crawling through a tight tunnel. Where on earth was Tovi taking her?

"Just keep going," Tovi told her from behind. "The tunnel drops off after a while, so be careful you don't fall."

Great. That sounded perfectly safe. The further she went, the more unsettled she became. More than her usual uncertainty. Something... touched her. A force or spirit or something unnameable. It pushed against her heart, clawed at her ribs. But there was no way back, not with Tovi behind her. She kept going until she reached the drop he warned her of. Carefully, and with great difficulty, she climbed down from the tunnel. This side seemed even higher than the other. It would be difficult to get back up without Tovi's help. What if that was what he wanted? To trap her here so he could never lose her again?

She shook away the morbid thought. Her imagination was getting the better of her. What would be the point?

Blind, she could only hear as Tovi landed on the ground beside her. "Just a moment," he mumbled, his footsteps headed away from her. And then there was a spark, a flare, as a torch burst to life.

Rolina winced at the sudden light, but as her eyes adjusted, she saw where she stood. This was not the rough, natural caves she was used to. It was carved. Smooth and ornate. Tall and twisted pillars and little alcoves in the walls. Some sort of table in the center. An altar? A vase sat in the center with curling handles and strange patterns. Figures were painted on the face, but couldn't make out much detail as she walked nearer. That horrible, dark uncertainty crept over her. Heart pounding, she looked into the vase. It held some sort of liquid that she hoped was not blood. It didn't smell like blood, but her gut twisted into knots all the same.

"It's some sort of temple, I think," Tovi explained, walking around the edge of the room. "Maybe all this stuff is offerings." His torch lit up the alcoves carved in the walls, revealing glittering coins and golden idols. Ornate boxes that could hold any number of treasures. "I found it a few years ago and, well, I thought it was the sort of thing you would find interesting. Never thought I'd actually get to show you though."

"You don't... feel that?" Rolina asked him, looking back down at the dark liquid in the vase.

He nodded a little too casually, "It's like that at first. Kind of like something wants to reach out and choke you."

"At first?" she squeaked out, backing away from the vase.

Tovi crossed the room and put a reassuring hand on her back, "It only wants to frighten you, but I don't think it can actually do anything."

"It?" she snapped, glaring at him.

He gestured with the torch to the vase. "I probably should have warned you not to touch it, sorry."

"Why not?" she asked, taking a wary step away from him.

"Because it's creepy," he answered as if it was obvious. "Do you really think I would have left all these riches alone if I didn't think something would happen? I don't know for sure, but I'm not stupid. Eldurians worship demons, you know."

She knew better than he did, actually. "You think this is a demon temple?"

He nodded, then continued, "I think it's why we're here, but for some reason I can't bring myself to tell them what I found."

Rolina would have been excited if it weren't for that wretched *something* clawing at her heart. "What do you mean? The rebels are looking for a demon relic?"

"They're looking for magic, and they heard there was something here," he told her, walking towards the vase. "It has to be this, I'm sure of it, but..."

"But even though you believe in the rebellion, you're afraid of it falling into their hands. Into anyone's hands," she finished his thought, daring to join him by the vase. "Why tell me?"

"Because right now, you're my friend. The one I loved and lost and missed. You're just Rolina, and I don't want anything to happen to you."

Rolina slipped her hand back into his, "Come on, let's get out of this place. I can't stand it."

Tovi helped her up into the tunnel and they were off. Back toward the rebels. Back towards her little cavern cell. Now heavy with a new burden. They were after magic. Magic like Spirit, the first known earth born in centuries. Magic like that horrible vase and whatever demonic power it held. Magic like the stone Tovi mentioned, whatever that may be.

If he really wanted to be who they once were, he would tell her. As children they never a keep a thing to themselves, no matter how important or secret it was supposed to be. "Tovi," she asked quietly, "Can you tell me anything about the stone they're looking for? Why it's important?"

"I don't know. None of us do, really. Just that there's a stone that needs finding because it's magic could help us," he shrugged as they kept walking. "Don't know what it looks like or what it does. Makes you wonder though."

"Wonder what?"

"What the higher ups are keeping from us soldier boys." He answered so immediately and sincerely that Rolina didn't doubt him. He was worried. Deeply. That was a start. A hole to work at until she tore through the illusions of Duke Cadogan's lies. Until she got her Tovi back.

As the flicker of torches appeared in the distance, Rolina paused. She looked up at the first person she ever called friend, her heart sinking. "We can't be just Rolina and Tovi once we reach the cavern."

He nodded, expression somber.

"Then before they're gone, let Rolina give her friend something she always wanted to, but never had the chance," she said, taking his hand in hers. Rolina leaned forward and pressed a soft kiss against his lips. "Goodbye, Tovi Tavner."

"Goodbye, Rolina Cotter," he breathed against her lips. Then together they walked back into the world. The space between them wide, but warm.

32

Pet

Rolina walked into her cell, happy that no one threw her this time. Tovi gave her a small, solemn nod before locking the door. She turned away, wishing she could hold onto him. But he had made his choice to fight for the rebellion and changing his mind would take more than the few hours they shared. Still, if she could protect him from the war, she would.

"They took Twila again?" It wasn't quite a question as she surveyed the cell. Just her and Spirit once more.

He nodded from his place on his cot, looking as bored and timid as ever. Rolina didn't feel like being alone, so she walked over and sat beside him. Spirit eyed her, but didn't say anything against it. "You alright?" he asked quietly.

"Just sad," she admitted, staring towards the door. What would happen to him? He was just a soldier, like any other. Her mind flashed to the infirmary with Eli. The way he worked to set the rebel's broken leg. It made sense to her now. Rebel or not, she wanted every bit of luck and mercy for Tovi. She wanted someone who would choose a smile just for him.

"Did he ask you the same stuff?" Spirit asked, breaking her from her thoughts.

"No, um, I think he was just trying to soften me up." As she said the words, she realized they could very easily be true. He could be working their past friendship against her. She hoped not, but how could she trust him? It had been less than a day since he threw her on the floor of this very cell.

"At least he didn't hurt you," Spirit offered, giving her a weak smile.

"I don't think he will." She leaned against the rough cave wall and sighed, "Eden can't get here soon enough."

"He's really coming?" Spirit leaned forward slightly. "I heard you say something about him to the princess, but I didn't know if you meant it, or were just trying to make her feel better."

"I meant it," she assured him, sitting straighter. What was she doing, wallowing and worrying when she would be free soon? She needed to keep her chin up and wait.

"He'll help us? I've heard he's not very nice," Spirit said, half-whispering as if Eden might hear him and be insulted.

Rolina laughed, "He's not, but he likes me."

"Like how Dimitri likes you?"

It was *very* different than how Dimitri liked her, but she couldn't exactly tell him that. "Yes. Neither of them are very open, but that doesn't mean they can't care about people. Why do you think Dimitri is so good at what he does? It's because he wants everyone to have the best life possible. Because he wants to help and give people the tools they need to be strong and happy."

"But that's different than really loving someone," Spirit said, sitting forward. He was getting more comfortable with her. No longer using his knees as a shield all the time. "How did you do it? How did you make someone like that care?"

When they spoke about the guardians the day before, he didn't push her for more, though she told him very little. Why did he care so much about Dimitri? About how to get in his good graces.

If *she* wanted information from a prisoner, she would plant someone in the prison. A friend. A liar. To gently steer the conversation towards that information. She shook the thought away. Paranoia getting the better of her. "I don't know, we just get along. He likes having me around and I like being around."

"But what is he like? Really?"

The question grated her nerves. Why did he care? "Dimitri's favorite color is yellow." A useless piece of information. Harmless, even if her doubts proved true.

Spirit half-smiled, "Seems too happy a color for a man of his reputation."

He didn't push. Rolina's heart eased. He was only curious. "He has this-" She cut herself off. She almost mentioned the yellow jadestone he wore every day. Now that she knew it was potentially valuable, she needed to keep it to herself. "There are a lot of yellow flowers in the gardens," she said instead, "I think Mercury chose them for him."

"That's sweet. People always say she's sweet," Spirit mumbled.

"She is," Rolina smiled, her suspicions slipping farther and farther away. "A few years ago, Iero was in one of his homesick moods and so she gave him this silvery-white marble apple that came from the Frostlands." An apple like his favorite fairy tale. One of the many ways Mercury proved she noticed little things.

"Was it magical?" Spirit leaned forward. A bit more than simple curiosity.

Rolina's doubts returned in force. "I don't think so." What did Spirit care? It was only a chunk of marble.

And marble was a stone. Like the one the rebels wanted.

"I need to stretch my legs," Rolina sighed, reaching her arms over her head as she stood and walked across the room. Putting a few paces of distance between her and the boy. It was nothing. She was overthinking it. Spirit was a sweet, abused boy who healed her and Twila. He wasn't a rebel.

"It's nice either way, I just thought it might be magical like in the story," he said, watching her move across the room.

"You know *Alexander and the Apple Tree*?" she asked, uncertain if it was enough to make her trust him. To believe he was innocent.

"Doesn't everyone?"

She chuckled. The sound was forced. Stretched thin. "I can never tell the difference between common fairy tales and the weird stories Maddy used to tell me growing up." Even if Spirit was a rebel, he couldn't hurt her. He was so small and skinny. But he could call for the guards outside. Perhaps she shouldn't get so close to the door. But it was her only possible route of escape. *Pas*, she wished Eden was there already. "What about you?" she couldn't give anything away if she got him talking instead of her. "Do you remember anything from before you were taken?"

Spirit rushed through the answer, "Not really. Does Mercury give people valuable gifts often?"

He would not let the stupid story go. "Only once in a while," Rolina lied. Mercury was one of the most generous people she knew.

Spirit's eyes narrowed. "I knew this would happen."

"Knew what would happen?" Rolina decided it was better to stay near the door. Something scratched her arm as she moved. The fork she stole the day before, still tucked out of sight. She fiddled with the button on her sleeve, trying to position the fork for an easy retrieval. Far from an ideal weapon, but she would take it over nothing.

"Usually I take my time. Make friends. Build trust," Spirit stood and stretched his arms lazily. "But you went and said Eden the Brutal is on his way."

They shouldn't have spoken so freely in front of him when they first arrived. But Twila was distraught. She wasn't thinking. Neither of them were.

"So I rushed it," he shook his head, walking slowly towards her. He needn't hurry. She had nowhere to go. "I pushed too hard and you've figured it out."

Rolina dropped the act, "You're one of them." Back against the door, Rolina wished she could remember any handy, emergency lock-picking tips Iero may have let slip.

"It doesn't matter." When did his voice turn so confident? No more acting. No more hiding behind his knees and mumbling to draw out sympathy. "Trust me, it's in your best interest to talk to me," he continued, reaching behind his back. He retrieved a knife. Skinny or not, the blade put him at advantage in the confined space. There was only so much a fork could do.

He took a step closer.

Rolina gripped the door handle.

Spirit laughed. Useless or not, she had to try. "I like you, Evensong. You're... naive in the sweetest way. So I'll give you another chance. Tell me the emperor's plans, or suffer the consequences."

Rolina wanted to stand tall and unafraid but her legs shook. Trapped. Armed with only a fork. Stuck between Spirit and the door. No path out. "Do it then," she dared, her voice stronger than her trembling legs.

"I could kill you," he stepped closer. "Is your life worth their secrets?"

Rolina set her jaw firm.

"They really have you whipped," he mused, but it was the same for him and the rebels. "A little stray dog they took pity on. Too grateful to see their flaws."

"I'm not a dog," the words came out strained. Too tight in her throat.

"Oh but you are," he purred, twirling the knife between his fingers. "Dimitri's pet. He calls you Prayer, doesn't he? Are you his little pet Prayer?"

Prayer.

She heard the word in Dimitri's voice. Dimitri's Prayer. Not a pet. A daughter. A daughter of the most powerful man in history. Everyone else believed it, why shouldn't she? Time to inherit that power. Wield it. Find her own. Tears streaked her face. Her legs stopped shaking. Her eyes lifted to meet Spirit's, full of the fury of an empress. "Hurt me if you like. You'll be the one left bleeding in the end."

"If that's how you want it, little dog." Spirit surged forward.

Nowhere to go. She let the fork slide from her sleeve to her hand. Braced for the pain as she looked for an opening. Instead, a pressure at her back, pushing her forward. The door! Her eyes widened as she spun to face it. Guards dragging Twila back to the cell.

Spirit was distracted as well.

Rolina lunged as she rotated back around. Using her momentum to drive the fork deep into Spirit's chest.

The boy stumbled back, crying out in pain.

Rolina didn't have the time to see if he fell. "Run!" she bolted through the door, seizing Twila's arm. Yanking the princess free of the stunned guards. Twila cried out in shock. Rolina's strength lay in speed. Eden always said so. Small made her quick. She only hoped Twila could keep up.

"What's happening?" Twila cried, stumbling after her. Behind them, Spirit shouted at the guards to give chase.

"Spirit's a rebel," Rolina huffed. Where had she seen the prisoners? The guards talking about little Blaire Seely? She chose a path on instinct, following the lights from before. The tunnels grew brighter and brighter. There! The door. Rolina prayed to the Keeper her parents were behind it. "We have to make a stop!" Rolina told her friend, barreling towards the guards.

Fear flashed across Twila's face, but she did not slow. They separated, targeting one guard each. Rolina gripped her guard by the hair and smashed his head against the cave wall. She did not have Eden's strength, but the craggy wall did the work for her. The man slumped to the floor.

Twila, untrained, but brave, shoved the second guard and punched him as he tried to regain his balance. "Ow!" she rubbed her knuckles as she kicked the man between the legs.

Rolina snatched a ring of keys from her guard's belt, shoving it in the door as Twila worked to render her guard unconscious. Local boys. No match for the emperor's daughter and the princess of Illandia. Rolina threw the door open.

"Come with us!" she cried to the prisoners within. "Now!" The confused prisoners cowered at first, then saw the unconscious guards on the floor. A rescue. Rolina hardly had a chance to jump out of the way before they rushed through the door.

"Do you know the way out?" Rolina asked Twila on the slightest hope her connection to the rebels gave her more information. Freeing the prisoners was one thing. Escaping was another. At the very least it added confusion to the chase.

Spirit and the guards were gaining. They needed to move.

Her eyes fell on a face she had not seen since she was six years old. Her father. Carrying a young girl with an injured leg. Beside him, her mother.

"I think they brought me in from this direction," Twila said, taking Rolina by the hand. When Rolina did not move, Twila gave her a solid tug, "Evensong!"

Plenty of time for a reunion after they escaped.

Spirit and the others were just behind them.

The passage ahead was too narrow for such a large group.

As Twila worked to hurry them along, Rolina heard a voice speaking in a foreign, yet familiar tongue. The language Maddy used to cast his spells. Spirit. Rolina's heart leapt to her throat. She turned to see him preparing a spell. His hand blazing with electric energy. He pulled back his arm, aiming for the group. No. Not the group. Her and Twila.

"No!" she shouted, pushing Twila out of the way. The energy slammed into her chest. Shooting through her body. The pain pulsed from her chest to her extremities and back again. Over and over as she fell to the ground.

"Evensong!" Twila started towards her.

"Get them out of here!" Rolina screamed through the pain.

Twila hesitated, looking down at her convulsing friend. She was a princess, taught from birth to put her people above herself. These people were not her own, but the instinct remained. She ran, ushering the group along without another look back.

"After them!" Spirit growled, but his pursuit stopped. As pain shot up and down her body, Spirit stood over her. Watching, breathing heavy. "I would have shown you mercy," he said, lowering himself to the ground. With a snap, the pulsating magic vanished. His hands dug into her. Flipping her over, pressing her head against the floor as he straddled her. "Your loyalty is disgusting," he snarled in her ear, tracing the knife against her back, ripping her shirt and Eden's jacket open in a clean line.

Body quaking, she clenched her jaw, unwilling to show him the fear he desired.

He laughed, light, pleasant. "Dimitri keeps such well-trained pets," he teased, stroking the knife along her spine. When he saw how the touch made her quiver, he smiled like a cat playing with a mouse.

The knife dug into her back.

Rolina screamed. Scalding pain ripped through her body. Worse than the magic, worse than anything. Hot blood poured. Dripping down her back. Her sides. The floor. Drenching Spirit's hands as he carved. She thrashed, desperate to free herself. He was stronger and she couldn't think through the pain. Could hardly feel anything but the searing burn. Screaming, Rolina wished for relief, to pass out, to go numb. Her nightmares showed more mercy.

Satisfied with his work, Spirit pressed in close, his chest against her freshly marred skin. He put his lips to her ear and whispered, "Feel like talking now, pet?"

33

Into the Caves

Eden wiped the blood from his hands onto his long, gray coat. Bound to a chair provided by the soldiers of Ev, the beaten form of the kidnapped rebel, spitting gobs of blood. It was messy, it was crude, it was nothing Eden hadn't done before. By now, the rebels would know their scout was gone and the imperial men of Gaj had something to do with it. Eden did not care. He had what he needed. Information on the entrance to their hideout in the pass. The rebels would not harm anyone else.

Eden stood and walked out of the tent, catching the attention of a wide-eyed, young soldier nearby. "Clean that up for me," he ordered, gesturing at the tent. He left the rebel alive, but it wasn't pretty, and he wondered if the soldier would have the stomach to do what needed to be done.

That was not his concern. Rolina needed him like she never had before. He would not fail.

Voices caught his attention before he made it more than a few steps. Across the camp. He turned his gray eyes to find Lieutenant Darragh and several of his soldiers facing another group. By the way the newcomers stood, Eden knew they were soldiers. Real soldiers. Not like Darragh and his platoon of idiots. They were steady, uniform, alert.

And as he came closer, he saw the symbol on their chests. A ram. The symbol of Illandia. In the center of them stood a familiar face.

King Farran Darville.

Eden resisted the urge to roll his eyes and strode through the imperial soldiers to stand beside Lieutenant Darragh. Face to face with the king. Darragh started to say something but Eden raised a hand to stop him, addressing Farran directly. "Are you here for your daughter, or to cause trouble?"

"I came for both Twila and Evensong's sakes," he said, holding Eden's gaze.

"Then we're allies for the moment," Eden said, turning on his heels and starting back towards the mountains. "Come. Leave your men here, they'll only slow us down."

Farran tossed a glance at his soldiers, "You heard the man. Wait here." Then he followed after Eden. The king and the guardian walked on in silence.

Burning. Bleeding. Rolina passed through waves of semi-consciousness and delirium. If only she could wake up. If only she could understand why she could not command her body to move. But in moments of lucidity, she understood. It was not a dream.

Spirit dragged her by her leg over the jagged floor of the tunnels, each scrape and scratch digging into her wounds. Silent tears slid down her face, but she had not the strength to cry out. Her only peace came in the hope Twila managed to bring her parents to safety.

The blood would kill her before Eden came to save her. She lost too much. She knew by the dizzy thoughts and weak body.

A fleeting glance of her parents was all she would get. A shame. She would have liked to say hello.

Spirit stopped dragging her, and in her vague awareness she thought they were back in the cell. He leaned over her, watching with satisfaction as the life left her eyes. "Not yet, dear," he purred, rolling her onto her stomach before touching her wounds. By the same, warm magic he used to heal her bruised chin and Twila's shoulder, he stopped the flow with one touch of his blood soaked hands. But this time, he did not end the pain.

By capturing the rebel soldier, Eden had alerted the others to the presence of a real threat. The rebel patrols increased. Searching the area for their lost comrade and the enemy responsible. Eden hid behind a rock cluster like before, this time with a rebel king he ought to stab. The opening to the caves - according to the unfortunate rebel he interrogated - was beneath a low outcropping. A gap so small and well hidden it could not be noticed without direction. But miles and miles of caves and caverns could be found inside. The perfect hideout.

He and Farran crept closer to the heart of rebel activity. To the place the captured soldier described. But the small entrance proved difficult to locate, and Farran himself didn't know the exact spot. Too many rebels about for a proper search. But Eden didn't need to find the exact place anymore. He had someone who could ask.

"Come on then," Eden said, walking out into the open. Farran followed behind as the rebels began to notice them.

"Stop!" one of the rebels demanded, a group of them forming a half circle blocking their path. "Who are you and what is your business here?" Some of them noted Eden's hell born eyes and kept a step further away than the others.

"You don't recognize your own king?" Farran said, his voice laced with an anger deep enough to be dangerous. Good. Eden preferred his allies lethal. Before they could ask for proof, Farran held out his right hand, his middle finger graced with a golden signet ring. "You fools have made an error and taken my daughter into custody. Release her. And while you're at it, I'd like to speak with your commanding officer."

"Right this way, Sir," the rebel said, something smug in his voice that set Eden's instincts on edge. Something was off.

But they were moving forward. Towards Rolina. He could deal with whatever they threw at him.

"We apologize for the rough entrance," the rebel said before dropping to the ground and slipping under a large rock. The gap between the rock and earth was small and obscured by other rocks around it. No wonder no one had found the place.

Farran huffed in annoyance then slipped through. Eden, broad-shouldered and large, struggled his way in after.

His feet landed in a cave tunnel. Taller and wider than expected. Partially lit by torches on the walls. Only a handful of guards in the tunnel, leaving it near empty. Eerie. As they proceeded, Eden scanned the darkness for danger. His hell born eyes saw into the black tunnels ahead as the others strained to see in the dim light.

A few hundred paces in, the cave split. The guardian listened. There were more voices to the right, in the distance. A quiet, near imperceptible murmur. They took that tunnel. Eden could only hope they kept the prisoners close. Easier to keep an eye on them, to catch them if they slipped past their guards. On the other hand, they may have stowed them somewhere deep and hidden. To isolate. To make them feel alone and uncared for. People spilled their guts for a little bit of human interaction if left alone in the dark long enough.

Brighter lights caught their attention from ahead. The tunnel opened into a cavern, set up as a central base of operations. Tables on one side where a handful of soldiers ate and socialized. On the other, a command center. A table full of maps surrounded by sour-faced men with high ranks. Weapon racks lining the wall. There were three separate tunnel openings. One between two weapon racks. The others near each other, just beyond the dining tables.

Eden took in every bit of information he could as the rebel led them to the officer's table. If they had to make a break for it, the tunnel between the racks would do. Fewer soldiers standing by, and a touch closer to their current position. And something about it called to him. A scent he couldn't quite catch. A heartbeat he couldn't quite hear.

Tasa pulsed in her sheath for blood.

Eden rested his hand on the blade, sending his own thoughts to the sword to wait. There would be blood soon enough.

"Your Majesty," an officer said, visibly displeased the king of Illandia was there in person.

"I don't have time for pleasantries," the king said, getting straight to business, "You have my daughter, release her. As well as Lady Evensong. We don't want the kind of attention that will draw from the empire." The kind of attention that brought a guardian into their stronghold. "And while I'm here, I'd like to know why you've been taking innocent villagers hostage."

The officer took a step closer. A bit too confident. Too threatening. "What makes you think I have to listen to a single word you say?"

Eden blinked. He knew something was wrong, but the outright defiance threw him.

"I am your king."

"We all know who really has the power, *sir*," the final word was laced with so much venom that Eden knew there would be no reasoning with him.

A thrill pulsed from Tasa's blade, up through the handle, and into Eden. *Blood.* He would give her all the blood she desired.

"I don't think you understand-" Farran began.

"I don't think I care," the officer said, then waved to the nearest soldiers.

They hadn't finished their first step closer before Eden drew Tasa. A second later Farran had his own sword in hand. But the king's other hand went to something on his belt. A small bottle. He ripped it from the belt and threw it into the larger group of soldiers by the tables. As it shattered, a jolt of lightning ripped through the air, sending splinters of wood showering and blasting men apart.

Feinin lightning in a bottle.

Eden swore and dove into the confusion. Tasa departed a head from its corresponding shoulders before the poor rebel had a chance to reach for his sword. Others were on their feet, heading his way. Though the rebels were shaken from the lightning, they only saw two men. They could take care of two men. They could if Eden was human. He stabbed

Tasa between a man's ribs, his Hell born strength driving the blade to the hilt.

At the sound of more shattering glass, rocks split beneath a trio of soldiers running Eden's way, vanishing them in a chorus of screams. More soldiers rushed in. More Feinin spells hurled their way. Each one a favor returned, a gift from the Fae. The king was a fierce ally. A stronger enemy.

Two soldiers closed in on Eden from either side. Joy beat from Tasa into his hand. Eden sidestepped the frightened rebels, slicing Tasa behind and through the first. As the soldier fell, the second rushed in. Eden adjusted his grip and faced him. He crushed Tasa down atop the soldier's weapon, breaking the blow before it reached him. Cutting through to his skull. He fell beside his comrade.

More rebels rushed in, and with them, two more bolts of lightning. The king was showing him up. It was easy to hide behind lightning bolts and borrowed magic. Safe. At least Eden had the decency to risk his own body in the fight.

Pushing past a smoldering and shattered table, Eden set his sights on a cluster of enemy rebels by his chosen tunnel. He smiled and dove in, Tasa singing in his hand. He tore apart the soldiers, piece by piece, until he stood in a mound of flesh and blood, his body drenched in red.

He looked up to find few enemies remaining. A slice, a stab, and the fight was over.

Tasa pouted.

"Come on!" Eden ordered, surprised at the indifferent look on the king's face after they finished slaughtering his own men. Practiced indifference, he hoped. Not genuine numbness.

Best to find Rolina before more rebels crawled out of the woodwork -well, stonework, he supposed. He darted toward the mouth of the tunnel. Before he made it, he heard shouts and thundering footsteps. The guardian braced himself for more enemies, Tasa singing in his hand. But the group of people who poured from the tunnel were unarmed and frightened. The farmers. Someone set them free.

They froze when they saw the results of the battle. Rebels strewn across the cave floor.

"Eden!" a voice cried. From the back of the group, none other than the princess of Illandia appeared.

"Princess Twila?" Hope jolted through his chest, his eyes leaving her to scan for Rolina.

"They still have Evensong," she said through labored breath, as though reading his thoughts, "She saved us, you have to get her out."

Before either could say another word, the king was there, scooping her into his arms. "Twila," he breathed, pulling her close against his chest.

"Father? I thought you were still in The Eternal Forest?" Even as she questioned him, her arms squeezed him tight.

"Did you honestly think I could wait around and hope things would work out?" He pressed a kiss to her forehead. Eden had never cared for either of them, but he couldn't deny there was something warm in watching them reunite. A kind of affection he had never shared with his own kin.

Touching as it was, Eden didn't care. He wanted Rolina safe. "There are still rebels outside and through the tunnels," Eden told the hostages. Twila and Farran broke apart, but their hands remained laced together, "You can't fight them, hide and I'll come back for you. For now," he gestured to the racks of weapons lining the walls, "arm yourselves."

"She's through there," Twila said, starting back the way she and the farmers came.

"You're not coming with us," Farran said, stopping her in her tracks.

"I *have* to help her. She saved me from..."

"Stay and help these people," he ordered.

Her eyes darted to the farmers. Terrified. Uncertain. In need of a leader. Twila nodded then turned to Eden, "I used a glamour to hide us as they passed, so they'll be confused, distracted and scattered looking for us. Use it."

"I will," Eden took a step towards the tunnel.

"Eden," Twila called, stopping him in his tracks. Her voice was raw, on the edge of cracking, "She's hurt." Then she faced the frightened farmers and ordered, "Do as he says."

Rage roiled under his skin. But there was no time for anger, only action. Eden didn't give them another word before continuing down the tunnel, almost surprised when Farran followed him.

"I told you," the king said, sensing Eden's surprise, "I came for both of them."

They met little resistance in the tunnel. A rebel, here and there, searching for the escaped prisoners.

Eden and Farran found several promising doors, but when they dispatched the guards and broke through, they found nothing of interest. Their commanding officer's chambers, a storage room, and once, simply more cave. Eden assumed the door was to prevent things getting in. Tasa thrummed in his hand. Hell born instinct calling him to delve into the dark. To see what might be lurking there.

Rolina came first. He shut the door and moved on.

They found one door - more heavily guarded than the rest - with something worthwhile inside. More prisoners. Not the one Eden hoped for, but they needed rescue all the same. Eden pointed down the tunnel and told them where to find the weapons and the other escapees. The next door held prisoners as well, and he told them the same.

Around another twist in the tunnel, a scent hit Eden. Blood. Fresh. Familiar. His sharp senses recognized the subtle differences in the blood of different people. Knew it to be Rolina's. Anger flared beneath his skin as he followed the trail to the end of the tunnel. An odd shaped door jammed into it. His own blood stirred looking at it. This was the one. Rolina was there. Eden heard a shriek from within.

He kicked the door open.

Eden knew anger. Knew pain and hatred. But seeing Rolina, pinned to the ground, blood running onto the stone floor, he found a new depth of rage. A rage centered on the boy straddling her. Cutting a line into her perfect skin.

Reason shot out of Eden's head. He tackled the boy, slamming him into hard stone. The boy yelped. Eden liked the sound. His fist pounded into the boy's face. Again. Again. He was vaguely aware of Farran rushing to Rolina's side, of hurried words and the pop of a bottle being opened. Eden's instincts worked on their own, beating the boy until his face was little more than a bloody mess.

He coughed blood.

If Eden had been more coherent, he might have noticed the boy's hand turning red. The steam wisping into the air. He pressed it into Eden's arm, burning through his coat, his shirt, his skin. Eden smacked the boy's hand away, but it was enough of a distraction to give the boy time to utter a spell. He lunged forward and shoved, knocking Eden to the ground. How could this skinny boy hit so hard? Another hurried spell escaped his lips. The boy vanished.

"*Hiek*!" Eden swore, searching the empty air.

He shut his eyes and inhaled deeply. Dried blood and fresh, mixed and metallic. Eden dove. He crashed into cloth and skin, carrying the boy into the wall. A spot of blood appeared on the stone half a second before the boy became visible.

He spat blood into Eden's face, swinging his arm to hit Eden in the ribs. Eden stood his ground, slamming the boy into the wall before jerking his arm back for another punch.

Electricity jolted through Eden's body. He found himself falling, twitching, convulsing. No control. Nothing but a rising sense of panic. The boy muttered a few words that sent Farran flying across the room. Then he was atop Eden, grinning. He shook his hand in the air in front of him. It grew red with heat. Pressing his searing hand against Eden's throat, he proclaimed, "Never thought I'd kill a guardian."

"You won't," Rolina growled. Sometime during the fight, she managed to crawl forward. To snatch the discarded knife. With a wave of adrenaline and her last ounce of strength, Rolina drove the knife into Spirit's skull.

He fell as hard as she did. Bloody, empty. But she was the one left breathing.

34

Sorrow

Warmth. Rolina's heavy eyes opened. She lay face down on a military cot, the left side of her face pressed against a pillow. Legs. Two pairs standing nearby. Pressing her hands on the cot beneath her, she attempted to push herself into a sitting position. Pain. Shooting up her spine. Her arms buckled beneath her.

A shuddering cry escaped her lips. The legs came further into view, dropping down to her level. Eden and a man she didn't recognize. "Keep still darling, I'll have your back patched up in no time," the man said gently, then hopped back to his feet. She heard him mumble something to himself about sutures. A doctor. But she couldn't feel him stitching. Some sort of magic or herb must have numbed her back.

Eden ran a hand through her short hair. "*Kier, iha puell.*"

"*Kier*, Eden," she replied, her voice weak.

"We brought in the local physician to stitch you up," he explained, resting his chin on the cot. His hair had grown long, and his beard unruly - part of it singed off in the fight with Spirit. Flecks of blood and dirt speckled his face. But his eyes were the same soft gray. People thought them cold. Rolina did not. Rolina wanted to fall into those eyes. To grab him by the shirt and pull him into a kiss. But her injury would not let her move. And they were not alone.

"How bad is it?" Rolina asked, tears pricking her eyes.

"Bad," Eden answered, never one to sugar coat things. "Haven will be able to fix it," he promised, but the smallest hint of sorrow flashed across his face before he added, "Until then, you won't be able to walk."

"What?" Her heart twisted in her chest. The tears fell.

"You and I both know Haven can work miracles, but your injury is too severe for the average healer. That freak cut through to your spine," Eden explained, gripping her hand in his own.

Paralyzed. Spirit paralyzed her. "You're sure Haven can heal me?" Panic tightened her throat, the words barely made it through.

"Yes," Eden promised, not a speck of doubt in his voice.

His confidence did little to relieve her. Not as the memory of the caves rushed back to her. Rolina's gut twisted. She had forgotten, the pain and exhaustion overwhelming her. She killed Spirit. Actually killed him. It was not a dream. "He was Eli's age."

"And he would have killed us," Eden reminded her.

He was a child. Rolina had the blood of a child on her hands.

He offered no more words of comfort. The pain too fresh. Eden knew she wouldn't hear them. So he let her cry, sitting in silence beside her. The doctor finished his work and wisely slipped away to leave them alone.

After a time, she wiped away her tears. Pushed the image of the knife in Spirit's skull to the back of her mind. Like her nightmares. She could pretend it wasn't real if she ignored it. She wanted to go home and scrub away the memory of blood on her hands so bad she almost forgot why she came. Almost. "My parents. Did Twila get them out?"

Eden smiled. "That was brilliant. All the guards were scattered about looking for their escaped prisoners. Farran and I hardly had to lift a finger getting to you."

"They're safe?" Rolina asked again.

"Yes," Eden said. The ache in Rolina's chest eased. Her injury, the journey, running away in the night, worth it. Worth every step. Every cut. Every bruise.

"Wait, did you say Farran?" Rolina asked. The haze in her mind cleared enough to recall a man rushing to her aid when Eden came to rescue her. He had a bottle and made her drink. Feinin healing magic, bottled up as a gift to the king. She hadn't even recognized Farran through the pain. Hadn't realized whose loving hands had saved her.

Eden nodded, but his brow furrowed, "It was strange, they treated him like he was nobody. But those were his soldiers. At least some of them."

But they weren't his anymore. Not since Cadogan took Nox. Not since Farran had his child ripped away from him. Rolina opened her mouth to explain, to tell Eden what she knew, but the words stopped in her throat. Promises were sacred to the Feinin, and Rolina had promised not to tell. Twila may have been only half-Feinin, but that was enough. And what would become of Nox if Kandston realized the empire knew? If they thought Farran had gone against their demands. She had to think about it more, weigh if the promise was worth breaking.

"Your family is outside with the other rescued prisoners being treated and accounted for. I didn't tell them about you yet. Thought you should rest before I brought them in."

Excitement thrummed through Rolina, shoving away her worries. "I'm awake now," Rolina would have bolted out of the tent to find them if her body allowed it. Eager to see more than a glimpse of their faces. What would she say? All those years apart. It didn't matter. She needed to see them. Needed to know they were alive and safe.

"Are you sure?" Eden was already on his feet.

"I want to see them," she confirmed, watching him duck out of the tent.

Alone, the silence brought fear with it. Reminded her of Spirit. Of what she had done.

The tent flap flew open, banishing her fear before it broke her. A woman ducked inside with glistening eyes. Her hands lifted to her mouth and she gave a small cry. "Rolina?"

"Mother!" Once again, she wished to leap from the cot. To throw her arms around the woman, heart pounding with absolute love. One look destroyed any doubt of the woman's identity. Aside from a few extra wrinkles, and the streaks of gray in her deep brown hair, she was the perfect image of the woman Rolina once knew.

Behind her, a man entered, followed by a young girl on a crutch. The same girl she saw him carry out of the cell. Her eyes fixated on the man, his hair the same gold of her own, now dotted with gray. "Father?" Tears welled in her eyes.

Their bodies were bruised and scratched. Their frames skinnier than she remembered. Starved. Abused. Her gut flared with rage. She reminded herself they were safe now. She and Eden made them safe. Her eyes landed on the girl.

Rage gave way to confusion.

She had the same striking features of Eli. The same dark brown hair, the same green eyes. Rolina looked back and forth between the girl and her parents. She couldn't be older than eleven.

"You're dead," her father said, stunned by the young woman before him.

Eden slipped inside, leaning against a post supporting the tent. Silently watching the interaction.

"No." What else could she say? She knew the longer he studied her, the less he could deny it. She looked just like them. Her father's hair, her mother's eyes. She and Eli both had their mother's nose. So did the girl. More family resemblance. More undeniable proof. It *was* undeniable, wasn't it?

"It's her," her mother crossed the tent and dropped beside the bed. She slipped her arm over Rolina's injured body, holding on as tight as she dare. Her mother's voice shook, "My girl."

Her father joined them, eyes shining with awe. He pressed kiss after kiss on her cheek and forehead. Forgetting their broken bodies, they wrapped their arms around her. Careful of her wounds, but close. Tight. Nothing else mattered. Only parent and child. Only warm touches and the gap of her absence repairing itself. An empty decade refilling. Then the world crept back into their minds. The embrace broke. Rolina's parents huddled close by the cot.

"What happened to you?" The woman began fretting over her wounds, examining the bandages and bruises.

"How are you alive?" her father asked, his fingers laced with hers. Unwilling to release the newly reclaimed treasure.

Words surged in Rolina's mind. A thousand stories and explanations. Where to begin? Did she even have the energy? The breath? Perhaps she should have listened to Eden. Rested a while longer. Thought things through. "It's a long story," she said at last, unsatisfied with her own answer. "Eli is alive too. And safe," she offered, hoping to push their questions aside while they took in the good news.

Her parents looked to each other. Wonder in their eyes. A miracle. Both their children, alive. *All three*, Rolina corrected herself, eyeing the girl standing on the edge of the tent.

"That man," her mother whispered, casting a less-than subtle glance at Eden, "That's Eden the Brutal."

"He knows you," her father added, a question in his voice.

"Uh," she glanced up at Eden, knowing he could hear every whisper with his hell born ears. Too much to explain. Too much at once.

"It's alright," her mother slipped her arm around her again, whispering as she clung to her, "If you can't talk in front of him I understand. We'll find another time."

The words struck her. Did they think she was held captive? Abused and manipulated. That she had to kick and claw her way home to them. She was not some traumatized victim. She was a selfish girl who let her parents think her dead while she danced with noblemen and chatted with fairies.

Something childish in her assumed they would carry on fine without her. Miss her only in brief moments, as she missed them. She never considered the depth of losing a child. Of losing two. The happy delusion of The Eternal Forest slipped away from her. She gazed upon her parents like an open wound. Life had never been easy for them, but she could have made it better. Could have woke Eli late in the night and marched him home years ago. If only she had been brave sooner.

"Um," her father dropped her hand and waved the girl over. She let him tug her by the sleeve to stand in front of Rolina. "I know this will be a bit of a surprise," he began, but as he looked from Rolina to the girl, she knew it would not. She had already figured it out. "This is your sister."

She may have guessed as much, but hearing it aloud sent a new feeling through her. A hesitancy mixed with something she couldn't name. "Hello," Rolina greeted her awkwardly. Should they embrace? Shake hands? They were strangers, but family. Neither greeting felt appropriate, and Rolina couldn't move anyway. They remained still, staring at each other.

"Hello," she replied, just as awkward. "I'm Sorrow."

"Sorrow?" Rolina blinked.

Behind her family, she saw Eden raise an eyebrow.

"I've heard about you," the girl continued, either oblivious to Rolina's reaction to her name, or used to others reacting the same. "And Elian. Never thought I'd meet you."

"You'll meet Eli too," she promised. Did they name Sorrow for their grief? For the loss of her and Eli? For the children thought dead? A tinge of guilt flickered in her chest.

Sorrow shrank back towards their father. Done with conversation.

Was she always so awkward and timid? Or did the situation alter her demeanor? Rolina hoped she had the chance to find out. And yet, something red and glaring sparked in her gut. Her parents had another child. Another daughter to replace her. With dark hair like Eli, and many of their mother's features. Their mother and Eli shared olive toned skin, but the girl had pinker skin like Rolina and her father. Rolina hated the link between them. The tiny bit of evidence they were related. She tried not to. She failed.

"That's enough," Eden stepped forward, fixing his cold eyes on each of her family in turn. "She needs rest."

"But-"

Eden shot her father a look, cutting him off. "Soon as the area's secure, we leave for The Eternal Forest. You and your family may come, if you choose."

Rolina's heart leapt. Her family in the forest. Everyone she loved in one place. They could see Eli. Make him new memories to replace the ones he lacked.

"You want us to go with you?" her father stood, looking Eden in the eye, though he was about a foot shorter. Rolina had a sudden, childish impulse to know if she was taller than her father. But her injuries kept her glued to the cot.

"I don't *want* you to come," Eden said, sending a chill down her father's spine by fixing his icy gray eyes on the man. "I'm telling you it's an option."

Confliction flashed in her father's eyes. They had a life here. A farm to tend. He had his wife and daughter to think about. But Rolina was his daughter too. He wanted to be with her more than anything in that moment. One glance at her wounds, at the daughter once lost, at the woman who freed him, and he nodded his head. "What do you think, girls? Ever wanted to see The Eternal Forest?"

Her mother stood beside him, reluctance in her face. They were farmers, not adventurers. But she set her jaw firm and said, "I want to see my son."

"Then I suggest you run home and pack any essentials," Eden said it like an order, gesturing to the exit, "We could leave as soon as tomorrow." They might have fought to stay by their daughter if Eden did not take a single, imposing step towards them. Towards Sorrow. She came first. The daughter they were used to protecting. "I'll send word when we're heading out. Be here and ready within an hour of receiving word, or we're leaving without you," Eden added as they hurried away.

"Why did you make them leave?" Rolina asked, a harsh edge to her voice. She only just had them back. He may have offered to bring them to the forest, but she wanted them now. Here.

"You looked scared," Eden said, coming to sit beside the cot. "And you do need rest."

"Why would I be scared of my own family?" Rolina snapped.

"I don't know," he shrugged.

She knew she was nervous, but she wasn't scared. Was she?

"I'd be scared if I saw my parents again too," Eden said, a small smile slipping onto his dirty face. "Of course, they were evil and have been dead for a few thousand years, so..."

Rolina half-laughed. Staring into his gray eyes, she forgot her worries. Forgot the blood on her hands. Forgot... everything. "Would you kiss me already?"

Eden's smile widened. He glanced towards the entrance, checking they were truly alone, then pressed a kiss on her lips. "I've wanted to do that for months."

Rolina scrunched her face up in disgust, "When was the last time you had a bath?"

He shrugged, "Before I left."

Rolina mimicked gagging, "Maybe you should at least wash your face before you go around kissing girls."

"You asked," he chuckled, studying her bruised face. "I should have come sooner. They never would have touched you."

There were many things they both should and should not have done. Rolina didn't care. Not as she stared into his face. The face she missed more than anything. "I'm sorry too," she said, but her smile was full of love. And a bit of guilt, "I was wearing your jacket before. It... ripped." Spirit sliced it in two.

Eden shrugged again, "Got plenty of jackets. Only one you." He put his chin on the cot again, staring into her eyes. "I wasn't kidding. You should rest."

"How could I sleep, when I could be looking at you?" she asked, wishing she could move, could lean in and kiss him again.

"I could leave," he started to pull away from her, but she caught his arm.

"Stay."

"I'll have to turn away then," he said, then shifted around so his back rested against the cot. He tilted his head back where she could almost see his face. "I'm glad you're safe, *Iha puell. Lydan syk.*"

Eden wasted a great deal of time teaching her Eldurian curses and profanities over the last year, but sometimes, she caught on to other words. Kinder words. *Iha puell.* Beautiful girl. He had been calling her that since he came back from Eldur, the same idle way he said it to Alice and the other horses. Sweet. Innocent. Beloved.

Lydan syk was fairly new. Words given to her only months before. Whispered in the dark the night before he left for Bane. She spent an hour digging through Maddy's chaotic library the next day before she found a Syytan/Eldurian dictionary. The words were rare, too kind for their cruel lips. Terms of endearment too loving. Tears pricked her eyes hearing them, just as they had that first time she read them in Maddy's dictionary. Words meant for her alone. Words spoken by the man beneath the soldier.

Lydan syk.

My own heart.

There would be time soon. Time for lazy days in the garden. Time for hidden kisses in the dark. Time for life and love. Time for them. First there was a war to end. First there were lives to save.

First there was a nap to take.

Rolina flashed a small, secret smile, the one crafted especially for him, and slipped her arm over his shoulder. Ignoring the grime and dried sweat as her hand found its way to his chest. He slid his own hand over hers. Rolina shut her eyes, feeling the rise and fall of his chest beneath her hand.

Under the smell of months old mud, of the blood of a hundred dead rebels, the sweat and filth, it reached her. A smell like a campfire. A smell like Eden.

The scent of embers and smoke washed over her.

Acknowledgements

It is my joy to thank God that this book exists at last! How many times have I prayed over these words? How many times have I asked for your help, your motivation, and your wisdom? How many times did you push me along this path and reassure my heart that it was meant for me? Thank you.

Mom and Dad. Thank you. You taught me to read. You taught me to write. You sat through nonsensical tales and plotless plays. When I used to staple papers together, fill them with nonsense, and call them books, you called them books too. Over the last few years, you've let me be a bum and spend your money and live in your house and eat your food all so I could focus on writing. I've had so much room to write and learn and turn dreams into a novel. It's your love that made this book happen.

Mom, thank you for typing Happy Cats, the stupidest, greatest story I have ever told. Thank you and also how dare you for naming Sorrow. I hate/love that name.

Dad, thank you for giving me the time and space to write this book. I've been worried about what would happen if I worked so hard and nothing came of it. But you know something? If you've been worried too, you haven't shown it, and that has made me so much more confident that I could do this.

Okay boys, it's your turn. Thank you to my brothers, Brian, Ethan, and Aaron, none of whom have read this book yet. That's right, I'm doing the guilt thing. Read it! But really, all of you have let me talk your ear off about this book and so many other stories I have planned.

Sometimes you've even been helpful. In case you're wondering, yes, I do base characters off of you.

Next up, the girls! Thank you to my sisters-in-law, Sarah and Danielle. You beautiful, bookish nerds! Thank you for reading earlier, jankier drafts and helping me fix them up into something readable. I like you better than the boys now, because you two actually read the book.

Thank you to my book club buddies, Noelle and Alison. I can't even begin to express how helpful your thoughts and suggestions were. It's nice to have friends as obsessed with books as I am who aren't afraid to tell me the flaws in my writing. This book is so much stronger now than the draft I gave you guys.

Thank you to my cover artist and friend, Daniel. I still can't get over how perfectly matched your art style is to what I originally imagined. I know how much work goes into a single piece of art so thank you, thank you, thank you! The cover is perfect.

Jeff! The monkey in the wall! Thank you for taking my author photo. I've always liked your photography and still have the photo you took of me for Much Ado. I miss hanging out at the studio with you and the rest of the theater fam.

Now for my emotional support crew. Thank you to my dogs, Kelsey and Mia, who used to lay near me while I wrote and always let me hug them when I was sad or depressed. I miss you both. Thank you to my puppy, Sasha, who sometimes lays near me while I write, but usually tries to steal my socks instead. Like Kelsey and Mia before you, you are an excellent hugger, baby girl. Thank you to Macks and Mikey. Though I haven't seen you in a long time, when I think of you, I know that I am so loved, I once inspired music. And though most of them can't read yet, I must thank my nieces and nephews, Cecily, Azrael, Astrid, Kai, and Griffin. Your mere existence is help enough. Your hugs are pretty great too. I love you each, and can't wait for time to tell the stories of who you are.

Last but far from least, thank you Alex. You found me when I was broken and put a sword in my hand. People think white knights are a thing of fairy tales, but your existence proves them real. So Alex, my knight, my hero, thank you.

Character Guide

Rolina Cotter (Roh-lee-nuh Kaa-ter)/Evensong Antaires (Ee-vuhn-song An-tair-eez):

Born in Gaj, Ev to simple farmers. Her and her brother were lost on a journey with their father and found by the Imperial Guardians. From that point on, they were raised in The Eternal Forest by the High Emperors.

Elian "Eli" Cotter (Ehl-ee-uhn "Ee-lie" Kaa-ter)/Bryer Antaires (Bri-er An-tair-eez):

Rolina's brother. Raised alongside her in the forest where he picked up a skill for healing.

Dimitri (Dih-mee-tree):

The High Emperor. The immortal ruler of Syytala alongside his sister, Mercury. He claimed his rule by killing the emperor before him.

Mercury (Muhr-kyur-ee):

The High Empress. The immortal ruler of Syytala alongside her brother, Dimitri. She claimed her rule by killing the emperor before her.

Iero Anluan (Ee-air-oh Ahn-lahn):

Imperial Guardian from The Frostlands. Selected as an Imperial Guardian for his compassion. He was made immortal and his name changed to Iero Anluan at eighteen as part of his initiation as a guardian.

Eden Anluan (Ee-den Ahn-lahn):

Imperial Guardian from Eldur. Selected as an Imperial Guardian for his brutality. He was made immortal and his name changed to Eden Anluan at twenty-one as part of his initiation as a guardian.

Madara "Maddy" Anluan (Muh-dar-uh "Mahd-dee" Ahn-lahn):

Imperial Guardian from Viska. Grew up as an earth born student at The Wizard's Academy. Selected as an Imperial Guardian for his intelligence. He was made immortal and his name changed to Madara Anluan at twenty-five as part of his initiation as a guardian.

Haven Anluan (Hei-vn Ahn-lahn):

Imperial Guardian from Kandston. Selected as an Imperial Guardian for his kindness. He was made immortal and his name changed to Haven Anluan at twenty-seven as part of his initiation as a guardian.

Kail Anluan (Kayl Ahn-lahn)/Teagan Edris (Tee-gun Ih-drees):

Imperial Guardian from Kauneus. A mix of various Fae races and a bit of human. Selected as an Imperial Guardian for his beauty. He was made immortal and his name changed to Kail Anluan at twenty-two as part of his initiation as a guardian.

Bolwerk Anluan (Bohl-wairk Ahn-lahn):

Imperial Guardian from The Southern Plains. Selected as an Imperial Guardian for his strength. He was made immortal and his name changed to Bolwerk Anluan at thirty as part of his initiation as a guardian.

Daingeon Anluan (Daen-jee-ahn Ahn-lahn) [Deceased]:

Imperial Guardian from Taivas. Selected as an Imperial Guardian for being an embodiment of freedom. He was made immortal and his name changed to Daingeon Anluan at thirty-two as part of his initiation as a guardian. As a Taivan, Dain had large, birdlike, brown wings and could often be found napping high up in trees in The Eternal Forest.

Kila Anluan (Kee-luh Ahn-lahn) [Deceased]:

Imperial Guardian from Onschuld. Selected as an Imperial Guardian for her determination. She was made immortal and her name changed to Kila Anluan at twenty-four as part of her initiation as a guardian.

Skyli Anluan (Skee-lee Ahn-lahn) [Deceased]:

Imperial Guardian from Ev. Selected as an Imperial Guardian for his generosity. He was made immortal and his name changed to Skili Anluan at 408 as part of his initiation as a guardian. In human terms, he looked about twenty-seven.

Satama Anluan (Sah-tah-mah Ahn-lahn) [Deceased]:

Imperial Guardian from Elska. Selected as an Imperial Guardian for her wisdom. She was made immortal and her name changed to Satama Anluan at twenty-three as part of her initiation as a guardian.

Ráj Anluan (Rai Ahn-lahn)/ Varun Udo (Vah-ruhn Oo-doh) [Deceased]:

Imperial Guardian from Valtameri. An adventurous Valtamerian with a love of drifting in ocean currents and getting lost. Selected as an Imperial Guardian for being an embodiment of peace. He was made immortal and his name changed to Ráj Anluan at twenty-nine as part of his initiation as a guardian. Before being chosen as a guardian, he had never stepped foot (or fin) on land.

Farran Darville (Fahr-ruhn Dar-vihl):

King of Illania and father of three half-Feinin children. Aligned with the rebels and Duke Cadogan against the Empire.

Twila Darville (Twai-luh Dar-vihl):

Daughter of Farran and best friend of Rolina and Ramar. Her half-Feinin heritage slows her aging slightly and gives her the ability to create simple glamours.

Nox Darville (Nox Dar-vihl):
Son of Farran and brother of Twila and Aurora. His half-Feinin heritage slows his aging slightly.

Aurora Darville (Uh-ror-uh Dar-vihl):
Daughter of Farran and sister of Twila and Nox. Her half-Feinin heritage slows her aging and allows her some simple Feinin abilities from her mother's clan.

Aine Darville (Ahn-yeh Dar-vihl) [Deceased]:
Queen of Illandia and mother of three half-Feinin children. Sought to bring the humans and Feinin together to create lasting peace and friendship.

Roan Cotter (Rohn kaa-ter):
Father of Rolina and Elian, husband of Sky. A simple farmer from Gaj, Ev.

Sky Cotter (Skie kaa-ter):
Mother of Rolina and Elian, wife of Roan. A simple farmer from Gaj, Ev.

Luther Cadogan (Loo-ther Kah-dug-gan):
Leader of the rebellion. The half-elven duke of a large province in Kandston, Cadogan used his influence and power to spread lies and rumors about the High Emperors in order to manipulate the people across Syytala. A clever and intimidating man who wants nothing more than to overthrow Dimitri and Mercury.

Tovi David Tavner (Toh-vee Day-vid Tav-ner):

Rolina's childhood friend and son of the owners of the local tavern in Gaj, Ev. Used to go exploring in the caves with her. Rolina named her horse after him.

Spirit (Spihr-iht):
A captive of Kandston.

Hel (Hel):
A potential ally with an army.

Sikker (Sik-kur):
A potential ally accompanying Hel.

Ramarajan Amin (Rah-mar-ah-jahn Ah-meen):
Holy Prince of Onschuld and son of the Holy Prophet. Best friend of Rolina and Twila. Ramar commands his own troop of soldiers, The Holy Guard, which the empire hopes to enlist in defending against rebel expansion.

Guide to Syytala

Syytala:

The continent of Syytala is made up of twelve distinct kingdoms of widely varying climates and cultures. Thousands of years ago, after a massive Fae migration, the continent and it's human inhabitants were severely altered through magic, allowing humans to survive in extreme and magical environments alongside their new Fae companions. Eventually, the kingdom was united as one empire by The Wizard's Council of Viska who imbued their new High Emperors and their protectors, the Imperial Guardians, with imperfect immortality.

The Eternal Forest:

Home of the High Emperors and the Imperial Guardians. Full of secrets and magic. Law states that anyone who enters uninvited is to be executed.

Ev:

A lovely, hilly kingdom lined by mountains along the coastline.

Un: A booming town full of merchants and traders looking to capitalize off of visitors to The Eternal Forest.

Zey: A city known to draw the criminal element.

Gaj: A small farming town edged by mountains. Rolina and Elian's hometown, and current residence of their parents, Roan and Sky Cotter.

Bane: A small hillside town similar to Gaj beside a deep, open valley.

The Hunting River: A large river that crosses through Ev, The Eternal Forest, and all the way down across The Southern Plains. The Montathi of the plains follow it in their nomadic migrations regularly, and many citizens of Ev rely on it for survival.

The Frostlands:

Homeland of Iero Anluan. A kingdom of ice and snow known for its military strength and difficulty to invade. The humans there are magically adapted to the environment and don't do well in heat without an enchantment to aid them. Currently ruled by worryingly young King Daniel Aleksandrov after his father died of a fast-acting illness.

Eldur:

Homeland of Eden Anluan. The kingdom is volcanic and rocky. An inhospitable place to all humans but those magically adapted to the heat. Much like Frostlanders suffer in the heat, Eldurians do not take well to cold. Ruled by several noble houses that rise and fall in power through the years. House Fianna was fortified by Eden's rise to Guardian. Though it's power also fluctuates, it has never fallen entirely out of influence.

Viska:

Homeland of Madara Anluan. A place that promotes education and discovery. Ruled by a council of wizards who often forget that magic is not always the greatest weapon, nor the greatest tool. This council was responsible to the Making, the event that granted the guardians and High Emperors their imperfect immortality.

Kandston:

Homeland of Haven Anluan. Located on the eastern edge of the continent, the further inland, the less populated and more farm-like the towns. Closer to the coast, cities are more populous and diverse. Like all the kingdoms of Syytala, Fae are common here, but not as common as many other parts of the continent.

Illandia:

A feudalistic kingdom currently ruled by King Farran Darville. Situated south of Eldur, it has historically been key in defending The Eternal Forest from Eldurian invasions.

Onschuld:

Homeland of Kila Anluan. A desert kingdom known for its skilled cavalry and harsh environment. Ruled by The Holy Prophet, Nirved Amin, father of the Holy Prince Ramarajan Amin. Leadership is hereditary, but not always passed from parent to child. Once a generation, a person of royal blood is born with the sigil of Tvor upon their back. This marks them as the next ruler and prophet to the god of the desert, Tvor. These markings can be found on any member of the royal family, no matter how remote, though usually a close relative, such as a child or niece/nephew of the current holy prophet. Tvor's chosen are said to hear his voice.

Elska:

Homeland of Satama Anluan, Dimitri, and Mercury. A kingdom known for its beauty and art, especially its expert armorsmiths. It is ruled by a matriarchal hereditary line. Though all children born of a Queen of Elska are taught to find a place of importance in the kingdom, it is always a female heir that rises to the throne.

Kauneus:

Homeland of Kail Anluan. An enchanted jungle, deeply saturated by the magic of the Fae. This is where Fae beings are most concentrated. Some species tend to rule themselves and avoid other Fae, while others love to intermingle and gather. There is no real central leadership in Kauneus, though certain groups and clans have their own political structures. Decisions regarding the kingdom as a whole are decided by anyone who chooses to show up at meetings in their holy place, and everyone's votes and opinions count equally.

Valtameri:

Homeland of Ráj Anluan. An underwater kingdom inhabited by water Fae as well as humans who were severely altered by magic to be more akin to fish. They are a very peaceful country, as it is near-impossible to invade, and its people love to be of help to others. Ruled by a council of Elders.

Taivas:

Homeland of Daingeon Anluan. Half the kingdom is situated on enchanted clouds that never drift away from their place above The Red Mountains. The half in the sky is inhabited by air Fae and magically altered humans with wings. The Red Mountains below are inhabited mainly by dwarves. Many of the jewels they mine are used in the construction of Taivas' beautiful, heavenly cities. Both the dwarves and the humans have separate leaders, but they meet together often to make decisions about the kingdom as a whole.

The Southern Plains:

The largest kingdom in Syytala, but not very populous for its size.

The Montathi: A nomadic race of human-like beings with blue or green skin. They follow the Hunting River in their migration and are excellent herders and hunters. Bolwerk is a Montathi, and prone to getting stir-crazy when forced to stay in the same place too long.

Imimoya: A kingdom far in the south. Their biggest contact is with the Montathi and the Valtamerians. They are largely peaceful and do not like to interfere with other kingdoms.

The Drowning Sea:

A Volatile sea to the southwest of Syytala, known for storms, pirates, and mysterious creatures.

Draven's Cove: A small island with a reputation for housing pirates. Named after a famous Pirate captain from the west who made the place his home.

Photo by Jeff Truong

Hannah Williamson is a California based, Christian author with a love of fantasy and magic. She loves winter nights with a mug of hot cocoa, a warm blanket, a good book, and a dog to snuggle with. She also has a passion for adventure and can often be found rafting through raging rivers, jumping out of planes, hiking through woods, or on some other strange adventure. When she is not adventuring, she is usually dreaming up stories, playing games with her family and friends, sketching, knitting, crocheting, or - when she absolutely has to - working on homework. If you spot her in the wild, be sure to say hello.

www.ingramcontent.com/pod-product-compliance
Lightning Source LLC
Chambersburg PA
CBHW060629310726
48982CB00003B/723

* 9 7 9 8 9 8 6 2 2 5 4 0 1 *